BLOODSCRIPTS

WRITING THE VIOLENT SUBJECT

Elana Gomel

THE OHIO STATE UNIVERSITY PRESS
Columbus

Gomel, Elana.
Bloodscripts : writing the violent subject / Elana Gomel.
p. cm. — (The theory and interpretation of narrative series)
Includes bibliographical references (p.) and index.
ISBN 0-8142-0949-1 (alk. paper) — ISBN 0-8142-5119-6 (Paper : alk. paper) —
ISBN 0-8142-9017-5 (CD-ROM)
1. Violence in literature. 2. Holocaust, Jewish (1939–1945), in literature. 3. Literature, Modern—20th century—History and criticism. 4. Detective and mystery stories—History and criticism. I. Title. II. Series.
PN56.V53G66 2003
809'.93355—dc21
2003008508

Cover design by Dan O'Dair
Typeset in Adobe Electra
Printed by Thomson-Shore, Inc.

The paper used in this publication meets the minimum requirements of the American National Standard for Information Sciences—Permanence of Paper for Printed Library Materials. ANSI Z39.48-1992.

9 8 7 6 5 4 3 2 1

The Theory and Interpretation of Narrative Series

This book is dedicated to my grandmother, Ethel Starominski, who has outlived the twentieth century and survived five wars, two revolutions, state terror, and genocide.

We all look to fathom the mind of a mass-murderer and to understand what makes him commit such heinous crimes.

Yet which of us can honestly say that in his Hobbesian heart of hearts, he does not already have the answer?

– *PHILIP KERR, A Philosophical Investigation*

Contents

Acknowledgments

So many influences, intellectual and otherwise, have gone into the writing of this book that it is impossible for me to acknowledge every single source. Nevertheless, some special thanks are in order. To Professor Hana Wirth-Nesher, whose support and encouragement have been invaluable. To Dr. Robert Griffin, without whose loyal friendship and challenging critique this book would not have been written in its present form. To Professor Brian McHale, who opened my eyes to the beauty of narratology. To my editors at the Ohio State University Press, especially James Phelan and Peter Rabinowitz, whose comments have helped greatly in shaping the final version of the book. To my students at Tel-Aviv University for their interest and enthusiasm, with apologies to those who suffered nightmares as a result of my syllabi. To Daniel Kluger for the illuminating discussions of detective fiction. To my mother, Maya Kaganski, for giving me the courage to ask hard questions. To my sons, Ariel and Eliran, for giving me the empathy to deal with the answers. And to Dr. Stephen A. Weninger, for intellectual companionship, shared interests, and the love of a lifetime.

Introduction: Stories to Die For

A world at war. . . . I wish I could make you see the whole thing, the amazing scale of it. The bombs falling. . . . Parades and music, crowds cheering, whole cities falling down. . . . It was sublime.

– *Carol O'Connell,* Shell Game

I. SUBLIME SUBJECTS

Contemporary culture is permeated by violence, not only visually but narratively as well. So many popular fictions revolve around the physical act of inflicting damage on the human body. The same is true of narratives of history, which increasingly abandon the rhetoric of power, statehood, or global trends to focus on violence. Genocide becomes a key concept of political discourse. As Michael Ignatieff points out in his discussion of ethnic wars, we "have lost our narrative" and what is left is the "simple" story of violence (98).

But the story of violence is far from simple. The best proof of its complexity is the fact that we find it so difficult to describe its protagonist. The violent subject, as a murderer, a mercenary, a terrorist, a soldier, or a martyr, has become one of the main foci of postmodern culture's fears and desires. And yet, the vocabulary of cultural studies offers little in the way of understanding the trajectory of his—or occasionally her—self-narrative. There are many questions. How do they do it? Why do they kill? How does it feel, being a murderer? But there are few answers.

A new strategy of reading confidently promises to illuminate violence's heart of darkness. Sociobiology reads the body of the violent criminal as a palimpsest of heredity and environment. Poring over brain scans and DNA charts, it looks for the textual flaws in the composition of the subject.[1] But unwittingly it replicates the failed fin de siècle project of Lombroso's criminal anthropology. Better technological tools do not guarantee better results.

The main insight of contemporary cultural theory is precisely that: the subjectivity located outside the individual, outside a specific body, with its irreducibly individual entanglement of genes and memories. Language, discourse, and narrative are the sites in which the self is—precariously—woven together out of the disparate strands of other people's stories. And it is in the field of narrativity that the enigma of the violent subject may be approached as a cultural phenomenon and not a supposedly biological deviation.

The human subject is constructed by a life story. Such stories project different modalities of the violent self. These modalities, these genres of subjectivity, hold the key to the way violators are perceived by others and by themselves. The generic prototypes of the murderer's life-story are to be found in horror fiction and film, in detective stories, in thrillers, in "true crime" apocalyptic fantasies, and all the other narrative genres dealing with violence. Literary murderers are not pale reflections of some essential violent psyche. On the contrary, actual murderers are stories of violence made flesh.

This is not to lay the blame for war and crime at the doorstep of the media. My goal is not to castigate narrative representation[2] for supposedly inciting violence. Rather, it is to look at the diverse ways in which narrative representation makes us into subjects capable both of violence and of resistance to it. Just as being a man or a woman is the end result of the process of social construction, so is being a killer. Like gender identity, a violent identity is a narrative of the self that has to conform to certain cultural, political, and generic expectations.

Bloodscripts explores incorporation of violence in narratives of identity. My focus is on genres of subjectivity rather than on more conventional generic divisions of the narrative field. In the chapters that follow I discuss genres of violence, both in their contemporary incarnations and with reference to their nineteenth-century roots, as illustrative of the specific violent subjects that are the focus of this study. In other words, my aim is neither to provide a complete guidebook to the culture of violence—a task daunted by the sheer size of the field—nor to write a history of the narrative representation of murder. Rather, it is to analyze how violence interacts with narrative to generate identity.

Several limiting definitions are in order. By violence I mean physical violence, murder or serious bodily harm inflicted in a face-to-face interaction. This, of course, excludes much of modern warfare, but recent events have shown that Baudrillard's "virtual war" has not supplanted old-fashioned slaughter. Nor, I believe, can it. As the stories that I will discuss show, it is precisely the personal, even intimate, contact between the victim and the perpetrator that shapes the aesthetic, narrative, and ultimately ideological impact of violence.

There are two sides to each violent interaction: the dimension of instrumentality and the dimension of excess. The latter is clear in so-called motiveless violence, such as the private torture and serial killing that constitute the subject of the first two chapters in the book. But instrumental violence seems far more pervasive: soldiers, terrorists, professional criminals, all would claim that their violence is a means to an end, whether collective or personal. However, I will argue that instrumentality does not exclude violent excess. Whatever its pragmatic purpose, experience of violence involves ecstasy or intoxication, sometimes paradoxically coupled with revulsion and horror, in which doing harm to another's body becomes an end in itself. I call this non-instrumental aspect of violence "the violent sublime." The book analyzes how narratives of identity acknowledge the violent sublime and how they represent its impact upon the coherence of the self.

By "narratives of identity" I do not mean memoirs or autobiographies. My focus is on the narrative molds of selfhood provided by culture and available to the subject in order to make sense of his or her experiences. Identities are stories. This is an argument familiar both from cultural studies and from psychology. Narratologists claim that, as Mark Currie puts it in *Postmodern Narrative Theory,* "the only way to explain who we are, is to tell our own story . . . we learn how to self-narrate from the outside, from other stories" (17). Psychologists, following the lead of Donald Spence in *Narrative Truth and Historical Truth,* emphasize the significance of narrative coherence for mental health. A subject incapable of telling his or her story is a flawed, incomplete, or pathological subject.

The narrative approach to subjectivity is quite common in the practical discipline of criminology, including the much touted "profiling." Criminologist David Canter frames his discussion of serial murderers in the general claim that "human life unfolds through a series of episodes" (221) and that subjectivity is constituted through a process of perpetual internal storytelling. "The stories we tell each other and ourselves about ourselves do have great power in giving shape and meaning to our lives. It is the narrative form of these accounts, not their elegance or veracity, that is crucial to understand" (Canter 227).

Canter profiles serial killers through formal analysis of their self-narratives. Similarly, Richard Rhodes argues in his recent book *Why They Kill,* based on the theories of criminologist Lonnie Athens, that subjectivity is a narrative construct, elaborated and transformed over time: "Selves are not given. They are constructed. They are built, modified, altered, refurbished, even replaced over time" (Rhodes 55). Even the most violent criminal possesses what Athens called the "beautiful narrative" of the self (Rhodes 62). This "beautiful narrative" is created through the process of inner conversation with the "phantom community," which consists of the internalized significant others in the person's life. The crux of violent behavior is that the phantom community of perpetrators encourages and supports their violence, offering "different, violent meanings to their social experiences" (Rhodes 84). In other words, if the self is a story told to an internalized audience, the violent subject adapts to his interlocutors' expectations by casting himself in the role of the "bad guy."[3] Within the subject's phantom community, cultural narratives of selfhood become internalized as scripts of behavior.

Athens's choice of the term "beautiful narrative" suggests coherence, measure, and harmony. But in fact, his and Canter's analyses of specific murderers' stories indicate that this is not the case. Rather, the narratives both of them adduce are marked by a struggle between the protagonist's search for a perfect form and the ineluctable disturbance created in this form by the act of violence. Another aesthetic term seems to suggest itself for the narratives of the violent self: sublime. Juxtaposed to the beautiful in the aesthetic theories of Kant, Burke, Lyotard, and others, the sublime is a modality of representing the unrepresentable. The beautiful is an aesthetic effect created by harmony, measure, and proportion. The sublime, on the contrary, is that which exceeds representation, that "which can't be shown, or presented" (Lyotard 1991, 89). It is my contention that the self-narratives or violent subjects are not beautiful but rather sublime, shattered and (imperfectly) reconfigured by the impact of an experience, for which ordinary means of representation are inadequate. Violent subject-stories constitute a very special subset of narratives: narratives structured by their own impossibility.

The Trope of Murder

In Tony Parker's book *The Violence of Our Lives: Interviews with American Murderers,* murderers tell the stories of their lives. Their narratives are shaped by instantly recognizable generic patterns—the melodrama of victimization, the boastful memoir of the unrepentant social enemy, the romance of erotic obsession. But there is a snag every time the killer struggles to articulate the pivotal event in his or her life, the murder itself. The typical responses: "I know what I did was wrong, and I don't know why I did it" (117; the husband who shot his wife); "I've lost count of how many psychiatrists have interviewed me before the trial and time and time again after it for the first few years. But when they did, it always came down to the same question: 'Why did you do it?' That was always the bottom line. My answer to it too was always the same; 'I don't know why I did it, I thought you were supposed to tell me.' I don't have any insight into it, and I don't have much remorse or regret for it either" (171; the man who raped and killed an old woman during an aimless break-in). "The price I'd paid for being stopped for a minor traffic violation was the thing no one could understand, and least of all me" (197; the successful young lawyer who ran over the cop who stopped him for speeding).

Criminals' confessions illustrate one way in which an act of violence disturbs a narrative of subjectivity: by undermining causality. Many murderers cannot answer the most basic question we ask ourselves about our own and other people's actions, "Why?" It is also the first question the public asks when a particularly horrific crime is committed. Even when the murderer is insane, our hunger for causal explanation is not assuaged; we still want to know the etiology of his murderous psychosis. But none of Parker's subjects is diagnosed as mentally ill; they are articulate and alert. They are also aware of their own narrative deficiency. One of them, Jeff Hessler, a Vietnam veteran and a drug dealer, finds a perfect model for his life story in e. e. cummings's gnomic poem "LISN bud LISN." When asked to explain, he replies: "I guess it's the incoherence of it that sums me up" (186)

This "incoherence" is endemic to the first-person narratives of violent criminals. The notorious Boston Strangler, describing the ghastly details of his murders to the police detectives (who had to be convinced that this smarmy, apologetic housepainter killed thirteen women), can answer any question except the question "why?" "There was no need for it to happen. . . . There was no reason for being there, period. There was no reason for her to die. Nothing was taken away from her, no money, no nothing. . . . How can I explain it to you?" (Frank 331).

He cannot explain it either to his investigators, or to himself. Later on he even pleads with the police to find the reason for him: "Why? Why? Why does it have to be me? . . . when my children grow older, I want them to get an understanding of me. . . . There's got to be a reason. I don't think you're born like this. Why did I start? Why did I stop?" (Frank 386).

We may feel skeptical about anything a mass murderer says; perhaps all these cries of confusion are self-serving lies. But the pattern is too ubiquitous to be easily dismissed. Even when nothing tangible, such as an insanity plea, can be gotten out of it, criminals stubbornly insist on the contingency of their crime. And if a rational reason is advanced, it often seems to be insufficient even to the perpetrator himself.

A break in causality characterizes criminal subjects. But another kind of incoherence mars narratives of ideological killers. They find no difficulty in explaining the "why" of their actions. But they stumble, stutter, and often fall silent when it comes to the "how."

Rudolf Hoess, the commandant of Auschwitz, wrote his autobiography while awaiting execution in a Polish prison. It has been pointed out that Hoess is often less than truthful, but the question that interests me is not his veracity but his narrative competence. As he states at the beginning, his aim is "to reconstruct from memory a true account of all the important events and occurrences in my life and of the psychological heights and depths through which I have passed" (Hoess 20). Such an account adheres to what Hoess sees as the narrative truth of his life rather than to the historical truth.[4]

The main narrative model that Hoess adopts is the soldier's story, endlessly reproduced in the writings of the *Freikorps,* to which Hoess belonged in his youth. Such writings typically exhibit the pattern of initial loneliness, trial by fire, male bonding, and martyrdom in the name of an Idea, all of which Hoess faithfully applies to himself, finding in his "service" in Auschwitz the highest expression of the soldierly virtues: fidelity, purity, dedication. But when he finally gets down to describing the actual running of the camp, something cracks. The writing becomes disjointed and the narrative flow is dammed, eddying into repetitions, evasions, inconsistencies.

It is not that Hoess tries to minimize the magnitude of his crime: he provides the exact figures, speaks about the "processing capacity" of the gas chambers, and seems to glory in the unimaginable scale of the slaughter, even to the point of exaggerating the number of his victims. But he cannot tell how he felt when looking at the piles of corpses, despite his professed intention to focus on his own psychological states. Hoess knows exactly why he killed more than a million people. Nazi ideology provides a convincing explanation, to which he steadfastly adheres even after the collapse of the Reich. He does indeed believe, up to his execution day, that Jews are vermin and not really human beings. Coupled with his enormous emotional investment in the image of himself as a loyal soldier, the ideology holds together his depleted self.[5] He knows what and why, but he cannot tell how: "During this first experience of gassing people I did not fully realize what was happening, perhaps because I was too impressed by the whole procedure" (137). This grotesque combination of bureaucratese and emotional somnambulism characterizes the autobiography as a whole, making it one of the most chilling texts ever written. There is a void at the core of the Nazi killer's subjectivity, generating a narrative in perpetual flight from its own horror.

Jorge Luis Borges's short parable "Deutsches Requiem" draws upon such narratives to make clear their underlying pattern: justified and explained—or explained away—violence still creates a gap in the subject's self-perception. The story is the first-person apologia of an unrepentant torturer and murderer. Otto Dietrich zur Linde, opening his statement of self-justification with a barrage of illustrious names of Western culture, represents the madness of civilization that produces its own nemesis in the Nazi "faith of the sword." But even more strikingly, he represents a new kind of killer, whose elaborately defended violence seems at the opposite pole to the random brutality of tough-luck criminals. And yet, his self-narrative, like theirs, is marked by "incoherence," only of a different kind. If one of Parker's criminals, despairing of self-explanation, talks of "a hole . . . where there used to be a human mind" (Parker 186), the urbane and articulate Linde has a hole where there used to be a human heart.

Linde claims to have no natural predilection for violence. This is a constant feature of Nazi self-narratives: Eichmann indignantly denied he ever took any pleasure in killing, and Hoess's only spark of emotion comes when he describes his reaction to the flogging of a prisoner in Dachau. He claims to have gone "hot and cold all over" and yet being "compelled" to watch this unbearable spectacle. For both Hoess and Linde, murder is a self-sacrifice that they bring to the altar of their "faith." Both pride themselves on their "toughening" that comes at the cost of psychological anguish. They are not naturally violent men. They are men who use violence to remake themselves in the image of their ideal.[6] According to Jean Amery, an Auschwitz survivor, men like Linde "were not sadists in the narrow sexual-pathological sense. In general, I don't believe that I encountered a single genuine sadist of this sort during my two years of imprisonment in Gestapo and in concentration camps" (Amery 34). They were, according to him, "philosophical" sadists, torturing and killing out of ideological conviction.

Both Linde and Hoess are such "philosophical" sadists. For Linde, the violence of Nazism is "an act of morality, a purging of corrupted humanity, to dress him anew" (Borges 144). Dreaming of a purifying apocalypse, Linde sees himself as a New Man in a world about to be born: "this era, comparable to the initial epochs of Islam and Christianity, demanded a new kind of man" (Borges 143). Linde is Hoess's narrative truth that can never be matched by the messy historical truth of any actual human being. Linde's murderous self-righteousness is Hoess's unattainable ideal. But at the same time the ruptures in Hoess's autobiography are magnified by a gaping hole in Linde's story.

Linde sets out to torture and kill the Jewish poet David Jerusalem, whose work he tremendously admires. Jerusalem's ordeal in Linde's "laboratory" is supposed to put a seal on the killer's transformation into a Nazi *Übermensch:* "if I destroyed him, it was to destroy my compassion. In my eyes he was not a man, not even a Jew; he had been transformed into a detested zone of my soul" (Borges 145). But just as he is about to describe what he has done to the poet, there is a line of dots. A note, purportedly by the story's fictional "editor," enigmatically states: "It has been necessary to omit a few lines here" (ibid).

Is Linde's description unreadable? Or is it, perhaps, unwritable? Any reader familiar with what came to light during the Nuremberg Trials is capable of filling the gap with words: torture, starvation, brutality. But these are only words. Linde's narrative, like Hoess's, is interrupted not by squeamishness or shame but by its own impossibility. It stops at the point in which language fails to convey the experience of extreme violence. The shocking row of dots in the text is a typographical equivalent of the trope that marks—or mars—all self-narratives of killers. This trope is ellipsis.

Ellipsis is a narrative technique defined by Gerard Genette as an omission from the discourse of some time elapsing in the story. Genette distinguishes between story, which is the sequence of the narrative events in a chronological order abstracted from the text, and discourse, which is the events as actually represented. An ellipsis occurs when there is an event that we know must have happened, since we can infer it from the overall shape of the story, but which is omitted from representation.

As Fredric Jameson convincingly argued in *The Political Unconscious,* formal narrative conventions are meaningful in themselves. The narrative form, apart (and sometimes in opposition to) the ostensible content, is a "frozen" ideology, the result of "sedimentation" that inscribes relations of power and systems of belief through structural devices and techniques. The ellipses that mar killers' individual stories indicate something general about the relation of violence and narrativity: an aspect of violence that cannot be incorporated into discourse. Necessary, even pivotal, to the story, the violence remains outside discourse, indicated but not shown; spoken about but not described; hinted at but not explicitly named. And this aspect has a disturbing impact on the coherence of the narrative and, consequently, on the coherence of the self created through this narrative.

This narrative disturbance is expressed differently in different violent subjects. For the criminals who wonder why they killed, the impact of violence amounts to an annihilation of personality. A subject with no inner logic is a subject in ruins. The Nazis, on the other hand, preserve the continuity of the self but at the price of its richness and depth. The subjectivity that emerges from their narratives is a hollowed-out ideological construct, hiding the secret that it cannot articulate. This ideological self appears as a defense against the corrosion of violence, the defense that is both necessary and inherently unstable. And when it crumbles, the consequences can be similar to the narrative collapse experienced by the criminal. This is illustrated by a remarkable episode in Martin Gilbert's *Nuremberg Diary.* When in the course of the trial the prosecution showed a film taken by the American soldiers in the newly liberated death camps, the reaction of the accused was quite unexpected. Gilbert was astounded to observe the elite of the Third Reich sweat, tremble, grow pale, and even cry. Later Ribbentrop tearfully told him: "Hitler couldn't even have looked at such a film himself" (Gilbert 49). Of course, next morning they staunchly denied responsibility for anything, but it seems that for a moment they were confronted with a sight for which the *lingua tertii imperii*[7] provided no words.

For both criminals and ideological killers violence is formative of identity. Jeff Hessler's defining himself as a "bad and violent and dangerous man" (Parker 174) and Rudolf Hoess's defining himself as a soldier of the Fuhrer claim genres of violence as their genres of subjectivity. But these genres are structured around a gap that language can gesture at but cannot suture.

For the criminals, this gap all but devours identity ("the incoherence of it sums me up"); for the Nazis, it is masked—but not obliterated—by a new kind of subjectivity, the ideological self, that is supposed to incorporate violence in its system of values. But whatever form the ellipsis of murder takes, it indicates that physical violence cannot be part of a "beautiful narrative" of the self. The narrative it produces is indelibly marked by the impact of the victim's violated body. For this is ultimately what the two kinds of killers have in common. Whether outcasts or pillars of their communities, whether repentant or smug, whether behind bars or in positions of power, murderers share one thing: the physical relation with another human being that results in his or her pain, suffering, and death.

Books and Bodies

Setting side by side criminological texts and cultural studies of violence, it is difficult to shake off the feeling that they relate to entirely different activities. Following Derrida's famous reference to the "violence of the letter," cultural scholars insist that violence is inherent in the very nature of discourse.[8] In their Introduction to the appositely named collection *The Violence of Representation,* Nancy Armstrong and Leonard Tennenhouse summarize this view: "writing is not so much about violence as a form of violence in its own right" (2).

Criminologists, on the other hand, are well aware that real violence is very much a matter of bodies coming into close and intimate contact with other bodies. Coroners, forensic scientists, police, and FBI investigators, feeding the public's insatiable appetite for the grisly details of their work, vie with each other in providing testimony to the physicality of violation. William R. Maples, a forensic anthropologist, opens his book with a precise catalog of the "everyday things I see on the job: crushed and perforated skulls, lopped-off limbs and severed heads, roasted and dissolving corpses, hanks of human hair and heaps of white bones" (1–2).

As opposed to cultural scholars, criminologists see language not as a tool of violence but as a shield against it. Maples explains how his daily encounter with horror has not managed to inflict any appreciable psychological damage. It is precisely the "letter"—science, knowledge, and ratiocination—that allows him to endure the sight, smell, and touch of the violated body. He describes an autopsy as "reach[ing] with both hands into the rotting remnants of some dreadful crime, rummag[ing] through the bones and grasp[ing] the pure gleaming nugget of truth that lies at the centre of it all" (2–3). Ronald Markman, a forensic psychologist, also claims that his function is to defuse the horror of violence by providing a rational and coherent explanation of the killer's motivations: "Of course, all my years of training and experience had prepared me to answer such questions, to evaluate and describe the event [of violence] in more elaborate terms, in words that sounded scientific—words that made it sound predictable and even part of some kind of order" (13). Discourse, language, reason are a protection against the impact of the violated body. This protection may be inadequate but it is necessary. Even if "the pure gleaming nugget of truth" turns out to be simply another sliver of bone, even if the testing of the man who stabbed his newborn son generates so much psychobabble, it is still necessary to try to make sense of the senseless materiality of violence.

In adjudicating a clash between two disciplines, it is worthwhile to ask whether they really study the same object. And it seems that criminologists and cultural scholars are, in fact, looking at different aspects of violence. The concept of the "violence of the letter" centers on the "violent meanings" that perpetrators attach to their acts.[9] The "everyday things" of the forensic anatomist, on the other hand, are the material traces of the act itself. Where the cultural scholar reads the text of violence, the criminologist looks at its spectacle.

Text and spectacle affect us in different ways. In the spectacle of violence its physicality comes to the fore: we are seeing bodies like our own being cut open, pulled apart, bleeding, suffering, in pain. The spectacle of violence reminds us of our own mortality; reminds on a basic, visceral level that circumvents all the justifications and explanations of discourse. The body appears in the lacunae of language.

Aristotle's classical definition of tragedy employs three terms: reversal (*peripeteia*), recognition (*anagnorisis*), and *pathos*. The last one is often translated as "suffering," but it actually means the spectacle of violence: "the destructive or painful action, such as death on the stage, bodily agony, wounds and the like" (25). Reversal and recognition are moral and psychological transformations, while pathos is a physical action, which is not only perpetrated on the body of a character but actively engages the bodies of the audience. In the implicit physicality of catharsis, the purging of excessive emotions, Aristotle recognizes the irreducible corporeality of violence.

Pathos is what people react to when they throw up at the sight of blood. It is arguable that nausea is the true foundation of morality. Despite the clichés concerning "the beast in man," most animals are much less violent than human beings because almost every species has a built-in biological brake on intraspecies aggression. Anthony Storr in *Human Destructiveness* argues that if "all human disputes were confined to fistfights, there would not only be fewer deaths but fewer instances of cruelty" (113). He quotes Konrad Lorenz's *On Aggression* to the effect that human beings are defective animals whose "inhibitory mechanisms against injuring and killing one's own kind are poorly developed . . . and easily overcome because man is not armed with dangerous natural weapons like tusks and claws" (ibid). Despite the dangers of sociobiological arguments, this one makes sense, if only because it indeed corresponds to the well-known fact, also pointed out by Storr, that many people abstain from violence simply because they have no stomach for it and that a man who drops incendiary bombs on cities and villages might very well balk if ordered to pour gasoline over a child and ignite it.

In his book *On Killing* psychologist Dave Grossman claims that most soldiers throughout history were unwilling to kill and found ingenious ways to avoid doing it. While basing his conclusions on the extraordinarily poor firing rates during the Civil War and World War II, explicable only by the silent "conspiracy to miss," Grossman also adduces psychological and psychiatric evidence to prove the "existence of a powerful, innate human resistance toward killing one's own species and the psychological mechanisms that have been developed by armies *over the centuries* to overcome this resistance" (Grossman xxix).[10] In other words, people have to be taught to kill. There is no violent beast chained inside each of us; on the contrary, such distinctly human institutions as language, narrative, and ideology generate violence by weakening the residue of animal inhibitions against attacking members of one's own species. Insofar as violent meanings are used to overcome the wordless reluctance of the body to be engaged in a close and violent interaction with another body, "the violence of the letter" is indeed responsible for the tide of blood that is the history of civilization.

But Grossman's thesis begs a simple question. If we are all physiological pacifists, where does the pleasure of violence come from? We know that some people become addicted to killing. Before we brand such people as genetic freaks (as Grossman himself does), we should remember the overwhelming evidence for the psychological "ordinariness" of some of the worst mass murderers in history. If there is no "instinct" of aggression and violence is a by-product of civilization, why is it so persistently coupled with sexuality, which does rest on the irrefutable bedrock of the body's innate capacity for pleasure? Grossman seems to undermine his own case when he quotes a comment by a Vietnam veteran who scorns the academic research on violence because the scholars are "like a world of virgins studying sex, and they got nothing to go on but porno movies. And it *is* just like sex, 'cause the people who *really* do it just don't talk about it" (Grossman 2).[11] If the experience of killing were simply revolting, there would hardly be a need for this titillating silence.

The comparison between violence and sex is both right and wrong. It is wrong because the act of violence is not physically pleasurable in the same way in which the act of sex is. Grossman's interlocutor describes the nausea and shock following the loss of one's "virginity" in violence. Except for some truly pathological cases, violence is not orgasmic. But if orgasm is seen not as a physiological reflex but as a state of self-eclipse or self-shattering, sex and violence do appear to have common features. Leo Bersani's essay "Is the Rectum a Grave?" argues that sex is a "radical disintegration and humiliation of the self" (217). In sex the body temporarily obscures the mind, taking away the participants' ability to conceive of their bodies as mere extensions of their conscious wills. And in this sense violence is "like sex," only more so.

Jean Amery speaks of torture as the total eclipse of language by the body: "Whoever is overcome by pain through torture experiences his body as never before. In self-negation his flesh becomes a total reality. . . . [O]nly in torture does the transformation of the person into flesh become complete. Frail in the face of violence, yelling out in pain, awaiting no help, capable of no resistance, the tortured person is only a body and nothing else besides that" (33).

In her important book *The Body in Pain,* Elaine Scarry analyzes the "inexpressibility" of pain, the way in which "in serious pain the claims of the body utterly nullify the claims of the world" (33). Pain destroys language. And through this destruction the body in pain emerges as absolutely, uncompromisingly real, real beyond the construction of language and discourse. Here is Amery again on the giant factory of pain that was Auschwitz: "nowhere else in the world did reality have as much effective power as in the camp, nowhere else was reality so real" (19).

In the Lacanian notion of the Real, one can recognize the unarguable reality of the body stripped of its linguistic defenses, the body in pain. Slavoj Zizek glosses this notion as follows:

> The Real is therefore simultaneously both the hard, impenetrable kernel resisting symbolization *and* a pure chimerical entity which has in itself no ontological consistency. . . . The Real is the rock upon which every attempt at symbolization stumbles, the hard core which remains the same in all possible worlds (symbolic universes) but at the same time its status is thoroughly precarious; it is something

> that persists only as failed, missed, a shadow, and dissolves itself as soon as we try to grasp it in its positive nature. . . . All its effectivity lies in the distortions it produces in the symbolic universe of the subject: the traumatic event is ultimately just a fantasy-construct filling out a certain void in a symbolic structure. (169)

The Real, in other words, adumbrates the violated body in both of its aspects: as the story and the spectacle, the narrative elaboration and the silence of trauma, the representation and the ellipsis. But if the victim of violence actually experiences the utter reality of pain, the perpetrator vicariously tastes the Real through another person's suffering.[12]

Can one become addicted to the Real? If the spectacle of the violated flesh does indeed convey what language cannot express, "the radical humiliation and disintegration of the self" in pain, this explains the nausea of the audience and the trauma of the perpetrators. As Georges Bataille points out, rational prohibition of violence would not work unless there were some irrational emotion involved as well: "if some violent negative emotion did not make violence horrible for everyone, reason alone could not define those shifting limits [between legitimate and illegitimate violence] authoritatively enough" (Bataille 56). But this "negative emotion" can flip over into an addictive state of self-transcendence. The visceral impact of violence, which occasionally sends frontline soldiers into combat shock, may also create willing assassins, serial killers, and genocide junkies. All of them crave the self-transcendence of violence, vicariously tasted through the suffering of their victims.

Amery lucidly analyzes the psychology of torturers and killers. He points out that they are not immune to the wordless power of the violated body. Second-hand, they experience the disintegration of the self and the silencing of language in the total reality of pain. But for them, as opposed to the victim, this experience becomes a source of pleasure because they are in control of it:

> [The torturer] wants to nullify this world, and by negating his fellow man, who also in an entirely specific sense is "hell" for him, he wants to realize his own total sovereignty. The fellow man is transformed into flesh, and in this transformation he is already brought to the edge of death; if worst comes to worst, he is driven beyond the border of death into Nothingness. With this the torturer and murderer realizes his own destructive being, without having to lose himself in it entirely, like his martyred victim. He can, after all, cease the torture when it suits him. He has control of the other's scream of pain and death; he is master over flesh and spirit, life and death. (Amery 35)

The violator erects his power on the bedrock of the Real. He transforms the indisputable physicality of violence into the indisputable nature of his own mastery. He steals the reality of suffering and appropriates it to make himself more Real than any human being has the right to be. He vanquishes the doubts, ambiguities, and evasions of language by positioning himself in the gap opened by violence in discourse. In torture "the vision of suffering [is converted] into the wholly illusory but, to the torturers and the regime they represent, wholly convincing spectacle of power. The physical pain is so incontestably real that it seems to confer its quality of 'incontestable reality' on that power that has brought it into being" (Scarry 27). Even the victim himself is convinced: "I also have not forgotten that there were moments when I felt a kind of wretched admiration for the agonizing sovereignty they exercised over me. For is not the one who can reduce a person so entirely to a body and a whimpering prey of death a god, or at least, a demigod?" (Amery 36).

In his 1921 essay "Critique of Violence," Walter Benjamin extols "divine" violence, the violence of excess, the irresistible, awesome, purifying sweep of annihilation: "Divine violence, which is the sign and seal, but never the means of sacred dispatch, may be called 'sovereign' violence'" (Benjamin 1921, 252). Benjamin's "sovereign" violence is Amery's "agonizing sovereignty." The torturer is divine. Punishing the prisoner or obtaining information is only a pretext for the "radical disintegration of the self," which allows him to touch the bedrock of the Real and to experience the intoxicating rush of absolute power. In the furnace of excess, the murderers are remade as gods.

The true power of a torturer is negligible compared to the power of political movers and shakers, but it is power of a different kind. When in *1984* O'Brien explains to Winston Smith that he can change reality, he is right: by reducing Smith to a pain-racked thing, he makes an irrefutable argument in favor of his own ontologically superior being. Richard Rhodes describes how Vietnam veterans simultaneously mourn atrocities they have committed and betray their nostalgia for the godlike power of killing: "To be like a god is to escape, at least momentarily, human contingency; no wonder berserk, malefic violence feels ecstatic" (Rhodes 308). Contingency is experienced through the shifts and treacheries of language. The material body is solid and real, and the power over the body is the only real power there is.

But this power still has to be narrativized through language if it is to enter the social circulation of meanings. No subject can remain in the wordless ecstatic realm forever. And once violence returns to self-representation, it needs an aesthetic modality that can capture its irreducible ambiguity, both as a story and as a spectacle, both as "violence of the letter" and the violation of the body. In considering, as De Quincy has done, murder as fine art, we find its aesthetic idiom in the language of the sublime.

The Violent Sublime

In his A *Philosophical Enquiry into the Origins of Our Ideas of the Sublime and the Beautiful* (1757), Edmund Burke states: "the idea of bodily pain, in all the modes and degrees of labour, pain, anguish, torment, is productive of the sublime; and nothing else in this sense can produce it" (79). In his *The Inhuman* (1988), a manifesto of postmodernity, Jean-François Lyotard makes exactly the same connection between the sublime and physical pain and privation: "The aesthetics of the sublime is still more indeterminate: a pleasure mixed with pain, a pleasure that comes from pain" (98).

The sublime is one of the most contested terms in cultural theory today, trailing a long and complicated history. Originating in the Hellenistic treatise of Dionysius Longinus, the notion of the sublime became central to eighteenth-century aesthetics. The influential theories of Edmund Burke and Immanuel Kant developed the philosophy and psychology of the sublime, based on the distinction between the pleasurable and the terrifying modalities of aesthetic experience. Greatly oversimplifying, it is possible to say that the sublime opposes the beautiful in the same way as the awe occasioned by a volcanic eruption opposes the quiet enjoyment of a flowering meadow. The Romantic sublime was often found in the contemplation of mountain vistas or infinite stretches of the starry skies.

From the beginning of its history, the sublime has been linked both to transcendence and to violence. Dionysius talks about the "irresistible strength" with which the sublime strikes the observer (Ashfield and De Bolla 22). Kant, despite his insistence on the "disinterestedness" of aesthetic judgment, describes what he calls "the dynamic sublime," that is, the sublime of Nature's power, in terms of "a might," which is perceived as "an object of fear" (119). And Burke derives the sublime from "the ideas of *pain, sickness,* and *death*" (36).

Whether confined to stray metaphors or elaborated into a philosophy, the nexus of transcendence and violence persists in the discourses of the sublime. It is not accidental that the revival of the sublime occurred in the twentieth century, shadowed by wars, revolutions, and genocide. The paradoxes of the sublime are central to Lyotard's diagnosis of the "postmodern condition" (Lyotard 1984) and to Zizek's analysis of totalitarian ideologies. According to many cultural critics, the oversaturation of popular culture and the visual media with violence generates an aesthetic universe in which the sublime is the reigning principle. "If any human act evokes the aesthetic experience of the sublime, certainly it is the act of murder," claims Joel Black (14).

In the response to a sublime experience, two stages are to be distinguished. The first is the sense of the unspeakable and unrepresentable, an interruption of language, a suspension of thought. For Kant, the sublime is produced "by the feeling of the momentary inhibition of the vital forces followed immediately by an outpouring of them that is all the stronger" (98). The sublime is a lacuna in the symbolic order: "what [the sublime] leads to is a failure in representation through a massive disturbance as the texts, in trying to present the unpresentable, veer toward collapse" (Mishra 20).

This stage of collapse, however, is succeeded by an "outpouring"—of emotions, words, images. If the sublime is a wound in discourse, it is a wound that immediately stimulates a healing process. Even though language fails to encompass the sublime, it persists in trying. In the reaction to the sublime the mind asserts its power by coming against its own limits: "Sublime is what even to be able to think proves that the mind has a power surpassing any standard of sense" (Kant 106).

The sublime is the unrepresentable that clamors for representation; it is that which exceeds language but provokes speech. Lyotard describes the dynamics of pleasurable impotence, whereby the paradoxical aesthetics of the sublime becomes more seductive than the sensible aesthetics of the beautiful:

> the faculty of presentation, the imagination, fails to provide a representation corresponding to this Idea. This failure of expression gives rise to a pain, a kind of cleavage within the subject between what can be conceived and what can be imagined or presented. But this pain, in turn, engenders a pleasure, in fact a double pleasure: the impotence of the imagination attests a contrario to an imagination striving to figure even that which cannot be figured, and that imagination thus aims to harmonize its object with that of reason—and that furthermore the inadequacy of the images is a negative sign of the immense power of ideas. (98)

Lyotard brings together the two kinds of the sublime that Kant distinguishes from each other: the mathematically and the dynamically sublime. The first relates to "the cognitive power," the second, to the "power of desire" (Kant 101). The mathematical sublime is evoked by the vastness of the universe and the regularity of natural laws. The dynamic sublime, on the other hand, is produced when we regard Nature as "might" and as "object of fear" (Kant 119). For Burke, the dynamic sublime is a by-product of power: "I know of nothing sublime which is not some modification of power" (Burke 59). Specifically, it is the power to inflict pain: "But pain is always inflicted by a power in some way superior, because we never submit to pain willingly. So that strength, violence, pain and terror, are ideas that rush in upon the mind together" (60).

In Lyotard, the two seemingly incomparable kinds of sublime objects are yoked together: infinity and pain, eternity and power, abstraction and the body. The failure of the imagination in the face of an Idea of infinite magnitude mirrors the imagination's incapacity to come to grips with the Real of pain. The inability to represent divinity is shadowed by the inability to represent violence—not to indicate, name, describe, or show—but to convey the phenomenological experience of killing and being killed.

The ellipsis of the violent subject's life-story is a scar of the sublime. Violence both wounds the narrative and stimulates its recovery. In parallel with the aesthetic trajectory of the sublime, the narrative dynamics of violence is twofold: the fragmentation of the subject, followed by recovery and renewed sense of power. The initial trauma shatters the plot of the self, producing gaps, lacunae, silences, and inconsistencies; but the sublime sense of power generates a narrative reconstruction, which, nevertheless, bears the traces of the initial fragmentation. This is the source of the critical paradox, in which violence is simultaneously claimed to be overrepresented (as in many discussions of media violence) and unrepresentable (as, for example, in Elaine Scarry's study of torture and war). It is precisely the profusion of violent stories that testifies to the rupture produced by violence in the fabric of discourse.

The murderer's self-narrative is shaped by the poetics of the sublime. Slavoj Zizek describes the subject of totalitarian ideologies as possessing a "sublime body" composed of "the *sublime* material . . . that other 'indestructible and immutable' body which persists beyond the corruption of the body physical . . . exempted from the effects of wear and tear . . . always sustained by the guarantee of some symbolic authority" (Zizek 18–19). All murderers aspire, at least momentarily, to this "sublime body," or rather sublime self, which is created through identification with the power of violence. In order to avoid recognizing himself in the pain of the victim, the violator misrecognizes himself in the sublimity of the "experience that does open violence to the human image" (Des Pres 163). One masters terror by becoming its source: "the mind sheds its fear and exults in a strength it gained by internalizing, or identifying with, terror's own power" (169). Murderers are sublime subjects.

But the sublime appears in many guises, from the dark chaos of the Gothic novel to the blinding clarity of the visionary apocalypse. Similarly, the sublime subject has many forms, depending on the way in which violence is incorporated into the overall shape of his life-story. These forms are socially, culturally, and textually overdetermined, producing the different genres of the violent self. In the second part of the introduction, I will look at these genres in more detail.

II. FACES OF MURDER

> *I would also like to mention that as a result of the considerable psychological pressures, there were numerous men who were no longer capable of conducting executions and who thus had to be replaced by other men. On the other hand, there were others who could not get enough of them and often reported to these executions voluntarily.*
>
> *—Gustave Fix, member of Sonderkommando 6*

In every narrative interaction of violence, there are three participants: the perpetrator, the victim, and the regulator, the regulator being the police or other investigative agencies in case of unlawful killing and the state or a political organization in case of genocide, terror, ethnic cleansing, or war. The victim's body represents the intractability of the material Real. The regulator represents the law of discourse. The violent subject's story is plotted between these two poles.

The genres of violence prevalent in contemporary culture project several distinct modalities of the violent subject. First, there is a subject whose opposition to the law is so extreme that he is presented not just as a social but as a narrative outcast, defying all conventional stories of the self. Such a subject paradoxically merges with the mutilated body of the victim, which marks the area outside the Symbolic, the realm of language and representation. The monsters of horror fiction, vampires, werewolves, and zombies; some serial killers in thrillers and true-crime biographies; and even such rogue soldiers as Kurtz in Coppola's *Apocalypse Now* (though not necessarily the ideologically motivated Kurtz of *Heart of Darkness*) are instances of the violent subject who has positioned himself outside the law, in the realm of the corporeal sublime.

Another modality of the violent subject, while still opposing the social regulation of violence, acknowledges the law and distances itself from the excess of wanton cruelty. The rational killers of the classic detective story, trying to outwit the detective or the police, share liberal society's view of violence as limited, instrumental, and disciplined. The symbiosis between the perpetrator and the regulator is farther developed in the hard-boiled thriller, in which the detective often resorts to physical violence in order to uphold the law. But it is precisely this complicity that discloses the paradox at the heart of the disciplinary appropriation of violence: the law becomes entwined with its opposite, failing either to confine or to eliminate it. A narrative "spillage" of the sublime marks stories of rational murderers, whether in Agatha Christie's whodunits or in courtroom and spy thrillers, in which the ostensibly instrumental application of violence always exceeds its pragmatic determinants.

Finally, there is the subject of violence who becomes the law. In science fiction and dystopia there are numerous representations of societies in which wholesale violence is not only endorsed but positively required, and in which the violent subject is elevated into the Superman. But such societies belong in the realm of historical memory as much as that of the imagination. The Holocaust, the most shocking example of genocide in Western history, was perpetrated by people who sought the self-transcendence of violence as part of their ideological program and wrote it into their normative narratives of selfhood. Nor is Nazism the only such ideology; communism, especially in its Stalinist incarnation, is another. And the post–Cold War world is swarming with ideologies and regimes that attempt to utilize the power of the violent sublime in order to restructure their subjects in the mold of a New Man. Lyotard's putative death of the "grand narratives" or Jameson's death of the utopia only mark the mutation of the giant state-ideological Leviathans into a multitude of pesky little monsters. Terrorist organizations everywhere promulgate their own recipes of the millennium through tribulations. In every utopia of blood, the regulator and the perpetrator of violence become one, and every trace of the victim's material body is purged from discourse.

Bloodscripts explores three main types of the violent subject, three genres of the murderous self. Superimposed upon the bewildering variety of violent texts in postmodern culture, these types, I will argue, provide a heuristic grid for mapping out the narrative kingdom of violence. Any such map will be necessarily partial and incomplete, and the choice of specific texts will often be the result of personal taste. However, the overall design of the book reflects what I see as both formal and ideological structuring of the narrative field of violence. Below I will introduce the three violent genres of subjectivity through three well-known literary characters, then briefly discuss their cultural genealogies, and end with an overview of the book's individual chapters.

Three Killers

Bill Sikes, a thug and a criminal, is totally shattered by the murder of his lover Nancy in Charles Dickens's *Oliver Twist* (1837), losing his status in the underworld, his name, his sanity, and his life. Judge Lawrence Wargrave in Agatha Christie's *Ten Little Indians* (1939), having privately executed nine people he deems guilty of murder, writes a meticulous account of his activities and then neatly disposes of himself with a bullet through his head. Rodion Raskolnikov in Fyodor Dostoevskii's *Crime and Punishment* (1866) is redeemed and reborn into a new life after the brutal butchery of two helpless women.

Each novel frames the subjectivity of the murderer in a specific narrative structure proper to its genre. *Oliver Twist* is a melodrama, a loose string of tear-jerking episodes. But even this little coherence is lost when murder intrudes. Dickens, always a writer of prodigious visual imagination, transforms his scenes of violence into striking tableaux, lurid set pieces, whose intensity defies the exigencies of the plot. Neither Sikes's sickening brutality nor his subsequent hallucinatory flight is given any psychological explanation. Whatever crawls out from the blood-splattered room is no longer Bill Sikes but a nameless Thing, a monster and an outcast, shunned even by his criminal accomplices and haunted not by remorse but by self-directed horror and nausea. Spilling of blood robs him of his individuality and makes him an exemplum of violence at its deepest ontological level, as a rebellion against the human commonality of the flesh. And it is as such an exemplum that he dies in front of the avidly watching crowd, closing the circle of violence: a body for a body.

The twentieth century rediscovered the "dark" Dickens, the Dickens of murder, execution, and mob rampage. And the aesthetics of this Dickens is uncannily similar to the aesthetics of horror fiction and film. The Technicolor bloodshed of the twentieth-century cinema is prefigured by the hallucinatory vividness of Dickens's murders. The scene of Nancy's killing in *Oliver Twist* is a prime example of violence's assault on the eye. The ghastly sight of the mangled body—"mere flesh and blood, no more—but such flesh, and so much blood!"—is so horrifying the murderer himself cannot bear to look at it (Dickens 1837, 423). But look he must all the same, irresistibly drawn to it. And so must we, the readers, a captive audience, fascinated and sickened by the quivering reflections of sunlight in the pool of blood.[13]

On the one hand, the body in pain is an object of irresistible curiosity, strange fascination. The probing eye of the audience aligns itself with the murder weapon, laying open the defenseless flesh. On the other hand, the eye can become a wound, a channel through which our own vulnerability is forcefully brought home to us when we suddenly recognize ourselves not in the violator but in the helpless and suffering victim. If the eye is an instrument of aggression, it also becomes a site of punishment. The murderer is caught in the shifting dynamics of visibility. Sikes is haunted by a vision of Nancy's eyes. In his botched attempt to escape from the lynching crowd, he slips and hangs himself because he hallucinates that she is looking at him. The murderer's horror of being seen, which also torments other Dickens's criminals, such as Jonas in *Martin Chuzzlewit,* is more than a fear of discovery. It is a symptom of the ever-present danger of exchanging places with the victim.

The reason for such a reversal in Dickens is the shared corporeality of both victim and murderer. The murderer disavows his own body by inflicting pain on the body of the Other. The murderer is a person who, to adapt Sartre's famous words about the anti-Semite, wishes to be "pitiless stone, a furious torrent, a devastating thunderbolt—anything except a man," a human being whose body is potentially as soft and vulnerable as the body of the victim

(Sartre 54). In the murder scene Nancy tries to escape the blow by embracing Sikes, but this reminder of their physical intimacy only enrages him. The polluted body of the streetwalker sets off the purity of Sikes's inexorable will. But after her death it is Sikes who becomes a leper and an outcast. Her revenge is his reembodiment.

Perpetrated on the body, punished through the body: for Dickens, murder is not a moral but an ontological crime. Dickens's murderers cannot change, cannot repent, cannot atone for their crime. Once blood is spilled, the murderer becomes a creature apart, "hunted down," as in the title of one of Dickens's detective stories, and his destruction is inevitable. Even an occasional fallen woman can be redeemed, but a murderer is beyond forgiveness. Dickens was in favor of prison reform, energetically campaigned against public executions, and was aware of the excessive strictness of the law. But for him, as for the legal reformers of the 1830s and 1840s, violent crime, especially murder, was a category apart, distinct from crimes against property. A murderer separates himself from the human community, defined by the common vulnerability of the flesh.

In Dickens's *Our Mutual Friend* (1864) Riderhood, a despicable little crook, almost drowns and is pulled out of the water by the hostile crowd. His rescuers do their best to resuscitate him but promptly kick him out when he regains consciousness. As an anonymous body, poised on the brink between life and death, he is the subject of tender solicitude. As Riderhood, he is a pariah. "Not one has the least regard for the man; with them all, he has been an object of avoidance, suspicion, and aversion; but the spark of life within him is curiously separable from himself now, and they have a deep interest in it, probably because it *is* life, and they are living and must die" (503). It is this "spark of life," the impersonal vitality of the body, that constitutes for Dickens the essence of humanity. Murder is a crime against the body, and the body of the criminal fails him by undergoing a change that sets him apart from ordinary human beings. The retribution suffered by Dickens's murderers—Bill Sikes, Jonas Chuzzlewit, Bradley Headstone—is strangely akin to a disease: they are plagued by hallucinations, lapses of memory, bouts of fainting. A grotesque corporeal transformation becomes their mark of Cain. The instant metamorphosis undergone by Bradley Headstone is typical: "Rigid before the fire, as if it were a charmed flame that was turning him old, he sat, with the dark lines deepening in his face, its stare becoming more and more haggard, its surface turning whiter and whiter as if it were being overspread with ashes, and the very texture and colour of his hair degenerating" (872). The revulsion other characters experience towards Dickens's murderers is visceral and instinctive. They are treated as if they, indeed, were lepers or plague carriers, or better still, monsters.

Agatha Christie, the undisputed queen of the classic detective story, squeezes violence into the straitjacket of logic. Like the rest of her oeuvre, *Ten Little Indians* is a brainteaser with an exquisitely worked-out plot, but it stands out by virtue of focusing on the personality of the criminal. In most classic detective stories the murderer is dramatically revealed by the know-all detective and hustled away to the unseen trial and execution. In *Ten Little Indians,* however, there is no detective: Judge Wargrave's first-person account that closes the novel provides the solution to the series of seemingly inexplicable murders on isolated Indian Island. The judge is both the murderer and the executioner, exposing the ineluctable violence of the law itself. The opposite of the brutishly inarticulate Bill Sikes, the judge is lucid and eloquent. His polished narrative minimizes the corporeal aspect of violence. He has killed nine people, some of them in close physical contact, but he describes these murders in the impersonal voice of a technician. Preoccupied with murder's know-how, he is oblivious to the grossness of the violated body. And the text collaborates: in the third-person narrative of the crimes, there are no blood splatters, no oozing brains, no incontinent agony. When people die, figures are removed from the game board. It seems that the judge's impeccable logic and self-control tame the horror of murder that destroys Dickens's killers. Not only is the execution rational but so is the motivation. The victims are all murderers who, for various reasons, cannot be punished by the legal system. Since the death penalty is legal at the time, Judge Wargrave merely corrects an annoying hitch in society's handling of criminality.

But the judge's account of himself, so smooth, rational, and reassuring, is built on a gaping contradiction, a shocking paradox, which he himself candidly exposes: "From my earliest youth I realized that my nature was a mass of contradictions. . . . I have a definite sadistic delight in seeing or causing death. . . . From an early age I knew very well the lust to kill. But side by side with this went a contradictory trend—a strong sense of justice. It is abhorrent to me that an innocent person or creature should suffer or die by an act of mine" (Christie 1939, 164).

Violence and the law are tied in a Gordian knot: slaughter requires the underpinning of justice, for only the guilty must suffer, and yet at the same time the initial impetus of the judge's pursuit of justice is the inborn love of bloodshed. His narrative reveals a rational and orderly personality, which is structured around the dark nucleus of sadism, crucial to the plot and yet inexplicable in terms of its logic.

Unlike the monstrous killers of Dickens, confined in the category of the Other, Judge Wargrave, a solid, useful, upper-class citizen, is Everyman. And so are the other inhabitants of Indian Island: a prim governess, a fashionable doctor, a retired general, a respectable spinster. And each one of them is a murderer. The question that the text implicitly asks is "Who is incapable of violence?" The answer is "Nobody."

But if the monster's subjectivity, by definition, is beyond the reach of human apprehension, the subjectivity of Everyman should be instantly accessible to all. So how are we to relate to the judge's self-confessed madness? The position of the implied reader in Christie's novel is an uncomfortable one, for while we are gently beguiled by a mind game (rather than grossed out by a violent spectacle), we eventually find ourselves caught in the web of the judge's twisted logic. A monster may be seductive, but a disciplined killer is compelling. If the strategies of exorcism and expulsion can rid society of Bill Sikes's delirious violence, what can work against the rational slaughter of Indian Island? Judging by the denouement of the novel (which was also published under the title *And Then There Were None*), only total annihilation.

The judge's suicide results from the paradox of violence as both necessary and inimical to social discipline. His death resolves the *aporia* of the genre he represents, the genre of the classic detective story, in which a rational subject rationally commits the most irrational act of all, murder. Throughout the text, the horror of violence is both emphasized by the creepy atmosphere of the island and minimized by the careful exclusion of the physical aspect of the killings. But it breaks out in the last pages, in which the judge, foreseeing the condition of his own corpse, describes the future gun wound in the middle of his forehead as the "brand of Cain" (173). Like Bill Sikes, branded by violence, the normative, disciplined, lawful subject is eventually transformed into an object of horror and disgust. And the medium of this transformation is physical corporeality. Judge Wargrave is not troubled by qualms of conscience, but the corpses with which he litters Indian Island (including his own) speak louder than words.

Ten Little Indians presents both the subjectivity of the murderer and the act of physical violence in a manner diametrically opposite to the dark Gothic of Dickens. Where the latter emphasizes irrationality, the former is reasonable; where the latter revels in gore, the former represses bodily pain and suffering. Showcased in Dickens, the corpse in Christie becomes little more than a plastic prop. But it is precisely the complexity of narrative strategies involved in the repression of the corporeal that testify to its centrality. Eventually, the rational subject of violence is revealed as a smooth-talking madman, and the violated body is restored to its macabre glory. All the strategies of ratiocination collapse when the urbane judge suffers the same fate as the brutal criminal. While different in so many respects, Dickens's and Christie's novels converge on one crucial point: there is no place in society for a subject of violence.

But amazingly, such a place is found in what is often considered the most morally elevated novel about violence ever written. Dostoevskii, a fervent

Christian, does what Dickens, with his superficial yuletide sentimentality, and Christie, with her healthy metaphysical indifference, are unwilling to do: he not only forgives a murderer but allows him to emerge from butchery spiritually purified and morally reborn.

Dostoevskii's most important novels, *Crime and Punishment, The Brothers Karamazov,* and *The Possessed,* deal with murder. But this is a different murder from that of Dickens or Christie: its motivation is essentially ideological, even when (as in *The Brothers Karamazov*) there is personal malice involved as well. In *Crime and Punishment* Raskolnikov is motivated by a "Napoleonic" idea, which he explains in his article as a "permission to kill" for exceptional individuals, the "law-givers and builders of new humanity" (282; trans. mine). Seeing himself in the august company of the Solons, the Mohammeds, and the Napoleons, Raskolnikov is a prescient image of what Nietzsche's Zarathustra would call later the "higher man" (Nietzsche 323). And just like the Nietzschean Superman, Raskolnikov needs violence to recreate himself: "The evilest is necessary the Superman's best" (Nietzsche 322).

Raskolnikov is not a "natural-born killer," like so many of Dickens's monsters. He is a delicate and sensitive man, a true intellectual, marked by an inborn empathy with the oppressed and the downtrodden. A vivid dream about the torture of a helpless horse makes him cry. But he commits two ax murders, which, in their sheer brutality, top Bill Sikes at his worst. What makes him capable of this revolting bloodshed is his "Idea." And when, after the murder, his body reacts in the same involuntary way as the bodies of Dickens's unenlightened butchers, with nausea, illness, and eventually a physical collapse, Raskolnikov perceives this as a humiliating defeat. The spirit is willing, but the flesh is weak. He has failed his idea by not being strong enough to become a "lawgiver," to transcend the mob's prejudices against violence, which he despises: not because he is enamored of violence for its own sake but because he is sick of what Nietzsche was to call "human, all too human."[14]

Dostoevskii, of course, is adamantly opposed to Raskolnikov's worldview, which is essentially the same revolutionary utopianism he savages in *The Possessed.* But he has his own ideological ax to grind. And ironically, the novel that is supposed to illustrate the failure of utopian violence unwittingly demonstrates its triumph. Raskolnikov killed the old moneylender and her pathetic sister in order to restructure his own subjectivity, to emerge from the violent ordeal as a Superman, free of weakness and fear. And this is what eventually happens, only the ideal he uses as a model for his nascent self has changed. He wanted to be Napoleon; instead, he becomes Christ.

Raskolnikov's violent bildungsroman eventually leads him to a spiritual rebirth. The fractured personality of a murderer is glued together by repentance and atonement and emerges in a strikingly different, purified, transcendent form. The longed-for transformation is achieved by assimilating Raskolnikov's story into the master-narrative of Christianity. The "Napoleonic" script he attempted to write for himself has proven to be too fragile to absorb the visceral shock of killing two human beings. But the Christian narrative, promising rebirth and regeneration, is far sturdier; not only does it allow the murderer to live with himself, but it actually establishes his crime as the basis for a new utopian subjectivity. The last sentences of the novel promise a new story, the story (or history) of "man's renewal" (558; trans. mine). Was it not what Raskolnikov wanted from the beginning?

Crime and Punishment is a political novel in the guise of a psychological one, analyzing the dynamics of the ideological self-fashioning through violence. Its interpretation of the Christian narrative aligns it with utopian ideologies of Dostoevskii's own social and cultural milieu. The novel is a story of political violence and its success—not in achieving its purported social goals but in changing the personality of the perpetrator. As opposed to Sikes's visceral aggression, Raskolnikov's violence is ideologically motivated—but so is his salvation. He sees murder as a tool of self-fashioning, a means of recreating himself in the image of his superhuman ideal. And he succeeds: all that is necessary is to exchange the wrong ideology for the right one. Rodion Raskolnikov, meant as the opposite of the "possessed," ideological assassins and pure-minded terrorists, becomes their mirror-reflection.

Three faces of murder: the inarticulate monster, the man next door, and the true believer. The three novels written within a hundred-year span illustrate the types of violent subjectivity that have largely—though not exclusively—defined (post)modernity's attitudes to murder. And now the three killers have taken over popular culture. Bill Sikes, blood-splattered and flesh-rending, lumbers through horror films and orchestrates the serial killer scares. The urbane judge, the least likely suspect in the rational game of murder, presides over the empire of the detective stories and still rules the beleaguered liberal jurisprudence that refuses to accept that murderers are genetic freaks. And Rodion Raskolnikov, the killer on behalf of an Idea, has wrought more havoc in recent history than many an advance in military technology.

The generic conventions of their stories are shaped by the divergent ways in which they incorporate the violent sublime. Bill Sikes is a Gothic monster, whose engagement in torture killing annihilates him as a human subject. He is reduced to the purely corporeal existence and excluded from the Symbolic. His violence is doubly unlawful: illegal but also disavowed by the narrative itself.

Judge Wargrave is his opposite, the law made flesh. The choking exactitude of his narrative is the means of disciplining violence. But in a paradoxical inversion, which the novel itself cannot fully grasp, the disciplined subject produced by such a well-trained plot is a killer. Christie's novel is a classic detective story, which D. A. Miller in his *The Novel and the Police* sees as a genre of discipline, participating "in a general economy of policing power" (Miller 2). If the monstrous Sikes lives out the violence at its most nakedly physical, violence as torture, Judge Wargrave represents the disciplinary subject of the violence hidden, disguised, kept out of sight, but still indispensable to the workings of the modern state.

Finally, Raskolnikov is an ideological New Man, consciously using violence as a means of remaking himself in the image of his political ideal. Unlike Wargrave's law of discipline, Raskolnikov's ideology does not hide its dependence on bloodshed; it revels in it. And he is the only one who actually succeeds in pursuing his own narrative trajectory as it leads him into a better and brighter futurity. Raskolnikov is a killer on behalf of utopia.

What all these narratives have in common is a disturbance created by the violent sublime. But each is affected by it in a specific way. Violence may shatter the subject's life-story, creating a mute, incoherent, and threatening Other. It may transform him into a New Man. And when it does neither, it generates a paradoxical and uncanny double self, outwardly indistinguishable from anybody else but harboring a deep and ominous secret. These three narrative patterns exemplified by the three killers provide the structural skeleton of *Bloodscripts.* I will call these patterns the *subject of torture*, the *subject of discipline*, and the *subject of ideology*. The rationale for these names lies in a modern history of violence, as sketched out by Michel Foucault and his followers.

From the Scaffold to the Death Camp

Public torture was, of course, a common event in the premodern age. Despite the often voiced contention that the present era is more violent that its predecessors, the spectacle of physical violence, legally sanctioned and socially accepted, was an inseparable part of people's everyday experience for hundreds of years. Rhodes pointedly notes that not so long ago "children attended public displays of *real* violence for moral uplift" (Rhodes 319). Whatever the ostensible purposes of such displays, there is no doubt that they had a profound emotional impact. On the one hand, as Leon Sheleff points out, torture had a pragmatic aspect in its linkage to the "law of proof" (299). On the other hand, as Foucault vividly describes in the opening chapter of *Discipline and Punish,* such a proof resided not so much in the information extracted under duress as in the shocking visibility of the violated body itself. Bill Sikes, who stages his own public hanging, epitomizes the violent subject at his most corporeal and, therefore, most visible. He is still directly linked to the spectacle of the scaffold.

In a rather short historical period, according to Foucault, public torture gives way to discipline, which marks a decisive divorce between power and physical violence, commented upon by Hannah Arendt in *On Violence*. Physical violence, while of course still indispensable to power, is kept out of sight, and the soul rather than the body becomes an object of disciplinary techniques. While torture collapses crime and punishment into a spectacle of suffering (for the torture of the criminal often reproduced the damage done to the body of the victim), discipline separates them by a long period of psychological anguish, whose stages—guilt, remorse, rehabilitation—constitute a narrative of the subject's transformation. Whereas torture shocks the rebellious subject into obedience, discipline produces obedient subjects. The first rests on the naked visual display of the body in pain, the second, on the narrative "translation" of the scene of violence into a plot. Excluded from the daily experience of the vast majority of the population, raw violence becomes an invisible yet indispensable foundation of power. Judge Wargrave, enmeshed in complex, elaborate, and rigid narrative frameworks—both of classic jurisprudence and of classic detection—exemplifies the invisible but pervasive violence of discipline.

However, Foucault's scheme only goes so far. It does not account for the most visible and frightening subject of violence today: the ideological killer. The seemingly never-ending fascination of the Holocaust may owe more to the hideous enigma of its perpetrators than to the wrenching suffering of its victims. The debate on the nature of the ideological killer clamors on, swaying between the poles indicated by Hannah Arendt's "banality of evil" on the one hand and Kant's "radical evil" on the other.[15] In this debate the Nazi often appears to be a metonymy for the army of murderers too vast to comprehend: from Stalin's henchmen to the perpetrators of the genocide in Bosnia and Rwanda; from the soldiers of a would-be millennial empire to terrorist freelancers. In the wake of 9/11, the terrorist has assumed the dominant place in the popular imagination, somewhat displacing the Nazi Übermensch. But his cultural genealogy is rooted in the same search for utopia, so that there are surprising and yet real connections between bin Laden and Raskolnikov, Mohammed Atta and Otto Dietrich zur Linde. For despite the inflated rhetoric of the "clash of civilizations," the perpetrators of today's terrorist atrocities are no evil aliens from some faraway Muslim galaxy: they are a product of the cultural convergence and ideological globalization that have disseminated the lure of the sublime utopian subject worldwide. The ideology that justifies killing is different in each case, filtered through the indigenous tradition and local grievances. But whether it is religious fundamentalism, radical nationalism, social justice, or racial purification, the terrorist's political agenda is only half of his narrative. The second half, far more important, is the implicit quest for self-transformation through the divinity of bloodshed. And it is precisely because this quest unifies seemingly disparate movements with contrary political aspirations that I decided against inclusion of a separate chapter on terrorism in this book.

The fear of being instantly outdated, as terror is being redefined on a daily basis in presidential speeches and political summits, is only part of this decision. More important is the desire to stand back from the current political turmoil in order to discern the common narrative pattern that unites disparate historical outbreaks of ideological violence. There is not a single terrorist movement today that does not have its defenders who point out the "justice" of the movement's ostensible goals. But precisely because one person's terrorist is another's freedom fighter, the overt agenda of mass violence cannot fully explain its modus operandi—not only because ethically the ends do not justify the means but also because ideologically and psychologically the means *are* the ends.

My subject in this book is this "deep" level of ideological murder that restructures the perpetrator's subjectivity. To reach it, one has to cut through the verbiage of reasonable and perhaps even sympathetic rhetoric of social or national rights, to probe the "surplus" violence that is channeled into the self-fashioning of the violator. For Nazism and Stalinism the existence of this surplus violence has been convincingly demonstrated by the disclosure of the tremendous scope of the genocide, far exceeding any pragmatic goal. While both are by no means dead as ideologies, their immediate political contexts are remote enough for us to see that the rights and wrongs of the Versailles treaty or the precarious geopolitical situation of the Soviet Union cannot account for the Holocaust and the Terror. But discussions of contemporary terrorism are often hijacked by politics, as if murder and suicide were rational means to achieve rational ends.

Lingering on the political dimension of ideological violence can obscure its true motivation. The suicide bomber and the perpetrator of genocide, cultural differences notwithstanding, share a taste for transcendence through violence. Their sublime selves are bought at the price of physical annihilation, of others and even themselves, if necessary. The sublime self is fashioned through a narrative dynamics of a utopian transformation, which is encouraged and supported by the group of fellow believers, whose mutually reinforcing convictions protect them from horror or remorse.[16] The core narrative structure of the violent subject of ideology remains the same, no matter what ideology he adopts. The Nazi camp guard, the Gulag functionary, the thug in

Bosnia, the genocidal butcher in Rwanda, the radical Islamic terrorist, all attempt to shatter the old law through violence in order to inaugurate the new law that will justify their metamorphosis into sublime New Men.

Bloodscripts attempts to portray this violent *subject of ideology* through specific examples of the Holocaust and its perception in popular culture, with some references to Stalin's Terror as well. While not engaging directly with bin Laden, I will look at his narrative predecessors who still haunt the popular imagination, with their incomprehensible cruelty, their glory in bloodshed, and their symbiosis between law and violence. It is not accidental that the handiest insult in the current terrorist controversies is "Nazi," each side flinging it at the other with scant regard for historical accuracy. Purists may roll their eyes but the vox populi has a point: the Nazi is in fact the paradigm of terror as a means of self-transformation.

And not only the individual perpetrator but also the community infected with ideological violence exhibits the same features, regardless of the political justification of it. Violence is not hidden as in the disciplinary state; on the contrary, it is proudly flaunted. But at the same time something is omitted from representation. Citizens of Hitler's and Stalin's empires knew about the concentration camps; they even knew what was done there, but they preferred not to know how it was done. And while the terrorist times his strike to coincide with the prime time news, his own self-representation substitutes dedication, sacrifice, or despair for the atrocity that is so plainly visible on the screen. The visibility of ideological violence is not the same thing as the Foucaldian spectacle of the scaffold, for it refuses to name what it has done in order to preserve its own discursive coherence. Ideology engenders the rhetoric of the *open secret,* something which is known to everybody but spoken of only in an oblique, indirect, euphemistic way. If discipline has to repress the sight of violence, ideology thrives on it but in strictly controlled doses, regulated by the authority, which derives its power from the monopoly on the violent sublime. While the ideological state possesses this monopoly by definition, the terrorist has to rely on the in-group of fellow believers and sympathizers, whose willful blindness may be more effective than imposed censorship.

The *subject of torture*, the *subject of discipline*, and the *subject of ideology* are the modalities of the violent self that I will explore in this book. They are not to be seen in terms of historical progression but of narrative classification. Genres are "sedimented" ideologies, to use Jameson's term, bearing inscriptions from different historical periods in their formal strategies.[17] Moreover, contrary to

Foucault's assertion, torture, discipline, and ideology have coexisted throughout much of the modern and postmodern periods. The disappearance of the scaffold has not eliminated the spectacle of violence, and ideology has not supplanted discipline but rather intertwined with it. In the universe of stories, which we inhabit, all kinds of violence coexist and interact, just as they coexist and interact in the global political and social landscape. The diverse narrative texts analyzed in the book reflect—and construct—the diverse self-narratives of violent subjects.

In the next section I will describe in detail the order and composition of the book's chapters, providing the reader with a guide to the maze of stories in which the horror of violence meets the pleasure of the text, the maze of bloodscripts.

Mapping Hell

The progression of the chapters follows the diminution of the sublime incoherence of violence in relation to the regulatory power of narrative. I begin with the texts in which the sublime is unleashed, resulting in a fragmented or incomprehensible identity, and end with those in which the sublime is harnessed to an ideological master-narrative, producing a collective script of subjectivity. To put it differently, I follow the path—structural if not historical—from the subject of torture to the subject of ideology.

In all generic classifications mixtures are probably more common than pure specimens. It is the same with genres of subjectivity, where each type is surrounded by a fuzzy border of intermediate forms. The book is structured in such a way as to allow for both heuristic precision and for appreciation of the richness and scope of the narrative field it explores. Each of the six chapters that follow describes the intersection of violence and identity in a specific narrative genre. Each chapter setting out a "pure" paradigm is followed by a chapter on the transitional type. While somewhat artificial, this scheme provides a roadmap for the reader to navigate among a variety of texts that are discussed in the book.

The texts are many because murder has so many faces. And yet, as I hope to show, these faces are like pictures in a family album, linked together by resemblance, descent, and wandering genes. Leafing through such an album, certain regularities soon begin to appear: Ted Bundy has the eyes of Dracula, and Dr. Hannibal Lecter the forehead of Holmes and the smile of Moriarty. The narratives of violent subjects are indeed a family in Wittgenstein's sense of the word: a set of verbal objects held together by multiple connections and shared traits, even though not every member of the set necessarily has all or any of these traits.

I begin with the genre whose explicitness in representing the physical side of violence has placed it in the same situation as the spectacle of the scaffold in the early modern period: abhorred by many and shamefacedly patronized by many more. Surely few public hangings drew a crowd the size of Stephen King's readership. Descending from the Gothic, horror fiction and film explore the violent excess of torture and mutilation. Chapter 1, "The Visible Man," discusses the subject of torture as incarnated in horror's monster. The monster is a walking oxymoron, an impossible subject, hovering on the fault line between language and silence. Like the ideal Victorian child, it is often seen but seldom heard. The chapter focuses on the imbalance between spectacle and story in horror fiction and argues that the genre's visual emphasis is linked to the violent sublime. Like its ancestor, the eighteenth- and nineteenth-century Gothic novel, horror fuses violence and transcendence. But in this fusion the human identity of the perpetrator melts in the ecstasy of the unspeakable. The tension between vision and word in horror expresses the clash between the violent sublime and narrativity. The chapter links the conventions of modern horror with the paradigmatic Gothic texts of the fin de siècle, such as Oscar Wilde's *The Picture of Dorian Gray,* H. G. Wells's *The Invisible Man,* and Bram Stoker's *Dracula.* It traces the postmodern resurgence of the monster in the fiction and films of Clive Barker, a contemporary British writer and director.

The popularity of horror is contested today by several hybrid genres of violence that attempt to fit the monstrous subject into a psychological, medical, or legal explanatory framework. By doing so, they generate a correspondingly hybrid violent subject, who combines the Gothic opacity of the monster with the transparency of the disciplined self. The most important of these genres is what is known as "true crime," largely dedicated to serial killers. The serial killer, whose violence is both mysterious, horrifying, and yet at least potentially explicable, provides a transition from the subject of torture to the subject of discipline.

In chapter 2, "Serial Killing and the Dismemberment of Identity," I discuss the narratives of serial killing. The subject of intense curiosity and no less intense fear, the serial killer has become a postmodern cultural hero. This chapter argues that the importance of the serial killer in contemporary culture stems from the paradox of his subjectivity. Seemingly random, the serial killer's actions are nevertheless supposed to correspond to some plot of psychological causality. There are two groups of such plots, the killer as monster and the killer as victim, whose historical and cultural genealogies the chapter traces in some detail. But both types of plots manifestly fail to account for the violence that exceeds any determinants, thus leaving the killer's selfhood in the state of flux and confusion that is misperceived as freedom. The chapter is panoramic, surveying a number of texts: nineteenth-century treatises on criminal anthropology by Cesare Lombroso and his followers; textbooks of criminal psychology; best selling true-crime books by John Douglas; and equally best selling novels by Thomas Harris (*The Silence of the Lambs*), Patricia Cornwell (*Postmortem*), Caleb Carr (*The Alienist*), and others.

The genre that exemplifies the cultural construction of the subject of discipline is the classic detective story. A cerebral and rationalistic genre, the classic detective story is a disciplinary narrative par excellence. It trims the plot down to a rigid formula, eliminating not only graphic descriptions of violence but desire, contingency, and accident. And yet at the heart of even the most bloodless detective story lies a corpse. The ultrarational detective story is a testimony to the disturbing power of violence, as it labors to produce a violent subject who is simultaneously totally rational and totally Other. The uncanny underside of the classic detective story, with its doubling, paradox, and inconsistency, reveals both the limitations of discipline and its covert reliance on the excluded and rigidly policed physical violence. In chapter 3, "The Library of the Body," I discuss the way in which narrative attempts to discipline violence by binding it to the plot of ratiocination. The chapter traces the rise of the disciplinary subject of violence in the classic detective story of the late-nineteenth and early-twentieth century, focusing on the works of the four defining writers of the genre: Edgar Allan Poe, Arthur Conan Doyle, G. K. Chesterton, and Agatha Christie.

The formulaic detective story that I discuss reaches its peak in the period between the two world wars, its own golden age. Today, while having a flourishing offspring that more or less conforms to its original rules, the detective story has also developed in new directions under the influence of its rival, the hard-boiled thriller of Dashiell Hammett and Raymond Chandler. The classic Golden Age texts inscribed the disciplinary paradigm of the violent subject with unmatched clarity. The hard-boiled thriller and the film noir originally registered the crumbling of this paradigm in the unsettled social environment of mid-twentieth-century America. Precisely because the hard-boiled conventions respond to social violence, I have chosen to relate to them through an unusual generic offshoot that combines features of the hard-boiled thriller and utopia. I will call this offshoot the *investigative dystopia* and use it to chart the transition from the subject of discipline to the subject of ideology.

In chapter 4, "Utopia Noir," the sublime "I" clashes with the private eye; Sam Spade takes on the SS Übermensch. Following the traditional plot structure of the thriller and featuring a private detective as the protagonist, such dystopias investigate not an ordinary crime but state-sponsored genocide. Through the narrative of discipline, they attempt to confront the bloody havoc wrought by the New Man in pursuit of his sublime self. But the secret that they pursue is the open secret of atrocity, the knowledge of the crime that is available to all and acceptable to none. And the subjectivity of the perpetrator that emerges from such texts is very different from the detective story's criminal, who accepts his punishment as part of his own disciplinary narrative. Rather, it is the detective who ultimately becomes the sacrificial victim, acting out the temporary defeat of discipline by ideology. I consider several recent investigative dystopias and situate them in the context of the classic utopian/dystopian tradition, from Wells to Orwell.

In chapter 5, "Doctor Death," we encounter the New Man face to face. And as we enter utopia, we find ourselves back in the horror country. If the subject of horror fiction is a monster, the subject of utopia is a creator of monsters. The monster unleashes violence and is destroyed by it; the creator of monsters controls violence and makes others bear the brunt of his sublime self-fashioning. The pain, ugliness, and mutilation of his victims are the necessary counterpart to his glorious rebirth in the image of his ideal.

The New Man was born from the spirit of science. Dr. Mengele, the notorious Nazi torturer-physician, has become an emblem of Nazism. His story is retold in the literary texts I analyze: Rolph Hochhuth's The *Deputy,* Ira Levin's *Boys from Brazil,* Lucius Shepard's "Mengele," and others. Rather than reflecting Mengele's actual biography, however, these works look for inspiration in H. G. Wells's science fiction novel *The Island of Dr. Moreau* (1896). This rewriting of the representative New Man as a monster-maker through dystopian science fiction reveals both the historical genealogy and the narrative composition of the Nazi subject of ideology. The intertextual continuity between twentieth-century atrocity and nineteenth-century fantasy of self-transcendence accurately reflects the ideological link between Nazism and the bio-ideologies of Social Darwinism and eugenics. Such ideologies hollow out the positivism of science to make room for the "biological sublime" predicated on the scientific superman's identification with the ruthlessness of post–Darwinian nature. The violence unleashed by the "applied biology" of Nazism is what happens when a search for knowledge is transformed into a search for identity. The figure of Mengele/Moreau, the remote and horrifying Doctor Death, is an eidolon of the Nazi New Man who finds purity in massacre and sublimity in torture.

Doctor Death is only a specter today, but a specter stalking postmodernity. The aftermath of his reign has been marked by what is aptly named "the memory wars." In chapter 6, "The Singularity of History," I analyze the memory wasteland left in the wake of violence. Returning to the issue of representability or unrepresentability of violence, I focus on the current controversy regarding the trauma of the Holocaust. Raging with particular ferocity in the last two decades and generating such scandalous highlights as the Paul

De Man and Benjamin Wilkomirski affairs, the memory wars have moved back and forth over the no-man's-land of historical trauma. What is the proper response to the Holocaust: silence, incoherent stuttering of the traumatized survivor, or imaginative storytelling? In this chapter I analyze the clash of traumatic memory and narrative imagination in the light of its dominant trope, the metaphor of "the black hole."

The black hole is the breakdown of the space–time continuum that represents the breakdown of historical narratives under the weight of an intolerable trauma. While such a breakdown is perceived by many as the only authentic response to the Holocaust, I argue it mirrors the central narrative device of the perpetrators' self-narratives, ellipsis. The "memory wars" are essentially a battle of the ellipsis. Should this hole in the discourse be reverently preserved—and, if possible, enlarged—or should it be filled with a restored narrative, even if this narrative can never aspire to the status of the absolute truth? I argue that in presenting genocide as ineffable and sublime, the critical discourse of trauma creates parity between victims and perpetrators and obscures the ideological nature of violent self-transcendence.

As opposed to the critical glorification of silence, popular culture appropriates the Holocaust as a proper subject for storytelling. This storytelling increasingly fits into what many see as scandalously incongruous generic molds: fantasy, science fiction, and the fairy tale. Holocaust fantasies literalize the metaphor of the black hole, using it as a narrative device or part of the projected fictional world. In doing so, they confront the issue of action and choice that "trauma studies" disavow. In opting for imagination over memory, popular culture reconstructs history as a field of conflicting subject positions rather than a blank space of victimization. It combats the dangerous seduction of the violent sublime by resorting to "strong" narrative patterns and restoring the traditional narrative division into protagonists and antagonists, heroes and villains. And yet, in doing so, it courts the inevitable falsification of memory.

The last chapter offers a parallel analysis of the critical discourse of trauma (by Shoshana Felman, Dori Laub, Kali Tal, and others) and of Holocaust fantasies (J. R. Dunn's *Days of Cain,* Jane Yolen's *The Briar Rose,* Lisa Goldstein's "Breadcrumbs and Stones," and the film *Life Is Beautiful*). It closes the circle by returning to the issues of chapter 1, but situates the problematic of speech and silence in a political and historical context.

Each chapter in the book highlights a specific form of violent identity and looks at a different selection of narratives. But there are common threads that link them together. First is the notion of the sublime. Whether emphasized as in horror, repressed as in the detective story, or utilized as in utopia, the violent sublime is central to the narrative construction of the violent subject.

Even when the golden age detective story attempts to deny the sublimity of violence by squeezing it into the procrustean bed of instrumental rationality, all its conventions are shaped by this denial, creating ineluctable rifts and strains in the textual fabric.

The second general concern that runs through all the chapters in the book is the relation between body and narrative. Linked to the first one (for the sublimity of violence is the result of its corporeal nature), my understanding of this issue differs from the extreme "constructionism" of such theoreticians as Judith Butler. While the body is indeed constructed in discourse, it also constructs discourse. Pain, suffering, violence, and death can only be apprehended through socially and ideologically contingent narratives. But the violated body speaks in the language of silence. In particular, as I argue in chapter 1, it manifests itself in the visual impact of physical violence.

The concept of corporeality leads to the conundrum of individuality. Among the "solutions" to violence an important place is occupied by the biological discourse of differentiation that purports to explain aggression by locating it in individual and collective deviance. I see biology as an ideology rather than as an irrefutable science of the corporeal human subject. It is not a solution to the enigma of violence but part of the problem. This issue is spotlighted in chapter 2 (on serial killers) and chapter 5 (on the Nazi New Man). In both cases, I emphasize free agency and argue that biological explanations of violence actually contribute to its spread by offering highly problematic scripts of individual behavior. It is particularly true in the case of Nazism, where biology becomes a foundation for the utopian ideology of a murderously sublime subject.

Finally, an important issue—indirectly raised throughout the book and brought to the fore in the last chapter—is the ethical dimension of the nexus of violence and narrativity. If narrative provides the templates of violent identities, contains the visceral horror of killing, and allows murderers to function as social subjects, would it not be better to do without it altogether? The answer, also implicit in the project itself and elaborated in the conclusion, is "no." There is no return to storyless innocence. Human beings are narrative animals, finding themselves only through the lineaments of a tale. The attraction of violence lies precisely in the phantasmagoric escape from the strictures of narrative coherence, into the timeless realm of the sublime. If violence enters culture through narrative, it is also through narrative that it is apprehended and resisted.

The Visible Man

Knife in the head before, now in the hand
Makes little difference. Pain is never personal;
As love or anger unconfined, it takes
Part in each moment and person, unconditioned
By time or identity, like an atmosphere.
There is no giving or receiving, only
Pain and creation coming out of pain.

—SIDNEY KEYES, "Gilles de Rais"

BOOKS OF BLOOD

"Everybody is a book of blood," says the epigraph to Clive Barker's six-volume collection of horror stories, *Books of Blood*. "Wherever we are opened, we are red."

Here, it seems, horror is finally honest about itself. What is it if not one giant book of blood, fixated on the tortured, mutilated, grossly violated body? What other genre could produce "splatterpunk" novels and "slasher" movies? Many people's discomfort with, if not outright revulsion from, horror literature and film stem precisely from what is seen as a gratuitous pleasure in graphic scenes of torture, a pornography of violence. Horror fiction, it is often claimed by its critics, is not really fiction but rather a pretext for sating the reader's perverse appetites with pictures of violence. In pornography, plot, characterization, and other elements of narrativity wither to fig leaves on the obscene body of sexual description; similarly, it is said, horror jettisons all literary pretensions in pursuit of graphic bloodshed.

However, Barker's mammoth collection demonstrates that the spectacle of violence does not necessarily dam the flow of words. The indefatigable storytelling activity of Stephen King, another world-famous horror writer, pits narrative ingenuity against the speechlessness of visual shock. The body is both "red" and "read."

Horror's violent subject is born in this tug-of-war between story and spectacle. Horror, whether as fiction or film, emphasizes visibility: it is structured around the spectacular body of the monster. The word "monster" comes from the Latin "monstrum," i.e., "portent," deriving from *monere,* "to warn." A monster is a warning flag of danger, striking the eye with terror: "the traditional idea of the monstrous was strongly associated with visual display, and monsters . . . were to be seen, not heard" (Baldick 45). But on the other hand, horror is a popular narrative genre. Thus, the horror text is strained by the opposition of spectacle and narrative, of what Peter Brooks called "the imaginary versus the symbolic order" (207). Even in horror cinema, where the scales are naturally tipped toward the spectacle, there is the same tension between the Imaginary and the Symbolic. The violent sublime is inscribed in the gap between the conventional structure of the narrative and the shocking visibility of the monster's body, which, I will argue, is both the body of the perpetrator and that of the victim.

The paradoxes of violence shape the paradoxical identity of the monster.[1] The monster is a living oxymoron, created by the collapse of a binary dichotomy, such as linving/dead (the undead vampire) or human/animal (the werewolf) (Carroll 34). Scholars of horror have pointed out that the monster is a subject beyond humanity, occupying a position that Judith Butler calls "the humanly unthinkable" (1993, 8). Often, "the humanly unthinkable" is understood in terms of a specific moral panic, as in Butler's own discussion of gender bending. But whatever sexual taboos the monster transgresses, its violence creates a deeper disruption in the structure of discourse. The "humanly unthinkable" subject is the one who has committed deeds that "put their perpetrators outside of the pale of humanity," with any history of torture, genocide, or serial killing providing a sufficient catalogue of such acts (Sheleff 16). Horror translates the abstraction of ethical excommunication into the concreteness of visual impression: when a slimy shape rises from the swamp, we do not need to be told that it is "outside the pale of humanity."

But the monster's ultimate transgression is of the one boundary that actual, as opposed to fictional, violence cannot cross. In horror fiction and film, the monster is often not only a fantastic reflection of the subject of torture but also an image of the victim. The monster expresses the commonality of the flesh that underlies violence: we are all books of blood, we are all potential monstrous displays. Its terrifying and obscene body is simultaneously the ruined corporeality of the victim and the ruined subjectivity of the perpetrator. This might appear perverse and often is. But the perversity of horror discloses the true seduction of the violent sublime, which is the escape from the slippery discriminations of morality into the incontestable materiality of the body.

Volume 1 of Barker's collection opens with the eponymous tale "The Book of Blood." In this tale a fraudulent medium is attacked by the enraged ghosts whose messages he falsifies. Determined that the world should know the truth, they use his body as a parchment on which to write the stories of their predicament. Grotesquely scarred with their inscriptions, the medium's body is transformed into "their [the dead] page, their book, the vessel for their autobiographies" (11). He becomes a living script. The female psychic investigator, in love with the medium, assumes the role of the enraptured reader of the body/text: "She would read them all, report them all, every last syllable that glistened and seeped beneath her adoring fingers, so that the world would know the stories the dead tell" (16).

The medium's grotesque body is both a spectacle and a sign. It is pornographic, not in the sense of producing a specifically sexual pleasure in the audience, but rather as a fetishistic object that straddles the boundary between verbal and visual. In her discussion of pornography, Linda Williams describes the genre as structured by the opposition of visual stasis and narrative drive. On the one hand, she claims, pornography is a "frenzy of the visible," in which the naked body "provokes a disturbance in the text" (43). On the other hand, pornography is "just another way of speaking about and constructing the apparent 'truths' of sex" (122). As a story, the pornographic text projects a certain modality of the gendered, sexualized subject, with which it invites its readers to identify. But its efforts to generate a smooth flow of textual identification are disrupted by the spectacle of the body. This body, with its sex organs that have no intrinsic meaning but that, nevertheless, simply and indisputably *are,* interferes with the misogynist or banal message of the text. In its visual emphasis pornography strives to capture the irreducible *thingness* of the body; but as a text (whether verbal or cinematic) it is structured by the cultural meanings of sex and gender. While gesturing at the sexual body, pornography covers its nakedness with stories.

Just as all human bodies are endowed with genitals of one sort or another, they all have viscera. They can be cut, opened, brutalized in various ways. They are all material and mortal. As shows, horror fiction and film convey the irreducible materiality—and vulnerability—of the body. As stories, they construct, in various ways, the "truth" of violence and victimization. But the visual impact of violence interferes with their ability to inscribe coherent identities. Like "the spectacle of the naked or nearly naked body . . . [that] retards any possible forward narrative drive" in pornography (Williams 71), the violated body in horror undermines narrativity.

A way to conceptualize the spectacle of violence is through what Barthes calls "the third meaning" of a visual image. "The third meaning" is "a message without a code" (36). Also called by him "the denoted image," it is what exceeds the symbolic or representational function of a display and yet accounts for its power to hold the gaze. The "denoted image" is composed of a network of visual elements, untranslatable into a verbal narrative. Barthes's formal definition has an advantage over Freudian and Lacanian analyses of specularity because it is not grounded in a specific theory of psychosexual development. All such theories may be contested on various grounds. But there is no contesting the fact that a mutilated human body is the object of a horrified and fascinated gaze. When we see it, we stare, or we avert our eyes, unable to bear its "message"; we throw up or run away or remain rooted to the spot; we may laugh, jaded by too many such images, or we may cry. But we are not indifferent, and the message gets through, even though we may be unable to say what it is. There are many codes used to translate this human reaction to violence into discourse, but none of them can quite capture the impact of seeing the violated body. Calling him a "denoted image" is a rather antiseptic way of describing Barker's character, scarred and mutilated, bleeding on a filthy floor. But when blood flows, asepsis is what is needed.

The interaction between the spectacle and the story in horror suggests that the current critical consensus over the construction of the body in discourse needs some modification. This consensus (which, of course, is not undisputed) claims that the materiality of the body is created in, and through, language: culture endows us with the capacity "to read the inscribed messages of socially constructed bodies" (Burroughs and Ehrenreich 1). Judith Butler's highly influential analysis of the body describes it as a "variable boundary, a surface whose permeability is politically regulated, a signifying practice . . ." (1990, 139). It seems that Barker's tale offers an allegory of such theories, with the medium playing the role of the passive "socially constructed body," and the angry incorporeal ghosts descending upon him like the furies of the Foucaldian discourse. However, the tale demonstrates not only the power of the discourse over the body, but also the power of the body over discourse. The body validates the writing rather than the other way around. The ghosts' stories are true because they are written on the flesh. The medium told lies in order to hide his inability to communicate with the dead, and his tales, like all spiritualist communications, were ambiguous, obscure, and suspect. But the book of blood is incontrovertible by virtue of the terrible spectacle it presents. Words are slippery, but there is no arguing with wounds.

The female investigator recognizes her own corporeality in the medium's violated body. The caresses she lavishes upon the mutilated flesh highlight the intensity with which violence brings home the knowledge of the body's irreducible materiality. In a sense, the investigator represents the audience of horror, whose involvement with the spectacle of violence has baffled and disgusted many high-minded critics. But such critics often fail to distinguish between the reactionary or puerile message of the text and the visual impact of the violated body, whose truth is all the more potent because it cannot be articulated.

Butler claims in *Bodies that Matter* that the materiality of the body is merely the result of a discursive "process of materialization that stabilizes over time to produce the effect of boundary, fixity, and surface we call matter" (9). But this "effect" is far more efficiently produced by a moment of pain than by hours of such verbal persuasion. We may be told that the body contains moist mechanisms that work independently of the mind. But we are truly convinced of the *thingness* of the body when we see it open—and red. To see is to believe; to see violence is to believe that we are material and mortal.

The victim of torture "is only a body, and nothing else beside that" (Amery 33). Physical violence endured with no possibility of resistance or reciprocity makes the flesh the only reality there is: "only in torture does the transformation of the person into flesh become complete" (ibid.). In the silence of the victim's pain "the edges of the self become coterminous with the edges of the body it will die with" (Scarry 33). Of course, any physical pain has the effect of reminding the sufferer of his or her corporeality. But sickness can be symbolized away, transformed into a seal of purity, like consumption in Henry James's *The Wings of the Dove* or stigmata of desire, like cholera in Thomas Mann's "Death in Venice." For the victim of violence, especially violence unmotivated, unearned, unexpected, there is no escape into language. The death of language in the brutality of suffering pervades Primo Levi's *Survival in Auschwitz.* In the *Lager,* which is essentially a giant torture chamber, "the reality was revealed to us: we had reached the bottom. . . . Nothing belongs to us anymore . . . if we speak, they will not listen to us, and if they listen, they will not understand. They will even take away our name . . ." (22). Outside language, locked in the brutal *thingness* of physical suffering, the victim confronts—and becomes—the Real.

Survivors of torture, rape, and attempted murder are a special minority. They are admired but also feared because they have touched the bedrock of humanity. Like Oedipus after his self-blinding, they become witnesses to the unspeakable. But while nobody would willingly follow them into the anguish-filled realm of "total reality," the desire to see their quest is what underlies the Grand Guignol spectacle. We may condemn this desire, but we cannot deny its existence. The popularity of horror comics, films, and novels is only a recent incarnation of the age-old popularity of the spectacle of the scaffold. Public torture was still an acceptable method of punishment in the eighteenth century. Public execution was only discontinued in England in the middle of the nineteenth century. The visual industry of violence today is a direct continuation of this trend (and its many critics should consider that in this case a fake is definitely preferable to the real thing). The artificiality of the horror film mitigates the raw impact of the violent sublime but does not completely neutralize it. And society needs this impact, while simultaneously deploring it. The spectacle of the violated body fulfils an important function in the construction of identity by providing a model for being in the body, being a body.

Jean Baudrillard asserts that in postmodernism the body disappears, eaten away by what he calls "the ecstasy of communication." In the obscenely visible space of the electronic media and the Internet "this body, our body, often appears simply superfluous" (153). Baudrillard's view is essentially nostalgic, harking back to the Golden Age of corporeality that never was. Mortality has not been abolished by electronic communication. But the development of the society of the spectacle, coupled with increasing personal security from violence, have made it inevitable that new means of experiencing the "total reality" of the flesh will be found in the realm of visual representation. Contra Baudrillard, it is possible to claim that what he calls "the obscenity of the visible" creates the modern and postmodern material body rather than destroys it. Horror's obscenely visible book of blood is what we read in order to learn how to be "a body and nothing else besides" (Amery 33).

JUST LOOKING

In H. G. Wells's *The Invisible Man* (1896) there is a scene that links violence and vision in a particularly striking way. Griffin, the Invisible Man, an outcast genius who becomes a terrorist and a murderer, is set upon by an enraged mob that beats him to death. And as his invisible body suffers kicks and blows, it curdles back into visibility. Like a photographic negative, his absent corporeality is developed by pain.[2] The secret interior of his body is displayed for all to see:

> Suddenly an old woman, peering under the arm of the big navvy, screamed sharply. "Looky there!" she said, and thrust out a wrinkled finger.
>
> And looking where she pointed, every one saw, faint and transparent as though it was made of glass, so that veins and arteries and bones and nerves could be distinguished, the outline of a hand, a hand limp and prone. It grew clouded and opaque even as they stared . . .
>
> And so, slowly, beginning at the hands and feet and creeping along his limbs to the vital centers of his body, that strange change continued. It was like the slow spreading of a poison. First came the little white nerves, a hazy grey sketch of a limb, then the glassy bone and intricate arteries, then the flesh

> and skin, first a faint fogginess and then growing rapidly dense and opaque. Presently they could see his crushed chest and his shoulders, and the dim outline of his drawn and battered features. (Wells 1933, 305)

With the help of a mysterious chemical process, Griffin has previously made himself invisible. Escape from visibility for him equals escape from the body. Griffin is an albino, with no money or class, shabbily dressed, painfully aware of being the object of mocking and prying stares. And so he opts for the radical solution of total invisibility, which to him represents freedom from the detested burden of corporeality. To see but not to be seen; to ravage others' bodies, while having no body to feel the sting of retribution—this is Griffin's dream, shattered at the moment he realizes that an invisible body is a body still, vulnerable to heat, cold, hunger, and most of all, pain. His subsequent violence is an attempt to complete his project, to foist, as it were, the remnants of his own corporeality onto the despised bodies of the human herd. At the end, his project is turned against him, as violence becomes the means to reveal his pitiful nakedness to the group of spectators, all of whom are protected from his reciprocal gaze.

This scene epitomizes the spectacle of violence, central to the aesthetics of horror. At work here is a double movement of identification and disavowal. On the one hand, Griffin's mutilated body elicits a visceral response from his killers, forcing them to identify with his pain. On the other hand, the scene establishes a new social hierarchy, as the would-be invisible dictator is now an object of scorn and derision. For a victim, to be seen is a condition of abjection. But in this abjection also lies the victim's only power.

Violence may be incorporated into the discourse of domination. As such, it becomes a signifying activity, symbolizing something other than itself: the might of a state, the victory of an ideology, the triumph of an individual. But in the sight of violence there is also a "surplus" emotional affect, which is not reducible to the symbolism of the vanquished victim. The spectacle of the tortured body is greater than the story that it is supposed to illustrate. Griffin's death may be understood in several different ways: as just retribution; as hate crime; as society's self-protection. But none of these explanations can quite capture the feelings of the mob petrified by their own bloody handiwork when it becomes fully and brutally visible.

Perpetrators often respond to the spectacle of violence by banishing it outside language, in the hope that such banishment will remove the moral issues posed by the act of homicide. However, in many horror texts, conscience turns out to be far easier to pacify than the guts that rebel at the shock of spilled blood. In Oscar Wilde's *The Picture of Dorian Gray* (1891), the dialectic of language and spectacle in violence structures the aftermath of Dorian's murder of Basil Hallward. In order to keep what's left of his sanity, the murderer deliberately separates the sight of the dead body from language. The body is the "thing . . . seated in the chair, straining over the table with bowed head, and humped back, and long fantastic arms" (466). Refusing to name the corpse, Dorian also refuses to name himself as the agent of Basil's death: "He felt that the secret of the whole thing was not to realize the situation. The friend who had painted the fatal portrait to which all his misery had been due had gone out of his life. That was enough" (ibid). But exiled from language, "the thing" implacably hovers on the fringes of Dorian's field of vision. Dorian can only get some temporary peace of mind by having the corpse destroyed without a trace by a chemist friend. And then he becomes burdened with another dead body as the chemist, whom he blackmails into helping him, commits suicide. What Dickens in *Oliver Twist* calls "an item of mortality" cannot be gotten rid of easily. Like Dorian, other horror-fiction murderers are also haunted by the bodies, rather than the spirits, of their victims. In F. Marion Crawford's classic ghost story "The Screaming Skull" (1911), for example, the malefactor is graphically killed by the skull of the title, while in M. R. James's "Martin's Close" (1911) it is the entire corpse that is on the prowl. This convention is an exaggeration of the reaction of such murderers as Bill Sikes who are unhinged by the sight of the flesh and the blood—"such flesh and so much blood"—of the victim (Dickens 1837, 424). The "sight of his victim, his first victim, bloody and pitiful at his feet" makes the Invisible Man abandon for a time his schemes of world domination (Wells 1933, 292).

Paradoxically, the Symbolic becomes a haven from the wordless sublimity of violence. If the subject of violence feels that his psychic integrity is being dissolved by the "sight of his victim," he will attempt to anchor his identity in a story. He will seek a narrative to keep the horror of the violated body at bay and to reduce it to a mere cipher of powerlessness. Polish writer Stanislaw Lem gives a striking description of the difference between the visual and the cognitive impact of murder on the behavior of the SS killers during the execution of the Jews. The lower ranks beat and abuse the condemned men, but the officer is invariably polite. He is also the one who carries out the shooting with no flicker of hesitation:

> Although he spoke to us, you see, we were not people. He knew that we comprehended human speech but that nevertheless we were not human; he knew this quite well. . . . The simpler ones among his men did not possess this higher knowledge; the appearance of humanity given by our bodies, our two legs, faces, hands, eyes, this appearance deterred them a little from their duty; thus they *had to butcher those bodies to make them unlike people's.* But for him such primitive proceedings were no longer necessary. (Lem 1983, 65–66; emphasis mine)

The "simpler ones" are intoxicated by the sight of human beings being reduced to the "thing," the deindividualized bloody object. This intoxication is what prompts them to engage in sadistic abuse, but it is also what makes them disturbed and uneasy afterwards. The officer, however, is immune to the spectacle of violence because he is equipped with an ideological narrative that blinds him to the actual sight of the victims. He does not see the "thing"; he looks straight through it to the abstractions of racial science. Being immune to the fascination of violence makes him also incapable of empathy.

The officer is a New Man, a subject of ideology, rather than an ordinary killer. His underlings, like the mob who killed Griffin, are far more representative of nonideological reactions to, and participation in, violence. The Medusa-like fascination of the violated body is powerfully described in Dickens's *A Tale of Two Cities* (1859), the French Revolution novel replete with images of staring eyes, gorgon faces, sights that cannot be endured and yet must be seen. The crowds that gather around the guillotine are animated not only by vengeful rage but also by "a species of fervour or intoxication" that eventually prompts some of them "to brave the guillotine unnecessarily, and to die by it" (310). This intoxication, the delirium of the show of violence, represents for Dickens an attempt "to collapse the limits of the self as it is conceived in subject-centered terms" (Kucich 200). This collapse is both sought and abhorred. This is the dialectic of horror whose pleasure is predicated on revulsion and shock.

Griffin's battered body represents a defeat of language by the spectacle of violence. Just before his death, already half-mad with rage and privation, he issues a number of declarations, threatening the population with terror. "Death, the unseen Death, is coming" (Wells 1933, 293). Like his mysterious books holding the secrets of invisibility, these "strange missives" are invested with the magic of the Symbolic, a premonition of a new order, to which this would-be New Man is desperate to ascend out of the mire of his own corporeality. This magic is made void by his death, the proclamations meaningless, the books undecipherable. What is left is an anonymous body beyond language in all its ghastly visibility. Death is not unseen.

In his proclamations, refusing to divulge his real name, Griffin calls himself "Invisible Man the First," promising a new era, "the Epoch of the Invisible Man," a reign of anonymous tyrants (293). This is the namelessness of power, in which the proper name of the ruler is supplanted by a general title. Ironically, however, Griffin is ultimately granted another kind of namelessness: that of the victim, as his individuality is obscured by the terrible sight of his "crushed" body. There is the anonymity of language and the anonymity of the spectacle, and Griffin's entire career may be plotted between the two. He aspires to lose himself in language, becoming a word rather than a man, an unseen Terror, an intangible symbol of pure power. All he achieves is to become a "bloody and pitiful" sight (292).

In being both an image of violence and a symbol of power, Griffin exemplifies the duality of the violated body, which, like the duality of the Lacanian Real, is "at the same time that of corporeal contingency and that of logical consistency" (Zizek 171). In other words, the body is both an intrusion of mute and incommunicable pain that shatters language and a token of social communication, traded in the stock exchange of ideological narratives. Thus, it possesses a double fascination. In terms of "logical consistency," the book of blood tells the story of difference: the difference between the powerful and the powerless. But as an image of "corporeal contingency," the book of blood is beyond words. It inhabits the ecstatic realm of the sublime.

"I AM EVERY DEAD THING"

Horror's tales of violent excess probe the desire that leads ordinary human subjects to lose themselves in this realm, to seek the condition of sublimity that is also self-erasure. Horror texts not only detail the transformation of a man into a monster but also uncover its underlying dialectic of repulsion and attraction. Nobody is born a subject of torture: this is a condition that people achieve because they aspire to it. And the generic tradition of horror investigates the nature of this aspiration.

Contemporary horror is an offshoot of the Gothic novel of the late eighteenth- through early-nineteenth centuries. Since the blood-and-thunder excesses of Ann Radcliffe and "Monk" Lewis, preoccupation with violence has been the backbone of the genre.[3] The shadow of Jack the Ripper hovers over the great horror thrillers of the fin de siècle. Their contemporary descendants, steeped in visual culture, are obsessed with graphic torture and mutilation. Despite the conventional critical emphasis on sexuality, it is violence that constitutes the one stable topos of the genre.[4] True, Dr. Jekyll becomes the monstrous Mr. Hyde to ease the intolerable burden of middle-class repression and hypocrisy; Dracula's female victims are seduced by his Sadeian charms; Dorian Gray exchanges identities with a work of art ostensibly in order to live a life of sensual pleasure. But while the beginning of monsterhood may be sexual, its subsequent development invariably leads to violence. Dracula is a killer; Lucy, the angelic beauty turned into a vampire by his love bite, preys on children; both Jekyll–Hyde and Dorian Gray commit senseless and atrocious murders. Beyond eroticism, horror discloses the existence of another desire, more difficult to pinpoint, which is sometimes designated by the empty phrase "motiveless violence." No human action is motiveless; what is meant by the phrase is rather that the motivation of a murderer exceeds both the rational calculus of profit and the Freudian calculus of sex.

The Picture of Dorian Gray explores the trajectory of the violent desire and its consequences. It suggests that the murderer wants to be a monster and that monstrosity does not mean freedom from the annoying restrictions of the superego. Rather, it means a far more radical freedom from the self. The monster is a subject who succumbs to the seduction of pure materiality, seeking escape from the Symbolic in the wordless revelation of the violent sublime.

Wilde's novel has been variously seen as immoral or as excessively moralistic. But almost all critics agree that Dorian's bargain to exchange identities with his own portrait is a means to an end. Hedged in by the taboos of a homophobic society, Dorian seems to seek nothing more extraordinary than the possibility of enjoying himself in peace. However, those who, like Eve Kosofsky Sedgwick, see the novel as a parable of homosexual desire, find it difficult to explain Dorian's subsequent transformation from a placid hedonist into a near-psychotic killer (67–91). He has what he wants: why can't he just be happy, instead of driving Sybil Vane to suicide and knifing Basil?

The key is "what he wants." And it is certainly more than a few clandestine trips to the brothels of Soho. Dorian's wish is to be an objet d'art, to exchange the mutability and uncertainty of discourse for the materiality of painting. He wants to escape time, to remain frozen in "this particular day in June" (391). Impervious to aging, forever fixed in his perfection, Dorian would become the body of the Real, the corporeal self-presence untroubled by the divisiveness of consciousness. To acquire the immediacy of a spectacle, Dorian gives up his temporal—and hence narrative—subjectivity.

Before some nameless force grants his desire, Dorian cries out: "I would give my soul for that!" (391) His "soul," in this novel of a devil's bargain without Devil or God, is his humanity, predicated on change, mutability, and mortality. And instead of being the means to an end, the loss of the soul is an end in itself. It is not the price Dorian reluctantly pays for his transformation, but the transformation for which he has to pay a price. And the price is murder.

Dorian first commits a murder by proxy, driving Sybil Vane to suicide. But his metamorphosis into a body without a soul is only completed when he stabs Basil Hallward, his best friend and the painter of the fateful picture. After the stabbing, Dorian experiences the ultimate evacuation of subjectivity. There are no feelings left: no craving, no hope, no memory, no remorse. Basil's corpse is a "thing," but so is Dorian himself. He is a beautiful object, just like the beautiful objects that he collects and that he pities for their impermanence. In the moment of violence, he becomes that phantasmagoric flesh that, poised outside language, appears to beckon with the promise of immortality and omnipotence.

But being a purely corporeal subject is impossible. Dorian eventually realizes that being "a body and nothing else besides" paradoxically means renunciation of bodily pleasures: "But I seem to have lost the passion, and forgotten the desire" (492). Desire and passion are products of the mind, physical sensations filtered through the soul. And Dorian's soul is missing.

Dorian's desire is perverse, not in the homophobic sense of the Wilde trials, but as a murderer's desire is perverse because it apes the horror of the victim. For Amery and Levi and every other torture victim, being an object is the ultimate degradation. For Dorian, it is the ultimate bliss. The victim has both his soul and his body destroyed; the perpetrator believes he can amputate the soul and enjoy the self-presence of the body at the expense of somebody else's suffering. But once violence is unleashed, it spares no one. Dorian ends up as just another anonymous corpse. "Lying on the floor was a dead man, in evening dress, with a knife in his heart. He was withered, wrinkled, and loathsome of visage" (503). In order to experience his own corporeality as sublime, the torturer destroys the bodies of others: "the goal of the torturer is to make . . . the body emphatically and crushingly *present* by destroying it" (Scarry 49). But this absolute presence of the body, unclouded by language and consciousness, is achievable only in death.

Every time Dorian commits an act of violence, his picture undergoes an additional transformation, becoming as monstrous as the bodies of his victims. When he spills blood, blood appears on the portrait's hands. The fairy tale simplicity of this visual image expresses the link between the murderer's desire and the victim's body. The murderer wants to be as Real as he perceives the victim's body to be. In a sense, the murderer wants to *be* the victim. Cleansed of his limited subjectivity, he aspires to the condition of the sublime, in which "the body affects the soul" and in which the body ultimately consumes the soul (Lyotard 1991, 99). Thus, his monstrosity is the monstrosity of all flesh. It symbolizes not so much the distortion of morality as the inescapability of mortality.

Horror's monsters have been often defined through their deviance from the "standard" human corporeality. However, for all their baroque bodily shapes, they share one salient feature with humans: materiality. Even spiritual entities, such as ghosts, enter horror fiction only through their material manifestations. The monster's corporeal difference acts as a defamiliarizing device (in Viktor Scklovsky's sense of the word), to return us to the unfamiliarity of our own bodies, whose irreducible materiality the mind stubbornly refuses to accept. Dorian's body, so alluring and yet so monstrous, is the body as a "thing," exiled from language and narrative by violence. There are many other horror texts that explore the same trope. The protagonist of Ray Bradbury's story "Skeleton" (1945), for example, becomes obsessed with the thought that he has a monster inside him, a Halloween horror, "one of those jointed, snowy, hard things, one of those foul, dry, brittle, gouge-eyed, skull-faced, snake-fingered, rattling things that sway from neck-chains in abandoned webbed closets" (184). The "thing" is ordinary human bones. The monster of horror is frightening not because it is the distant and impossible Other but because it is the Other who is a constant and unavoidable companion of the conscious self. The monster is the human body, with its capacity to violate, to be violated, and to thrill in wordless identification with violence. On a small and carefully circumscribed scale of aesthetic experience, horror does what Scarry describes torture as doing: the body is set against the psyche, "made a weapon against [the self], made to betray [the self] on behalf of the enemy, made to be the enemy" (48).

LANGUAGE OF ANGELS

Imprisoned in the Imaginary, the monster in horror has a strained and equivocal relationship with language, in particular with the language of self-description. The monster is a creature that is seen for what it is but who cannot give a coherent account of itself. Sometimes when a monster is disguised as an ordinary human being, this narrative deprivation coincides with its transformation into a "thing." In tales of the werewolf, for example, a radical physical change that heralds the onset of violence vitiates the subject's self-consistency to the point of amnesia. Returning to the human form, the werewolf often has no memories of its nocturnal phase. But on the other hand, as a narrative genre, horror needs to equip the monster with some sort of narrative identity and link its violence to a specific moral, epistemological, or sexual transgression. Thus, the monster's body becomes "infinitely interpretable . . . a machine that, in its Gothic mode, produces meaning and can represent any horrible trait that the reader feeds into the narrative" (Halberstam 21). But the running of this "machine" is never smooth, as narrative interpretation is impeded by the violent spectacle. The meanings that horror produces aggregate around a core of semantic emptiness that is the monster's visible body. The monster eludes the straightjacket of narrative interpretation through the enigmatic "message without a code" of its visibility. Some horror texts explicitly dramatize the conflict between spectacle and language by linking the appearance of the monster with a disturbance in the temporal and causal progression of the narrative.

M. R. James's ghost story "The Mezzotint" (1904) and the film *A Nightmare on Elm Street* (1984) oppose ordinary time to the time of the monster. The monster appears in a picture (in James's story) or in dreams (in the film), in a realm where order, duration, and causality are so scrambled that no narrative of origin can be reconstructed even in retrospect. The two observers of the moving mezzotint wonder whether they are looking at the past or the future: "Has it happened already, or is it going to come off?" (46). In Freddie-haunted dreams there is only the endless "now" of a nightmare. But this realm is not "illusory" in any poetic sense; having been killed in a dream or in a picture, the victim remains dead. The two monsters defy the temporal and moral order at once: both are victims and victimizers simultaneously. In James's story the skeletal intruder who is seen in the picture stealing into a building and kidnapping a child is a poacher, judiciously executed by the child's father. Similarly, Freddie Krueger of *Elm Street* is a child abuser, murdered by enraged parents, who subsequently invades their children's dreams. Violence and victimization are tied in a circle, in which discriminations of guilt and innocence become meaningless. The monster and its victims literally merge into one. The creature of "The Mezzotint" always appears with the boy firmly clasped in his arms, while the film's teenagers, murdered in their dreams, are caught like flies in Freddie's viscous body.

Freddie Krueger devours temporality; other monsters destroy language itself. Many horror creatures simply do not speak. But even when the monster is quite voluble, there is some mysterious slippage in its self-expression. The classic paradigm of the loquacious monster is Frankenstein's creature, and of the silent monster, Dracula. As eloquent as a star lawyer, Frankenstein's fiend easily mounts a convincing defense of himself, arguing away such trifling matters as the murder of a child. But his smooth and coherent account of himself is undermined by the unbearable spectacle he presents. The creature's uncanny and horrifying appearance affects even those who are well disposed toward him, so that the tension between spectacle and speech becomes central to the novel. Dracula, on the other hand, is firmly entrenched in his monsterhood by being denied access to language. He is the only major character who is not a narrator in Stoker's novel. The few things he says are conveyed to us by his enemies, filtered through their incomprehension or hostility. Deprived of a self-narrative, Dracula is totally absorbed in the visual appurtenances of his monstrosity: fangs, bloody hands, bats, and rats. It is not an accident that while cinema has been unsuccessful in finding an appropriate visual equivalent of Frankenstein's creature (Boris Karloff's neck screws are quaint rather than frightening), the vampire has become a major part of the iconography of popular culture. Since Stoker, of course, there have been many attempts to write a vampire's first-person narrative, with Anne Rice's *Interview with a Vampire* and its sequels being only one example. But all such texts fall into what might be called Frankenstein's trap. If the monstrous self is presented as transparent, coherent, sympathetic, it is not a monster. If it is presented as alien, mute, incomprehensible, it is not a self.

The result of this trap is a grotesque psyche, paralleling the monster's grotesque body. Grotesque corporeal images emphasize the patching together of incongruous parts. The psychic grotesque "moves inward towards an individualized, interiorized space of fantasy and introspection. . . . Emerging with the concept of the Romantic sublime, the category of the uncanny grotesque is associated with the life of the psyche and with the particular 'experience' of the 'strange' and 'criminal' variety . . . " (Russo 8). The grotesque character is one of the "many partial, dual, multiple and dismembered selves scattered throughout literary fantasies [that] violate the most cherished of all human unities: the unity of 'character'" (Jackson 82).

The connection between the grotesque self and the grotesque body is explored in Clive Barker's short novel *Cabal.* Its heroine, Lori, contemplates the ideal body of Western culture and rejects it in favor of its monstrous counterpart:

> Dreams of the perfected anatomy—the soap opera face, the centerfold body—had distracted her with promises of true happiness. Empty promises. Flesh could not keep its glamour, nor eyes their sheen. . . . Against that the monsters of Midian—transforming, re-arranging, ambassadors of tomorrow's flesh and reminders of yesterday's—seemed full of possibilities. (188)

The parameters of Lori's choice are set by Mikhail Bakhtin, a Russian cultural scholar, in his distinction between the classical and the grotesque body. But for Lori the choice of a grotesque body also indicates an escape from the straitjacket of a normative identity. Midian, the city of monsters where she and her lover, Aaron Boone, also known as Cabal, eventually find refuge, is a perpetual carnival of weird and wonderful flesh, an enclave of ecstasy, exuberance, and excess in the desert of "centerfold bodies." The grotesque body is "full of possibilities" because it houses a personality free of guilt, compulsion, and repression.

In the course of the novel Boone's body undergoes multiple transformations, collapsing all binary dichotomies that are used to define the self and the Other. Infected by a shape-shifter's bite, pumped full of bullets, cut open in a police autopsy, Boone's body remains triumphantly alive. He violates the boundary between human and animal (by becoming a cannibalistic "beast" when seduced by the scent of blood); one and many (he is renamed Cabal, an "alliance of many" [243]); inside and outside (he breathes out a "veil of smoke" that melts down and reshapes his flesh [119]). And while only implicit in *Cabal,* the monster's transgression of the gender boundary is explored in many other Barker texts, always in terms of liberation tinged by horror or violence colored with exaltation.

"Skins of the Fathers" (in volume 2 of Barker's *Books of Blood)* offers an origin myth of gender indeterminacy that posits monstrosity as a counterweight to patriarchy. The patriarchal descent is supplanted by an alliance of women and monsters. Those "fathers" who jointly beget a son on the willing body of a woman are irreducible to the ordinary definitions not only of gender but even of physiological sex. But in their grotesquerie, they are things of beauty and wonder: "Creatures too fantastic to be real, too real to be disbelieved; angels of the hearth and threshold. One had a head, moving back and forth on a gossamer neck, like some preposterous weather-vane, blue as the early night-sky and shot with a dozen eyes like so many suns. Another father, with a body like a fan, opening and closing in his excitement, his orange flesh flushing deeper as the boy's voice was heard again" (138–39).

Midian and "the angels of the hearth and threshold" are alternatives to the society of the centerfold and patriarchy (139). They are an attempt to imagine and reimagine the violent sublime as utopia. Barker does not minimize the violence of the monster, but he sets it against the greater violence of social discipline. In *Cabal,* the violence of the Symbolic is represented by the monster-hunter and psychopathic killer Decker. He is a sterile and implacable authority, whose purification of the monstrous body takes the form of wholesale slaughter. It is in opposition to such an authority (with its "classic," "closed" corporeality) that the monster's transgression appears as seductive and liberating. But the monster's rebellion is ultimately not against a specific discursive formation, a specific ideology, but against discourse itself.

The monster's spectacular body and speechless self hold out a promise of release from the prison of language. Monsters are postmodern angels. They point to a world beyond words, in which "the violence of the letter" is overcome with the greater violence of the spectacle. In Rachel Pollack's story "Angel Baby" (1982) a woman raped by a monstrous angel gives up her ordinarily human life to bear his autistic child. The angel comes from the world without language, in which "you did not need any reason for anything" (141). Purged of feelings and causality, bathed in the perpetual glow of a never ending apocalypse, this is a world of the Real: "Everything humans did had to mean something because humans couldn't stand it otherwise. Only the angel did things that didn't mean something else, something explained in words or feelings" (154). Desperately longing to enter the angel's realm, the heroine welcomes his brutal assault in the hope of getting at least a glimpse of the wordless "world of lightning." But she is still too human to bear its splendor; only her son, with the "metal coldness" in his eyes, is vouchsafed an access to it (158). Like Barker's monsters' offspring, he will become a prophet of the unspeakable. But to do so, he will have to learn to speak. In order to be comprehensible, the language of angels has to be translated into ordinary speech or, at least, into those shared discourses that have traditionally grappled with the sublime.

THE MEDUSA'S HEAD

Since of all the genres of violence horror is most responsive to its shattering impact on identity, it is always close to those areas of experience that involve excess or transfiguration, or both. In other words, horror is particularly concerned with desire and divinity. In this section I will explore the role of sexuality in horror's depiction of the violent sublime, and in the next one I will look at some monstrous gods.

The spectacle of violence often has the same effect as the Medusa's head in the Greek myth of Perseus, petrifying the onlooker. This image has been a recurrent starting point for explorations of the interrelation of violence and gender. The Medusa's head in *A Tale of Two Cities* is a metaphor for the fascination of the countless heads rolling off the guillotine under the avid stares of the mob. And long before Freud, Dickens is aware of the sexual connotations of the image. He links it with the dancing, blood-splattered women of the Revolution, the castrating furies at the knife edge between violence and sex.

In Freud's short essay "Medusa's Head" (1922; published in 1940), the sight of the Medusa becomes the tableau of sexual difference. What turns the male spectator to stone is the castrated female genitals:

> To decapitate = to castrate. The terror of Medusa is thus a terror of castration that is linked to the sight of something. Numerous analyses have made us familiar with the occasion for this: it occurs when a boy, who has hitherto been unwilling to believe the threat of castration, catches sight of the female genitals, probably those of an adult, surrounded by hair, and essentially those of his mother. (273)

"To decapitate = to castrate." An equation can always be turned around and still remain valid. Freud uses sex to explain violence. But can violence explain sex? In Thomas Ligotti's horror story "The Medusa" (1996), a man obsessed with the eponymous creature of the title is finally reunited with it in the "rose-tinted heart" of his own private hell (376). Whatever Ligotti's Medusa is, it is not what the protagonist derisively calls "the image par excellence of romantic panic" (365). Rather, the enigmatic Medusa seems to be horror itself, irrespective of its cause, haunting us "just *this side* of . . . the Real" (375). Ligotti's post-Freudian tale tries to undo the connection established by classical psychoanalysis between horror and sexuality. What holds the gaze of the male spectator in the Freudian model is the recognition of sexual difference. What

Dregler, Ligotti's protagonist, eventually sees in the mirror is his own naked, contorted, violence-scarred body, "the thing itself" (376).

The recognition of sexual difference through the image of the Medusa involves an irreducible element of violence. The female genitals are reinterpreted as a site of mutilation: "the absence [of the penis] is the cause of the horror" (Freud 1922, 273). Femininity is a trace of violation. And not satisfied with seeing the wound of the female genitals, the gaze of the masculine subject commits further aggression by trying to penetrate the mysterious interior of the female body. The "absent" genitals draw the gaze inwards, inviting the opening up of the dark visceral cavern. The "bodily cave," writes Mary Russo, "is culturally identified . . . with the female and the maternal" (116).

But in *The Invisible Man* it is a male body that is opened up, its viscera displayed to the audience's gaze, its "bodily cave" invaded. What makes this violent feminization possible is Griffin's victimization. From a disembodied (and implicitly masculine) Power, he has been reduced to an inert (and implicitly feminine) Thing. But in the humiliation of his downfall, his passive body becomes invested with a compelling magnetism. The savage attackers are now as petrified by Griffin's shamelessly exposed materiality as the boy in Freud's parable of gender is petrified by the mother's castrating genitals. Invisibility is the power to act but visibility is the power to be.

The opened-up body is "abject," as Julia Kristeva argues in *Powers of Horror*. The abject is the unclean body of the birthing mother. The affect of horror, claims Kristeva, results from "something *horrible to see* at the impossible doors of the invisible—the mother's body. The scene of scenes here is not the so-called primal scene but the one of giving birth, incest turned inside out, flayed identity" (155).

But is the violated body horrible because it reminds one of the maternal body or vice versa? In other words, what is the real "scene of scenes": giving birth or killing? Kristeva situates the discussion of the maternal in the context of her analysis of Celine's anti-Semitism, making an implicit connection between abjection and genocide. Would giving birth be terrifying to an observer if, by a biological accident of human anatomy, it were not accompanied by pain and bleeding, producing a natural simulacrum of the "flayed identity" of the victim of violence? The scene of "birth" in the first *Alien* movie (1979), with the creature bursting out from its male "mother's" abdomen in a shower of blood, flouts the logic of gender to make a point about our attitude to the interiors of our own bodies. In the *Alien* films, feminine and maternal abjection becomes a wandering signifier attached to any character who loses control over her own corporeality. It has taken four films (so far) to sort out the permutations of gender and violence and to restore, more or less, the alignment between abject femininity and biological femaleness.

Violence creates its own hierarchy, which cannot be neatly aligned with the hierarchy of sex. There is the gender of violence, as well as the gender of sex, and the two are not the same. In her book *The Rites of Man* Rosalind Miles argues that violence is a necessary component of masculinity, a contention that is patently untenable, for not all men are killers and not all killers are men. However, Miles's argument can be reversed: masculinity is not always violent but violence is always masculine, even if perpetrated by a woman. Today, with popular culture overrun by single white females and leather gear vampirettes, a violent woman is still awarded an honorary phallus. Stephen King calls his character Carrie "Woman, feeling her powers for the first time and, like Samson, pulling down the temple on everyone in sight" (170). Carrie's defiance coincides with the onset of her menses, but her violent womanhood is still conceptualized by her creator in terms of masculine heroism. The violator is always manly because his body is intact, while the body of the victim is open, receptive, and penetrable. Thus, the male victim acquires the abject maternal body, the "flayed identity" of the birthing mother.

Of all contemporary horror writers, Clive Barker is most aware of the possible disjunction between ordinary gender and the gender of violence. In his novella "The Hellbound Heart" (on which the *Hellraiser* series of films, directed by Barker himself, is based), the abject body is not merely male but explicitly phallic. Frank, a reckless womanizer, is captured and dismembered by the strange androgynous creatures called the Cenobites he accidentally conjures up in his pursuit of forbidden pleasures. He becomes a patchwork of bodily parts, an animated anatomical exhibit: "the body has been ripped apart and sewn together again with most of its pieces either missing or twisted and blackened as if in a furnace. There was an eye, gleaming at her, and the ladder of a spine, the vertebrae stripped of muscles, a few unrecognizable fragments of anatomy" (212).

The feminization of the male victim hardly requires a proof: one has only to consider the sort of verbal and physical abuse (including castration) that the victors commonly heap upon the vanquished. A more interesting and provocative question is whether anybody may *want* such feminization. Even posing this question sounds like blaming the victim. But here as well, horror suggests some unsettling answers. If Dorian and other assorted killers want to become monsters by committing acts of violence, some horror characters achieve monsterhood through victimization. In *Cabal* the monstrous inhabitants of Midian, displaying a dazzling collection of opened-up, mutilated, twisted, ripped bodies, are mostly male. Their violation has endowed them with the magic of anarchic fertility, commonly associated with femaleness. The abject body is a fecund body. And like the imaginary invulnerable body of the killer, the victimized body transcends mortality. In Barker's "The Madonna," two men wandering into a deserted swimming pool discover the Virgin Mother, ceaselessly giving birth to monstrous children and surrounded by young girls who suckle her creations. The Madonna is not even remotely human; she looks like "something slow and molten . . ." (Barker 1987, 195). Having been touched by the Madonna's magic, the two men undergo a spontaneous sex change but respond to it in opposite ways. Ezra Garvey, a man's man, commits suicide by trying to "slice off" his transformed genitals. Jerry Coloqhoun, a gentle dreamer, welcomes the change: "There were miracles in the world! Forces that could turn flesh inside out without drawing blood; that could topple the tyranny of the real and make play in its rubble" (206). Miracle is "turn[ing] the flesh inside out" without dying; dissection without blood; violence without pain. And in this transubstantiation of torture, feminine passivity is eagerly embraced.

Barker's stories make explicit what tamer horror texts only hint at: victimization is power. If women are made into honorary men by wielding guns or carving knives, men are made into women by submitting to the same. This is a commonplace; but what is far less frequently noted is that both men and women might trade their actual gender for the femininity of violation in the hope of tasting the sublime. Barker's tale, with its images of monstrous maternity, recalls the famous predecessor of *Dracula,* Joseph Sheridan Le Fanu's vampire story "Carmilla" (1870). Like Barker's characters, its female protagonist seeks miracle in abjection. Laura, the first-person narrator and heroine of the story, goes to her death willingly and with pleasure. Assaulted by the beautiful vampire Carmilla, Laura is by turns seduced and brutalized, wooed with tender love, and dragged like a lamb to the slaughter. Carmilla is lover, sister, friend but, most of all, mother.[5] Her enchanting realm, glimpses of which Laura gets in her delirium, is like the realm of Barker's Madonna, a maternal space of mingled beauty and horror, carrying her away on the stream of its "unaccountable fascination" (Le Fanu 307). Laura is Carmilla and Carmilla is Laura: in the pre-Oedipal kingdom of the vampire, there is neither separation nor identity.

There is both pleasure and power in victimization, as a famous episode in Stoker's *Dracula* (1896) demonstrates. When Jonathan Harker is about to be attacked by three vampire ladies, he is instantly transformed into a Victorian bride, awaiting with bated breath her consummation: "There was something about them that made me uneasy, some longing and at the same time some deadly fear. I felt in my heart a wicked, burning desire that they would kiss me with those red lips . . . I was afraid to raise my eyelids, but looked on and saw perfectly under the lashes. The fair girl went on her knees and bent over me, fairly gloating" (39).

This scene has been interpreted in terms of every sexual perversion known to psychology.[6] But there is another way of reading Harker's sexual masochism: as a strategy of empowerment. Were he allowed by his author to cross the barrier of a vampiric rape, Harker, like Lucy, would eventually be transformed into a powerful, immortal, irresistible being. For Harker, a little clerk ordered around by everybody, from his London employer to the Transylvanian Count, an effective feminine mystique would be preferable to a frustrated and impotent masculinity.

Other victims of horror show how evil endured becomes a prerequisite for evil inflicted. Frankenstein's creature stridently claims the status of an abused child. The Invisible Man has been on the receiving end of taunts and blows for most of his life. In M. R. James's ghost story "Martin's Close" (1911) an implacable toadlike creature is the phantom of a poor retarded girl killed, for no particular reason, by a wealthy gentleman.[7] But more than the psychological balance of suffering and revenge is at stake here: the empowerment of the victim coincides with a physical transformation into an abject body. The vampire is the most striking example of such transformation. Each vampire has been a victim once, and each victim is a future vampire. A vampire, of either sex, is a phallic mother, giving birth to its offspring at the very moment of a murderous assault. Despite his perpetually erect fangs and virile mystique, Dracula, in the climactic scene of his takeover of Mina, becomes a nursing mother: "With his left hand he [Dracula] held both Mrs. Harker's hands, keeping them away with her arms at full tension; his right hand gripped her by the back of the neck, forcing her face down on his bosom . . . The attitude of the two had a terrible resemblance to a child forcing a kitten's nose into a saucer of milk to compel it to drink" (Stoker 249).

This maternal power is rooted in the Medusa-like fascination of the spectacle of violence. Robbed of agency, the victim is invested with the passive fascination of an object, having become what Kristeva calls "something *horrible to see* at the impossible doors of the Invisible" (155). Having lost his ability to elude the gaze, the Invisible Man, in the humiliation of his public torture, acquires the ability to make people look at him. As the viewers of fashion television know, this is not an inconsiderable power, especially in the absence of any other. Like a beautiful woman, a mutilated corpse rules the gaze. The executioner unwittingly turns his victim into the Medusa's head that can unman him with its ghastly sight. And the femininity of violence can be more powerful than the femininity of sex. Nancy's looks earn her the paltry living of a prostitute and Bill Sikes's blows. But the spectacle of her mangled body forces her abuser to hang himself in the public square.

There is something undeniably seductive, a sort of poetic justice in a world bereft of most such consolations, in horror's empowerment of the victim through abjection. But there is danger in it as well. The dumb schoolgirl of the horror flick, going down into the cellar to meet the monster, seeks submergence in the violent sublime and drags the audience with her. Having had their fill of second-hand shivers, the spectators go home unharmed, but the schoolgirl remains in the cellar forever. She is only a fictional construct, of course; but who is to say that the idea of violence as a transfiguring experience has not leaked out of the confines of the movie theatre, into the mind of some would-be murderer or suicide? Here is Barker's character from "The Madonna" lured by the glimmer of the sublime on the other side of violent death:

> There was light ahead. How far it lay, he couldn't calculate, but what did it matter? If he drowned before he reached that place, and ended his journey dead, so what? Death was no more certain than the dream of masculinity he'd lived all these years. Terms of description fit only to be turned up and over and inside out. The earth was bright, wasn't it, and probably full of stars. He opened his mouth and shouted into the whirlpool, as the light grew and grew, an anthem in praise of paradox. (Barker 1987, 209)

Plunging into the whirlpool of violence, the victim seeks a metamorphosis into the Medusa's head: the shape of mingled horror and beauty, that can revenge the pain and humiliation endured by the victim's ordinary human body. If victimization is the epitome of powerlessness, perhaps it can be turned inside out to become an invincible armor. The Medusa lures its devotees into the "rose-tinted heart" of horror, in which Dregler, forever fused with the Real, exists in a timeless realm, bereft of "his world and his words" (Ligotti 376).

The sublime exaltation of violence, dissolving gender and overturning social hierarchies, can become an object of desire for both the perpetrator and, shockingly, for the victim as well. This desire is ruinous for the individual, who, becoming the lawless subject of torture, is ultimately exiled into the wilderness outside the social field of narativity. But what happens when the craving for the violent sublime becomes social and collective? Can a community of monsters exist?

GOD'S BODY

Horror's monsters are ordinarily loners. M. R. James's ghosts (like M. R. James himself) prefer their own company; Pollack's angel strikes on his own; King's "It," the ultimate monster, the embodiment of everybody's worst fear, is sui generis. However, in Frankenstein's creature's longing for a family and community, in the Invisible Man's dictatorial aspirations, in Dracula's plans of conquest, and in Barker's Midian, we are beginning to discern the outline of a monstrous body politic. And as we shall see later, such a body uncannily mirrors the lineaments of utopia. Bypassing the subject of discipline, the subject of torture and the subject of ideology join hands in building the brave new world of permanent violence.

Barker's visionary glorification of the liberating violence of torture in opposition to the stifling violence of discipline follows a long philosophical, political, and literary tradition. It is paralleled by Walter Benjamin's distinction between "mythic" violence, which is the violence of the law, and "divine" violence, which is the violence of excess, transformation, and rebellion:

> Just as in all spheres God opposes myth, mythic violence is confronted by the divine. And the latter constitutes its antithesis in all respects. If mythic violence is lawmaking, divine violence is law-destroying; if the former seeks boundaries, the latter boundlessly destroys them; if mythic violence brings at once guilt and retribution, divine power only expiates; if the former threatens, the latter strikes; if the former is bloody, the latter is lethal without spilling blood. . . . Mythic violence is bloody power over mere life for its own sake; divine violence is pure power over all life for the sake of the living. The first demands sacrifice; the second accepts it. (1921, 249–50)

Despite the absence of any contemporary references in the essay, its politics—in the shadow of World War I, following the recent Revolution in Russia, and surrounded by the volatility of the defeated Germany—are not difficult to fathom. The "mythic" violence of war is to be defeated by the "divine" violence of revolution, with its promise of a utopian transformation. However, in a more comprehensive sense of the *politics of the body,* Benjamin's essay also makes clear what is at stake in viewing violence as an instrument of utopia. Revolutionary ethics has to deny the integrity and inviolability of the human body and regard it as malleable and expendable:

> Man cannot, at any price, be said to coincide with the mere life in him, any more than it can be said to coincide with any other of his conditions or qualities, including even the uniqueness of his bodily person. However sacred man is (or however sacred that life in him which is identically present in earthly life, death, and afterlife), there is no sacredness in his condition, in his bodily life vulnerable to injury by his fellow men. (1921, 251)

With the benefit of hindsight, it is easy to point out the historical results of the large-scale application of "divine" violence or to ponder the irony of Benjamin's own fate.[8] However, what is more interesting is the rhetorical attempt in this passage to burst, as it were, the boundaries of the individual body, to extend it beyond death, to blur the distinction between the actual physical individual and the body politic. Benjamin's "imaginary anatomy," to use Lacan's expression, is the anatomy of the monster, fluid, protean, and unbounded.

The monster is simultaneously a sideshow and a revelation. In the political discourse of "divine," liberating violence, the implicit rhetoric of corporeal monstrosity interacts with an explicit apocalyptic thrust. Hannah Arendt emphasizes the apocalyptic (in the sense of "revelatory") dimension of utopian violence:

> Not many authors of rank glorified violence for violence's sake but these few—Sorel, Pareto, Fanon—were motivated by a much deeper hatred of bourgeois society and were led to a much more radical break with its moral standards than the conventional Left, which was chiefly inspired by compassion and a burning desire for justice. To tear the mask of hypocrisy from the face of the enemy, to unmask him and the devious machinations and manipulations that permit him to rule without using violent means, that is to provoke action even at the risk of annihilation so the truth may come out—these are still among the strongest motives in today's violence on the campuses and in the streets. (1970, 65)

The violence of radical revolt is the revelation of the truth. The language of unmasking points to the utopian desire for the clean page, the new beginning, and the end to secrets and lies. But, paradoxically, the secret that needs exposing is precisely the absence of physical violence in democracy, the fact that the "enemy" manages "to rule without using violent means" (Arendt 65). The complaint of the revolutionary is not that there is too much violence in society, but that there is too little.

This is the point forcefully made in D. H. Lawrence's *Apocalypse* (1931). A Nietzsche without irony and depth, Lawrence denounces "the vast anti-will of the masses, the will to negate power" (17). Cut off from the vital Cosmos and locked in a Baconian hell of science and rationality, the modern man (or rather the modern male, for Lawrence has different prescriptions for women) is deprived of his "natural proud self of power" (21). He is tyrannized by words, bound by the Lilliputian web of rules and regulations. The main flaw of society, as seen by Lawrence, is that it relies on prohibition rather than on force: "The community is inhuman, and less than human. It becomes at last the most dangerous because *bloodless* and insentient tyrant" (Lawrence 21). In Lawrence's version of what John Fraser calls "a simple dichotomy between oppressive 'order' and liberating 'revolt,'" the goal of the revolt is to supplant the subject of discipline by the subject of torture (43). The "natural self of power" is the self that can kill without pangs of conscience or fear of jail. Violence is not a regrettable stain on utopia. Violence *is* utopia.

In Foucault's description of public torture, the institutionalized spectacle of violence generates a social epiphany in which the ghastly spectacle of the torn and bleeding flesh becomes an indisputable signature of power. The truth is incarnated in the suffering body, whose text has an inestimable advantage over the text of a written proclamation or a legal code. It is free of ambiguity—no "différance" here, no slippage of meaning. The visceral shock of seeing the blood, the wounds, and the hanging entrails leaves no room for argument. Franz Kafka's well-known parable "In the Penal Colony" (1919) describes a torture machine that literally writes on the body, slowly and painfully executing its victim by carving on his flesh the text of the Law. The text cannot actually be read; it is obscured by gushing blood. But precisely for that reason, it cannot be disputed. The language of violence cannot lie: whatever the suffering body says, becomes true by virtue of its suffering. The torture machine reveals the truth of the power that "not only did not hesitate to exert itself directly on bodies, but was exalted and strengthened by its visible manifestations" (Foucault 1975, 57).

It is in its revelation of the truth that the trauma of torture can be rewritten as utopia. For Barthes the visual impact of a spectacle combines the traumatic destruction of language with the paradisiacal innocence of image. On the one hand, "a pure denotation" exists "at the level of absolutely traumatic images . . . The trauma is a suspension of language, a blocking of meaning" (30). On the other hand, "the denoted image can appear as a kind of Edenic state of the image; cleared utopianically of its connotations, the image would become radically objective, or, in the last analysis, innocent" (42). In the extreme spectacle of torture, trauma is transmuted into utopia by its "Edenic" purification of language from ambiguity. And thus torture and radical violence in general can become objects of desire for people with no sadistic inclinations. The most terrible thing about Kafka's penal colony is the idealism of the officer who runs the torture machine. The depth of his devotion is measured by his ultimate self-sacrifice: when the new governor abolishes torture, the officer lays himself down under the machine's harrow, seeking the enlightenment that violence brings.

However, this enlightenment is transient precisely to the extent that it is not verbalized. Insofar as the monstrous body politic attempts to hold itself together only by the sublime spectacle of torture, it is as impossible in its collectivity as the single monster in its fantastic corporeality. The more social violence appears as divine, the speedier is its disintegration into senseless butchery.

In Barker's darkly visionary story "In the Hills, the Cities" (presciently written in 1984), a couple of gay lovers vacationing in Yugoslavia encounter two monstrous giants at war with each other. These are walking cities in which the bodies of their inhabitants are lashed together to create a sublime Leviathan, a literal body politic: "They could see the way the roped bodies pushed and pulled against each other in solid cords of flesh and bone. They could see the intertwined people that made up the body: the backs like turtles packed together to offer the sweep of the pectorals; the lashed and knotted acrobats at the joints of the arms and the legs alike, rolling and unwinding to articulate the city" (Barker 1986a, 207).

This monstrous body politic is created through the self-torture of its inhabitants who stretch themselves on the rack for the greater glory of the community. Here mutilation and self-mutilation, pain inflicted and pain endured, sadism and masochism are fused together in a violent epiphany that transcends the puny "uniqueness of [a man's] bodily person" (Benjamin 251). the hills as it goes, the walking city is preceded by a sweeping tide of blood and avalanche of broken flesh resulting from its clash with its rival. Its sublimity draws one of the lovers, Mick, to join the giant, sacrificing his life, like Kafka's officer, for the apocalyptic ecstasy of torture. Mick is tired of his problematic identity, of the pettiness of his mundane existence, of his unsatisfactory and compromise-ridden love life. The pleasure of sex cannot compete with the exaltation of violence; it is too transient, too sentiment-dependent, too enmeshed in the muddle of human relationships. Far better to lose himself in the utopian body of death than to be confined to the humble body of life.

> The Englishmen remained where they stood, watching the spectacle as it approached. Neither dread nor horror touched them now, just an awe that rooted them to the spot. They knew this was a sight they could never hope to see again; this was the apex—after this there was only common experience. Better to stay then, though every step brought death nearer, better to stay and see the sight while it was still there to be seen. And if it killed them, this monster, then at least they would have glimpsed a miracle, known this terrible majesty for a brief moment. It seemed a fair exchange. . . .
>
> The earth was gone from beneath [Mick]. He was a hitchhiker with a god: the mere life he had left was nothing to him now, or ever. . . . Love and life and sanity were gone, gone like the memory of his name, of his sex, or his ambition. (Barker 1986a, 207–9)

Being "a hitchhiker with a god" offers the ecstasy of the "oceanic" that Freud described in *Civilization and Its Discontents* (5). The *oceanic* is a renunciation of individuality, a feeling of "oneness." Feminist psychoanalysts link it to the baby's experience of the plenitude of the maternal body in the pre-oedipal stage. But Klaus Theweleit points out that killing may be just as powerful a source of the "oceanic" as mother love: "What Neruda says of the ocean ('And you lack nothing') is realized for Junger in the battle-machine: lack is transcended" (Theweleit 2, 155). The "battle-machine" is a collective body generated and sustained by violence visited first on its individual members and then on unlucky bystanders. Benjamin's "divine" violence does create a god but it is a god-as-monster.

In Barker's novel *Imajica* God the Father appears as a city of flesh and bone: "What were those gleaming folds at the windows if they weren't skin?; what were those arches if they weren't bone? What was that scarlet pavement, and that light-shot stone, if it wasn't flesh? There was pith and marrow here. There was tooth and lash and nail" (1066). Imprisoned in the material and maternal body of violence, Barker's characters search for freedom, finding it, like the child in his fairy tale *Thief of Always,* in the separation from both parents. To be born is to emerge from the "oceanic" dissolution either in the waters of the womb or in the blood of violence. Theweleit calls the murderous fascist subjects "not-yet-born," meaning that they prefer the ecstasy of belonging in the sublime body of a "battle-machine" to the inevitable humdrum of individual existence (155). Like the components of Barker's monstrous city, such not-yet-borns are simultaneously victims and violators. And the greater the pain they endure, the greater the pain they are willing to inflict.

In attempting to fight the mythic violence of discipline with the divine violence of excess, Benjamin and Lawrence face the paradox of the flesh made word. Both see violence as a means to reveal the Edenic truth beyond the lies and prevarication of language. But in looking for such truth in the bleeding body of the victim, one discovers that while wounds indeed speak louder than words, their meaning is not necessarily clearer. The sublime impact of violence may be felt only in silence; once it is made basis for a communal politics of any kind, the tortured flesh is translated into a political doublespeak, the "oceanic" becomes part of battle drill, and God is reborn as an army. Barker's walking and warring cities utilize their "terrible majesty" in the service of a petty village feud. Kafka's torture machine is programmed to write in blood Sunday school platitudes.

In the image of God's body as a monstrous body politic created by violence, horror comes closest to utopia. Seemingly opposite, these two genres meet in the realm of torture, both drawn by the fascination of the violent sublime. Dystopia, utopia's dark twin, constantly slides into horror, as in George Orwell's *1984* and Yevgeni Zamyatin's *We.* Horror, when it ventures into the realm of the social, becomes dystopia, as in Barker, Kafka, and Dan Simmons's *Children of the Night.*[9] If the ordinary monster is a subject both created and destroyed by violence, the divine monster is a community of such subjects, requiring constant infusions of fresh blood to sustain their impossible existence.

SEQUELS

Popular culture has to satisfy its audience's desire for reassurance, stability, and conformity. Popular horror may tease us with a glimpse of the sublime, but it can never adopt its aesthetics as wholeheartedly as does the avant-garde. For every visionary book of blood, horror produces ten run-of-the-mill monster hunts, in which the "creature" is allowed its share of killing before being brought down by a righteous avenger. The paradox of horror is that this most subversive of all literary genres can also be the most philistine. Dracula is eliminated and the middle-class Victorian paradise is restored; all the Edwardian ghosts are exorcised; Freddie Krueger is defeated; and the killer angels of the film *Dogma* are recalled to heaven. And yet, despite its overt longing for the status quo the very narrative form of horror is intrinsically unsettling. As opposed to the detective story, horror has no strong narrative strategies to subdue the violent sublime. On the contrary, its plot constructions are normally slack; its fictional worlds paradoxical and inconsistent; and its strategies of explanation attenuated to the point of absurdity. The narrative form of horror showcases rather than represses the violated body. Horror is a realm of paradoxical and enigmatic plots, illogical transitions, and dreamlike sequences. It is a genre underpinned by oxymoron, "a figure of speech which holds together contradictions and sustains them in an impossible unity, without progressing towards synthesis" (Jackson 21).

Like the psychological consistency of the subject, the consistency of horror's fictional world collapses under the weight of the violent sublime. This process is vividly dramatized in Christopher Priest's novel *The Extremes* (1998). The heroine's addiction to the virtual reality game of Extreme Experience, in which she relives scenarios of serial killing, results in the textual universe of branching simulacra, a labyrinth of high-tech nightmares. This is Baudrillard's world of endless imitations, except that it is created not by the absence of the body but precisely by its traumatic presence. Motiveless, insistent, and addictive violence shatters Teresa's selfhood and demolishes her story.

The supernatural and fantastic aspects of horror undermine the ontological stability of the projected fictional world. In horror's deployment of the supernatural (different from the deployment of fantasy), it functions not so much as an index of a self-consisted "other world" but rather as an incomprehensible and inexplicable intrusion. The supernatural in horror marks the semantic locus of paradox, where the clear-cut distinctions of real and unreal, existent and nonexistent, objective and subjective begin to merge. Terry

Heller locates the aesthetics of horror in the endless oscillation between two possible readings, neither of which can be chosen over the other (169–71). The monstrous text is as paradoxical as its monstrous subject.

In Joseph Sheridan Le Fanu's classic ghost story "The Green Tea" (1872) the protagonist pursued by a spectral monkey cries out in anguish against the alien and incomprehensible system, which is destroying him: "But as food is taken in softly at the lips, and then brought under the teeth, as the tip of the little finger caught in a mill crank will draw in the hand, and the arm, and the whole body, so the miserable mortal who has been once caught firmly by the end of the finest fibre of his nerve, is drawn in and in, by the enormous machinery of hell, until he is as I am" (Le Fanu 200).

Here opposites are brought together: the "machinery of hell" is likened to the homely machinery of the mill crank and, even more intimately, of one's own mouth. The result, however, is not the naturalization of the supernatural but the alienation of nature. Collapsed together with the "machinery of hell," natural order becomes as threateningly opaque as its opposite. Natural and supernatural mirror each other in the gray zone where familiar reality is subverted, but no alternative reality emerges. This is the domain of horror, the twilight space of joined but not reconciled opposites. Stallybrass and White describe the textual grotesque as "a boundary phenomenon of hybridization or inmixing, in which self and other become enmeshed in an inclusive, heterogeneous, dangerously unstable zone" (193). Le Fanu's text, with its absence of causality (the protagonist never knows why he is haunted), its multiple and mutually contradicting narrators, its intimate entanglement of the self and the Other, inhabits just such a "dangerously unstable zone." But as the narrative becomes broken, paradoxical, and grotesque, so does the protagonist's body, poisoned by green tea, shaking in fear, contorted in agony, and eventually bleeding from a self-inflicted wound.

In the postscript to Barker's *Books of Blood,* the equivalence of the horror narrative and the monstrous body is made explicit. A hired assassin flays the ghost-inscribed medium, attempting to separate the body and the text. But the flayed skin continues to bleed, and the tide of blood becomes a tide of words, sentences, and stories. This grotesque image sums up the poetics of horror, whose narratives are both generated and undermined by the ineffable spectacle of the tortured body.

Barker's apparent inability to wrap up his collection with a tidy closure is not just a sign of creative exuberance. A book of blood needs a postscript. The messy, opened-up body of the text oozes sequels like bloodstains. Unlike the trim detective story, horror can rarely be contained within a trim Aristotelian plot, with a beginning, middle, and end. Straining for closure, horror bursts its own boundaries, each successful text hatching a brood of sequels, from

Alien 4 to *Blair Witch 2*. No sooner is the monster decisively eliminated then it reappears anew.

Not only horror, of course, indulges in sequels. From the soap opera to any successful blockbuster, popular culture uses sequels as a marketing ploy. But the sequels of horror almost always involve actual death and resurrection: since the monster is most often physically eliminated, its return indicates the rebirth of the monstrous body, not just the repackaging or extension of the original text, as in other genres. Sequels to *Star Wars* may deal with plot and setting continuity and introduce new characters at will, but sequels to *Alien* necessitate the resurrection of the alien itself. Freddie Krueger's absurd indestructibility is the stubborn return of the (corporeal) repressed, haunting the dreams of suburbia.

The horror sequel is a reflection of our ambivalence toward violence. Sickened by torture, we turn away, only to sneak another look at the sight that is both intolerable and compelling. Condemning bloodshed, we are held spellbound by its magic. Casting out the monster, we secretly dream of becoming it.

I will end this chapter with a postscript of three images. These are glimpses of the torturer's paradise, of which horror's book of blood is a testimonial—and a warning.

The first image is from Barker's story, "Jacqueline Ess: Her Will and Testament." Jacqueline Ess, a bored and depressed housewife, discovers in herself a magical ability to wish people's bodies into new shapes. Followed by a trail of grotesque mutilations—hated, worshipped and desired—she becomes a modern equivalent of the mythological Terrible Mother. Her only true mate is a man who is willing to pursue the sublimity of desire to its consummation in death:

> And thinking they were together, her will was made flesh. Under her lips her features dissolved, becoming the red sea he'd dreamt of, and washing up over his face, that was itself dissolving: common waters made of thought and bone.
>
> Her keen breasts pricked him like arrows; his erection, sharpened by her thought, killed her in return with its only thrust. Tangled in a wash of love they thought themselves extinguished, and were. (Barker 1986b; 116)

This is divine violence guarding the doors of true bliss. For these characters, the "red sea" of blood is a reasonable price to pay for the Promised Land of the sublime, in which mundane identities are extinguished. But so many—perhaps all—drown on the way.

The second image is from Oliver Onions's horror classic "The Beckoning Fair One"(1911). Paul Oleron, an unsuccessful writer, rents a lovely house haunted by an intangible succubus, an amorphous feminine essence that seems to echo Oleron's unborn literary character. Bewitched, Oleron courts the creature—and ends up murdering his best friend, a woman journalist whose florid and all-too-real body stands in the way of his transcendental consummation. Commenting on Oleron's pursuit of the violent sublime, the narrator says:

> To the man who pays heed to that voice within him, which warns him that twilight and danger are settling over his soul, terror is apt to appear as an absolute thing, against which his heart must be safeguarded. . . . Mercifully, he has never far to look for safeguards. Of the immediate and small and common and momentary things of life, of usages and observances and modes and conventions, he builds up fortifications against the powers of darkness. He is even content that, not terror only, but joy also, should for working purposes be placed in the category of the absolute things; and the last treason he will commit will be that breaking down of terms and limits that strikes, not at one man, but at the welfare of the souls of all. (Onions 66)

Searching for "absolute things," one is apt to find oneself with a dead body wedged in the kitchen cupboard. This is the ethics of the mundane. But does not "the welfare of the souls of all" sound terribly philistine and old fashioned, compared with Jacqueline Ess's power of unleashing the "red sea"?

The third voice is that of a real-life murderer in prison talking to a political scientist who investigates "the nature of evil." It turns out evil is an irrelevant category for a man who has tasted the sublime: "I didn't care whether I killed the guy or not. I just wanted to be his God for a little while" (Alford 28).

2

Serial Killing and the Dismemberment of Identity

A census taker tried to quantify me once. I ate his liver with some fava beans and a big Amarone.

—*DR. HANNIBAL LECTER in Thomas Harris's* The Silence of the Lambs

INCOHERENT SUBJECTS

We can start with Foucault's famous and endlessly circulated statement in *The Order of Things:* "It is comforting, however, and a source of profound relief to think that man is only a recent invention, a figure not yet two centuries old, a new wrinkle in our knowledge, and that he will disappear as soon as this knowledge has discovered a new form" (xxiii).

Man the Universal Subject, a cookie cutter mold of technological and post-technological identity, stamping out simulacra of individuality. But why should we be "comforted" and experience "relief" at the thought of his imminent dissolution? Perhaps because, at least from Adorno on, the subject of reason has also been identified as the subject of violence. The universal Man of the Enlightenment has been reconceptualized as the universal killer, armed with the most potent of weapons—representation. In their introduction to the collection typically entitled The *Violence of Representation,* Armstrong and Tennenhouse offer the basic formula of this approach: "The violence of representation is the suppression of difference" (8).

In this particular reading of Foucault, the discursive constructedness of identity is directly responsible for corporeal violence inflicted by some postmodern subjects upon others. In his recent book *Serial Killers* and in the series of articles that preceded it, Mark Seltzer applies this insight to the fascinating and grisly phenomenon of serial killing, variously identified also as "stranger killing" and "lust murder." For Seltzer the enigma of the serial killer's personality consists in "an experience of typicality at the level of the subject": "The serial killer, I will be arguing, is in part defined by such a radicalized experience of typicality within. Simply put, 'murder by numbers' (as serial murder has been called) is the form of violence proper to statistical persons" (1993, 30–31).

Violence of representation, representation of violence, and violence per se smoothly link into an unbroken chain, leading from statistics to mayhem and from typology of subjects to fingerprinting putrefying bodies. My goal is to put a hitch into this chain, to question the easy fit between discursive molds of identity and the individual self-experience of serial killers, and to suggest that representation may be not so much the cause of violence as a post factum defense against it.

The difference between the serial killers and the monsters I discussed in the last chapter is that the serial killers exist. This is not such a trivial observation as it may appear, for it has important consequences for the narrative construction of identity. Being purely fictional constructs, horror's monsters are passive mirrors of the particular cultural interpretation of violence that I analyzed under the heading of "the subject of torture." Serial killers, on the other hand, besides inhabiting the interlocking genres of the thriller and true crime, are also self-aware subjects who actively engage in their own self-representation. Their autobiographies provide a fascinating glimpse of the way in which narrative molds of identity fit actual human beings. And what they suggest, I will argue, is that while it is impossible to have identity outside narrative, individual agency may well reside in the cracks and fissures of narrative discourse. Torn between two conflicting plots of their violence, serial killers exercise their freedom of choice by refusing to choose. Their murders are as sublime as the spectacle of the violated body in horror, and they exert a similar influence on the coherence of their narratives. But a fictional vampire may be a walking oxymoron; the actual Ted Bundy must somehow reconcile the violent sublime with a life-story. The (inevitably failing) attempt to do so constructs the serial killer as a hybrid subject of violence, occupying the unstable boundary between torture and discipline.

The serial form of violence is conditioned not so much by the monolithic coherence of representation as by its breakdown. The behavior of a serial killer is not a direct outcome of any social construction but a random choice, which is retrospectively and partially incorporated into a generic narrative of identity. His repeated ritualistic violence, then, becomes a means of reinforcing this identity but achieves precisely the opposite, its complete disintegration. Rather than being generated by representation, corporeal violence offers a resistance to it. On the one hand, the narrative of the serial murderer is a product not so much of what Seltzer calls the general "wound culture" of postmodernity as of specific scientific narratives of deviance whose conflict and interaction I will analyze below. On the other hand, these narratives, the representational molds of the criminal self, always fail to explain and thus to contain the excessive and irrational violence whose unruly opacity constitutes their raison d'être. In fracturing scientific discourse, the violent sublime exceeds its determinants, creating a self whose freedom lies neither in some impossible essence beyond the reach of cultural conditions nor in the uniform resistance to monolithic representation, but rather in the inconsistencies, gaps, and fissures within representation itself.

While the actual incidence of serial killing remains small compared to other kinds of violent crime, the literature on the subject is enormous. This literature spans the entire spectrum of narrativity, from fiction to science, bounded on the one end by the best-selling mystery novels of Thomas Harris, Patricia Cornwell, James Patterson, and others, and on the other end by criminological explorations of the serial killer's mind. By far, the largest part of the spectrum is covered by the murky genre of "true crime," predominantly consisting of the biographies of every significant serial killer of the last thirty years. With a string of blockbuster films on the subject, from Hitchcock's classic *Psycho* to *The Silence of the Lambs, Seven, Kiss the Girls, Hannibal,* and others, the serial killer looms disproportionately large in the contemporary universe of discourse.

Whatever their genre, writings on the phenomenon of serial killing often stress its representative role. The killer becomes what the protagonist of Caleb Carr's novel *The Alienist* portentously calls an image of "all that is dark in our very *social* world" (592). Maria Tatar, in her analysis of the iconography of lust murder in the culture of the Weimar Republic, points out its "virtually ubiquitous presence," which she derives from the ubiquity of misogyny (4). A number of writers subscribe to the argument that serial killing is a recent phenomenon brought about by the conditions of modernity. Colin Wilson, for example, boldly states that "there were no sex killers before the late-nineteenth century" and links this new phenomenon with his somewhat idiosyncratic diagnosis of the modern malaise (3). Finally, Seltzer suggests that the postmodern creation of the "pathological public sphere" with its confusion between public and private, action and image, natural and technological, body and machine is the underlying cause of the proliferation of Jack the Ripper look-alikes. His project traces "the links between the problem of serial murder and the more general problem of the body in 'machine culture' . . . the forms of repetitive and addictive violence produced, or solicited, by the styles of production and reproduction that make up machine culture" (1993, 92). Jeffrey Dahmer becomes the monstrous offspring of "machine culture," a latter-day Frankenstein's creature. For Seltzer serial killers are "emptied" of their psychic interiority by social forces and their violence "might be taken as the traumatized intimation, at the level of the subject, that his interior states are nothing but outer or social forces and fantasies turned outside in: the subject, as it were, flooded by the social and its collective fantasies" (1998, 126).

All such schemes, however much at odds with each other, share one feature—emphasis on a tight causal connection between killer and social milieu. They are all driven by the necessity to "explain" the serial killer in terms that assimilate the corporeal particularity of violence to some abstract modality of meaning. This explanation generally takes the form of a narrative of origin. Such narratives, freely exchanged between literature and science, treat violence as a symptom or an outer manifestation of a hidden truth, an oblique symptom of an intelligible cause.

However, taken as a whole, the bulk of the available cultural narratives of serial killing is fissured by unresolvable contradictions. The stories are not merely different from each other but incompatible, representing the killer as either a monster or a victim, either a chameleonic "man of the crowd" or a hideous mutation, either the product of severe psychopathology or somebody "abnormally normal" (Seltzer 1998, 106). The problem is not a shopping list of identities, which every postmodern subject supposedly carries around. The difference between the serial killer and other such subjects is that his narrative of the self is structured around an act of radical physical violence that cannot be fully accommodated by any explanatory model. Quoting Hannah Arendt's observation about the banality of Nazi evil, Seltzer claims the serial killer represents "the replacement of the soul and, in this case, the soul of evil, with knowledge systems, expert and scientific" (Seltzer 1998, 107). However, necrophilia, dismemberment, and cannibalism are not banal (and neither was Nazism). The unexpected appearance of the "soul of evil" alongside "knowledge systems" testifies precisely to the insufficiency of any kind of causal model, whether psychological, cultural, biological, or sociological, to account for the serial killer's violence.

Rather than offering a choice of identities, the discourse of serial killing piles all the models together in a vain attempt to cover up the emptiness at its core. The result is incoherence. Seltzer notes how pop culture representations of serial killing tend to deploy mutually exclusive clichés indiscriminately and then gravitate toward "nonexplanation and noncomprehension as a way of conserving the mystery of evil" (1998, 120). However, his own reference to the "soul of evil" seems to suggest that the fault lies not only with the shallowness of pop psychology but with the nature of the serial killer's violence itself.

As opposed to the violence of war, state persecution, or terrorism, the violence of the serial killer is devoid of political imprimatur: it is nonideological and therefore, at least partially, situated outside the discursive field of power. Seltzer compares the putative psychology of the serial killer with that of the fascist male described by Klaus Theweleit. But the fascist always acts in a group where extreme violence is rendered meaningful within the group's weltanschauung. There is a profound difference between the state-sponsored concentration camp and the private torture house because the latter is not subordinated to any collective goal. Serial killers are sometimes represented as Storm Troopers in search of an ideology (see Fox and Levin). What they may be looking for is the kind of selfhood the fascist male possesses, the selfhood that, reinforced by external ideology, can contain extreme violence without being blown up into pieces.

If all narrative constructions of identity fail, the resulting subjectivity is bound to be a narrative failure too: splintered, incoherent, and fragmented. As Cameron and Frazer point out, serial killers' accounts of themselves are "representations, often consciously constructed, which draw on cultural as opposed to individual resources" (71). But when these "resources" are radically self-contradictory, the resulting account is necessarily hybrid, monstrous, and mutant. Thus representation, rather than being a seamless conduit between social compulsion and individual violence, becomes a site of their conflict.

But it is precisely the resistance of the serial killer to representation that acts as incitement to representing him again and again. In his encounters with an array of forensic specialists, psychologists, medical examiners, criminologists, scriptwriters, and authors, the serial killer functions as a figure of the Real, soliciting explanations and defying or deflecting them. And yet his own paradoxical and tormented subjectivity is delineated precisely by those narratives of violence whose perpetual renewal is the result of their perpetual failure to contain their subjects.[1]

NERO ON THE COUCH

In his essay "Pen, Pencil and Poison," dedicated to the career of the serial poisoner Thomas Griffiths Wainewright, Oscar Wilde chooses a particularly effective way to vex his audience. It consists in refusing any psychological speculation on the motivations of the man who was a promising journalist, a talented artist, an admired dandy, and a mass murderer. Any contemporary work in the same genre, from paperback biographies of Ted Bundy and John Gacy to Hannah Arendt's *Eichmann in Jerusalem,* begins and ends with the question that Wilde nonchalantly brushes aside: why? Nor was this preoccupation with the killer's subjectivity any less evident in Wilde's own time, since both naturalism and the sensation novel made it one of their hallmarks.

Dickens and Bulwer-Lytton, both of whom explored the minds of malefactors at great length, are mentioned in the essay. But Wilde abides by his own dictum that the true mystery lies in the surface, not the depth, and flouts the reader's expectations of a plunge into the abyss of sin or madness. Instead he dissects Wainewright's style.

Discomfiting the audience is Wilde's aim, and his success is the measure of how widespread the assumption is that murder has to be not so much displayed, condemned, or even punished, as explained. Much of nineteenth-century psychological realism bears witness to the power of this assumption —from *Adam Bede* to the novels of Balzac. Precisely because the murderer's psyche is seen as aberrant and opaque, it functions as a test case for the power of psychological analysis, which derives its prestige from kinship with the epistemology of science. Wilde notes that Wainewright's more famous predecessors in the field of mass killing, Nero, Tiberius, Cesar Borgia, "have passed into the sphere of art and science" where they are free from sanctimonious expressions of moral horror but not from the sharp scalpel of "disinterested curiosity" (856). Wilde's own piece, however, refuses both moral condemnation and psychological explanation, becoming an unsettling comment not so much on the killer himself as on the drive of "art and science" to assimilate his murderous peculiarity to some grand scheme of meaning.

The killer's resistance to this drive is his epistemological crime. In Caleb Carr's retrothriller *The Alienist,* set in Wilde's own epoch, Dr. Lazlo Kreizler, the "alienist" of the title, is a medical man-cum-psychologist-cum-detective— the combination that has become de rigeur for the serial killers' hunters in contemporary popular culture, signifying the rejoining of science and detective fiction, the blending of Sherlock Holmes and Dr. Watson into a single hybrid figure. Kreizler hunts down a serial killer of boy prostitutes in fin de siècle New York, presciently employing the techniques of contemporary criminal profiling. However, when the killer is captured and interviewed, both Kreizler and his assistant experience increasing frustration, for the criminal refuses to yield the final mystery: not the how, where, and when but the why. Not that he is evasive; he simply does not know himself. When he is mortally wounded, the alienist desperately attempts to wring a death bed confession, only to hear: "I have never known . . ." (574). The psychological scalpel yields nothing and neither does the surgical one: the killer's dissected brain shows "no evidence of either congenital abnormality or physical trauma" (589). All the patiently assembled knowledge of the killer's identity and modus operandi is worthless compared to the one thing the alienist craves: the secret of his subjectivity. But this is the secret that is hidden from the subject himself, and so the narrator's description of Dr. Kreizler as the "man who knew [the killer] as well as he knew himself" (570) becomes profoundly ironic. The ending of the book displays none of the detective's exuberant smugness, so common in the Golden Age mysteries of Doyle and Christie. Rather, Dr. Kreitzler sounds tired, defeated, and disappointed: "We'll never know now. Ah, Moore—there are so *many* things we'll never know, now . . ." (592).

Both Wilde's teasing renunciation of the desire to know the murderer and Dr. Kreizler's foiled drive to satisfy it, are testimonies to the fascination of the serial killer's benighted subjectivity. This fascination is different from the opacity of the Foucauldian Other of madness who is positioned outside the boundaries of discourse, confronting the classical subject of the Enlightenment "without a possible dialogue, without a common language" (Foucault 1961, 111). A majority of apprehended serial killers do not fall under the McNaghten rules defining legal insanity. Though the rhetoric of madness is an important one in the public controversies surrounding serial killers' trials, most of them are quite competent to engage in a possible dialogue with their society and, in fact, actively do so.[2] A serial killer is a subject who speaks not an alien tongue but a horrifyingly mangled version of the common language, the version that rings unsettlingly familiar but never quite coalesces into meaning. Thus, the necessity and urgency of translating the killer's motivation into discourses of art and science stem not from absolute difference but from uncanny similarity. And it is precisely because of this similarity that his resistance to meaning becomes an epistemological scandal of epic proportions.

The way in which the sublime excess of any murder provokes equal excess of ratiocination will be discussed in the next chapter with regard to the classic detective story. But if all murder has a kernel of irrational mystery, serial murder appears to be irrationality squared. It is not only the sheer brutality of Dahmer's actions but their senselessness that staggers the imagination. Confronted with Dahmer's charnel house or that of his British counterpart, Dennis Nilsen, the public and the media alike insist on answering "the perennial question of how could they bear it, how could they do it?" (Cameron and Frazer 148). When John Douglas, the media-celebrated FBI special agent who was the real-life model for Jack Crawford of *The Silence of the Lambs* and one of the founders of the methodology of criminal profiling, is asked this question, his answer is a rhetorical sleight-of-hand that establishes the serial killer's rationality but denies that this rationality is rational to anybody but the killer himself: "[the serial killer] is not 'insane' because he is rationally faithful to his own ideas and values. The perpetrator of this type of crime differs from the rest of us in his character and thinking. We find it difficult to comprehend that someone would *want* to do something so horrible. But that's the way it is" (1997, 265).

Faced with such double-talk from the authority, the public at large has recourse to two seemingly contradictory but, in fact, closely related strategies of emotional response. On the one hand, it consumes increasingly large quantities of new material, always eager for new and improved explanations of serial murder. As Wendy Lesser puts it, in reading about murder "we want to ask big questions; more than anything else we want to get *answers* to big questions" (13). Yet on the other hand, she also points out that we get irritated by too facile solutions: "Any explanation for murder that too easily explains away the mystery is likely to strike us as suspect" (69). When a new series of murders occurs, the first public response is to rush to psychiatric and criminological experts clamoring for an explanation, only to deride the experts' diagnosis when the murderer is finally caught. This dynamic was particularly clear in the case of Peter Sutcliffe, the Yorkshire Ripper, in which the jury refused to recognize the psychiatrists' contention that the murderer was mentally abnormal. Popular fictions often adroitly exploit this double dynamics, throwing to the reader a handful of explanations, while virtuously preserving the fig leaf of mystery. In Mark Morris's *The Secret of Anatomy,* the protagonist who witnessed the mass shooting by a crazed gunman is "infuriated and appalled" by the media profiling of the killer: he feels that the media "has moved in on this situation and diminished it with their slick neat theories, imposing order on a chaos they couldn't possibly comprehend" (269). This does not prevent the novel itself from imposing "order on chaos" for all of its formidable length, inventing more and more complicated theories to account not only for this specific act of slaughter but ultimately for all of the world's evil.

Even the rejection of a specific narrative does not mean renunciation of narrativity. The man on the street who evinces healthy distrust of fashionable psychiatric theories of the criminal's mind does not thereby remain bereft of explanations. The jury in Sutcliffe's case, as Cameron and Frazer point out, threw out the experts' opinion and applied a different paradigm, that of a willful commitment to evil. Precisely because the serial killer's actions are not unstructured, they cannot be simply banished from the universe of meaning. A series of murders for pleasure is guided by a tight inner logic that assures the repetition of the crimes according to some sort of pattern, but this logic seems to be inassimilable to any collective narrative of art and science. Deciphering the killer's motivation means bringing him back within the purview of such a narrative. An explanation rewrites his opaque inner logic in terms that are collectively intelligible and thus fixes not only the murderer's aberrant identity, but also the identity of the bystander who can now define himself in opposition to what is no more a shapeless mystery but rather a determined signifier of either sickness or evil. It does not matter how grim or apocalyptic the narrative of explanation might be. As long as it makes sense, we keep at bay both the flippancy of Wilde and the epistemological angst of Dr. Kreitzler. As Wilde's essay slyly suggests, we use pen and pencil to revise the incomprehensible scribbling wrought by poison or, in the case of Wainewright's successors, by blunter instruments.

NATURE AND THE POLICE

Many sciences, including psychology and criminology (but also paleontology and evolutionary theory), are modes of storytelling. What unites them is commitment to "reconstruct[ing] events in the past-sequences presumed to be unique or so hugely cyclic that they are beyond experiment" (Landau ix). Thus, what serves as an explanation for these sciences is not an abstract law to which every particular instance can be reduced as its manifestation but a unique narrative, which obeys the general law only insofar as it is ruled by causality. However, such stories are also molded by generic expectations. Stephen Jay Gould writes: "We think that we are reading nature by applying rules of logic and laws of matter to our observations. But we are often telling stories—in the good sense but stories nevertheless" (1991, 251).

Gould's own position is not the radical relativism advocated by some cultural scholars who see scientific narratives as just-so stories rooted in nothing but the social balance of power. However, his somewhat wistful recognition of the "literary bias" reveals a hunger for what Lyotard calls "strategies of legitimation." Narratives may be more or less interesting, tragic or comic, canonical or subversive, but how do we know they are right?

In Stanislaw Lem's *The Star Diaries* a scientist, driven to distraction by just such questions, literally tortures matter to extract its secrets. The remedy is extreme but logical. Nature, devoid of consciousness and subjectivity, responds to our queries in a way that seems overdetermined by the form of the question itself. Now, if nature but had a voice, if it could tell its own story, if, in fact, a scientific enigma could be arrested and interrogated, perhaps the threat of relativism would finally be averted. What better strategy of legitimation than a legal sanction?

Lem's joke is based on the similarity between the ethos of science and that of crime detection, between investigation and interrogation. The nexus between science and the police, which Foucault conflates into the common "scientifico-disciplinary mechanisms," is vividly reflected in the nineteenth-century paradigmatic figures of Great Detectives as scientists *manqué,* Augustus Dupin with his disquisitions on theory of probabilities and Sherlock Holmes with his chemistry kit (1975, 193). Both the scientist and the detective are in pursuit of the elusive "truth" and both are, essentially, tellers of tales. Gould's description of the scientist as a master storyteller is echoed by John Douglas: "a detective's job is to collect as many little bits of information as he can and then work them into a logical, coherent narrative of the crime. That's the reason I've always found good detectives to be among the best storytellers" (1997, 293).[3]

Douglas is one of the founders of what was originally called the FBI Behavioral Sciences Unit at Quantico, where combined methods of psychology, forensic medicine, and criminology are used to chart profiles of violent offenders. Criminal profiling, as employed by Douglas and his colleagues, is a practical methodology. Its theoretical underpinnings, however, are rooted in criminal anthropology, which emerged in the nineteenth century as part of the project to make humanity intelligible. "Beginning with the middle of the nineteenth century, people have been speaking more and more of the criminal in the same naturalistic sense which, in our days, found its culminating expression in Professor Cesare Lombroso" (De Quiros 1). In his early history of criminal anthropology, De Quiros links its emergence with psychiatry and population statistics, that is, with all those "human" sciences that share the "old preoccupation and longing to discover in man the relations between body and soul, the correspondence between spirit and matter" (2). Sciences of man went hand in hand with the reconceptualization of crime, both theoretical and practical: "that moment when the sciences of man became possible is the moment when a new technology of power and a new political anatomy of the body were implemented" (Foucault 1975, 193).

What distinguishes the narratives of human sciences from the narratives of natural sciences, however, is the presence of a protagonist. If natural sciences are allegorical, relying on personification to tell their stories of the struggle of evolution or the birth of the solar system, human sciences are novelistic, appropriating the strategies of psychological description to analyze their self-aware and vocal subjects. Sherlock Holmes and Augustus Dupin do not have to be content with inferences since they have the criminal's narrative to confirm or undermine their own. The detective's "logical, coherent narrative of the crime" has as its strategy of legitimation the criminal's confession. The tripartite plot of the classical detective story—murder, investigation, exposure—traditionally culminates in the explanation of the criminal's motive.

However, as we have seen in *The Alienist,* this convention often fails in detective fictions dealing with serial killers. And it fails in ways strikingly similar to those in which the first-person narratives of monsters fail in horror fiction. The killer is either totally silent or unnaturally voluble and, in either case, his first-person narrative is corroded by the intrusion of the violent sublime.

In Patricia Cornwell's series of best-selling mysteries whose criminals always turn out to be serial killers rather than any common or garden variety lawbreakers, there is a conspicuous refusal to grant the antagonist a voice. The resolution is a swift execution by the heroine, the forensic pathologist Dr. Kay Scarpetta, rather than a traditional confession. In other texts, on the contrary, the killers clamor for the podium. In Harris's *Red Dragon,* Robert Walker's *Darkest Instinct,* and James Patterson's *Kiss the Girls,* to name but a few, whole chapters are narrated from a serial murderer's point of view. However, such narratives are striking by the exactitude with which they conform to the detective's profiling of the criminal. They fail to provide any subjective perspective and merely reproduce the paradoxes inherent in the detective's reconstruction of the killer's motivation. This tautological construction is particularly evident in *Darkest Instinct,* in which the murderer's attempts to preserve the bodies of his victims are glossed by another female forensic pathologist, Dr. Jessica Coran, as follows:

> "if you want my opinion, the hand is just the beginning of an escalation."
> "An escalation of what?"
> "His attempt to preserve flesh, to preserve a victim whole. . . ."(220)

When her perplexed interlocutor asks for what purpose, Jessica replies: "We've got to stop looking for purpose; this bastard's purpose is totally a construct of his own making, having no validity outside his brain" (220). In other words, the criminal's aberrant behavior is a proof of his madness, which, therefore, explains his aberrant behavior (like Dr. Scarpetta, Dr. Coran is supposed to double as a "mindhunter" in the tradition of Douglas, acting as a sort of unwitting parody of the psychiatric and criminological discourses). However, in the parallel chapters narrated from the viewpoint of the criminal, this dubious diagnosis is slavishly confirmed, since he does indeed try to preserve his victims whole for a purpose which has "no validity outside his brain": in the time-honored tradition of *Psycho,* he wants to reincarnate his abusive mother.

If in horror fiction the rationally inassimilable "residue" of violence is displaced on the monster-as-spectacle, in serial-killer thrillers and true crime books the visual aspect is muted (though, as we shall see, not absent). Even a run-of-the-mill shocker, such as *Darkest Instinct,* cannot make the murderer look like a product of the special effects industry and retain minimal plausibility. Instead, madness comes to function as a substitute for true monstrosity. While a majority of real-life serial murderers have been judged legally sane, a majority of fictional serial killers, especially those who are granted a narrative voice, are delusional, their outlandish psychoses soaking up the excess of the violent sublime. But when it comes to actual killers, where baroque madness is not an option, narrative buckles under the weight of violence.

At the opening of their second nonfictional book *Journey into Darkness,* John Douglas and Mark Olshaker attempt something both ambitious and gruesome: a first-person simulated narrative of a real-life sex killer, the man who savagely murdered U.S. Marine Suzanne Collins. The narrative is remarkable for its chilling sanity. At the end of it Douglas defends his experiment of putting himself in the mind of the killer: "If you understand—not in some academic, intellectual way, but in a visceral, experiential way—then maybe we can begin to make a difference" (6). The verisimilitude of such simulation is seen as a primary tool of the detective. In identifying with the mind of his quarry, Douglas, a "mindhunter," follows the time-honored tradition of his fictional predecessor, Poe's Augustus Dupin, who defines his method as "the identification . . . of the reasoner's intellect with that of his opponent" (216).

However, the more Douglas extols the success of his "mindhunting" technique, the more does it appear to be founded not on the intellect but on a mixture of novelistic imagination and something suspiciously like an unwholesome affinity with the serial killer's dark desires. The first-person narrative of Collins's killer, Sedley Alley, is immediately undercut by presenting a third-person account of his confession, which paints a strikingly different picture: according to Sedley, Collins's death was an accident. After a while, a third version emerges, promoted by Sedley's defense attorney: that he suffers from multiple personality disorder and that the murder was committed by one of the alternative personalities. Douglas is dismissive of both these explanations, but their very presence puts his own in question. Moreover, the epistemological status of his reading of Sedley's mind is further compromised by hints that there is something "horrible" about the whole exercise and that its very success indicates a disturbance in the detective himself. Douglas can precariously retain the moral and psychological distance from the killer only by walking a tightrope between scientific detachment and artistic dissimulation, between truth claims and fictional license. On the one hand, understanding the criminal's subjectivity is the sine qua non of criminal profiling; on the other hand, we are pointedly reminded that "human behavior . . . is not an exact science" (12).

The ambiguity that pervades Douglas's simulacrum of the sex murderer's self-revealing narrative is just as evident in those narratives, which are indeed penned by killers. Disconcertingly, in speaking of true experience, which might be expected to correct the "literary bias" of social narratives, serial killers appear to be as confused about their motivation as everybody else. Analyzing the serial murderer Dennis Nilsen's writing as extensively quoted in his biography *Killing for Company* by Brian Masters, Cameron and Frazer highlight its strangely vacillating and unreal quality: Nilsen not only seems not to remember the exact details of his crimes but more significantly "he has real difficulty in remembering *why* on earth he strangled the man in question" (150). Attempting to answer this question to himself in precisely the same way as the spellbound and repelled public attempts to wring the answer from bickering experts, Nilsen runs the whole gamut of options available to him: occasionally, he talks of "compulsion," occasionally of split personality, occasionally of freely chosen evil. Finally, the only way he can make sense of his own actions is to identify with society that sees him from the outside, a frightening and incomprehensible Other: "It would not do for me to escape just punishment. I am an irresponsible selfish bastard who deserves everything that is coming to him. Society has a right to call me a cold, mad killer. No other category fits my results" (151). Not only are the categories hopelessly confused (a "selfish bastard" is not the same thing as a madman), but more importantly, the resulting identification is nothing more that the tritest of all clichés. We would hardly congratulate a psychologist or a writer on their acumen if the best they could come up with in dissecting a criminal's mind was "a cold, mad killer." And yet this is not merely an identification but an identity, not a label but a lived experience.

Cameron and Frazer rightly emphasize that Nilsen's writing illustrates the impossibility of escaping the discursive categories that construct the Real. The only tools that Nilsen has at his disposal to construct himself as a subject of and in discourse are conflicting narratives of criminology, psychology, and fiction. But, perhaps more importantly, he is also aware that these narratives fail to encompass his experience and yet cannot use this experience to counteract their failure: "In his dilemma, finding that the language cannot adequately describe what he is and utterly failing to make up what the language lacks, Dennis Nilsen graphically illustrates the extent to which our reality is bounded by discourse. For at the same time that none of our categories 'fit the results,' so they all do: they all make sense to us, they all give us a way of understanding Nilsen's acts" (151).

But one cannot live with several mutually contradictory ways of understanding one's actions, especially if the actions in question are mass slaughter and necrophilia. At the end Nilsen's subjectivity becomes exemplary not so much of the "bad" or flawed subjectivity of the Other as of the impossible subjectivity of an object. Like nature, he obediently accepts any story that science chooses to tell about himself. Unlike nature, however, he casts himself into the identities projected by these stories, creating a generically hybrid and monstrously inconsistent selfhood.

There are two main modalities of the serial killer's narrative identity. Both have the imprimatur of science; however, their underlying assumptions and their basic plots are strikingly different. The serial killer's broken life-story vacillates between the two poles that might be called the Ape and the Minister, following the paradigms of Edgar Allan Poe's classic detective tales.

In Poe's "The Murders in the Rue Morgue" Dupin, the prototype of all the subsequent Great Detectives and the man who brings the knowledge of the

"Calculus of Probabilities" to sleuthing, finds the main clue to the solution of the crime precisely in what has left the police baffled: "the seeming absence of motive . . . the atrocity of the murder" (154). As he dispassionately examines the horribly mangled bodies of Madame L'Espanye and her daughter, he concludes that no human perpetrator could possibly commit so bloodily senseless a deed. Therefore, the perpetrator is not human. Q.E.D. Dupin, who likes to boast that "most men, in respect to himself, [wear] windows in their bosoms" (144), is under no obligation to turn his mental searchlight onto the orangutan apprehended for the murder. The beastly nature of the beast is a sufficient, if tautological, motivation for its violence.

It is instructive to compare this tale with "The Purloined Letter," in which Dupin solves the conundrum by penetrating the criminal's subjectivity, deeply identifying with his motives and modes of thought. But in this story Minister D. commits an elegant theft, not a disgusting butchery. It seems to let Dupin off the hook; even if, as he half confesses later, there is something criminal about himself, the criminality of a clever blackmailer is not the same thing as that of a lust murderer. However, in "The Mystery of Marie Roget" the body which he "reads" in excruciating detail is that of a rape and murder victim, and the criminal with whom he identifies is a man of superior intelligence and cunning, a moral brute, perhaps, but not a dumb animal. Yet the deed is as cruel as the murders in the Rue Morgue, suggesting that lust murders can be committed not only by monstrous orangutans but also by people very similar to the urbane and intellectual detective.

The two extremes into which the narratives of murder, particularly of serial murder, tend to fall identify the murderer as either the bestial monster or as the detective's double. In *Mindhunter* Douglas easily shifts from the serial killer as beast of prey to the serial killer as the guy next door. On the one hand, "It is the thrill of the hunt that gets these guys going. If you could get a galvanic skin response on one of them as he focuses in on his potential victim, I think you'd get the same reaction as from that lion in the wilderness" (1996, 25).

On the other hand, "It isn't always easy, and it isn't always pleasant, putting yourself in these guys' shoes—or inside their minds. But that's what my people and I have to do. We have to try to feel what it was like for each one" (ibid. 26).

Both paradigms generate narratives of genesis. If the killer is a beast, one has to find out, as Dupin does, where it comes from. If the killer is "one of us," onc has to account as Dupin does not—for his evil transformation.

The clash and interweaving of these narratives is prefigured by the conversation between Frankenstein and his creature on the bleak slopes of Mont Blanc. Frankenstein dismisses the creature as inherently defective and views his murderous rampage as an inevitable result of his tainted birth. However, the monster himself offers an entirely different interpretation in which "his vices are the children of a forced solitude" (147). The book remains open-ended, the two positions balanced against each other in a stalemate that generations of critics have attempted to break in vain. If for Seltzer the grand prototype of the serial killer is Dracula, I would suggest that Frankenstein's creature, forever caught between the poles of "born bad" and "made bad," offers a better model of the serial killer's position in postmodern culture.

In Patricia Cornwell's first novel *Post-mortem,* Dr. Scarpetta has a conversation on the nature of evil with her precocious ten-year-old niece.

> "Maybe he [the current killer] doesn't mean to hurt them, Aunt Kay."
>
> "There are some people who are evil," I quietly replied. "Like dogs, Lucy. Some dogs bite people for no reason. There's something wrong with them. They're bad and will always be bad."
>
> "Because people were mean to them first. That's what makes them bad."
>
> "In some instances, yes," I told her. "But not always. Sometimes there isn't a reason. In a way, it doesn't matter. People make choices. Some people would rather be bad, would rather be cruel. It's just an ugly, unfortunate part of life."
>
> "Like Hitler," she muttered. (39)

This is the Frankenstein debate all over again, in which the options are the ape and the minister, the naturally evil creature and the ordinary person who has gone bad because "people were mean" to him. And it is not likely to be settled any time soon.

NATURAL BORN MONSTERS

The view of the serial killer as a born monster goes back to Lombroso's criminal anthropology, which viewed the offender as a creature of a different species, indelibly marked by the stigmata of biological degeneracy. Enrico Ferri, Lombroso's son-in-law, explains the purpose of the new science: "as zoology is the natural history of animals, criminal anthropology is but the study of a single variety of mankind" (4). "Variety" here is understood in its primary biological sense: the criminal is, first and foremost, a body whose constitution lends itself to physical taxonomy. The secret of violence can be read in the shape of his skull, the form of his ear, the asymmetry of his face. The typological view of the criminal precedes Lombroso: Morel in 1847 talks about "the strange and unknown types which people our prisons" with the zeal of a naturalist discovering a whole new animal kingdom (qtd. in De Quiros 7). Lombroso himself studies criminality "among the lower organisms, detecting it even in the vegetable world," and focuses on the "embryology of the crime" (De Quiros 12). The rhetoric of criminal anthropology nudges it closer and closer to natural, rather than human, sciences since its primary goal becomes "the organic study of the criminal, both anatomical and physiological" (Ferri 7).

The end result of criminal anthropology is the incorporation of crime: removed from the sphere of moral or even legal judgment, it becomes the matter not of doing but of being. Paradoxically, criminal activity itself ceases to be of any particular importance in defining the criminal or adjudicating the proper punishment, for if the criminal is born, his actions are mere symptoms, superficial expressions of his immutable nature which precedes and determines any particular instance of lawbreaking. A criminal, in fact, can be detected before he commits a crime. This shift from activity to corporeality is exemplified in De Quiros's statement: "The criminal type, as the scholastics said of the soul, is in its entirety in the whole body and in each of its parts" (18). This, of course, is a profound break with the classical legal theory that views the criminal as a morally autonomous agent, whose exclusion from the community is the result of his own freely chosen misbehavior. "For classical theory, each being was a person, a subject of law, subject to law" (Pick 136). The criminal was a lapsed citizen and every citizen a potential criminal. Lombrosian criminal anthropology, however, renounces "the assumption that we can measure the moral culpability of the accused" (Ferri 165). Instead, the sole function of the judge is to be a competent taxonomist: "the one and only possible issue between the prosecution and the defence will be to determine, by the character of the accused and of his action, to what anthropological class he belongs" (164).

The criminal's "class" is his species. In nineteenth-century racial anthropology, polygenism views different races as different species of the genus *Homo,* creating a science-fictional world populated by racial aliens.[4] For criminal anthropology "born" criminals are "if not exactly . . . a degenerate species, at least . . . a degenerate variety of the human species" and the only "problem" they pose is the same as posed by any fast breeding vampire or werewolf, which is "to diminish their number as much as possible" (238–39). For the teratology of crime, every criminal is Frankenstein's creature, a misshapen "fiend." The body itself becomes the locus and breeding ground of evil.

What criminologist David Canter calls "the 'monstrous creation' vision of people" generates the poetics of display and menagerie. If serial killers are either "badly built or their original programming got out of control" (Canter 207), the defects, the "missing bits," can be exposed to "the exercise and decisions of the gaze" (Foucault 1963, 89). Conceived as a disease, criminality blossoms into a show as the "disease, emerging before our gaze, becomes embodied in a living organism" (ibid. 5). A serial killer is criminality personified, not an individual but an anonymous and typical representative of a species.

A lavishly illustrated coffee-table volume *Serial Killers* has recently been published by Time-Life Publishers. The book opens with a short introduction, titled "The Nature of the Beast" and printed above an enormous photo of two staring eyes. Turned into a beast of prey, the serial killer becomes the classical subject of the gaze: caged in a textual panopticon and pinned down by a definition. But if for Foucault incarceration in a see-through cage is one of the "technologies of individuals" which produce disciplined human subjects, the visual display of the serial killer makes him into an animal in a zoo, offering him a subject position on the murky biological boundary between humanity and beasthood.

Lombroso's theory of atavism explains criminality as a throwback to earlier evolutionary stages, thus literally turning the criminal into an animal: "in the criminal there are numerous anatomical traits, especially craniological, that suggest the structure of primitive men and even of the leading mammals" (De Quiros 14). Poe's orangutan would qualify as a full-fledged felon, after all. Despite its triteness, *la bête humaine* is far from a meaningless term of abuse. Rather, it expresses the shift from moral condemnation to biological classification. Stephen J. Giannangelo's rhetoric in *The Psychopathology of Serial Murder* is an example of how easily the "beastliness" of murder can produce the "beast" of a murderer:

> It has been said that the predatory behaviour of prey animals reflects "a neurological basis that is different from that of other kinds of behaviour." In other words, predatory aggression is different from other aggression, in that it "does not show rage and is not interchangeable with flight behaviour, but is purpose-oriented, accurately aimed, and the tension ends with the accomplishment of the goal." The calm, purposeful behavior of the accomplished serial murderer clearly reflects the actions of a predatory aggressor rather than the behavior of an excited, flight-stimulated organism. (23)

Since Giannangelo's purpose is precisely to show that the behavior of serial killers has "a neurological basis that is different from that of other kinds" of violence, his analogy with a predator collapses into an equation that, perhaps unintentionally, resurrects Lombroso's blunt claim that criminals are throwbacks to "leading mammals." In Douglas's comparison between a serial killer and a lion in the wilderness, quoted above, the same dynamics is at work: from the figurative to the literal, from the criminal being like an animal to the criminal being an animal. Animality indicates both the biological difference that defines the serial killer as "a single variety of mankind" and his accessibility to the naturalistic gaze.

The continuity between the contemporary "monstrous creation" paradigm of the serial killer and Lombrosian criminal anthropology is most evident in their shared opposition to traditional legal theory and practice. If the criminal is "a degenerate species," then the proper task of the court is not justice but classification. The criminal, not the crime, becomes the focus of the legal proceedings whose function is diagnostic: "to determine, by the character of the accused and of his action, to what anthropological class he belongs" (Ferri 164). In a move calculated to medicalize jurisprudence, Ferri boldly declares that "in every criminal trial the basis of inquiry is or ought to be formed by the data of criminal biology, psychology, and psycho-pathology" (170). He is indignant that ignorant magistrates poke fun at experts' minute examinations of prisoners' ears. In his recent book *Serial Killers,* Joel Norris cites twenty-three visible signs of genetic disorders in suspected serial murderers, which do, incidentally, include misshapen ears. Norris treats serial killing as "an infectious disease" and "a public health issue" (326). Killers are "physically and psychologically damaged people," displaying unambiguous stigmata of their monstrosity: "scars on their bodies, missing fingers, evidence of previous contusions and multiple abrasions on and around the head and neck area" (17–18). The killer is both the carrier of the disease and the disease itself, deadly to his victims but ultimately the victim of an "epidemic" himself: "the epidemic of serial murder is spreading. Passed on from generation to generation . . . serial murder is actually a disease that is thriving in American society" (Norris 38). Redefined as a hereditary taint, serial killing must free itself from the obsolete shackles of morality and pass from the hands of lawyers into those of physicians. The question of the killer's responsibility for his actions becomes irrelevant to the diagnosis of his inherent condition. Norris's critique of the McNaghten rules for determining legal insanity is couched in the terminology of scientific progress: "To premise a legal definition of insanity on the McNaghten rules is like applying nineteenth-century medicine to treating cancer or AIDS" (19). The irony, of course, is that Norris paraphrases the criticism of classical legal theory by Lombrosian criminal anthropology, thus, in fact, applying "nineteenth-century medicine" to his newly discovered malady.

Criminological descriptions of the serial killer as an embodiment of a deadly disease or a beast of prey pave the way for the serial killer as a monster. This is the mold for the serial killer in popular fiction and film. Perhaps the most famous popular-culture serial killer is Dr. Hannibal Lecter in Thomas Harris's *The Silence of the Lambs* and its sequels, played in the film versions by Anthony Hopkins. Lecter is a prodigy, an evil genius gifted with marvelously acute senses and an uncanny psychological penetration. But his many gifts, as in the case of Dracula, only underscore his essential monstrosity. In *Red Dragon,* the first book in the series, he is described by the protagonist thus: "He's a monster. I think of him as one of those pitiful things that are born in hospitals from time to time. They feed it, and keep it warm, but they don't put it on the machines and it dies. Lecter is the same way in his head, only he looks normal and nobody could tell" (56). Lecter, in fact, is even physically monstrous, though not in the spectacular way of the Red Dragon, another serial butcher whom he helps to track down. The Red Dragon has a "bat-like" face with a cleft palate; the dapper Dr. Lecter hides his six-fingered left hand.[5]

The assimilation of serial murderers to legendary monsters proceeds apace as, on the one hand, cultural scholars like Seltzer find Dracula and Mr. Hyde in every Ted Bundy, while on the other hand, true-crime writers suggest mythical monsters are merely serial killers writ large. Douglas writes, for example: "Serial murder may, in fact, be a much older phenomenon than we realize. The stories and legends that have filtered down about witches, and werewolves, and vampires may have been a way of explaining outrages so hideous that no one in the small and close-knit towns of Europe and early America could comprehend the perversities we now take for granted. Monsters had to be supernatural creatures. They could not be just like us" (1996, 30).

The last sentence exemplifies the ambiguity inherent in viewing the serial killer as a monstrous creation: monsters, by definition, are not "like us." The rhetoric of monstrosity, poised on the borderline between metaphor and medicine, forces such an extreme separation between the killer and the ordinary run of humanity that the former appears to be a force of nature, vicious and brutal to be sure, but as impervious to psychological analysis as Poe's orangutan. For Norris the serial killer is "a nonpersonality type—a nosferatu," Dracula without his fangs (71). He also explains the legends of vampires and werewolves as somewhat exaggerated but essentially accurate reflections of "individuals who seemed to kill out of a blood lust for the act of murder itself and not from any other motivation" (72). But if so, any attempt by the judicial system to treat "nosferatus" "as though they had volition and were capable of managing their own behavior . . . as though they were within the range of normal human existence," is misguided. For Norris, serial killers are literally the Undead "who seem to come alive only during the episodic cycle of murder" (60–61). Such a drastic denial of agency is bound to feed contempt for the judicial system, hopelessly mired in the old-fashioned ideas of choice and responsibility. The only certain cure for the plague of serial killing appears to be the one practiced by Dr. Van Helsing, to stop the spread of Dracula and his vampiric cohorts.

If the monstrous creation paradigm is problematic legally and morally, it is even more so narratively. A narrative is supposed to provide the satisfaction of an ending, to tie up all the loose ends in a decisive closure. But at its extreme, the notion of the killer as a natural-born monster is antinarrative. As a monster on display, the serial killer is frozen into an image whose circulation in culture becomes possible only as an endless reproduction of the same frightening icon, a serial proliferation of simulacra which unnervingly imitates the killer's own modus operandi. The serial killer acts out a fantasy whose realization involves a chain of substitutions, anonymous victims being merely disposable props in some violent tableau. The narrative of the killer's desire is looped into repetition. Similarly, the narrative of the public desire for the killer to be known, explained, and exorcised is looped by the typological model into reiteration of the same emblem of monstrosity. Denied the release of an ending, the discourse of serial killing fragments into a series of snapshots that exhibit violence but do not exorcise it. The literature of serial murder, both fictional and criminological, skirts perilously close to the sublime spectacle of fantastic horror.

One way to avoid this ruination of narrative is through the plot of secrecy, in which the serial killer and the police or the criminologist assume the classic roles that Stevenson called "Mr. Hide" and "Mr. Seek." A Mr. Hide's monstrosity must be hidden and invisible. If serial killers are, as Norris claims, "obviously physically and psychologically damaged people," the task of detection becomes simplified out of existence: arrest anybody who displays the telltale signs of the "disease" (17). The Lombrosian approach, with its emphasis on the visual, can become embarrassing: what is the function of the criminologist if any rookie can apprehend hereditary criminals by being on the lookout for large ears and prognathous jaws? Both in *Red Dragon* and in *Alienist,* in which the murderers are deformed, the reader, after a while, feels impatient with the slow-witted society that allows people branded with such an obvious mark of Cain to walk freely in its midst. The monstrous creation paradigm lacks narrative suspense, which, however, can be supplied by the poetics of hidden monstrosity.

Within this poetics, the signs of the serial killer's disorder are not self-evident stigmata but rather symptoms that Carlo Ginzburg describes as "infinitesimal traces that permit the apprehension of a deeper, otherwise inaccessible reality" (101). The meaning of violence is hidden within the criminal's secret anatomy, which necessitates the epistemology of dissection, bent upon rooting out the mystery that seems to be retreating deeper and deeper into the body. Now the criminologist pursues not the visible signs of monstrosity but faulty chromosomes, brain damage, chemical and hormonal imbalance. Apprehended serial killers are often subjected to a battery of psychological and physiological tests meant to elicit the secret of their deviance. There is nothing particularly new in this corporeal sleuthing of Norris's "new criminologists."

Lombroso's eureka moment, as he describes it in *Criminal Man,* occurs at the dissecting table when he reads in a criminal's misshapen skull the cause of his wrongdoings. From the moment of its birth, "essential" criminality is seen as both corporeal and elusive, blatant and hidden, invisible to the untrained eye but triumphantly revealed to the probing gaze and sharp scalpel of the scientist:

> This was not merely an idea but a revelation. At the sight of this skull, I seemed to see all of a sudden, lighted up as a vast plain under a flaming sky, the problem of the nature of the criminal—an atavistic being who reproduces in his person the ferocious instincts of primitive humanity and the inferior animals. Thus were explained anatomically the enormous jaws, high cheek bones, prominent superciliary arches, solitary lines in the palms, extreme size of the orbits, handle-shaped ears found in criminals, savages and apes, insensitivity to pain, extremely acute sight, tattooing, excessive idleness, love of orgies, and the irresponsible craving of evil for its own sake, the desire not only to extinguish life in the victim, but to mutilate the corpse, tear its flesh and drink its blood. (xiv–xv)

Within the narrative of the secret, the serial killer's body and psyche appear as double-layered, combining the deceptively normal surface and the monstrous depth: "the overwhelming majority of serial killers seem on the surface to be normal-looking individuals. . . . But in reality they are walking time bombs ready to ignite at just the right combination of events. . . . An individual who is on the verge of becoming a serial killer may seem like a dormant volcano. No one knows that beneath the usually bland exterior is a psyche in turmoil . . ." (Norris 40–41).

However, precisely because the work of the criminologist consists in opening up the killer, it bears an unsettling resemblance to the killer's own craving for opening up the victim. The criminal and the criminologist are locked together in a Jekyll-and-Hyde relationship, attested to by the persistent rumor that Jack the Ripper was a physician and incarnated in Dr. Hannibal Lecter, a brilliant savant of the criminal mind, including his own. Cornwell's Dr. Kay Scarpetta is a forensic pathologist whose work is extensively documented in the novels. In detailed descriptions of autopsies, the Scarpetta novels seek to titillate the reader with a show of corporeal vulnerability, while simultaneously positioning their heroine on the side of the angels: it is she, after all, who has to confront the serial killers' handiwork in order to aid their just punishment. But since the scene of the actual murders is generally left to the imagination, Dr. Scarpetta, in cutting open the victims' bodies, appears not so much the killer's nemesis as his proxy.

The doubling of the killer and the detective/physician/psychologist whose function it is to cure the "disease" of serial killing appears with stunning regularity in fictional works which otherwise seem to conform to the monstrous creation paradigm. Again, the roots of this phenomenon seem coterminous with serial killing itself. Not only Jekyll–Hyde but also Dr. Van Helsing, the fearless vampire killer, with his sharp stake, seems—surreptitiously—to mirror his adversary with his sharp tooth. In Arthur Machen's 1917 novella "The Terror," a suspected serial killer is profiled as "a madman only at intervals," with a "fluid and unstable" personality which is not a unity but "a mere polity, a state in which dwelt many strange and incongruous citizens," unaware of each other's existence (351). The man who expounds this theory ends up by suggesting that the lawyer who heads the investigation into mysterious deaths may be the culprit without having "the faintest suspicion that there is another Llewelyn within him, a Llewelyn who follows murder as a fine art" (352). The monster within the law-abiding citizen can appear as another personality such as the Red Dragon, whom the killer perceives as something external to himself or as the "real face" of the detective, as in James Patterson's *Kiss the Girls* where the serial rapist and killer Casanova turns out to be a police officer on the case.

The monstrous creation paradigm of the serial killer generates a paradox that explodes the very identity it assigns to its subject. The location of criminality in the body, meant to separate cleanly the normal and the abnormal human species, ends up blurring the very distinction it is supposed to uphold. Once the criminal anatomy becomes a secret anatomy, hidden in the deepest recesses of the body and accessible only to a diligent search, who can be completely sure of escaping its taint? The actions of the psycho-killer and the physician become structurally identical: digging for the secret of the Other that may turn out to be the secret of the self. The monster is one of us, after all.

A FINE LINE

In Cornwell's *From Potter's Field,* Dr. Scarpetta has a peculiar conversation with her psychologist whom she asks to dissect her latest adversary, performing on his mind the same operation she herself performs on the bodies of his victims. The psychologist says, simply and chillingly: "I don't give a damn why any of them do it . . . I think they should all be hanged" (255). The reason for this default of professional duty may be seen in the dialogue between Scarpetta and her niece quoted above. The niece defends the killer as a past victim, providing her own childish answer to the question "why": because "people were mean to him." A psychological analysis of a serial killer may lead to understanding and then to forgiveness. As Wendy Lesser tentatively suggests: "But is it not possible for murderers to be a different kind of victim . . . ?" (83).

Seen as a victim, the serial killer becomes the product of a childhood trauma, most often of abuse. The victimization paradigm and the monster paradigm are, in practice, not mutually exclusive. Most criminologists, even those committed to a genetic or physiological explanation of serial violence, readily admit the etiological contribution of the environment. True-crime books are omnivorous, adopting both explanations with ease. In a typically mixed presentation, Margaret Cheney in *Why—The Serial Killer in America* notes that "many such killers were severely abused as children," while at the same time referring to serial murder as "disease" (xi). Stephen Giannangelo, in a much more serious investigation of violence, gives equal weight to biological and environmental factors: "The combination of physical predisposition and environmental stressors helps develop a pattern of maladjustment with two major consequences: a distorted sense of self and the dysfunctional sexual component" (27). John Douglas, while stressing that serial killers are not "like us," is not particularly enthusiastic about straightforward biological explanations. Referring to the Speck case, in which the murderer had originally been supposed to have a genetic defect that was later disproved, he denies that any of "his" killers were biologically abnormal (1996, 21).

However, taken as narrative paradigms, the monstrous creation and the victimization stories are quite different, both structurally and ideologically. The psychologist's brusque refusal to understand the killer testifies to the fear of finding him pitiable or, worse, sympathetic. The conversation between Scarpetta and her niece recalls the anguished confrontation between Frankenstein and his creature, in which the origin of the monster's violence becomes the moral crux of their relationship. If the creature is "born bad," Frankenstein is right in denying all his pleading for justice and recognition as the low cunning of a hereditary criminal. If the creature is forced into violence by his parent's rejection and society's cruelty, he is a victim and then Frankenstein himself is rightfully to bear the blame for all the corpses he leaves in his wake. Despite the psychologist's disclaimer, "I don't give a damn," it does matter whether the killer her client is hunting is viewed as an evil alien or as an abused and traumatized human being.

Narratively too, the two paradigms produce quite different stories for their subjects. The monstrous creation narrative focuses on the aftermath of violence; it is the story of search and exposure. The "victimization" story works from the crime backward to account for the genesis of the killer. It allows a psychological identification with the murderer, which is stalled by biological determinism. A monster is the Other, incomprehensible and alien. His sublime subjectivity may be seductive, but it remains out of reach for an ordinary human subject. The victim of abuse, on the other hand, is instantly comprehensible. If we go back in time far enough, we encounter—as in *Alienist* and *The Red Dragon*—the serial killer as a helpless child. Even in *Postmortem,* where Dr. Scarpetta resolutely refuses to consider her niece's proposition that "people were mean to him first," the FBI profiler on the case brings back the victimization theory by suggesting that the "killer was from a 'dysfunctional home' and might have been abused, either physically or emotionally, by his mother" (78).

As the series progresses, Scarpetta seems more and more obviously torn between her professional need to understand the mind of the killer and her resolute denial of any human kinship with the monster. In *From Potter's Field* Scarpetta encounters a "malignant genius," Temple Gault, who seems beyond any psychological explanation. No profile for him, he just "does what he pleases" (39). Gault defies both models of serial killing: reared in a decent family, he cannot be easily seen as the product of a biological taint either, since he has a "good" twin sister whom he cold-bloodedly murders. A monster is a monster is a monster. When asked what Gault is, Scarpetta answers, "There is no description for what he is" (29). And while she diligently delves into Gault's childhood, all she discovers is the identity of his victim but not of himself.

However, the generic form of the crime thriller inexorably pushes Dr. Scarpetta to account somehow for Gault. And since she cannot do it, the text lapses into incoherence, petering out in an unconvincing gunfight. This is not an option for criminology. Science of crime requires an explanation of the killer's motivation, which always incurs the danger of sliding into empathy. On the one hand, according to Douglas, identification is the sine qua non of detection: "We must try to feel what it was like for each one" (1991, 26) Yet, on the other hand, "feeling like" can all too easily mutate into "being like." The horror of being sucked into the killer's mind through understanding it accounts for the narrator's outburst at the end of *Alienist:*

> I suppose that I, too, should have been deeply gratified at the results of this initial interview; yet as I watched Beecham answer Laszlo's questions—his voice growing ever more compliant and even childish, with none of the threatening, arrogant tone he'd used when we were his prisoners—I became powerfully irritated, disturbed at the very core of my spirit. This irritation soon became outrage, as if this man had no right to exhibit any pitiable human qualities in the light of all he'd done. Who was this enormous grotesque, I thought, to sit there confessing and sniveling like one of the children he'd slaughtered? (570)

Seeing the child-killer as a sniveling kid can flip into seeing any sniveling kid—including one's own childhood image of oneself—as a potential child-killer. Moore shoots the murderer in a futile attempt to reestablish the boundary between detective and criminal, victim and victimizer. The taint of violence, however, freely circulates across this boundary, carried precisely by those strategies of knowledge that have created it in the first place. In one of the episodes of the TV show *The X-Files,* the profiler who for three years has pursued a serial killer commits copycat murders after the killer is arrested, having been infected by his madness through a too-close penetration of his mind. The detective in Lewis Shiner's horror story "Love in Vain" realizes that the serial killer Charlie, whose gruesome exploits he investigates, is part of himself, in fact part of every male, an incarnation of sexual violence implicit in "normal" male sexuality. The mindhunter is both empowered and disabled by his affinity with his prey, as Douglas illustrates in an episode he recounts with wry humor. During a conversation with FBI agents, Richard Speck turns to the agents and says: "You fucking guys are crazy. It must be a fine line separates you from me" (1996, 21).

AM I EVIL?

The narrative aporia of *Frankenstein* prefigures the aporia of the serial killer's identity. The two paradigms described above cannot be reconciled, but neither of them is sufficient on its own. Both fail to account for the violence, which necessitates their deployment in the first place. Defining the serial killer as a monster offers a temporary relief from the emotional shock of murder: "Branded a maniac, beast, monster, or vampire, the sexual murderer often escapes psychiatric and legal definition by moving into a special category beyond human terms" (Tatar 26). However, neither criminology nor fictions of crime can accept this "special category" without giving up their raison d'être: the will to know. Their plots require the orderly progression from question to answer, from the killer's modus operandi to his identity. If the mind of the killer is an alien, impenetrable mystery "beyond human terms," this progression is stalled.

The victimization paradigm offers easy understanding but leads to the slippery slope of sympathetic identification, at the bottom of which the killer becomes "one of us." As Charlie says in "Love in Vain": "You can't never get rid of me because I'm inside you" (382). But even if the serial killer is Everyman, not every man is a serial killer. Even if inside each murderer hides an abused child, not all abused children grow up to kill. Both seductive and sickening, the pull of identification with the mind of the killer is checked by the gap between fantasy and deed. "Through murder and mayhem, the serial killer literally chases his dreams" (Fox and Levin 51). But though it may be argued that, as Jocasta says to Oedipus, "all men have dreams like this," obviously not all men go on to make these dreams real.

Thus, if the monstrous creation paradigm fails to account for the killer's similarity to the ordinary run of humanity, the victimization paradigm cannot explain his difference. Turned into a monster-hunt, criminology has to abjure its scientific claim to understand the serial murderer's psychology and motivation. Attuned to the killer's history of victimization, it fails to account for the unique horror of his violence. And mixed together, however pragmatically useful this may appear, the two paradigms create a narrative muddle. Their blending always fails as they work at cross-purposes, fracturing the text. The real nature of the serial killer is, perhaps, best acknowledged by these fractures, just as the Real can only be glimpsed in the rifts and cracks of the Symbolic.

The doubling of the serial killer in Thomas Harris's *Red Dragon* and *The Silence of the Lambs* provides a startling example of that. Lecter, the psychotic cannibalistic monster (who is also, as many critics have noted, the most appealing character in the books and the films) functions as the full-fledged Great Detective, while the FBI agents Clarice Starling and Jack Crawford play Watson to his Holmes. He appears as a hybrid of Dupin and Minister D., with the ravenous orangutan thrown in for good measure. But ultimately his subjectivity remains the only unsolved (and unsolvable) enigma of the novels, while he easily gets under the skin of everybody else, criminal and noncriminal alike. A mindhunter in his own right, Lecter reconstructs the twisted life stories of Red Dragon and Buffalo Bill, whose violence is ultimately explained as an outcome of severely abused childhood. They are sick, delusional, victimized. Red Dragon is physically deformed, but the text, after some vacillation, settles for the claim that his pathology stems from the rejection and mockery occasioned by his defect rather than from any biological taint. Both he and Buffalo Bill are descendants of Frankenstein's creature as he sees himself: monsters "made bad," not "born bad."

Lecter, on the other hand, seems to be just the opposite: Crawford defines him as a born monster whose evil is a result of some incomprehensible snag in brain chemistry. However, Lecter himself is quite aware of this explanation and mercilessly ridicules it in a remarkable conversation with Clarice Starling who seeks to "quantify" him: "Nothing happened to me, Officer Starling. I happened. You can't reduce me to a set of influences. You've given up good and evil for behaviorism, Officer Starling. You've got everybody in moral dignity pants—nothing is ever anybody's fault. Look at me, Officer Starling. Can you stand to say I'm evil? Am I evil, Officer Starling?" (T. Harris 1989, 20).

"Nothing happened to me" is the ultimate rebuff of all narratives of the killer's genesis. Neither made nor born a monster, Lecter freely chooses monsterhood. Lesser notes that the film audience cheers for Lecter and explains our "sympathies" with him by the process of psychological identification (51). However, Lecter has no psychology; he is a walking abstraction of autonomous, self-willed subjecthood, the generic Man of philosophy reincarnated as a mass murderer. Unlike Buffalo Bill and Red Dragon, he has no story, he is not shackled by the past or pinned down by an explanation. He flaunts his conscious and carefully tended evil as a badge of freedom from both nature and nurture. In a sense, his is the most traditional identity of all, the ahistorical incorporeal identity of a moral monad. And yet, in the age of scientific causality, of narratives of origin that strive to bind every subjectivity by a memory chain, Lecter's moral absolutism appears seductively anarchic. He is, in fact, Everyman, but Everyman as a *tabula rasa* of ethical choice, not as the hidden destructive presence beyond the reach of consciousness. He is not a serial killer inside each of us but a serial killer that each of us can become if we so choose. Lecter the gentleman killer holds the impossible promise of a nonnarrative identity, not conditioned by the past or glumly marching toward the unavoidable future, but created anew in each moment of choice. It is for the sake of this promise that we are willing to forgive his murders. This is why the author, with the connivance of the reader, kills off Buffalo Bill and lets Lecter go free, even though they both commit the same repulsive crime. Bill kills and flays women to make himself a suit of female skin; Lecter escapes imprisonment by tearing off a warder's face and wearing it as a mask. But Bill is an essentialist; he strives to fashion a real identity for himself because he believes becoming a woman will liberate his true self. Lecter is a *bricoleur* who creates disposable identities, an opportunist who refuses to be bound by the psychiatric bildungsromans he so deftly imposes upon others. For the culture tired of the stalemate between Frankenstein and his creature, it seems to be a relief to meet a monster who cheerfully says: "I am evil because this is what I have chosen to be."[6]

MEMORY CHAIN

Of course, a real-life Lecter would be quite a different matter. We applaud Lecter's sovereign self for the same reason we are seduced by the visionary appeal of horror fiction and film. But meeting the monsters of Midian (see chapter 1) in a dark alley would be a different order of experience. There were, in fact, serial killers who explicitly attempted to realize in their lives the antinarrative freedom of the sublime. Ian Brady, who, together with Myra

Hindley, committed the Moor Murders, was described by his biographer as "a disciple of the philosophy of amoralism and the absolute right of the individual to engage in whatever evil he chooses" (Cameron and Frazer 140). Cameron and Frazer describe Brady's goal as "masculine transcendence," a gender-inflected equivalent of the violent sublime. But they fall into the trap of perceiving this transcendence as a coherent paradigm that can, finally, provide an overarching explanation for all serial murderers—if not Buffalo Bill, then Dr. Lecter; if neither a born monster nor a victim, then, perhaps, a too-single-minded reader of Sade. But whatever Brady might have thought of himself, in the long run the sublime experience he sought exploded his identity as surely as the vacillation between different postures exploded the identities of Bundy and Nilsen.[7]

Presupposing that at any given moment one is confronted by two equally weighed ethical alternatives denies the importance of the self-awareness of the past. The dice of choice are always loaded by memory. Lecter's sublime self is impossible precisely because the memory of his past crimes contributes nothing to the current state of his personality. He has no story; his subjectivity is flattened out into the perpetual Grand Guignol show. But such subjectivity cannot be sustained over time.

Criminologist David Canter sharply critiques both the monstrous creation and the victimization paradigms, noting that both are of little practical use in apprehending criminals. In line with his narrative approach to psychology, he tries to pinpoint precisely what makes the serial killer's inner plot different from the life-stories of ordinary individuals.

> The question still remains. Are there different types of plot? Is there a finite limit to the plots available? How are the plots constructed? Also we have no firm, general answers to these questions, it is clear that the storylines that unfold for violent criminals are a limited subset of all possible life stories. Comedy and satire are certainly not for them and it seems unlikely that the optimistic objectives of romance fall within their realm of thought. Killers and rapists live broken, destructive, tragic lives. (234)

Thus, serial killers seem to have access to the grandest narrative of Western culture, tragedy. But, in fact, Canter's limited list of genres hardly does justice to the multiple generic molds of popular culture, which constitute the contemporary subject's reservoir of life-stories. Not Hamlet or King Lear but Dracula and Frankenstein are likely models for a narrative of motiveless violence. What Seltzer contemptuously calls the "pop-psychology" and "pop-sociology" of serial murder are new genres of selfhood that emerge in parallel with the generic explosion of mass culture.

But even within these genres, serial killers' self-narratives are generically contradictory, fragmented, broken beyond repair. Rather than tidily conforming to a particular paradigm, never mind how tragic, serial killers, as Nilsen's writings graphically demonstrate, seem to possess a number of irreconcilable stories, bits and pieces pasted together from a pile of random sources. Ted Bundy was generous with explanations of his murderous rampage for the benefit of the audience of experts, lawyers, friends, and general public mesmerized by the hideous enigma of this smooth, attractive, bright young man who charmed women at day and butchered them at night. He blamed pornography; he blamed his genes, he said that sometimes he felt "like a vampire," he talked of unspecified "unfulfilled desires" which transcended the sexual, he threw in a dash of mysticism, he declared himself to be "the most cold-blooded sonofabitch you'll ever meet" (*Serial Killers* 6–48). No doubt, many (or most) of these explanations were adopted for specific purposes, to impress the court, to charm a psychologist, or to stay the execution. But it would be wrong to presuppose that somewhere, underneath this ill-assorted pile of clichés, a real Ted Bundy was hidden, intelligible to himself if not to others. Rather, it seems, that as Cameron and Frazer put it, the "discourse by which sex-killing is made intelligible to us, whether it comes from the killer, a psychiatrist or *The Sun,* is not parasitic on some higher truth: it is the heart of the matter and the rest is silence" (xii).

But silence can be more powerful than words, the determining absence more central than the weakly cohering presence. Serial killing is never made fully intelligible because it is a locus where several discourses collide and shatter into mismatched fragments, which cannot be fitted together into a neat picture puzzle. Like their grand fictional archetype, Frankenstein's monster, serial killers are patchwork creatures, made of crudely stitched partial selfhoods that never solidify into a coherent narrative subjectivity. Canter suggests that we all have a "public" and a "private" narrative of the self, and what distinguishes violent criminals is the radical incompatibility of their "hidden narratives" with their public stories (233). While this Jekyll-and-Hyde model may account for somebody like Bundy, with other serial killers the "public" narrative amounts to hardly more than a threadbare social mask. Rather, what distinguishes a serial killer is the radical incompatibility of all the narratives of the self that make up his subjectivity. In the ritual enacting of his violent fantasy, the killer attempts to glue together his fragmented self with blood. However, the repetitiveness of his murders serves only to mirror the reproduction of loose stories, unanchored in the terra firma of reality, which float around his disintegrating self.

The fragmentation and aporia of subjectivity are not the exclusive province of serial killers. However, precisely the extremity of their self-construction and self-deconstruction and the glaring failure of human sciences to come to grips with their motivations raise the question of what is missing in the narratology of the self. As I have suggested, the missing category is the violent sublime. However, on the level of psychological motivation, its counterpart is randomness and free choice. Opting for the "high" of violence need not be anchored in any hidden irresistible compulsion. However, once made, such a choice has ineluctable consequences that deform the narrative of identity, pushing it as close as a human subject can come to the broken narrative of the sublime monster.

Having spent an inordinate number of pages on explaining the scientific principles of criminal profiling, having variously suggested that the typical serial killer is a beast of prey, a product of improper upbringing, and a plaything of irresistible and deviant sexuality, John Douglas pauses in the middle of describing the Hansen child murder case to deliver the surprising statement: "I have spent my career studying the complex motivations of criminals, but basically, all the prior influences on an individual resolve down to one key element: the *choice* to commit the crime" (1997, 98).

Choice is the one element of a narrative that cannot be predicted in advance since it does not obey the law of strict causality. By emphasizing choice, Douglas indirectly renounces his own project. All his psychological profiles are now bound to be approximate, stochastic, imprecise—mere convenient grids forced upon volatile reality. But by giving up the attempt to impose upon the serial killer a typological identity, he returns to him his individual subjectivity. This subjectivity now consists in the freedom to choose, but the choice it makes places it beyond all and every generic mold of selfhood available in the cultural repertoire. By choosing extreme, repeated, and aimless violence, the serial killer breaks away from the limitations of discursive identity, only to find himself stranded in the silence of no-identity, in the mute meaninglessness of the Real, in the wasteland of the sublime.

To answer "yes" to Lecter's question "Am I evil?" is to accept that there is no deep secret, no hidden truth in the serial killer's life-story. It is to view his self-chosen identity as irrevocably broken, the psychological equivalent of the hacked bodies of his victims. But this means renouncing the project of human sciences, especially criminology, which has been articulated by one of its early practitioners as follows: "the function of [criminal] psychology is widening to acquire knowledge not only of the conceptions of human beings of themselves but also of everything which occurs or has occurred within them, in other words, not only of their conceptions of, but also the whole of the objective reality of, their psychic life" (Bjerre 16). But if there is no such "objective reality," if the criminal's conception of himself is a sufficient determinant of his actions, and if, moreover, this conception is pliant and multiform, constantly revised by the choices of the hour, the project collapses. And together with it goes the institutionalized identity of the scientist, the mindhunter, the Great Detective who is uniquely equipped to penetrate the criminal's heart of darkness. This cannot be allowed to happen. Thus Douglas retreats from his notion of choice, going back to his increasingly more convoluted, increasingly more desperate attempts to solve, once and for all, the mystery of the criminal mind.

Both criminology and fiction follow him. Since to accept the indeterminacy of identity, the free choice of violence, and the mocking denial of causality exemplified by Dr. Lecter means abandoning their commitment to the scientific paradigm of rational explanation, narratives of serial killing quickly bring out a couple of representative Buffalo Bills, profile them out of existence, reduce the bodies of their victims to numbered exhibits of material evidence, and offer a new and improved theory of bad genes or bad upbringing. After every encounter with the indeterminacy of the Real, narrative picks up the shreds of its exploded models and patiently plods on to construct yet another impossible combination of monster and victim, as science and fiction endlessly weave their narrative nets around the mystery of violence without ever catching their prey.

3

The Library of the Body

We . . . have dreamt the world. We have dreamt it as firm, mysterious, visible, ubiquitous in space and durable in time; but in its architecture we have allowed tenuous and eternal crevices of unreason which tell us it is false.

—JORGE LUIS BORGES, *"Avatars of the Tortoise"*

THE SIGN OF FOUR

The classic detective story is the darling of literary formalism. First, it is one of the few genres whose origins are clear: by critical consensus, the genre sprang, fully formed like Athena from Zeus's forehead, from three stories written by Edgar Allan Poe in the 1840s: "The Murders in the Rue Morgue," "The Purloined Letter," and "The Mystery of Marie Roget." Second, the classic detective story is a highly formalized and extremely self-conscious genre, whose practitioners have been aware, almost from its very inception, of playing a game with definite rules. These rules have been articulated by W. H. Auden: "The basic formula is this: a murder occurs; many are suspected; all but one suspect, who is the murderer, are eliminated; the murderer is arrested or dies" (147).

This basic formula still structures a majority of detective stories published today. In the contemporary vast scene of crime writing, two main influences are to be distinguished: the classic Golden Age detective story and its rebellious offspring, the hard-boiled crime novel of Raymond Chandler and Dashiell Hammett. The classic (predominantly, though not exclusively, British) school embellished Auden's formula with additional ingredients: the Great Detective, an eccentric blessed with superhuman intelligence; his dumb sidekick, often functioning as the first-person narrator; the rationality of the murderer's motivation; and the strictly logical way in which the solution is reached. The heyday of the classic detective story was the so-called Golden Age between the two world wars. In the period between 1920 and 1939, the detective story accounted for one-quarter of all new novels published in the English language. The American school in the 1920s and 1930s rebelled against what it saw as the patent artificiality of the classic school and radically modified the formula, adding a certain gritty realism that found its perfect visual equivalent in film noir.

The classic tradition is very much alive today in work of the best-selling "queens of crime," P. D. James, Ruth Rendell, Elizabeth George, and others. The hard-boiled tradition has its own champions, such as Sara Paretsky and Sue Grafton. Crime literature dealing with serial murder, such as the novels of Patricia Cornwell and Thomas Harris I discussed in the previous chapter, combines the influence of both streams. But my focus in this chapter is exclusively on the classic detective story and, even more narrowly, on its four giants: Edgar Allan Poe, Arthur Conan Doyle, G. K. Chesterton, and Agatha Christie. The reason is not simply the ever swelling volume of crime fiction that makes any comprehensive overview very difficult. These four writers, covering among themselves a hundred years of modernity, from the mid-nineteenth to the mid-twentieth century, epitomize the construction of the violent subject as the subject of discipline in an almost pure form. Their epigones dilute their paradigm or crossbreed it with other narrative modalities in a cultural and historical situation, in which the subject of discipline finds himself in retreat. Discipline is contested both by the media's reign of horror and by the resurgence of violent ideologies, whose impact is magnified by the ever-present memories of the Holocaust. The conflict between discipline and ideology is the subject of my next chapter. But here I want to look at the disciplined killer in the moment of his full glory.

John G. Cawelti claims that "the detective story is a key *mythos* of the ideology of individualistic bourgeois democracy embodied in a unique formal pattern that ritually involves the reader in the celebration of the myth" (13). In what follows I will explore the subject of this "mythos," the triad of the detective, the criminal, and the victim. But before trying to disentangle the intricate—not to say uncanny and perverse—web of correspondences among the three, another question has to be addressed, a question so simple that it is seldom asked. Why murder? What is the relationship between liberal individualism and the detective story's raison d'être, violence? Why should democracy celebrate itself through incessant reiteration of the same drama of murder, investigation, and exposure? What exactly is being exorcised—or covertly acknowledged—through the detective story's contradictory impulses of strict rationality and Gothic sensationalism?

To answer these questions I will, in the following sections, consider such seemingly disparate aspects of the genre as game theory, penchant for Christmas, dismissal of ghosts, and Holmes's nonexistent sex life. All these aspects are informed by what I see as the dominant feature of the detective story: its repression of the sublime and the projection of the perfectly disciplined subject of violence. Such a subject is, of course, impossible. So, perhaps, is democracy. This might account for the popularity of both.

SUBDUING SENSATION

The detective story is often seen as form without content. Reading detective fiction is, then, "reading for the plot," for the aesthetic enjoyment deriving from the beauty and complexity of its construction: "[The detective story's] *raison* d'être is plot; and any element which is permitted to overshadow plot will weaken the effect of the whole, throwing it off balance and producing an ambiguous hybrid . . ." (Crispin 11).

Like Russian formalist definitions of poetry, such a definition of detective fiction stresses its self-referentiality. The genre is essentially autotelic, a narrative about narrativity: "It can be argued that classic detective fiction . . . perfected this ordering function of narration. . . . In fact, classic detective fiction is constituted by the very process and problem of storytelling" (Huhn 39).

The idea of the classic detective story as embodiment of the "ordering function of narrative" is linked to two other common ways of describing the genre: as a logical exercise and as a game. What unites all three is emphasis on structure as opposed to content. In fact, while in Huhn's definition the content is still present—a story must be about something, if only about itself—both games and logical exercises are founded on total evacuation of referentiality. Thus, the "method" of the classic detective, as epitomized by Poe's Dupin and Doyle's Holmes, becomes a species of formal logic. In *The Sign of Three,* edited by Umberto Eco and Thomas A. Sebeok, the contributors argue that Holmes was a "consulting semiotician," employing the logical technique called "abduction" (inference on the basis of a general rule, along the lines of "All men are mortal, Socrates is a man, therefore he is mortal").

However, semioticians, consulting or otherwise, have never boasted of a fraction of Holmes's fame. The detective story is a popular genre that has sold exceedingly well from the moment of its inception. The same public that remained profoundly skeptical, if not downright frightened, of science lapped up adventures of various Great Detectives, even though a lecture on the difference between deduction and abduction would most likely put it to sleep. In order to explain the contradiction between the intellectual exclusivity of the detective story and its market value, critics have seized on the concept of game. A mental workout can be entertaining despite its difficulty.

Like all the major constituents of the genre, the game metaphor was already present in the Great Detectives' three founding texts, Edgar Allan Poe's stories "The Murders in the Rue Morgue," "The Mystery of Marie Roget," and "The Purloined Letter." "The Murders in the Rue Morgue" begins with a lengthy discussion of what we today would call "game theory," and the unnamed narrator invites the reader to consider the entire story of his acquaintance with C. Auguste Dupin and Dupin's investigation of the grisly murders of two women "in the light of a commentary upon the propositions just advanced" (143).

However, Poe's "propositions" have a darker side that clashes with the sanitized ambience of intellectual playfulness. The entire disquisition hinges on the juxtaposition of two kinds of games. The first kind, epitomized by chess, is elaborate and complex; the second, such as draughts, is simple with few rules. Poe's paradoxical conclusion is that "the higher powers of the reflective intellect are more decidedly and more usefully tasked by the unostentatious game of draughts than by all the elaborate frivolity of chess" (141). The reason is that in chess the intellect is engaged with an abstract system of rules, while in draughts the players focus on each other: "Deprived of ordinary resources, the analyst throws himself into the spirit of his opponent, identifies himself therewith, and not infrequently sees thus, at a glance, the sole methods (sometimes indeed absurdly simple ones) by which he may seduce him into error or hurry into miscalculation" (142). In other words, Poe sees a game not as a purely intellectual pursuit but as a competition between two opponents in which pleasure derives from the victory rather than from the process of ratiocination. Cunning, ruthlessness, and psychological acumen count for more than logic. The game between Dupin and his adversary is not a chain of deductions but a duel. Violence is lodged at the very heart of rationality.

Agatha Christie's Hercule Poirot often irritates his sidekick, Captain Hastings, by his refusal "to play the game." In *Curtain* the Belgian detective dismisses Hastings's complaint of "unfairness": "Quite so, my friend! It is not fair! It is not sporting! It is not playing the game! Admit all this and pass from it. This is *not* a game—it is not *le sport*. . . . It is a question . . . not of your playing a guessing game, but of preventing a human being from dying" (59–60). While Christie's books are often seen as the purest examples of the detective story as an elaborate puzzle, her "artificial, contrived and fantastic" plots cleverly disclose their own darker underside, rooted not in the structure of logic but in the chaos of violence. Just as Poe's propositions on game theory turn out to be about the psychology of competition, Poirot's contemptuous "this is not a game" reveals the detective story's real subject: "a human being . . . dying."

Why should a discussion of chess and draughts in "The Murders in the Rue Morgue" be illustrated by two sickeningly mutilated human bodies? Why should abduction have something to do not with beans in a bag, as in Peirce's original example, but with corpses? Why should a "pure" narrative construction revolve around murder? All detective stories deal with crime; an overwhelming majority of them deal with violence. It is almost impossible to imagine a satisfactory whodunit without at least one dead body. This is so much taken for granted that only rarely does a critical discussion of the genre pose the question of the strained relation between logic and violence. And yet, writers themselves have been profoundly aware of it from the inception of the genre.

In "The Adventure of the 'Copper Beeches,'" Sherlock Holmes and Dr. Watson discuss the nature of their own narrative. Holmes initially praises Watson for dedicating his "reports" to "those faculties of deduction and of logical synthesis which I have made my special province." Watson, however, realizes that the compliment is misplaced: "'And yet,' said I, smiling, 'I cannot quite hold myself absolved from the charge of sensationalism which has been urged against my records.'" Holmes agrees and then takes his faithful chronicler to task precisely for that element of "sensationalism": "If I claim full justice for my art, it is because it is an impersonal thing—a thing beyond myself. Crime is common. Logic is rare. Therefore it is upon the logic rather than upon the crime that you should dwell. You have degraded what should have been a course of lectures into a series of tales" (272).

The generic dilemma of the detective story is set out clearly here: logic or crime, deduction or sensation, "a course of lectures" or "a series of tales." But, of course, both are necessary. The generic specificity of the detective story is created precisely by the sustained tension between its smooth and precise narrative exterior and its dark Gothic core. Few people would read Watson's accounts were they no more than scientific monographs of the kind Holmes himself is supposed to have authored. But at the same time, horror fiction, giving free rein to sensation, has never achieved the widespread appeal of the detective story. Despite their bickering, Watson and Holmes are the one couple that is never going to split. They have to stay together to balance the narrative in which crime and logic are kept in constant creative tension.

Among Doyle's most disturbing stories is "The Adventure of the Cardboard Box" (1893). The tale begins with an inoffensive spinster getting a mail delivery of two human ears pickled in salt and then evolves into a lurid narrative of adultery, incest, murder, and mutilation.[1] Like most Holmes stories, this one follows the set format of problem, investigation, exposure, and the criminal's first-person narrative that confirms the detective's brilliant deduction. It is introduced, however, with Dr. Watson's apology for even bringing such a story before the reader, his justification being that it is "impossible to entirely separate the sensational from the criminal" (307). The story is framed in terms of "chance and not choice" and displays with an uncommon vividness the tension between the logic of deduction and the chaotic, irrational, uncontrollable nature of violence the plot attempts to contain.

Before Holmes is invited on the case, he entertains Watson by reconstructing the latter's train of thoughts. This train has to do with violence and ends in Watson's conclusion that it is a "preposterous" method of settling disputes. The case that follows mocks this smug assumption. It taxes Holmes's power to provide a reassuring closure. The murderer's account, given in writing and thus invulnerable to the detective's interrogation, is driven by the passionate logic of obsession, disregarding the logic of causality. Jim Browner's murder of his wife and her lover seems both inevitable, given his personality, and yet also preposterous, founded on a series of chance slips and improbable coincidences, culminating in the final irony of the wrong sister getting the gruesome package.

The murder is a "strange and inexplicable horror" (311). It is a horror precisely because it is inexplicable. Violence, says Jean Amery, destroys our trust in the world, which includes "the irrational and logically unjustifiable belief in absolute causality perhaps, or the likewise blind belief in the validity of the inductive inference" (28). The function of the detective is to uphold these two blind beliefs at the face of such irrefutable argument as a mangled and dismembered human body: "'What is the meaning of it, Watson?' said Holmes solemnly, as he laid down the paper. 'What object is served by this circle of misery and violence and fear? It must tend to some end, or else our universe is ruled by chance, which is unthinkable. But what end? There is the great standing perennial problem to which human reason is as far from answer as ever'" (319).

"It must tend to some end, or else our universe is ruled by chance, which is unthinkable." This is the creed of the detective who fights chaos, accident, passion, and unreason. Sometimes he fails; more often, with the help of the author who clears away the too-obtrusive signs of violence, he succeeds.

THE INSOMNIA OF REASON

Dupin never sleeps. He is a creature of the night, Dracula *manqué* roaming the streets under the cover of darkness. But unlike the Transylvanian count, he is not seeking the heady pleasures of the chase. He is satisfied with "that infinity of mental excitement which quiet observation can afford" (Poe 144).

Why exercise a power of observation in darkness? In this perversity (which the narrator acknowledges as such) lies the key to the relationship between logic and violence in the classic detective story. The Great Detective must be a rationalist of the irrational. He is drawn not just to the night but also to what the night connotes in the Gothic: sensuality, mystery, and hunger. As opposed to the Gothic hero, however, the detective seeks out the irrational in order not to enjoy but to tame it. He sallies forth into the darkness to illuminate it with the light of reason.

Dupin boasts of his mental acuity, Holmes flaunts his logic, Poirot endlessly prattles about "order and method," and Chesterton's Father Brown extols common sense. All four are synonyms for reason: not just a general human faculty but a specific ideological construct, a post–Enlightenment sensibility that Foucault calls "the pure experience of order and of its modes of being" (1966 xxi). The function of this "pure experience of order" in the detective story is to counter another experience that goes by many names: chance, chaos, disorder, the irrational, and the sublime.

In Christie's "Dead Man's Mirror," when Poirot trots out a list of seemingly unrelated occurrences around the murder, another character asks irritably: "Are you going to tell me that that rigmarole makes *sense?*" (156). "Rigmarole" is violence devoid of explanation, the chaos of pure contingency in which things happen just so, without order or reason. Poirot's function is to "make sense." He brings "disorder into order" by fitting together "various improbably shaped and unlikely facts which, though seeming to bear no relationship to each other, yet did each have its properly balanced part in assembling the whole" (Christie 1956, 151). Christie's metaphor for this activity is assembling a jigsaw puzzle. But with a puzzle one knows that the "improbably shaped" pieces do fit together because the manufacturer guarantees it. There is no such guarantee attached to the universe. The assumption of "making sense" is an ideological assumption propped up by fear of its being otherwise. The function of the detective is to allay this fear.

Just how serious this task is, just how frightening the rigmarole can become, is clear from Chesterton's story "The Honour of Israel Gow." Father Brown is called upon to investigate the strange goings-on in the Scottish castle of Glengyle whose owner has recently died. The atmosphere is dark and getting darker as the priest and his companions discover various peculiar things: candles without candlesticks, torn prayer books, broken pencils. The horror is built up very effectively out of the senselessness of these things, which, while not scary in themselves, do not add up to any comprehensible whole. Even before the final gruesome discovery that the corpse of the castle's owner is missing its head, Father Brown succumbs to the fear of the nonsensical. Uncharacteristically for him, he begins to talk in the Gothic language of madness, torture, forbidden lusts, and black magic, imagining "the devil of the universe . . . sitting on the top tower of this castle . . . roaring like the Apocalypse" (83). With the discovery of the headless body, the normally placid Father Brown makes this dramatic announcement: "Something has fallen on us that falls very seldom on men; perhaps the worst thing that can fall on them. . . . We have found the truth; and the truth makes no sense" (85). The "worst thing" is not violence as such but the rigmarole of violence, the truth of its materiality that "makes no sense."

But when Father Brown does arrive at a logical and quite ingenious solution of the riddle, when all the pieces fall into place and a rational chain of events can be reconstructed, he is ecstatic: "Six hours in the spiritual abyss, and all because I never thought of the dentist! Such a simple, such a beautiful and peaceful thought! Friends, we have passed a night in hell; but now the sun is risen, the birds are singing, and the radiant form of the dentist consoles the world!" (87). The "pure experience of order" embodied in the form of the dentist delivers the implied reader from the hell of mere contingency.

The central opposition in the story is between the "radiant form" of reasonable violence and the dark abyss of its unreasonable double; between, so to speak, the dentist and the torturer. Though both inflict pain, the former does it for a cause and thus his actions are subject to causality. The latter, a homicidal lunatic, acts on contingency. And though the end result may be precisely the same (the lord of Glengyle is missing his head), the two kinds of violence are as different as the hell of horror and the heaven of the detective story.

The hell of horror is populated by demons, ghosts, vampires, and things that go bump in the night. But the radiance of the detective story's heaven flows precisely from the absence of angels or spirits of any stripe. It is an empty heaven, cleansed of anything not amenable to the law of reason. If the supernatural in horror is an aspect of the violent sublime, the absence of the supernatural in the classic detective story signifies its expulsion.

In "The Murders in the Rue Morgue" Dupin, in the face of the locked room with two frightfully mutilated bodies in it, dismisses a supernatural solution out of hand: "It is not too much to say that neither of us believe in preternatural events. Madame and Mademoiselle L'Espanaye were not destroyed by spirits. The doers of the deed were material and escaped materially" (156). This becomes the a priori axiom of the genre: "the doers of the deed were material." But why? Considering Poe's own supernatural oeuvre, why should a character be more skeptical than his creator?

At the beginning of *The Hound of the Baskervilles,* Dr. Mortimer expresses to Holmes his belief that the mysterious death of Sir Charles Baskerville is due to a supernatural influence. Holmes does not even deign to discuss this proposition, dismissing the suggestion with a joke. It is natural to think that Holmes here is speaking for his creator. But Sir Arthur Conan Doyle, author of *The Psychic Quest,* was a fervent believer in spiritualism who dedicated the last twenty years of his life to propagation of the spiritualist gospel. Even though his conversion to spiritualism was a gradual process, it was well underway by World War I. And yet even in the last Holmes collection, *The Case-Book of Sherlock Holmes* (1921–1927), there are no signs that Dr Mortimer's suggestion should have been treated seriously.

Whereas Doyle was a spiritualist, Chesterton was a devout Catholic. But Father Brown debunks claims of the supernatural with depressing regularity. More than once, he is confronted with a seemingly impossible crime, in which the criminal banks on what he considers to be a clergyman's credulity, only to be defeated by Brown's invincible common sense. As he says contemptuously in "The Dagger with Wings": "Perhaps his [the criminal's] only mistake was in choosing a preternatural story; he had the notion that because I am a clergyman, I should believe anything. Many people have little notions of that kind" (420). On the contrary, it seems, because he is a clergyman, Father Brown should believe nothing that is not rational. This paradox provides a clue to the role of reason in the classic detective story. The priest-as-sleuth exemplifies Chesterton's view of God as supreme designer who has created the universe according to a rational and orderly plan. The supernatural is excluded a priori because it is aligned with chaos that has no place in God's design.[2] Good is logical; evil is chaotic, irrational, and muddled. The universe, in other words, is structured like a whodunit.

This is clearly set out in the first two stories in the first Father Brown collection, *The Innocence of Father Brown* (1910). In "The Blue Cross" French policeman Aristide Valentin pursues the famous criminal Flambeau who is hiding in London. It turns out that Flambeau, disguised as a Catholic priest, attempts to steal a valuable relic from Father Brown, who deliberately leaves a trail of senseless disturbances that Valentin follows on a hunch. This allows Valentin to arrive on the scene of the attempted robbery in the nick of time and to arrest the criminal who is already half-converted by Father Brown's preaching (in the subsequent stories Flambeau abandons his criminal career and becomes a private detective). Valentin is very much a latter-day Dupin, a "thinking man" who achieves his remarkable successes by "plodding logic [and] clear and commonplace French thought" (11–12). Here he pursues a hunch. But the fact that this hunch pays off reveals the fundamental system of rational causality underlying the chain of seemingly unconnected events. Valentin's success is not a lucky chance but a denial of the very idea of chance and accident. In the conversation between Father Brown and Flambeau, it is the criminal who extols the unfathomable mystery of heaven, while the saintly priest defends the intelligibility of God: "reason is always reasonable, even in the last limbo, in the lost borderland of things. I know that people charge the Church with lowering reason, but it is just the other way. Alone on earth, the Church makes reason really supreme. Alone on earth, the Church affirms that God Himself is bound by reason" (20). I believe because it is reasonable. If Holmes can only hope that the universe is not ruled by chance, because the alternative is "unthinkable," Father Brown knows it is not because the Church tells him so.

Of course, such knowledge is inherently unstable, especially in the charged episteme of the early-twentieth century. The clear boundaries of the detective story buckle under the enormous pressures of the ideological battles of the time. Already the next story in *The Innocence of Father Brown,* called "The Secret Garden," revises the optimism of its predecessor. Reason alone, it appears, is not enough to lead one to the state of grace. In "The Secret Garden" Valentin the detective becomes the murderer. Such shifts are not uncommon, and later I will consider in some detail the doubling of the detective and the criminal. However, Valentin's fall is more extreme than most since he murders for ideological reasons: to prevent an American millionaire from bequeathing his money to the Catholic Church, which he loathes. If the mountebank of "The Dagger with Wings" and other assorted cranks and pagans (often of Eastern origins) exemplify the madness of superstition, Valentin exemplifies the madness of reason. His "great brutality of the intellect" (34) prompts him to commit a gruesome murder precisely because his logic is not restrained by faith. He is Dupin-become-Dracula, Holmes-turned-Moriarty, unable to sustain the delicate balance whereby the irrational is illuminated by reason, but reason is disciplined by the power of the law. Chesterton's Catholicism is only a specific incarnation of the wider disciplinary framework, which constrains the detective in the classic detective story. Holmes's unquestioned obedience of the law and Poirot's bourgeois attitude to murder are examples of the same configuration: reason that knows its proper boundaries, content to stay within a system of axioms that it does not dare to probe. If the supernatural is the mystery, which reason is called upon to discipline, faith, morality, and law are the mysteries, which discipline reason itself.

A perfectly rational world may be perceived in two contradictory ways: as a prison or as a refuge. D. A. Miller sees "the world of significant trifles relayed to one another in a minute causal network" as a universal panopticon of omnipresent power in which we are perpetually "put under restraint" (32). The opposite point of view is expressed in Krutch's famous observation that "Poe invented the detective story in order that he might not go mad" (quoted in Tani 10). Traditionally, the detective story has endorsed the second view, portraying the supernatural chaos of horror as frightening and repulsive. However, it is not unaware that the vigilance of reason breeds its own monsters. Some texts trace the fault line at which "the pure experience of order" slips into its opposite. Jorge Luis Borges's metafictional "Death and the Compass" (1942) takes to its logical extreme the genre's presumption of "making sense" and creates a labyrinthine universe of absolute causality, purged of all traces of randomness and accident. In "Death and the Compass" the archetypal criminal lures the equally archetypal detective—modeled on Dupin and Holmes—to his death by constructing an elaborate maze of clues at the core of which lies the detective's foreordained murder. The normal order of cause and effect has been inverted, so that the web of causality extends both to the past and the future, trapping the criminal, the detective, and the implied reader in a universal panopticon, in which, as in the paranoid delusion of a conspiracy buff, everything makes sense. Rather than being reassuring, this world of pure reason is horrifying, an oppressive jail, "a labyrinth, from which it [is] impossible to flee" (85). Absolute sanity flips over into insane compulsion, generating "superfluous symmetries" and "maniacal repetitions" (84).

The opposite of Borges's story is Ruth Rendell's brilliant *A Fatal Inversion* (1987), which spins an intricate plot out of a series of improbable coincidences, meaningless by themselves and yet leading up to an act of appalling violence. *A Fatal Inversion* and "Death and the Compass" tip in opposite directions the delicate balance of reason and unreason that sustains the detective story. The result is the same in both cases: a nightmare. In Ruth Rendell's novel (published under the pen name Barbara Vine), the characters, a group of young people living in a commune in the 1970s, are caught up in a web as inexorable as the one Borges's Red Scharlach spins out for his detective-victim. At the center of Rendell's maze there is also a murder. But this is a web with no design. No mastermind plans all the numerous small coincidences, wrong decisions, peculiar crisscrossing of destinies, which eventually lead to an irrational outburst of violence that irrevocably blights the characters' lives. Once the act of violence occurs, its consequences are inescapable and yet they cannot be predicted in advance, just as the narrative centrality of the murder does not preclude the fact that it is meaningless. The "why?" of the classic detective story simply has no place in a contingent world. "No one asked Adam why he had done it, then or later. He had done it, there was no point in asking" (1987, 302).

Stephen Jay Gould discusses *A Fatal Inversion* in his book *Wonderful Life* dedicated to the nature of evolution, as based on contingency rather than design. He calls *A Fatal Inversion* "a conscious text on the nature of history" (1989, 285). For the characters of Rendell's novel, buffeted by forces they can neither control nor comprehend, their fully historical world appears as a dark maze of horror. If reason and unreason are represented as a choice of nightmares, it seems natural that the detective story is trying so hard to steer a middle course.

NEAT WOUNDS

The duality of reason and unreason structures the entire fictional world of the classic detective story. With regard to the plot, it mutates into the juxtaposition of causality and contingency. Projected upon the level of characterization, it becomes the Cartesian dichotomy of spirit and body, or rather of body and brain. Logic, the detective's weapon, must tame the unruly passions of the corpus or, considering the genre's main preoccupation, the corpse.

Grooming is a necessary prerequisite for a detective story corpse. Decomposition is out; but even ordinary untidiness is barely acceptable: "Even violence itself, the books' reason for being, is somehow conformist, limited, unreal. A bullet-hole almost invariably is 'neat' (as a putt in golf, perhaps?), while scarcely a knife is on record that has not been embedded neatly between shoulder blades. Blood is generally a 'spreading stain' or a 'pool,' both fastidious expressions that convey nothing of the terrible glistening mess that is made by human butchery" (Watson 102).

In Christie's *Cards on the Table* (1936) a man is fatally stabbed in a room full of people. There is no outcry, no bleeding, and the dagger protruding from the body looks like "a particularly ornate shirt stud" (22). This cardboard dummy is, clearly, nothing but a pretext for the subsequent game of wit played with the reader, which proceeds according to patently artificial rules: four suspects, four detectives, and the solution found through the study of bridge scores. However, no matter how unreal, there must be a corpse.

Christie's self-caricature in the book, the famous detective fiction writer Ariadne Oliver, explains the secret of the successful whodunit: "What really matters is plenty of *bodies!* If the thing's getting a little dull, some more blood cheers it up" (55). And yet at the same time, Mrs. Oliver concedes that real murder is not "very much in [her] line" (80), since, as opposed to fiction, real life is "badly constructed" (28). In other words, the detective story must balance "blood" and "construction" in such a way as to convey just enough of the shock of the former to be successfully neutralized by the orderliness of the latter. If the scale is tipped on the side of blood, the result is horror. If the reader is starved for bodies, the result is boredom.

The suppression, by the detective story, of the violent sublime does not mean total exclusion. On the contrary, violent sights are a necessary part of its generic repertoire but in a weakened and circumscribed form. "Vaccination" is perhaps a better term than "evasion"; the detective story vaccinates its readers against the shocking reality of violence by doling it out in precisely measured quantities. Again, Holmes and Watson provide the best critical argument about their own text. In *The Sign of Four* Holmes rebukes Watson's "romantic" handling of the Jefferson Hope case, and when the doctor points out that the facts were romantic enough, Holmes replies: "Some facts should be suppressed, or, at least, a just sense of proportion should be observed in handling them" (65). "A just sense of proportion" is different from outright suppression.

In the same *Sign of Four,* however, violence intrudes into the text with a far greater force than usual, turning the novella into a hybrid near horror. Instead of a neat, bloodless prop, the corpse of the victim becomes an uncanny vision of doubling and dismemberment: "I stooped to the hole and recoiled in horror . . . Looking straight at me, and suspended, as it were, in the air . . . there hung a face—the very face of our companion Thaddeus. . . . The features were set, however, in a horrible smile, a fixed and unnatural grin, which in that still and moonlit room was more jarring to the nerves than any scowl or contortion" (78).

This "hanging" face signifies the Real: the tear in the linguistic fabric through which an unnamable trauma peeps out. Violence has wrenched the corpse's face from its moorings in the symbolic system and stripped it of name and identity. Suspended in the air, an object of fascination and disgust, it is a "thing in itself," a site of the sublime trauma of violence. The "thing" has to be veiled and yet at the same time displayed. This literary striptease is the detective writer's greatest skill: to admit just enough of the Real but never too much. Christie, who hones this skill to perfection, writes in the foreword to her novel *The Body in the Library:* "I laid down for myself certain conditions. The library in question must be a highly orthodox and conventional library. The body, on the other hand, must be a wildly improbable and highly sensational body" (5).

In this novel the body is indeed showcased in a way that contradicts the "decency" of the ordinary whodunit: "The face was heavily made-up, the powder standing out grotesquely on its blue swollen surface, the mascara of the lashes lying thickly on distorted cheeks, the scarlet of the lips looking like a gash . . ." (16).

Moreover, unlike *Cards on the Table,* the body here is not just the pretext of the investigation but the most important clue. In order to solve the crime, Miss Marple has to focus precisely on the stigmata of sexuality and deviance. Whereas in *Cards on the Table* the body and the text (the bridge scores) are kept separate, here they are collapsed. The corpse is divested of its horror not by evasion but by too-intent gaze.

Euphemism is defined as a word or phrase that "once meant, or prima facie still means, something else" (Holder vii). In other words, a euphemism not only misnames its referent but also diverts referentiality into a different channel. The object is doubled: the obscene or unacceptable meaning is covered up by another, which, however, does not nullify the obscenity but only decently veils it. Insofar as it is possible to extend this definition of euphemism to a set of literary strategies, it describes exactly the detective story's handling of violence: the corpse, without ceasing to be an object of horror, is doubled into an object of cognition. The genre begins with a primal scene of the euphemistic rewriting of the body. In Poe's "The Mystery of Marie Roget," physical violation is flaunted with a brutality unparalleled until the appearance of the police procedural a century and a half later, and yet at the same time the story counters the horror with an equally startling degree of cognitive detachment. "The Mystery of Marie Roget" deconstructs the genre at the moment of its inception. In the language of Russian formalism, it "lays bare the device" by literally laying bare the body. The corpse of a rape and murder victim is displayed before the reader in all its pitiful nakedness, its injuries carefully enumerated and classified, while Dupin and his unnamed Watson engage in feats of dazzling deduction.

And at the same time the body is not there at all. All the evidence Dupin possesses is the newspaper accounts of the crime; he never as much as stirs from his apartment to confront the grubby reality of the murdered grisette's life and death. Since these accounts are unreliable and self-contradictory, Dupin's work is essentially that of a literary critic. He has to pinpoint the slippages and inaccuracies in the narratives of Marie's murder, to unravel the metaphorical tangles, to argue with faulty logic. The corpse becomes a literary puzzle whose solution has as its object "the investigation of the truth" (169). But this investigation is enabled by the fact that the raw impact of Marie's violated body is already filtered through layers of medical, criminological, and journalistic discourse. In a sense, Dupin performs a postmortem of language, tracing the contours of the missing corpse through the fractures, lacunae, and knots it has left in the textual fabric. The body is the text; but when it is only the text, it disappears. Marie's corpse is the opposite of the torture victim's body. In Kafka's "In the Penal Colony" the sublime spectacle of the violated body overshadows the puerile text that the torture machine harrows into the condemned man's flesh. Marie's body, on the contrary, is reduced to its text; the beaten and bruised flesh veiled by a thick palimpsest of readable clues. But in the process of its deciphering, the body evaporates, leaving behind a sheaf of unreliable newspaper reports and an equivocal promise of the criminal's eventual apprehension.

In Ruth Rendell's *Kissing the Gunner's Daughter* (1991), there is an attempt to strip away the reassuring layer of textuality from the corpse. In the descriptions of the crime scene after an entire family is massacred, Rendell attempts to convey the visceral impact of violence, to reveal what the euphemism of "neat wounds" works so desperately to hide. One of her detectives stands in the bloody room bereft of speech: "He felt a blankness, a sensation of being stricken dumb, of all words being useless" (29). When words are taken away, all that remains is the mute protest of the flesh, shrinking in solidarity at the sight of the fellow flesh disfigured by violence: "It was a long time, an age, since he had felt actual physical nausea at such sights. On the other hand, had he ever before seen such a sight as this?" (ibid.). The trauma of the "sight" hollows out language; and yet, as Rendell's detective, Inspector Wexford, wisely recognizes, the shock of confronting the unnameable Thing may eventually lead to addiction. One can become hooked on the horror: "Those great dark splashes and stains were *real* blood. Was he privileged to see them, or unfortunate?" (97).

Is he? The murderer has to see his or her handiwork and, like the young girl in *Kissing the Gunner's Daughter* who participates in the slaughter of her family, may become first ill, then indifferent, then jubilant and craving more. But what about Inspector Wexford himself and all the other Great Detectives, the guardians of reason and law? How do they protect their own bodies from throbbing in sympathy with the mutilated flesh? How do they hold onto their language, protecting it from the corrosion of the sublime? How do they guard against the contagion of violence?

THE DETECTIVE'S BODY

The victim's body hides its corporeality by translating the stigmata of violence into legible signs. But the victim's part is easiest. The corpse only has to *be;* the detective and the criminal have to act. This acting inevitably involves their bodies. And thus both are caught in a complicated system of corporeal doublespeak.

The classic detective has gender but no sex. Dr. Watson, in the very first tale in Arthur Conan Doyle's groundbreaking collection *The Adventures of Sherlock Holmes,* dashes the reader's expectations of a traditional Victorian love story: "All emotions, and that one particularly, were abhorrent to his cold, precise, but admirably balanced mind. He was, I take it, the most perfect reasoning and observing machine that the world has seen. . . . Grit in a sensitive instrument, or a crack in one of his own high-powered lenses, would not be more disturbing than a strong emotion in a nature such as his" ("A Scandal in Bohemia" 117).

The detective is a logical machine, a human-shaped computer—the metaphor later literalized in Jacques Futrelle's Golden Age tales about Professor Van Dusen, called *The Thinking Machine*. To function efficiently, this computer requires a sterile environment, since its involvement with the material body and its passions results in pollution, malfunction, and failure. Watson's surprising tropes for love—grit and crack—indicate that it is specifically the physicality of desire that is dangerous to the detective's immaculate Logos:

"And if you have a form of fiction which is intellectual, then that form of fiction is fit for a Victorian man to read. . . . This was manly stuff. It accepted the physical world but kept clear that part of the physical world which was embarrassing" (Routley 23).

However, "manly stuff" did not endure for long. The generation after Doyle, both the writers and readers of detective fiction, showed the decisive trend of feminization, continuing till today. More importantly, however, the division of the physical world into the embarrassing and the nonembarrassing parts turned out to be difficult to effect. While Dupin, Holmes, and Father Brown are celibate, Christie's female sleuth, Miss Marple, is a confirmed spinster, and Hercule Poirot, aged, freakish, and sentimental, is proof against any sexual temptation. The second generation of the Golden Age writers rebelled against this convention. H. C. Bailey, Dorothy Sayers, Margery Allingham, Michael Innes, Ngaio Marsh, and others began tinkering with the Poe-Doyle-Christie heritage, attempting to make their detectives more human. In the process, the thinking machine acquired a wife and occasionally a family. Bailey's Reggie Fortune and Allingham's Mr. Campion are married, while Dorothy Sayers's Lord Peter Wimsey is the hero of a steamy love affair, which culminates in his marriage in *Busman's Honeymoon* (1937). Sayers's combination of the classic detective story and the women's romance has proven to be a winning formula, exploited with great success in the 1990s whodunits of Elizabeth George, whose aristocratic foursome of sleuths, two men and two women, go through all the possible romantic permutations among themselves, not to mention fleeting liaisons with strangers.

Such developments, however, are less revolutionary than might appear. In fact, they can be seen as an attempt to contain the disturbing implications of the original formula. Watson's statement hinges on the metaphorical opposition of the order of reason versus the chaos of desire. The romance sidesteps this opposition by producing the order of desire. It squeezes desire into very precise—and precisely gendered—boundaries. But the darkness at the heart of the classic detective story will not be so easily dispelled. The detective's romance simply covers up what the absence of a conventional love interest starkly emphasized, stranger and more obscure appetites.

There is something perverse about Dupin's and Holmes's celibacy, giving rise to various ribald speculations about the relationship between the detective and his faithful sidekick. As opposed to the Victorian Doyle, Poe appears quite nonchalant about the homoerotic implications of his night-cruising couple: Dupin's nameless friend candidly describes their relationship as "giving [himself] up to [Dupin's] wild whims with a perfect *abandon*" (144). However, like Holmes's and Watson's, this relationship is also mediated by a woman's dead body.

In "A Scandal in Bohemia" Watson qualifies his denial of Holmes's sexuality by pointing out that there was, after all, "one woman" for Holmes, and that one woman not only dead but "of dubious and questionable memory" (117). While the love story is rejected, another Victorian genre seems to insinuate itself into the text at that point: the melodrama of the fallen woman, laden with the images of the unchaste female bodies stretched out on the swampy river shore or starving in some cluttered attic. "A Scandal in Bohemia" suggests a dangerous attraction of the "reasoning and observing machine" to a woman's impure physique. Moreover, there is a strange slippage in this attraction, for though Irene Adler in this story is a clever criminal who outwits Holmes, the reference to her death aligns her with those dead females who furnish the traditional puzzle for the detective to solve. Dupin, after all, engenders the classic detective story on the dead bodies of three women: Madame and Mademoiselle L'Espanaye in "The Murders in the Rue Morgue" and Marie Roget in "The Mystery of Marie Roget." It is as if Holmes, through Watson, admits of being in love with the corporeality of the victim.

The perversity of the detective stems not from any unorthodox sexual practices but rather from the very juxtaposition of the purity of his thoughts and the impurity of their object: the violated (female or feminized) body. His eroticism is what might be called mental necrophilia. Providing him with a respectable outlet for his erotic energies only disguises the implications of his initial renunciation of love and family. By declaring that desire would be "disturbing" to the balance of Holmes's mind, Dr. Watson diagnoses his friend as suffering from an acute case of Cartesian dualism. Cloven by the gap between mind and body, spirit and matter, Holmes can only experience sexuality as an illicit attempt to bridge this gap. The only legitimate desire for him is the desire for the body that has been transformed into a sign; textualized, inscribed, written over with the obscure but decipherable script of murder.

This is not to engage in a Freudian reading, digging out the dark secrets of a fictional character's nonexistent unconscious. Rather, I suggest that the detective story may be read as an allegory of the desire of the disciplinary mind for the disciplined body. What Derrida calls "the violence of the letter" seeks embodiment in the actual violence inflicted upon the receptive and obedient, therefore feminized, corpus of the victim. But in a peculiar inversion it is the detective's own corporeality that perpetually eludes his all-seeing gaze. The missing body the detective hopelessly searches for is his own.

The collusion between the corporeality of the detective and of the victim is clear in Doyle's story "The Adventure of the Dying Detective," included in the 1913 collection *Reminiscences of Sherlock Holmes*. In order to trap a criminal, who commits murders by means of infecting his victims with the germs of an incurable tropical disease, Holmes pretends to be deadly sick. As usual, Watson is the narrator. Uniquely, however, his medical training allows him to assume the role of the detective as well. From a humble chronicler, Watson is transformed into the chief actor in the story. Normally, the narrative functions are unequally distributed between the two protagonists: to Watson belongs the not inconsiderable power of framing the narration through his exclusive point of view, but Holmes tops it with his control of the plot. In "The Adventure of the Dying Detective," however, Watson, at least ostensibly, appropriates both functions. He is the one who confronts the criminal, Culverton Smith, while Holmes, feverish and delirious, seems to have lost control not only of the action but of his own body as well. And it is through this reversal that the detective's own vulnerable corporeality is suddenly highlighted as the hidden source of the genre's anxieties.

Watson's profession is not accidental: if he is the physician of the individual body, Holmes is the physician of the body politic. Carlo Ginzburg famously relates the rise of the "evidential method"—detection of the hidden truth through study of seemingly trivial clues, which he finds at work in both Doyle and Freud—to medicine:

> In each of these cases the model of medical semiotics is evident: that discipline which permits the diagnosis of diseases inaccessible to direct observations based on superficial symptoms, sometimes thought to be irrelevant in the eyes of the layman. . . . It is worth noticing, incidentally, that the duo Holmes-Watson, the perceptive detective and the obtuse physician, represents the splitting of a single real person, one of the young Conan Doyle's professors, renowned for his extraordinary diagnostic abilities. (102)

In "The Adventure of the Dying Detective," Watson collapses the two halves of this single whole back into one: for once, he performs the same kind of work that Holmes so often performs on the body of the victim, on the body of Holmes himself. He reads the text of symptoms, employing to the full "the model of medical semiotics": "His eyes had the brightness of fever, there was a hectic flush upon either cheek, and dark crusts clung to his lips; the thin hands upon the coverlet twitched incessantly, his voice was croaking and spasmodic" (829). The cognitive mastery Watson enjoys over his friend is immediately translated into actual mastery: "'Holmes,' said I, 'you are not yourself. A sick man is but a child, and so I will treat you'" (829).

The dying detective's delirium brings to the fore the nightmare haunting the Thinking Machine, the nightmare of being locked in a material body. Even a computer is, after all, a metal box; even an engine is composed of the solid parts, which may, eventually, fail. Disease is a rebellion of the body but objects rebel too. "I wonder," says feverish Holmes, "how a battery feels when it pours electricity into a non-conductor?" (831). The "grit" of sexuality is only a metonymy for that stubborn materiality of the body, which no "reasoning and observing machine" can escape, precisely by dint of being a machine rather than a disembodied spirit. And while purification from sexuality is possible, the purification from corporeality is not. The nonembarrassing part of the physical world proves to be far more embarrassing than the Victorian underworld of sex, for an imaginary Holmes gripped by passion would be a less ignominious sight than a raving, gasping, helpless patient.

This is the detective's fall, becoming a passive body, on which others may practice the disciplinary skills. But having been brought to the ultimate low, he must rise again, lest the ideological framework of the genre explode. And "The Adventure of the Dying Detective" ends with an extraordinary closure, in which Holmes admits to practicing a cold-blooded deception on his only friend. There was no infection, no fever, no delirium; the telltale signs of the body in pain were all faked: "there is nothing which a sponge may not cure" (837). The detective reasserts his absolute control over the body—his own and, by extension, the body of the criminal and the victim—by turning it into a pliant, "writable" surface, which can bear an imprint of any text whatsoever. Holmes's unparalleled skill with disguises belongs in the same category of taming the body; in another story of his resurrection, "The Adventure of the Empty House"(1903), he rises from a faked death by putting on and then easily shrugging off the identity of an old man, which fools Watson again by its skillful counterfeiting of age and infirmity. Moreover, in "The Adventure of the Dying Detective" Holmes explains the seemingly gratuitous cruelty of his deception of Watson by the necessity for the latter to express genuine signs of anxiety when confronting the criminal: "You won't be offended, Watson? You will realize that among your many talents dissimulation finds no place, and that if you had shared my secret you would never have been able to impress Smith with the urgent necessity of his presence, which was the vital point of the whole scheme" (837). Watson, in other words, is put back in his place by being reminded how undisciplined and grossly material his own body is in comparison with the elevated corporeality of the detective. He could never counterfeit the tremor in his voice or the twitch of his lips. Holmes, however, is another matter. "To the last gasp he would always be the master" (832).

The story of the detective's death and resurrection is given an unusual twist in Chesterton's "The Resurrection of Father Brown" (1923), the tale that explicitly draws upon Holmes's paradigm. Unlike Holmes, who stages his own miracles, Father Brown becomes the victim of a conspiracy in some unnamed South American country. The aim of the conspiracy is to fake the detective's miraculous resurrection, which can be discredited afterwards in such a way as to cast obloquy on the Church. Like an incongruous Juliet, Father Brown is drugged with some mysterious substance that makes him appear dead, until he is dramatically resurrected in full view of a superstitious audience. Before that, however, he has been conned into writing to the publishers of his stories: "I am ready to die and come to life again like Sherlock Holmes, if that is the best way" (331). Waking up from the drug-induced coma, Father Brown, with his usual commonsensical wisdom, realizes what has happened and squashes the conspiracy in the bud by sending an appropriate telegram to his Bishop. However, the absence of miracle is, precisely, what is miraculous in the story. The little priest's coolness, self-possession, and self-detachment are as superhuman as Holmes's steely control of his body. Waking up in a coffin, most people would be more concerned with the state of their health than with the glory of the Church, and "canonized as a saint," a majority of mere mortals might be forgiven some twinge of vanity (332). That Father Brown is absolutely immune to both fear and pride aligns him with Holmes as an exemplum of self-discipline rather than with more traditional instances of Christian humility. The contrived note tells the truth: Father Brown is "like Sherlock Holmes." The dumpy, self-effacing man of God, created as an opposite of the flamboyant and arrogant private detective, turns out to be his hidden double, constrained by the law of the genre that demands that the detective's immaculate body be resurrected from the grave of the matter.

However—and this is precisely the paradox of the detective story—the body cannot be simply discarded; it must be obdurate enough to be disciplined and yet pliant enough to obey. The Thinking Machine is constantly suspended between these two opposing demands of rebellious corporeality and miraculous self-control.

Signs of the flesh are often admitted into the narrative as a concession to "medical semiotics." In fact, as if to offset the rigidity of the detective's self-discipline, such signs are often morbid, monstrous, exaggerated. There is something freakish about the detective's body. We know very little about Dupin's physique, but the narrator's frequent references to his "madness" and "eccentricity" beg for the correspondent corporeal marks according to the age's favorite "sciences" of phrenology and physiognomy. Holmes's striking appearance is described in great detail, but perhaps the clearest instance in which his physicality obtrudes upon the narrative is his cocaine addiction. A source of embarrassment to many critics, this addiction, however, is less interesting as a moral failure than as the pretext for an intensely vivid description of the Great Detective's vulnerable body: "Sherlock Holmes took his bottle from the corner of the mantelpiece, and his hypodermic syringe from its neat morocco case. With his long, white, nervous fingers he adjusted the delicate needle, and rolled back his left shirt-cuff. For some little time his eyes rested thoughtfully upon the sinewy forearm and wrist, all dotted and scarred with innumerable puncture-marks" (*The Sign of Four;* Doyle 64).

Not only do we get a disconcerting glimpse of the detective's steely physique "dotted and scarred" with self-inflicted injuries, but the subsequent conversation with Watson also calls attention to Holmes's body. In response to Watson's remonstrations, Holmes replies that, in the absence of "mental exaltation" provided by detective work, he requires the artificial stimulation of the drug, since his mind "rebels at stagnation" (64). Reason becomes a functional equivalent of cocaine; both are physiological stimulants craved by the detective's brain. This is the paradox of "medical semiotics": rooted in the body, it lacks the convincing lever to elevate certain bodily functions (such as those of the brain) above others (such as those of the genitals). Chesterton, of course, finds this lever in his faith; others found it in evolutionary theory with its imaginary ladder of progress from the lower to the higher faculties. But when Holmes, in his assumed delirium in "The Adventure of the Dying Detective," gasps out "Strange how the brain controls the brain!" (832), he articulates the central contradiction underlying the detective's supremely self-disciplined body.

In the next generation of Great Detectives, the residue of physicality became even more important: the freakishness was accentuated in some, while others inherited Holmes's charisma exaggerated into the charm of a romantic hero. Father Brown's short unprepossessing figure is meant to signify his unworldliness, but the constant stress on his "lumpy" appearance eventually achieves the effect of deformity. Ernest Bramah's Max Carrados is blind; Rex Stout's Nero Wolfe is so grossly overweight he cannot stir from his chair. Hercule Poirot's egg-shaped head, waxed moustache, and shortness serve as a comic way of introducing the detective's corporeality without the visceral shock of "scarred forearms."

On the other side of the scale is the detective-as-romantic hero, from Dorothy Sayers's Lord Peter Wimsey to Elizabeth George's Lord Thomas Lynley. The dashing and irresistible titled sleuth is the obverse side of the little Hercule Poirot with the egg-shaped head and enormous moustache. Both admit the body in carefully controlled and meticulously limited ways. Romantic sexuality or endearing freakishness equally adumbrates the paradox of the detective: the Thinking Machine locked in the cage of "meat."

CHRISTMAS MURDERERS

For all their importance, the victim and the detective are subordinated to the true center of the detective story, its raison d'être, the murderer. And it is in its delineation of the subject of violence that the genre most clearly reveals itself as a narrative of discipline.

While highly sophisticated in its plot construction, the characterization in the classic detective story may be described as realism "lite." The genre is "the swan song of old-style middle-class fiction, an attempt to freeze the last literary remains of the nineteenth-century novel" (Tani 26). The "remains" that are being frozen are what is left after an act of violence has shredded the psychological consistency of the character. And the extraordinary effort invested by the detective story in not letting these remains disintegrate into the rotten subjectivity of a monster or a serial killer is what accounts for the reassuring quality of the genre.

All popular literature, of course, may be seen as reassuring in the sense that it tends to collaborate with the reader's prior ideological convictions, but detective fiction is uniquely cozy—uniquely, that is, among the genres of violence. One can easily understand why a Mills and Boon romance tends to put its audience into the state of pleasant daydreaming, but it is not immediately clear why bleeding corpses, autopsies, fingerprints, chases, mounting suspicions, arrest, and as often as not a suicide should have a similar effect. And yet they do. Erik Routley explains this quality of the genre by reference to discipline:

> The detective story reader is not a lover of violence but a lover of order. . . . [He] does not love violence, and is not even primarily interested in what is bizarre. . . . It is not a matter of fear or guilt but of assurance. . . . And this feeling of surprising comfort is achieved not merely by the drawing of a satisfying rational diagram . . . but most of all by the disciplined dance of character which detection calls for and makes possible (223–24).

The connection between comfort and discipline is spelled out clearly here: the detective story is "cozy" because it provides "assurance." The assurance is not that justice will triumph (for formal justice is often flouted in both Doyle and Christie, whose criminals are as likely to eliminate themselves decorously as to put the state to the expense of a trial), but rather that the world and other people will ultimately make sense. Holmes's bleak "circle of misery and violence and fear" is turned into an arena where the implied author as the ringmaster puts his or her violent characters through the steps of the "disciplined dance."

The connection between character intelligibility, discipline, and reassurance is explored by D. A. Miller in *The Novel and the Police,* where, describing the "entanglements" of the novelistic form with the practices of police surveillance, he points out that the novel "interrogate" its characters in precisely the same way as the police interrogate criminals, attempting to elicit from them a full story of their being, marked by "continuity and repleteness"

(9). In other words, the very notion of character is disciplinary in nature. The disciplined dance provides reassurance by smoothing away the violence inherent in the very process of the narrative construction of identity.

But this is true about any character, no matter how blameless. When actual physical violence compounds the violence of the text, the stakes go much higher. Trembling Oliver Twist in Miller's example is hardly likely to arouse the reader's anxiety even if he does not manage to give a "continuous and replete" account of himself. But Bill Sikes is a different matter. And it is precisely with him, as we have seen, that Dickens's novel fails in its disciplinary role. The detective story sets out to rectify this failure. And if it manages to do for a murderer what Dickens does for a workhouse orphan, to provide him with a comprehensible story, the resulting surge of reassurance will be significant indeed.

In Christie's *Murder for Christmas* a particularly bloody and gruesome murder is committed during a Christmas family gathering. To compound the transgression, the murder is a parricide and the criminal is actually the police inspector investigating the case. And yet the overall impression of the book is of cheerful, old-fashioned fun. Like Dickens's "A Christmas Carol," Christie's novel invokes the frightening ghosts of the past, only to exorcise them through the vision of a happier, healthier future. This future is dependent on the process of investigation that restores authenticity to the characters. The Lee family is composed of unhappy hypocrites, each harboring a secret or playing a part. The grisly murder of the paterfamilias by one of his illegitimate sons provides the cathartic bloodletting, in the wake of which the therapeutic "interrogation and inquiry" take place, eventually producing a "full account" of each character, including the murderer (Miller 9). Only then may a true Christmas be celebrated. The greater the shock of violence, the more stringent is the narrative normalization of the character, and the emotional yield of this normalization is the Yuletide reassurance of "all's well with the world."

In Poe's story "Thou Art the Man!" the body of a murder victim is made to speak from beyond the grave in order to reveal its killer. It is a horror tale, not a detective story. But its culmination—the finger pointing at the murderer, the name named, the identity revealed—is the sine qua non of the classic detective story. This is how it always ends, with the definite, authoritative, and final answer to the question "whodunit?" The secret that the genre pursues is the secret of identity. The gesture of the corpse is the gesture of interpellation, calling upon the murderer to recognize himself as the man, or perhaps simply a man. The classic detective story is a narrative machine for producing a specific kind of self. What Foucault says about the panopticon may be applied to the plot of detection: it is "the abstract formula of a very real technology, that of individuals" (1975, 225).

This technology has several components. The first one is labeling: the criminal has to be named, identified, given a specific position within the fictional world of the text. From the free-floating signifier of the murderer which, via the process of suspicion, attaches itself in turn to almost every character in the text, the criminal has to be transformed into a stable, singular corporeal identity. This might be described as "disambiguation": the empty signifier has to coincide with the previously anonymous signified in a one-to-one relationship.

The second one is the assignment of a motive. "Find the motive, find the murderer" is Poirot's motto. He refuses to accept that, as in Ruth Rendell's novels, murder just happens. There must be a comprehensible, clear, and above all, rational motive. Again and again, throughout his fantastically long career, he gallantly defends the dilapidated citadel of utilitarian rationality against the rising tide of deep psychology. In a late novel, *Hallowe'en Party,* confronted with a seemingly psychopathological murder of a young girl, Poirot, despite all the evidence to the contrary, insists that "we still have to find the motive involved" (118). And of course, he is right and his opponents, speculating about nature and nurture in the makeup of sexual killers, are wrong. The "simpler" motive turns out to be greed and fear of discovery: the respectable middle-class engines of violence.

Moreover, there is a perfect fit between the manner of committing the crime and the criminal's personality. The "signature" of the serial killer is a remnant of the individualizing tendency of the detective story. "The murderer has, so to speak, signed his name by committing the crime," says Poirot in *Peril at End House* (40). When motive and manner perfectly coincide, when all the extraneous tangle of red herrings is cleared away, the detective stages a traditional denouement in which his finger unwaveringly points at the murderer. In this exposure an individual is produced who is simultaneously typical and unique, transparent and complex. "Thou art the man!" happily unites the generality of scientific classification (for the subject in question is instantly assimilated to the class of violent criminals) with the psychological discrimination of the realistic novel (for the murderer is defined by a particular, unique, idiosyncratic murder, which functions as the infallible index of his personality).

The detective story, thus, seems to be a perfect machine of discipline in producing what appears to be the two distinct kinds of subjects: the innocent and the guilty: "Rather than in rendering all its subjects uniformly 'normal', discipline is interested in putting in place a perceptual grid in which a division between the normal and the deviant inherently imposes itself" (Miller 18).

However, as we have seen in the example of Judge Wargrave, the situation is not so simple. On the contrary, the Judge is a baffling example of a disciplinary subject who is simultaneously totally normal—embodying both the judiciary and the narrative functions of normalization—and totally deviant, a pleasure murderer. *Ten Little Indians* betrays the secret of the genre: the normal subject is constituted precisely by its capacity for violence. The classic detective story may, then, be seen not as projecting two inherently different subject categories but rather as charting two different plot trajectories that any subject is potentially capable of taking. This follows from the very construction of the murderer in terms of a unique and coherent system of motivation. If the murderer is a perfect character, then any character can be a murderer.

In pursuing the narrative normalization of the violent subject, the detective story exposes the inherent contradiction of its own project. The discriminations of criminology, such as define the serial killer as a special biological kind, clash with the ideology of individualistic liberal democracy, which assumes potential equality of all social monads. The detective story leaves criminological profiling to true crime and the thriller. It does not endorse the category of the deviant and incomprehensible monster of violence. Rather, its formulaic plot functions as a dramatization of the ubiquity of violence, stemming from the very constitution of the liberal subject. The detective story shows that "ordinary psychological processes and normal, human motivations . . . are the primary sources of evil" (Staub 26). But in doing so, it undermines its own disciplinary grid, which establishes the categories of the normal and the deviant in the first place.

The classic detective story is perpetually tempted by horror's representation of the violent subject as a monster. When it succumbs to this temptation, the result is *The Silence of the Lambs.* But in general, the classic detective story valiantly resists the lure of Dr. Lecter and his look-alikes, not, however, without introducing characters who are poised on the very brink of monstrosity. But normally, such malefactors are used only to set off the main modality of the violent subject as the supremely rational subject of discipline.

THE BRUTE ON THE MOOR

In Doyle's *The Hound of the Baskervilles* (1902), there are two criminals. One is Selden, a brutal murderer, whose death sentence was commuted "due to some doubts as to his complete sanity, so atrocious was his conduct" (481). Selden escapes incarceration and hides on the barren moor, adding to the heavy atmosphere of menace blanketing this most Gothic of all Holmes's adventures: "Somewhere there, on that desolate plain, was lurking this fiendish man, hiding in a burrow like a wild beast, his heart full of malignancy against the whole race which had cast him out" (481).

It is not difficult to recognize in Selden both an offspring of Frankenstein's fiend, lurking in deserted places, and a progenitor of the monstrous serial killers we have encountered in the previous chapter. But the novel provides him with an even more spectacular genealogy, linking him to the prehistoric beast-man who had once inhabited that very moor: "Over the rocks, in the crevice in which the candle burned, there was thrust out an evil yellow face, a terrible animal face. . . . Foul with mire, with a bristling beard, and hung with matted hair, it might well have belonged to one of those old savages who dwelt in the burrows on the hill-sides" (Doyle 505).

Doyle here inscribes Selden within the fin de siècle favorite trope of "ontogeny recapitulates phylogeny," an all-purpose explanatory framework based on the notion that the development of the individual recapitulates the development of the species.[3] Selden is a "throwback," an atavism, whose savagery is the result of his arrested development.

However, Selden has nothing to do with the true mystery, the murder of Sir Charles Baskerville. The man responsible for this murder, the adversary who elicits Holmes's unqualified admiration, is Mr. Stapleton, the very opposite of the brutish Selden. Stapleton is a polished gentleman, a consummate plotter, a "cool and unemotional" player of games (492). Moreover, if Selden is defined through opposition to the civilization represented by Holmes and Watson—the opposition that amounts almost to species difference—Stapleton and Holmes are doubles. The criminal even taunts the detective with their similarity by introducing himself as Sherlock Holmes (477).

It seems that we are back to the split between "the ape and the minister" inaugurated by Poe. But Doyle complicates the scheme inherited from his predecessor. Selden may be animal-like, but he is no ape. The text undermines its own initial presentation of him as a bloodthirsty savage by adding yet another genealogy to Selden's already complex heritage. Selden as a literary character has the Gothic pedigree, leading back to *Frankenstein;* as a throwback, his evolutionary history links him to the Neolithic man, but as a human being, he belongs to a sympathetic and suffering family. Selden turns out to be the younger brother of Mrs. Barrymore, Sir Charles's stolid and respectable housekeeper. When Selden dies, his sister mourns him: "To all the world he was the man of violence, half animal and half demon; but to her he always remained the little willful boy of her own girlhood, the child who had clung to her hand" (531). The "half animal and half demon" is transformed into a pitiful human being by having what Frankenstein so strenuously denied to his creature: a loving family.

Stapleton, on the other hand, undergoes an opposite process. Initially, he is placed within the safest, most innocuous familial context of Victorian fiction: he lives with his sister. It turns out, however, that "Miss Stapleton" is really his wife, and the first glimpse we get of the brutality smoldering under his cool exterior is when he objects so violently to Sir Henry Baskerville's courting of his "sister," that Sir Henry calls him "a crazy man"(501). At the end we find out that the superrational Stapleton is a closet sadist who tortures his wife and was involved in some unspecified "infamy" in the school he kept. As Selden is raised to the status of full humanity through the intercession of his sister, Stapleton's abused sister-wife testifies to his real nature, calling him "the brute" (543).

Moreover, Stapleton is also a throwback. Like Selden, he is bound by murderous heredity, doomed to reenact the violence of his forebears. Stapleton is actually a Baskerville, a reincarnation of the wicked Sir Hugo who started the legend of the hellhound haunting the family. Reincarnation here should be understood in the strictly biological sense of the fin de siècle theories of heredity. If Selden recapitulates the history of the Neolithic man, Stapleton recapitulates the less distant but equally bloody history of the English gentry. When Watson marvels at the exact resemblance of Stapleton to Sir Hugo's portrait, Holmes responds: "Yes, it is an interesting instance of a throw-back, which appears to be both physical and spiritual. A study of family portraits is enough to convert a man to the doctrine of reincarnation" (533). Holmes expounds the "ontogeny recapitulates phylogeny" doctrine at some length in another story, "The Adventure of the Empty House": "I have a theory that the individual represents in his development the whole procession of his ancestors. . . . The person becomes, as it were, the epitome of the history of his own family" (566).

What this theory does in relation to Selden and Stapleton is to equalize them in a peculiar position of what might be called a "half-monster." Their bodies, while not outwardly deformed, become invested with an evolutionary history of violence; however, their humanity is not denied. Selden's pathos and Stapleton's rationality prevent them from sliding all the way down into the abyss of monstrosity or even into the limbo of broken selves inhabited by contemporary serial killers. Selden is redeemed by his loyal family, while Stapleton, despite his "craziness," does have a rational and respectable motive for murder: money. Neither monsters nor fully self-disciplined subjects, they epitomize the psychic anatomy of the detective story's murderer: the transparent veil of reason wrapped around the opaque core of violence.

Selden's atrocity is as far as the genre is prepared to go in exploring motiveless violence, and it is significant that he is not the murderer. Doyle's other criminals are often passionate, like Jim Browner of "The Adventure of the Cardboard Box," but never actually insane. Nor are Chesterton's, but in his case the "brute" reappears in a less innocuous guise as tainted not merely by bad blood but by bad race. The most egregious instance of this is "The Duel of Dr. Hirsch" (1913), which rewrites the Dreyfus trial as a Jewish plot. Dr. Hirsch, who pretends to be his own anti-Semitic adversary in order to cast opprobrium on the conservative cause, is a politicized version of Stapleton's brutality masquerading as sweet reason. Father Brown removes the mask and uncovers the Beast: "Seen thus in the glass the white face looked like the face of Judas laughing horribly and surrounded by capering flames of hell" (207). Chesterton's anti-Semitism means he does not have to account for Dr. Hirsch's wickedness. He is a Jew; this is explanation enough. But in using the detective story as a vehicle for ideological hatred, Chesterton pushes the limits of the genre. The detective story's monster is never monstrous enough. Anti-Semitism does much better in horror and fantasy, relieved from the necessity to walk the thin line between the opaque Other and the comprehensible self. The detective story's true protagonist is not the mad Dr. Hirsch, biologically programmed to do evil, but rather another doctor, the protagonist of Christie's *The Murder of Roger Ackroyd,* Dr. James Sheppard, who—even more successfully than Judge Wargrave—combines the functions of the criminal with those of the detective.

"A TWO-FACED HERMES"

Casting "a monstrous shadow," this figure presides over the denouement of Borges's "Death and the Compass," in which the criminal and the detective mirror each other across the boundary of violent death (83). Lonnrot and Scharlach are doubles, collapsing the careful division of roles that the traditional detective story maintains. Both men are—in turn—predator and prey, logician and avenger, killer and victim. With its numerous references to Dupin, Borges's tale makes explicit what is implicit in Poe: the uncanny undertext of the disciplinary discourse of identity.

I have already noted in the chapter on serial killers that Dupin's adversaries are either the totally Other (the ape) or the totally Same (the Minister D. and the unnamed killer of Marie Roget). It has, of course, often been recognized that Dupin and the Minister are "moral duplicates and may ultimately be two phases of the same mind" (Babener 324). However, seeing this doubling as merely another example of what Poe elsewhere called "the bi-part soul" misses the point: the similarity is so close that there is no Jekyll-and-Hyde split between the good and the bad parts. Rather, we are confronted with reproduction of the same psychological structure, the potentially endless coinage of identity simulacra.

This reproduction becomes the basis for the process of detection itself. Poe's game of draughts, the metaphor for a battle of wills between the detective and the criminal, presupposes that the detective "throws himself into the spirit of his opponent [and] identifies himself therewith" (142). Such identification is facilitated by the fact that there is little difference between the spirit of the detective and the criminal. Professor Moriarty, Holmes's adversary, is his exact counterpart, "a genius, a philosopher, an abstract thinker" (437). Holmes exults: "I had at last met an antagonist who was my intellectual equal" (ibid.). Their joint death in the Reichenbach falls, later revoked by their author, has a kind of narrative inevitability that cannot be overcome by Holmes's subsequent resurrection. The Holmes who comes back in "The Adventure of the Empty House" (1903) and continues chasing criminals for the next twenty-five years is a diminished copy of himself. Deprived of his criminal twin, he is simultaneously deprived of that symmetry, which, in Borges's terms, "fixes . . . death" (86). Without Moriarty, his stories become buffeted by melodrama and corroded by intimations of the supernatural. It is not that every detective needs a criminal mastermind, but every detective needs to confront a mind similar to his own. In Chesterton's "The Secret of Father Brown," the priest explains his method by stating that in his imagination he killed all the victims of the crimes he investigated: "I try to get inside the murderer . . . I wait till I know I am inside a murderer, thinking his thoughts, wrestling with his passions . . . Till I am really a murderer" (465–66).

But Father Brown is a killer only in the imagination; Hercule Poirot, seemingly even more upright and reliable than Holmes and Brown, is a killer in reality. He ends his illustrious career with a deliberate premeditated murder.

Throughout her oeuvre, Christie offers numerous hints that the detective and the murderer are birds of a feather. Christie's first tour de force, *The Murder of Roger Ackroyd* (1926), created a sensation: instead of being narrated by the detective's admiring friend, it was narrated by the murderer, but the reader did not realize that until the last couple of pages. This is a clever deconstruction of the dynamics within the Holmes-Watson duo. Despite his obvious intellectual deficiency as compared to the brilliant Holmes, Watson is essentially his alter ego, embodying the middle-class, respectable side of his friend, the very side that always keeps Holmes on the right side of the law. Watson, in other words, is the incarnation of the self-discipline that contains reason and prevents it from turning destructive. By making a Watson-figure into a murderer, Christie brings out the hidden potential of violence in the detective himself. Dr. James Sheppard, a Watson-turned-murderer, is indistinguishable from the original Watson. The cleverness of the novel lies in the fact that Sheppard's narrative voice is precisely the comforting, sentimental, slightly muddleheaded but essentially honest and reliable voice of the detective's sidekick. At some point Poirot tells him, "You must have indeed been sent from the good God to replace my friend Hastings" (81; Hastings is Poirot's Watson in Christie's early books). Sheppard never actually lies, not even in describing his last interview with Roger Ackroyd, in the course of which the latter is murdered. All he does is to use an ellipsis, the narrative trope of violence. In the last brief chapter, "Apologia," he talks of his skill as a writer, quoting again his description of the murder scene and commenting on it: "All true, you see. But suppose I had put a row of stars after the first sentence. Would somebody then have wondered what exactly happened in that blank ten minutes?" (220).

Insofar as Sheppard is created as a character through his own narration, this remark is a "laying bare" of his own narrative subjectivity, the subjectivity shaped by a missing typographical sign that marks the ellipsis of violence. Shaped around this missing center like a doughnut is Dr. Sheppard's Watson-like personality: the honest, upright, somewhat old-fashioned, not too bright but inquisitive and even slightly meddlesome general practitioner, an embodiment of Victorian and Edwardian virtues.

But the real giveaway of the detective's potential for violence is *Curtain: Poirot's Last Case.* The story of this novel is interesting: written in the 1940s (apparently as a sort of financial security for Christie's family), it was kept in a safe for thirty years and eventually published in 1975. In the numerous novels written after *Curtain,* Poirot becomes a ghost of himself.[4] He has already given away his secret, even though it is not available to the reader as yet. The secret is essentially the same as Father Brown's: I have killed all those people or rather, I may have killed all those people and the reason I have not is because I have been constrained by the straitjacket of the disciplinary plot. But once the straitjacket is removed—in this case, by Poirot's approaching death—murder ensues.

In *Curtain,* Poirot—now terminally ill—is reunited with Hastings at the scene of his first triumph, the country mansion of Styles, which is now a guesthouse. He is there to track a murderer among the guests. But the murderer is of a very peculiar kind. Modeled on Shakespeare's Iago, he is a perfect killer because he murders without violence. Norton, a small inoffensive man, instigates others to kill without ever tainting himself with actual blood. He leaves a trail of corpses but "*he could never be convicted of* a crime" (169).

Norton is the ultimate in the classic detective story's construction of the violent subject. He epitomizes all the efforts the genre invests in disciplining, taming, and controlling violence. No need for euphemism in describing his deeds because the deeds are nonexistent. There are only words, only a seductive web of manipulation, he weaves around his victims. Like the genre itself he produces corpses out of nothing, and before they are even glimpsed, they disappear again and dissolve into puzzles, literary allusions, stories. In fact, as Poirot explains in his own posthumous confession, the mainspring of Norton's behavior is his fear and dislike of actual violence, which results in his "developing a morbid taste for violence at second hand" (172). Like the detective story's reader, Norton is addicted to the violence safely distanced, safely explained, rationalized, and verbalized. But precisely what has been lauded as the genre's chief virtue—the "vaccination" against violence by providing a second-hand substitute—turns out to be a source of danger. For Norton is extremely dangerous. He is even more dangerous than Judge Wargrave, whose protection against the disciplinary law lay in his identification with the law's power. But this identification, occurring on the diegetic level of the text, could be undone: even a criminal judge may be punished like any other criminal. Norton, however, identifies with the extradiegetic law of narrative that designates certain subjects as victims. Unlike Wargrave, he is immune to the "mark of Cain," the irrational horror of spilt blood that corrodes the murderer's pellucid rationality. Norton does not spill blood. His own body escapes even the minimal sympathetic involvement with the death of the Other that damns the judge. He is not a "body without organs," in Deleuze's phrase, but rather a collection of organs—the brain, the tongue—without a body.[5] In order to be defeated, he has to be given back his corporeality—through an act of violence.

Poirot kills Norton by shooting him in the middle of the forehead. The same wound as Judge Wargrave's, it is also, in Hastings's words, echoing the judge's confession, "the brand of Cain" (188). But in order to put this brand there, in order to entrap the elusive murderous spirit in a vulnerable body, Poirot must acknowledge his own corporeality. His body is showcased from the beginning of the novel in a way that invites comparison with Doyle's "The Dying Detective": Poirot is now a "thin little man," crippled with arthritis, his "face lined and wrinkled," his moustache painfully artificial (13). But here there is no marvelous resurrection: Poirot dies of a heart attack, having deliberately removed his heart medicine from his bedside. The detective imitates the confessional suicide that ends the careers of innumerable criminals in the classic detective story. The identification is now complete; or rather, the detective and the criminal have exchanged places. It is now the criminal who withdraws from the bloody chaos of actual violence and controls action by pure logic and calculation. It is now the detective who has to involve himself with the recalcitrant materiality of the body and whose hands are stained with blood.

The detective's mastery of the plot dissolves in the terrifying sublimity of murder. In explaining his reasons for killing Norton, Poirot echoes the demented self-aggrandizement of Judge Wargrave: "I *am* the law!" (187). At the same time, he is lucid enough to realize that he is being infected by the madness of disciplinary reason that imperceptibly slides into the ecstasy of violence: "For the worst part of murder, Hastings, is its effect on the murderer. I,

Hercule Poirot, might come to believe myself divinely appointed to deal out death to all and sundry . . ." (179). In order to prevent this from happening, he must die himself before he completes the trajectory from the rational Dr. Sheppard who kills to uphold order, to the even more rational Judge Wargrave, in whom passion for order has metamorphosed into addiction to violence.

Poirot's final gesture is renunciation of knowledge: "But still I do not know. . . . It is perhaps right that I should not know. I have always been so sure—too sure. . . . But now I am very humble and I say like a little child 'I do not know . . .'" (187). This is the voice of Christie's classic detective story acknowledging its defeat, for the bulwark against violence it has so painstakingly built out of the precise structures of knowledge and reason has turned out to be worse than no protection at all.

What underlies the dance of substitutions, of the detective-turned-murderer and murderer-turned-detective, is the classic detective story's final pronouncement on the nature of the violent subject, succinctly summarized by Poirot: "Everyone is a potential murderer" (169). Turning away from its half-hearted attempts to delineate a typology of "brutes," to locate criminality in a Lombrosian monster, the genre embraces the liberal judicial view of violence as a necessary and inescapable component of any subjectivity. If so, the only way violence may be contained is via an external apparatus of law enforcement, the structure (and stricture) of discipline. The classic detective story's equivalent of this structure is the complex elaboration of its plot, the rigid encasement of characterization, the gag of euphemism, and the handcuffs of limited action. But all these devices, while confining individual violence, eventually set loose what Benjamin calls "the violence of the law." The question whether one is preferable to another is being arbitrated by history at precisely the same time as Poirot commits his first and last murder in the war-devastated mansion of Styles.

SLOUCHING TOWARD BETHLEHEM

Among the would-be murderers in *Curtain* is Hastings's own daughter Judith. She is one of those who almost succumb to Norton's campaign of insidious brainwashing, meant to liberate the murderer in each and every one of us. But Judith is also strikingly different from the rest of Norton's puppets. Those who actually commit crimes under his influence do it for the time-honored private reasons of the detective story: money, fear of blackmail, getting rid of an unwanted spouse. Judith, a trained scientist, does have a personal reason in wanting to kill sickly Mrs. Franklin: she is in love with her husband, a biologist of genius and Judith's boss. But this personal motivation is superseded by her firmly held ideological conviction (shared with Dr. Franklin) that certain lives are "unworthy of living." And unlike an ordinary detective story criminal, who prudently conceals his or her reason for wanting person X out of the way, Judith and Dr. Franklin hold forth on every possible occasion about their eugenicist gospel: "Lots of people I'd like to kill," said Dr. Franklin cheerfully. "Don't believe my conscience would keep me awake at night afterwards. It's an idea of mine, you know, that about eighty per cent of the human race ought to be eliminated. We'd get on much better without them" (49–50).

"Lives unworthy of living" is a Nazi catchphrase that became the slogan of the euthanasia campaign in 1939–1941, when at least 70,000 people were murdered for the reasons clearly and convincingly expounded by Judith: "I don't hold life as sacred as all you people do. Unfit lives, useless lives—they should be got out of the way. There's so much mess about. Only people who can make a decent contribution to the community ought to be allowed to live" (97).

Compare this with the points made in the 1920 book *Release and Destruction of Lives Not Worth Living* by Alfred Hoche and Rudolf Binding that later became the Bible of the Nazi eugenicist state: that the "ballast lives" and "human husks" of the incurably ill, mentally deficient, and "asocial" are "lives not worth living" and therefore killing them is a genuinely moral task (in Proctor 178).[6] Such views were, of course, not limited to Germany; eugenics was a respectable science with chairs in all major European universities, and the first country to enact eugenic legislation, including compulsory sterilization, was not the Third Reich but the United States. In preaching the eugenicist gospel in the country house sanctuary of the detective story, Judith and Franklin open its French windows just a little bit to the bloody storm of the racial war raging outside. It is no surprise that Hastings, treated to such a sermon from his beloved daughter, looks like "one who has envisaged a nest of snakes" (50). Pressing the point a little, it is even possible to read Norton's spellbinding tactics as an allegory of a far mightier Pied Piper who, at the very moment of the book's action, is sending millions to kill in his name.

However, Judith and Franklin are eventually exonerated from all suspicions. It is Mrs. Franklin herself, a weak, empty-headed, useless woman who succumbs to Norton's blandishments and accidentally brings about her own death. A seemingly "eugenicist" murder is committed but, in fact, it turns out to be a good, old-fashioned spouse killing (or would-be killing) with no ideological purpose in mind. The detective story approaches an ideological murder, only to draw away—no Raskolnikovs in Styles, let alone Himmlers or Hoesses.

The depiction of ideologically motivated criminality constitutes the subtext of *Curtain,* with Judith and Dr. Franklin, intellectual defenders of mass murder, successful, arrogant, and pitiless, being a sort of preliminary character sketch for the bio-utopian New Man. But at the end both are shipped off to Africa, there, presumably, to practice their theories on the benighted natives, while the scope of the novel dwindles back to the resolutely private sphere of the classic detective story. The genre of discipline admits its incapacity to discipline genocide.

Another such double text, adumbrating the possibility of a different kind of murder, only to escape back into the safe confines of domesticity, is Christie's 1940 *One, Two, Buckle My Shoe.* Here as well, the date of composition (and publication) is self-explanatory with regard to the historical anxieties the novel tries to cope with by simultaneous evocation and evasion. The England hovering on the brink of war, beset by fear and uncertainty, plagued by home-grown fascist sympathizers, creates a strange and unsettling background to the case of what looks like a botched political assassination but turns out to be the intended victim's plot to get rid of an inconvenient witness to bigamy. And it is the identity of the murderer that focuses the genre's aporia when confronted with violence whose determinants exceed the mythos of liberal democracy.

Alistair Blunt, a conservative politician and financier, is a bulwark of traditional English values, which Poirot enumerates in the slightly wistful tone of an admiring outsider: "sanity and balance and stability and honest dealing" (188). Poirot and his fellow Great Detectives have fought on behalf of these values, protecting the middle-class society, from which they have been barred by their own eccentricity or foreignness, or both. Blunt seems to be their fellow fighter and this is what makes him the target of potential assassination attempts by both the radical right and left. And yet Blunt is also a murderer who is responsible for the deaths of three people. In the last conversation with Poirot, pleading not to deliver him into the hands of the police, Blunt argues that he is "necessary to the continued peace and well-being of this country" (187). Poirot agrees, and yet insists that the lives of three people supersede the claims of the nation: "I am not concerned with nations, Monsieur. I am concerned with the lives of private individuals who have the right not to have their lives taken from them" (189).

This is the last stand of the detective story in face of the historical forces that threaten to open up its little country house sanctuary to the utopian vistas of the "New Heaven and the New Earth" (ibid.). This march into the millennium requires the inevitable sacrifice of "lives unworthy of living." Poirot's "bourgeois" insistence on the absolute value of individual life appears almost heroic in the bleak atmosphere of the catastrophe about to happen. In his uncompromising stance, the beleaguered mythos of liberal democracy battles the early-twentieth-century prevailing zeitgeist that focuses, in the words of historian Michael Burleigh, on "such supra-individual entities as the family, nations, or races, whose future well-being overrode the rights of individuals" (1997).

The battle is impossible to win because the detective has lost his adversary. The moment Blunt, that embodiment of "playing the game," begins arguing in the idiom of his radical enemies, claiming that national interests justify murder and that his victims are not quite "human beings" anyway, he becomes one of those New Men, who are impervious to the reach of liberal justice. Blunt may be brought to trial and executed but he cannot be disciplined and punished. All the tools of the classic detective story are blunted by his new subjectivity. Surveillance is impotent against a murderer who does not hide his deeds; reason cannot be used against a man who rationally argues the cause of irrationality; and repression is meaningless for a subject who is ashamed of nothing. The novel ends with Poirot's renunciation of his role of society's watchdog: his last request of the couple of young radicals who obviously represent Christie's fearful premonition of the "rough beast" of the future is that in their brave new world there should still be "freedom and pity" (190).

Of course, Poirot's renunciation was premature, as his flourishing postwar career demonstrated. "The New Heaven and the New Earth" perished in the furnace of World War II and in the protracted ice age of the Cold War. The detective has suddenly found himself triumphant once more, surveying the landscape pitted and scarred with the sites of multiple historical traumas but still amenable to democracy's disciplinary narrative. And yet these traumas, the wounds and scars of the New Man's sublime violence, are too insistent to ignore. Consequently, the postwar detective story, no matter how conservative in its adherence to the classic form, is underlaid by the unspoken mass murder and genocide.

Christie's 1940s novels contain another unwritten text, dramatizing the clash between the liberal detective and the utopian New Man, between the subject of discipline and the subject of ideology. This text is only implicit in her whodunits that eventually retreat from their own daring agenda. The novels that Christie could—or should—have written are actually written today, in the aftermath of the Holocaust and the Gulag, when the mythos of liberal democracy is retrenching its positions in head-on collisions with ghosts of the recent past.

4

Utopia Noir

"Hell of a world we live in, huh?" The proprietor was a thin black man with bad teeth and an obvious wig. I nodded, fishing in my jeans for change, anxious to find a park bench where I could submerge myself in hard evidence of the human near-dystopia we live in. "But it could be worse, huh?"

"That's right," I said, "or even worse, it could be perfect."

—*WILLIAM GIBSON, "The Gernsback Continuum"*

THE CHILD IN THE CELLAR

The conventional image of Utopia is of uniformly beautiful men and women in vaguely classical draperies perambulating across the Edenic landscape of green grass and shiny white buildings. In William Morris's *News from Nowhere* (1890), the protagonist realizes he has entered Utopia when he notices the clean-limbed, perfectly shaped bodies of its inhabitants. His exile back into the fallen world of history, however, is marked by the sight of the aging, filthy, and deformed body of a tramp. The utopian body is a body purified of all signs of sickness, mortality, and above all, violence. The latter is seen as a social malady, to be cured by the utopian medicine: "We are a healthy people generally," says an inhabitant of Morris's utopia, "so we are not likely to be much troubled with *this* disease," the disease of violence and criminality (71).

But despite its disclaimers, utopia is dogged by violence. Dystopia, utopia's mirror image, is obsessed with the violated body. A famous dystopian scene presents torture as the hidden truth of a supposedly utopian society: "If you want a picture of the future, imagine a boot stamping on a human face—forever," says O'Brien to Smith in Orwell's *1984* (215). The connection between utopia and violence has been explained away as an accident of history, the result of the perversions of Nazism and Stalinism. But is it?

Ursula Le Guin's short story "The Ones Who Walk Away from Omelas" (1976) implies that the connection between the marmoreal physique of the utopian "men like gods" and the jackboot-smashed face of a torture victim may be necessary and not accidental. The story pictures a utopian community blessed with health, happiness, freedom, and prosperity. But "in a basement under one of the beautiful public buildings of Omelas, or perhaps in the cellar of one of its spacious private homes, there is a room. It has one locked door and no windows." In this room sits a child: filthy, starved, sick, all but mindless from its continuing abuse. And all the good citizens of Omelas know of the child's existence, but they do nothing:

> They all know it is there, all the people of Omelas. . . . They all know that it has to be there. Some of them understand why, and some do not, but they all understand that their happiness, the beauty of their city, the tenderness of their friendships, the health of their children, the wisdom of their scholars, the skill of their makers, even the abundance of their harvest and the kindly weather of their skies, depend wholly on this child's abominable misery. (257)

Le Guin's parable is reminiscent of the conversation between Ivan and Alyosha in Dostoevskii's *The Brothers Karamazov,* in which Ivan claims that no universal salvation justifies a child's tear. But Le Guin, in the foreword to the story, denies the Dostoevskii connection and attributes her inspiration to a passage from William James's "The Moral Philosopher and the Moral Life," which she quotes in full:

> Of the hypotheses that were offered to us of a world in which Messrs. Fourier's and Bellamy's and Morris's utopias should all be outdone, and millions kept permanently happy on the one single condition that a certain lost soul on the far-off edge of things should lead a life of lonely torment, what except a special and independent sort of emotion can it be which would make us immediately feel, even though an impulse arouse within us to clutch at the happiness so offered, how hideous a thing would be its enjoyment when deliberately accepted as the fruit of such a bargain? (251)

The difference between the Karamazov brothers' conversation and James's ruminations is the difference between theodicy and utopia. Ivan frames his graphic description of child abuse in the traditional Christian problematic of evil, forcing his devout brother to admit that Christ's sacrifice cannot redeem the abusers. But James's passage, with his explicit references to the utopian tradition of "Messrs. Fourier and Bellamy and Morris," situates victimization in the secular context of an ideal society, in which "millions [are] kept permanently happy" by the violence done to the few. And as opposed to theodicy, it is not the source of evil but rather its function that constitutes the hideous enigma of utopia. Alyosha, in a recasting of the ancient lament of Job, cannot stand the thought that the all-merciful God allows children to be tortured. But in Le Guin's secular parable, it is the free will of the citizens of Omelas that keeps the child in its cellar. Enlightened by the historical experience James did not have, she knows that most of them will in fact eagerly "clutch at the happiness so offered." But she also believes that some will reject the bargain ("the ones who walk away" are those few who, having seen the child, leave Omelas and do not come back to its tainted happiness). But why should the child, or some other "certain lost soul," be tortured for the utopia to exist? What is the secret of Omelas? Or, in the light of the twentieth-century experiments in utopian politics, what is the secret of Auschwitz, the Gulag, or Cambodia's killing fields, where millions of children had to suffer in order to cure the body politic of its imperfections? It is not Alyosha Karamazov, desperately clinging to his dwindling faith in a world beset by violence, but rather Raskolnikov, with his violence-nurtured Idea, who can answer this question.

Raskolnikov knows very well that the New Man is baptized in blood. To produce a new utopian subject, one needs the power of the sublime. It is as a source of the sublime that the child's "abominable misery" becomes necessary for the happy citizens of Omelas. But their reactions vary: what is a sacrifice for a majority is a crime for a minority. There are two kinds of subjects in Omelas, the subjects of ideology, who thrive on torture, and the subjects of discipline, who are appalled by it. The texts I analyze in this chapter dramatize the clash between the two within the heterogeneous narrative field, in which utopia blends with crime fiction.

Beginning with the crime of utopian violence, the chapter proceeds with its investigation. Thus, the trajectory of my argument follows the plot of the investigative dystopia. This subgenre of crime fiction, as represented by four contemporary novels—Robert Harris's *Fatherland* (1992) and *Archangel* (1999), Donald James's *Monstrum* (1998), and Paul Johnston's *Body Politic* (1998)—will be the focus of the second half of the chapter. But before we join the private eye on his venture into the dark City of the Sun, we have to understand the background of his quest. The first half of the chapter deals with the classic utopias of the late-nineteenth and early-twentieth centuries, the narrative incubator of the sublime subject of ideology.

THE PRIMAL SCENE

Utopia and dystopia, argues Krishan Kumar, can be considered a single generic entity, for dystopia is "largely the creation of men for whom it represented the dark obverse of their own profound and passionate utopian temperament" (1987, 104). Dystopia is predicated "on the very terms of the modern utopia" (ibid. 110). The golden age of utopias, the late nineteenth and early twentieth centuries, is followed by the backlash of dystopias, the age of Zamyatin's *We* and Orwell's *1984,* in which precisely the "terms of the modern utopia" are charged with responsibility for the social disasters of modernity.

Today, after the collapse of Communism and the spread of globalization, utopia seems both old-fashioned and somewhat embarrassing.[1] The only way in which it manages to eke out a precarious existence is in the shape of what Jameson calls the "utopian impulse" as opposed to any concrete utopian vision: "the deepest vocation [of the utopian genre] is to bring home, in local and determinate ways . . . our constitutional inability to imagine Utopia itself, and this not owing to any individual failure of the imagination but as the result of the systemic, cultural, and ideological closure of which we are all in one way or another prisoners" (1982, 153).

We—postmodern culture, in other words—are prisoners in a disciplinary jail, atoning for . . . what? What is the crime, which has led to the incarceration of the imagination itself in the dismal cage of "here" and "now"? Jameson does not spell it out, but it is implicit both in his analysis and in Tom Moylan's more recent focus on the "critical utopia" that at least part of the blame for the crisis of utopia should be attributed to the failure of the twentieth-century utopian ideologies, Nazism and Communism. And this failure is not merely a military defeat or economic insufficiency but the revelation of the mass murder and genocide that accompanied both regimes, as it did the disastrous utopian venture in Cambodia. However, the present eclipse of utopian ideologies does not mean utopias or dystopias are no longer written. What it means, rather, is that in many cases such texts become past—rather than future—oriented. Instead of offering a glimpse of paradise beyond the prison's walls of globalization, they attempt to solve the mystery of the crime that has led to the incarceration in the first place. Memories of violence-tainted utopias haunt the postmodern subject whose genealogy is intertwined with the aborted birth of the New Man.

The trauma of violence may lead to either evasion or logorrhea, both gesturing at the ellipsis of the violent sublime I discussed in the introduction. Twentieth-century ideological genocide, especially the Holocaust, has generated both. In chapter 6 I will analyze the dialectic of silence and speech with regard to the Holocaust in greater detail. For now, it is sufficient to note how narratives of the postmodern subject both evade, and engage with, the crime of utopia. As I have argued above, the most influential account of the genealogy of the violent subject, Foucault's *Discipline and Punish,* turns a blind eye to the death camp. Foucault's nightmare of state violence seems to end with the nineteenth-century panopticon, a reassuringly low-tech apparatus of surveillance. In his other explorations of what he calls "bio-power," that is, the power that directly affects the human body, Foucault is primarily interested in sexuality and the management of population dynamics.

But Foucault also locates the impetus for his project precisely in that which is missing from his narrative. The main question, he notes, is why the concept of power is so central today. The answer is that power "is not only a theoretical question but a part of our experience," the experience that is shaped by the turbulent events of World War II and its aftermath. Foucault's examples of the historical events, responsible for the upsurge of the contemporary interest in the issues of subjectivity and domination, are what he calls the "two 'pathological forms'—those two 'diseases of power'—fascism and Stalinism"(quoted in Dreyfus and Rabinow 209).

The metaphor of pathology is revealing: "fascism and Stalinism" appear to occupy the same place in Foucault's own discourse that madness and disease occupy, according to him, in the discourse of the Enlightenment, the place of the excluded but necessary Other. There is no explanation for ideological mass murder in the disciplinary model of violence. Yet at the same time discipline is positioned in a covert but necessary relation to genocide. Foucault argues himself into a paradox when he attempts to make fascism and Stalinism both normal and exceptional. On the one hand, Auschwitz and the Gulag are a morbid exaggeration of the normal power relations: "in spite of their own internal madness, they used to a large extent the ideas and the devices of our political rationality" (ibid.). On the other hand, Foucault proceeds to argue that physical violence is essentially self-defeating as a strategy of power because it cannot produce new subjects; all it can do is to "pile up the dead" (ibid.). In a gloss on Foucault, Francis Barker claims that physical violence "acts directly upon the body or on things—it closes or minimizes the possibility of resistance . . . [and therefore] it limits the possibility of the self-creation for both self and other" (81).

However, Nazism and Stalinism were explicitly and consciously attempts at "self-creation." Foucault's and Barker's arguments are structured by disavowal rather than by logical consistency. Foucault's avoidance of the subject of genocide, paradoxically coupled with his recognition of the centrality of this subject in the postmodern experience of power, indicates the first stage in the West's coming to terms with the trauma of Nazism and Stalinism. The second stage, beginning roughly in the early eighties and continuing till today, is marked not by avoidance but by insatiable interest. In particular, this is true with regard to the Holocaust.

"The Holocaust," argues James Berger, "is the paradigmatic instance of an apocalypse in history" (59). He assembles an impressive array of quotes from

Theodor Adorno, Elie Wiesel, Jean-François Lyotard, and others that describe the Holocaust as the pivotal event of postmodernity, a catastrophic rupture, an event that "cannot be grasped or recovered, yet cannot be escaped" (61). There is, in fact, hardly any need to argue for this paradigmatic status of the Holocaust in the postmodern cultural imaginary, the status it has assumed after years of evasion and silence. Historian Michael Burleigh describes this as "the curious, super-nova like capacity of this subject [the Holocaust] to gain energy as the events themselves recede in time" (1997, 6). Whether expressed in silence or in a flood of words, the trauma of genocide shapes postmodern narratives of violence and evil. The unquiet past of mass murder invades the contemporary dreams and nightmares like a message from the stars in the science fiction film *Contact,* which reveals, in a blur of pixels, a swastika and then an image of the Fuhrer speaking.

Even the often-voiced claim that in Baudrillard's "society of simulacra" the physical body disappears can be related to the queasy sense of too many dead bodies cluttering the vistas of history. Francis Barker points out in his discussion of Shakespeare's *Titus Andronicus* that the lavish extravaganza of Elizabethan stage violence served "to divert attention away from . . . the [routine] elimination of huge numbers of population" (190). Simulacra of violence, in other words, might hide rather than supplant the real thing. The fact that postmodernism obsessively recycles images of genocide, turning them into part of the entertainment industry, does not make the genocide any less real. Rather, those images are a testimony to a huge historical trauma that fractures the development of the liberal disciplinary subject. For a time, this subject was challenged and seemingly overshadowed by a utopian subject of ideology, the New Man. And if discipline uses violence to mortify the body and train the soul, utopia destroys both bodies and souls in pursuit of their impossible unification.

THE BIRTH OF SUPERMAN

The centerpiece of both Nazism and Communism was the creation of a new kind of human being. Both aimed for an anthropological revolution, or what the French fascist thinker Drieu La Rochelle called "the revolution of the body."[2] Spurred by late-nineteenth-century evolutionary thought, the desire for a perfect society was transmuted into the longing for perfected man. The early-twentieth century radical ideologies, whether left or right, shared the utopian dream of the New Man that Slavoj Zizek called "man as harmonious being . . . a New Man without antagonistic tension" (5).

Perhaps the best way to introduce the New Man is through the utopian and science-fictional writings of the 1930s. Such texts, especially those published in England and the United States, escape the opprobrium of the ideologically tainted *Zukunftsroman* of the German radical right or of the socialist realism of the Soviet Union. At the same time, they display a number of features that unmistakably point to a common structure underlying the radical utopian longings across the political spectrum.

Olaf Stapledon's novel *Odd John* (1936) is particularly striking in view of its author's record as a pacifist and a liberal. Nevertheless, Odd John, for all his oddness, is a fitting introduction to the armies of the New Men that were soon to overrun Europe. John is a "mutation," one of the coming race of the *Homo superior* who are to dominate the "vast herd of cattle" that have the temerity to call themselves *Homo sapiens* (86; 187). He is endowed with a soaring IQ and some paranormal abilities, but what makes him a Superman is the unity of his being. He is not a prey to conflicting impulses, clashing desires, rebellious bodily processes, ceaseless prodding of the libido, and the subterranean subversion of the unconscious. His mind controls his body and his will controls his mind. He can not only squash unwanted emotions but also produce any emotional response he desires. He guides the motor development of his body in infancy and learns to swim, run, drive, make love, and work heavy machinery by sheer effort of will. Unlike old humans, whose psychological makeup is "a terribly unstable compound," John has managed to integrate his "whole being into a new and harmonious order" (83). His control over members of the inferior species is merely an extension of his absolute self-control. Other minds are as transparent to him as he is transparent to himself.

And this aspiring demigod is a ruthless killer. He attains his full spiritual maturity at the moment he commits his first (but not last) murder, killing the friendly policeman who interrupts the robbery John carries out in order to amass the fortune necessary to free himself from the hateful yoke of the "cattle." The murder is not done in a flash of anger or desperation but with a complete clearheadedness, with a liberating realization that "what must be, must be." The newly awakened, expanded self is free of atavistic guilt: "of remorse or shame it felt -nothing" (41). And this is only the beginning, for later John kills again, in cold blood and with the full approval of the implied author. These murders do not breed guilt because John sees himself and his fellow superiors as the only human beings on the planet. Morality does not carry across the interspecies gulf; as he explains to the narrator, "and just because I was really human, and had in me the possibility of some new and transcendent spiritual achievement, I was more important than all the rest of the sixteen hundred million put together" (86). This sense of biological difference explains John's perception of sex with humans as something inherently disgusting, poisoned "by the sense that this contact was with a brute, with something that could never satisfy his deeper needs, and might debase him" (63). His unconsummated affair with a beautiful woman suitably named Europa bears an uncanny resemblance to the scene in *Schindler's List* in which the commandant of Plazow concentration camp, Goetz, refrains from raping his Jewish maid because she is not "a human being in the full sense of the word."

John's spiritual superiority involves an experience of the sublime, an opening-up of the soul to Nature's infinity and might and a full identification with its irresistible power. It is "a sense of being the chosen instrument of Fate, of the Dialectic, of what might almost as well be called God" (75). He tries to explain this sense to his human slave (and the narrator of the tale) by comparing it to the mass movements that agitate the world at the time of the writing of the novel: the "hate that smashed the Tsar, and turned creative, and made Russia" (76) or the "revulsion from . . . rationality" in Germany and Italy, which, despite its numerous faults, is still a worthy expression of the "bewildered hunger of the soul" (77).

It is almost impossible to read this chilling portrayal of the New Man today without seeing its author as a fascist. But he was not; and neither were many other radical intellectuals who, in the period between the two world wars, longed for an apocalyptic transformation of human subjectivity, whose goal was sketched by Martin Heidegger: "What Nietzsche already knew metaphysically now becomes clear: that in its absolute form the modern 'machine economy' . . . demands a new kind of man who surpasses man as he has been hitherto" (quoted in Ashheim 268). Still unborn, the New Man is an object of worship, a new baby in the manger, but also the focus of narcissistic self-identification for those who see themselves as his forefathers: "Framed by swastika flags . . . is a statue. It is a man eight feet high, powerful, muscular, saluting with raised right arm; his left hand is clenched against his thigh. He is the typical 'Aryan.' 'Homo germanicus'—the new god in whose image the German admires and loves himself" (from "Fuhrers of the Future," an eyewitness report published in the *Manchester Guardian* in November 1937, quoted in Burleigh and Whippermann 236).

The New Man is an alternative to the other selves of Western culture: the Cartesian self, the nineteenth-century psychological self, and the Freudian self. All these selves are marked by inner division, the duality, multiplicity, or ambiguity of subjectivity. Dorian Gray wonders at "the shallow psychology of those who conceive the Ego in man as a thing simple, permanent, reliable, and of one essence" (Wilde 157). The soldier comes to enlighten the aesthete. The psychology of the people Klaus Theweleit called "the soldier males" is marked precisely by being "of one essence." The New Man is a dangerous dream of healing the wound of separation between body and mind, public and private, individual and collective, consciousness and desire. He discards

Cartesian duality in favor of impossible unity, "the perfect seamlessness between the natural body and the individual self . . . [the] denial of castration, loss, division" (Boscaglia 5). He rejects fragmentation and loss as the necessary foundation of selfhood. Such phantasmagoric unification of subjectivity is achieved by identification with what Des Pres calls "terror's own power." The New Man sees himself as a reflection of the suprahuman force of Nature (in Nazism) or history (in Stalinism). Their violence that sweeps aside all merely human obstacles becomes a model for the sublime self that transcends the law of "loss and division."

I will briefly examine the role of violence in relation to three aspects of the New Man: the connection between the individual body and the body politic; the politics of disgust; and self-worship. In all three aspects the New Man asserts himself in opposition to the liberal subject of democracy. Their clash becomes, therefore, the necessary conflict between two modalities of the self, two images of humanity, two species.

New Bodies for Old

Book Five of Plato's *The Republic* opens with this statement: "Such is the good and true city-state, and the good and true man is of the same pattern; and if this is right every other is wrong; and the evil is one which affects not only the ordering of the State, but also the regulation of the individual soul . . ." (167).

What is suggested here is the equivalence of individual and community: the harmonious order of the subject can be transposed, with no structural change, onto the body politic and vice versa. The "good and true man" is a hologram of the State and the State is "the good and true man" writ large.

In terms of utopia's self-consciousness, if not actual social policies, Plato is indeed the forefather of the modern ideal state. H. G. Wells, in *A Modern Utopia* (1905), acknowledges "Plato's profound intuitions" as the foundation for the contemporary radical projects of social regeneration (259). And what modern utopias, both left- and right-wing, inherit from Plato is, above all, the metaphor of the organic body politic, which Paul Johnston in his novel *Body Politic* reduces to its simplest form: "The ordinary citizens were the body of the city-state, while the guardians were its heart and brain and the auxiliaries its eyes and ears" (29).

In Wells's *A Modern Utopia* the living body politic is composed of four classes whose functions are described in terms of organic differentiation rather than division of labor: "The former two [classes] are supposed to constitute the living tissue of the State; the latter are the fulcra and resistances, the bone and cover of its body" (265–66). In Wells's later utopia, *The Shape of*

Things to Come (1932), the body politic becomes a monstrous superorganism, a polyplike entity subsuming the lives of its individual members:

> The body of mankind is now one single organism of nearly two thousand five hundred million persons, and the individual differences of every one of these persons is like an exploring tentacle thrust out to test and learn, to savour life in its fullness and bring in new experiences for the common stock. We are all members of the same body . . . more and more plain does it become to us that it is not our little selves but Man the Undying that achieves these things through us. (445–46)

The utopian minisociety of *Odd John* is not an association of individuals but an organic body, whose components are linked together by telepathy. The idea of an almost mystical unity between the individual and the collective is a common thread in all discourses of the New Man. In science fiction it takes the form of telepathic communion that, as Stapledon imagines in another work, *Star Maker,* will lead to the creation of a galactic supermind. The connection between the New Man and telepathy is fully elaborated in a later text, Theodore Sturgeon's *More Than Human* (1953), which depicts the advent of *Homo gestalt,* a telepathic entity with a single personality composed of several independent individuals.

The potent metaphor of social gestalt is ancient and deeply ingrained in Western culture. But it was given a new lease on life by the development of the fin de siècle bio-ideologies: Social Darwinism, eugenics, and scientific racism. Already in 1872 Winwood Reade coined the notion of the "One Man," the immortal subject of history, whose deathless body subsumes pain and suffering of individual cells in its ceaseless ascent to perfection: "As the atoms are to the human unit, so the human units are to the human whole. There is only One Man upon the earth; what we call men are not individuals, but components; what we call death is merely the bursting of a cell; wars and epidemics are merely inflammatory phenomena incident to certain stages of growth" (521).

This organic metaphor becomes central to the utopian socialism of the nineteenth and early-twentieth centuries. Here, for example, is Sidney Webb's contribution to *Fabian Essays*: "though the social organism has itself evolved from the union of individual men, the individual is now created of the social organism of which it forms a part: his life is born of the larger life; his attributes are moulded by the social pressure; his activities, inextricably interwoven with others, belong to the activity of the whole" (in Shaw 1889, 89).

Hitler in *Mein Kampf* offers his own version of the organic body politic: "the state is a national organism and not an economic organization. . . . [It is] the organization of a community of physically and psychologically similar living beings for the better facilitation of the maintenance of their species and the achievement of the aim which has been allotted to this species by Providence" (150–51). Webb, Wells, and Hitler make strange bedfellows. And yet the three of them articulate their disparate political visions in terms of the same organic metaphor: society as a vast living body and individuals as subordinate cells. As a Nazi ideologue, E. Gunter Grundel, succinctly put it, the New Man "does not live for himself but as an integral part of a living whole" (in Griffin 128).

This imaginary body is more than a fanciful way to describe social interdependence. The organic metaphor presupposes that the value and viability of a part derives from the greater life of the whole. The importance of the individual is purely functional, depending only on his or her "cellular" contribution to the political physiology of the "common stock." Within the stupendous body of "Man the Undying," individual differences are as unimportant as minute distinctions in the composition of single cells within the body of a human being.

But when a cell turns cancerous, it may endanger the whole organism. A malignant growth in the body politic has to be destroyed, and so the legal discourse of rights and obligations becomes supplanted by the medical discourse of health and sickness. The history of the uses to which the organic metaphor was put in justifying political persecution and genocide would make grim reading. Hitler's endless references to Jewish "vermin," "pestilence," and "parasites" express a coherent bio-ideological weltanschauung, deeply entrenched in Western culture and couched in the language of science. Hitler is quite unoriginal in his views; his only distinguishing characteristic is extreme literal mindedness, for what others see as quivering on the border of the figurative, Hitler straightforwardly translates into practical solutions. Webb may vaguely talk about ensuring "the sound health" of the social body, but Hitler and his cohort of health providers know exactly what it involved in such surgical intervention. Asked how he, a doctor, could participate in mass murder, Auschwitz physician Fritz Klein replied: "I am a doctor and I want to preserve life. And out of respect for human life, I would remove a gangrenous appendix from a diseased body. The Jew is a gangrenous appendix in the body of mankind" (quoted in Lifton 16).

Medicalization of politics not only justifies political violence but also protects the New Man from empathy. No matter how many die, the true subject of ideology is immune to the horror of self-identification with the victim's suffering body that destroys the subject of torture because he (the subject of ideology) possesses the sublime body modeled on the "national organism" itself. As each cell contains the DNA blueprint of the entire organism, each New Man mirrors the collective entity. Being immortal, he cannot see his own death in the deaths of others. O'Brien in *1984* succinctly describes how identification with the body politic becomes a shield against mortality: "'You are thinking,' he said [to Smith], 'that my face is old and tired. You are thinking that I talk of power, and yet I am not even able to prevent the decay of my own body. Can you not understand, Winston, that the individual is only a cell? The weariness of the cell is the vigour of the organism. Do you die when you cut your fingernails?'" (212).

But this does not explain why he tortures Smith instead of dispassionately cutting this infected hangnail of the social organism. On the face of it, the medical idiom does not encompass the gratuitous cruelty that was such an integral part of killing disguised as social healing. But it is precisely in this cruelty that the ideological narrative of the organic body politic reveals its covert reliance on the aesthetics of the violent sublime. No amount of verbiage can fully convince a murderer that the child he injects with phenol is "a gangrenous appendix in the body of mankind." The victim's book of blood speaks louder than the little red book of the leader. In order to defuse this residual emotional impact of the violent spectacle, the New Man has to incorporate this spectacle into his self-narrative as "toughening" (Hoess's favorite term) or inoculation. The sight of the enemy's unregenerate body in the state of utter abjection functions as a controlled experience of individual mortality, which is subsumed into the perpetrator's self-aggrandized identification with the collective. Le Guin's abused child has to be seen by all the citizens of Omelas, so that the visual shock will be redirected into strengthening the immortal "we" against this degraded, filthy, individual "I." The organic body politic can only exist through periodic infusions of violence, whose emotional energy reconstructs the phantasmagoric ties that keep this imaginary entity together.

The Politics of Disgust

The organic body politic constitutes a meeting point of different political utopias. Fascists, Nazis, Communists, right- and left-wing radicals of all stripes lay claim to "Man the Undying." This is not to collapse all political distinctions but to indicate the diffusion of a particular cultural construct whose attraction was felt across the political spectrum. Another common feature of all New Man ideologies is a profound disgust with democracy.

Disgust is different from hate. Hate is felt for an equal; and, of course, New Men of different political persuasions heartily hated each other. But their disgust was reserved for democracy, which was consistently perceived in terms of a stable set of metaphors: disease, femininity, chaos, swamp, and rot. The "femininity" of the crowd is a staple of the right-wing political discourse since Le Bon. For Hitler, social democracy is a "pestilential whore" (39), the free press is "scum," and the elected parliament is a "monstrosity of excrement and 'fire,' in which . . . the 'fire' seems to me at the moment to be burned out" (78). This scatological imagery is perfectly complemented by the notion of the crowd as a "woman" who has to be wooed by the strong-willed and clean-bodied suitor. Thus, the crowd becomes the antithesis of the organic body politic, a woman to its man. Theweleit describes the equation of the proletarian mass and woman in the right-wing *Freikorps* political vocabulary: "the mass may be variously encoded—with femininity, with the bestial, with dissipating contagious lust . . ." (Theweleit 2, 27).

However, precisely the same configuration is at work in some left-wing radical discourses. In *Man and Superman* (1903) George Bernard Shaw unleashes the full force of his contempt on what he calls "our political experiment of democracy, the last refuge of cheap misgovernment, [that] will ruin us if our citizens are ill-bred" (22). Democracy is a chaotic magma of inferior individuals, the "promiscuously bred masses" (23) that threaten to engulf the proudly erect New Man. As the only bulwark against this uncontrollable chaos, Shaw offers "a democracy of Supermen" (228). As late as 1947, in his last postscript to *Fabian Essays,* first published in 1889, Shaw repeats the same sentiments: "Fabianism thus becomes *Democratic Aristocracy* in strong opposition to *Underdog Authority or Government by the Unfittest,* which is the bugbear of the cultured classes today" (304). Shaw's explicit sexual agenda in *Man and Superman* seems very different from the Nazis' brutal misogyny. However, his vision of woman's social role is framed by eugenicist discourse, whose underlying assumptions echo the bio-ideologies of Nazism and its precursors. The politics of the metaphor are more insidious—and I would argue, more decisive—than the politics of the content.[3]

In H. G. Wells's 1927 Sorbonne speech "Democracy under Revision," democracy is represented as enfeebling: "Our modern democratic governments reveal as clearly that the onset of Modern Democracy did not mean a transfer of power from the few to the many, but a disappearance of power from the world" (36). In *The Shape of Things to Come* (1932), that many-headed hydra, the "Voter, the Mass, which was neither educated nor led" (130), is blamed for the collapse of European civilization, and even the future emasculation of the Soviet Union is confidently predicted due to the "ineradicable democratic taint of the Soviet system" (141).[4] Democracy is seen not merely as an inadequate or outdated political system but as a symbolic threat. Democracy is multiplicity to the New Man's hard-won unity; randomness to his control; pliancy to his hardness; indecision to his will. The femininity of democracy links the chaos of desire with the chaos of history.

In *The Shape of Things to Come* women are excluded from history. The one time when a woman plays a significant role in Wells's headlong rush into utopia, it is only to spoil it. When women appear to meddle in history, "we find the threads of human destiny running askew about a story of passionate love and passionate misbehaviour" (351). "Human destiny," which is supposed to progress inexorably toward the advent of the New Man, is derailed, loosened up, hopelessly tangled by women and desire. Like women, democracy is a thread "running askew," prey to chance, contingency, multiplicity, random choice. Democracy is the loss of control, which the New Man fears above all. Democracy by definition is the rule of Many, while the New Man is One. And in a complex chaotic system all clear-cut goals and definitions are blurred, approximate, adventitious. For the New Man control is the raison d'être of his being, the steely armor that keeps his phallic plenitude from shameful detumescence. And control means absolute certainty. After all, is it not clear "that there can be only one right way of looking at the world for a normal human being and only one conception of a proper scheme of social reactions, and that all others must be wrong and misleading and involve destructive distortions of conduct?" (364)? Women and other democrats, however, seem unable to grasp this simple truth: they insist on dredging up uncertainties, qualifications, unexpected complications, last-minute surprises.

The New Man's disgust with democracy is his disguised fear of history. For the Nazi New Man, as opposed to his Soviet counterpart, the contingency of history is epitomized by one single enemy, the Jew. In *Mein Kampf* the Jew is a universal solvent of all certainties, a shape-shifter, "a jelly-like slime which [is] divided up and poured through your fingers, but in the next moment collected again" (62). Jews are nowhere and everywhere, they are an annoying exception, a rebellious Particular that resists being assimilated to the truth of the General. Even for Wells who abhors Hitler's crude racism, Jews play the same role. When all ethnic particularity disappears in the "one body" of the Modern State, it is the disappearance of the Jews that is dwelled upon in great detail for the Jewish difference is Difference as such, a "willful separation from the main body of mankind" (1932, 398). The Jews stand for the stubbornness of variation and its disobedience to uniformity. The Jews become what Lyotard calls "the jews" to distinguish them from the real people: "'the jews' are within the 'spirit' of the Occident that is so preoccupied with foundational thinking, what resists this spirit; within its will, the will to want, what gets in the way of its will; within its accomplishments, projects, and progress, what never ceases to reopen the wound of the unaccomplished" (1988, 22).

Women, Jews, and democracy are different faces of the New Man's greatest enemy: contingency. In Odd John's contempt for the human "cattle" there is a hidden fear: what if he and the other superhumans are nothing more than a chance freak of development and not an inexorable advance of evolution?

What if there are no inexorable advances anywhere? What, in fact, if evolution is what Darwin says it is: a stochastic process of local adaptations, ruled by no overarching Law, and going in no particular direction? What if the narrative of history has no closure? The contempt for democracy is the New Man's horror at his own shaky ideological foundation, constantly threatened by the specter of chance, variability, and historical indeterminacy, just as his precariously unified psyche is threatened by the desire within and the femininity without.

To ward off the filth of democracy, one needs to be always clean. Dr. Mengele, whom I shall discuss in detail in the next chapter, was nicknamed "Mr. Clean" by Auschwitz inmates. Unlike other doctors and guards, often sloppily drunk and cracking up under the strain of killing, this model New Man was always immaculately dressed and aftershave-scented as he went to perform selections for the gas chambers. Purity is the New Man's obsession: purity in all its meanings, from the most innocuously literal (cold showers and "rational" clothing) to the most ominously metaphorical (cleansing the collective body from human vermin and parasites). The sliding from personal to racial hygiene is perfectly outlined in *The Shape of Things to Come.* First the New Puritans (the Air Control, the technocratic dictatorship of the future) "disinfect" all dwellings, get rid of those architectural excesses and ornaments Alfred Loos called "excrement" and leave behind "white bare streets" (376). Then they declare physical unfitness to be a crime. Then they institute a far reaching censorship over all books of the past, those "fever rags" (375), which spread the contagion of romance and critical thought. Then they outlaw all hedonism, all unconventional sexuality, all pleasure. And thus they achieve their goal: "to cleanse the human mind for good and all" (376).

The rhetoric of cleanliness reaches its peak in Nazism. Nazi portrayal of heroism is obsessed by "purity faced with putrefaction" (Friedlander 1986, 7). Putrefaction is caused by the presence of the Jewish infection within the national body. The infamous shot of plague-bearing rats interspersed with Jewish faces in the propaganda film *The Eternal Jew* clearly demonstrates the implosion of personal, social, and racial hygiene into a single lethal complex. Genocide, then, becomes a medical procedure, slaughter is equated with delousing and fumigation, and Auschwitz is nicknamed "Anus mundi" through which the emergent body of the "One Man" is purged.

What distinguishes the New Man's drive for purity is its total character. Everything must be scoured into transparency: minds (brainwashing), dwellings, bodies, and nations. There is no difference between dusty floors, polluted water, wrong thinking, miscegenation, and social turmoil. All are symptoms of the one underlying cause. For the New Man dirt is the foundational category of his metaphysics. Cristoph Steding, the author of *The Reich and the Sickness of Europe,* a book much admired by Heydrich and Himmler, talks about the "decay" of Europe and the infection of Jewry which leads to corruption of the body politic. And then he adds: "Thus the enemy today stands right in the heart of Europe, as he threatens to arise in the heart of every European" (in Griffin 153). The sickness of the collective body is identical to the sickness of the individual; the pollution of the community is the pollution of the body and vice versa. Theweleit compellingly analyzes how, for the "soldier male," the foul enemy stands for his own abhorred bodily and psychic interior, the streams of semen and blood, the flow of desire. The New Man is at war with the materiality of his own body that challenges his control, with everything unclear, ambiguous, untidy, secretive, and unique. Dirt, after all, is simply matter out of place. The New Man attempts to subdue his body, tidy up his psyche, regulate society. As a result, the quantity of waste grows at an alarming rate, for everything that does not fit into the scheme—both within and without—is relegated to what Stalin was fond of calling "the garbage-heap of history." The more one strives to keep clean, the greater is the pile of filth to dispose of. Finally, history itself becomes excrement.

However, in his quest for purity, the New Man is bound to splatter himself with gore. And the attraction of physical violence lies precisely in this: in the process of cleansing, one is allowed to wallow in filth. The soldier's fantasy of the immaculate fighting-machine corporeality results, as Theweleit demonstrates, in the orgasmic addiction to bloodshed. The grotesquerie of violence is the obverse side of the minimalist aesthetic of purification and control. But the self-narrative of the utopian subject cannot admit this grotesquerie without metamorphosing into horror. And thus the ellipsis of the violent sublime, so prominent in Hoess's and Linde's stories, comes into being on the grander scale of universal utopia. In *The Shape of Things to Come,* as the Air Control begins its drive to "cleanse the human mind" by killing a Catholic priest, the narrative abruptly breaks off, to resume after "seventy or eighty years," when the resistance is subdued. The textual gap swallows up the human litter, which must be swept out of the way if purity is to be achieved.

Worship of the Self

The anonymous newspaper report, quoted above, on the "Fuhrers of the future," describes the New Man as "the typical 'Aryan,' 'Homo germanicus'—the new god in whose image the German admires and loves himself." The object of the New Man's worship is that ideal—and unattainable—sublime self, which he glimpses only in the ecstasy of slaughter. Theweleit's soldier males of the *Freikorps* perceived themselves as the Supermen cast in the Nietzschean mold (see Ashheim 159). And their counterparts, scientists and physicians who run concentration camp laboratories and eugenicist programs, "saw themselves as 'children of the gods,' empowered to destroy and kill on behalf of their higher calling, as men who claimed 'spurious attributes of divinity'" (Lifton 449).

Violence is sublime, and sublimity holds the key to that ecstatic disintegration that Theweleit describes as the libidinal goal of the fascist New Man: "Only in the act of killing or dying—penetration or explosion—can he [the soldier male] burst his boundaries. . . . There must be a rush of blood, either within him or out of the other" (Theweleit 2, 185).

However, this disintegration is only the first step toward the final goal, which—however unattainable—is a total integration of the psyche. The sublime experience of violence explodes the old, self-divided, liberal democratic subject. And then ideology is used as the glue to assemble out of its shreds the "man of steel." This is what Himmler demands from the SS in his infamous Posen speech: to have seen "100 corpses together, or 500, or 1000" and yet to come out of this self-shattering experience with "no harm in our essence, in our soul, in our character" (in Remak 159–60).

The unification of the New Man's sublime subjectivity is assured by his identification with either Nature or History. For the Nazi New Man, spirituality consists in being what Lifton calls "nature's engine." And since Nature, for reasons that will be discussed in the next chapter, is perceived as cruel, the New Man's violence is part of the natural order itself. Shaw in *Man and Superman* articulates the desire to become the sublime, absolute, and irrevocable Power, which is above mere human contrivances: "This is the true joy in life, the being used for a purpose recognized by yourself as a mighty one; the being a force of Nature instead of a feverish selfish little clod of ailments and grievances" (32).

This "being a force of Nature" is what the New Man's spirituality is all about. The god he worships is his ideal self, whether called *Homo germanicus, Homo sovieticus,* or simply *Homo superior.* And this worship allows him to indulge in radical transgression, while having all his sins not just forgiven but magically transmuted into virtues. The New Man's spirituality offers him the ecstasy of self-annihilation and at the same time enables him to reclaim a unified, restored selfhood. He can flow with rivers of blood and remain firm as steel. This phallic plenitude, or what H. G. Wells calls, without a trace of irony, the "happy turgidity" of life, can only be attained by dedicating himself completely, body and soul, to the Idea, for anything else would "leave a man in the end 'deflated, collapsed into an aimless self'" (1932, 268). But dedication alone is not enough; it must be kept up by a constant current of violent excess that engorges the "aimless self." The New Man worships his own sublime body as if it were the Lacanian Phallus made palpable. And this all-body erection requires a steady flow of blood—somebody else's blood. The sublime subject fully exists only in confrontation with the lesser breeds on whom he can practice his technology of violent self-creation. Left in solitude, he is deflated, exposed for the unsteady phantasm that he is. Only by torturing others can "children of the gods" convince themselves of their own divinity.

The New Man was not unopposed. While many science fiction and utopian novels, from *Odd John* to *More Than Human,* depicted the beleaguered *Homo superior* tragically succumbing to the assaults of the lesser breeds, in the immediate aftermath of World War II the popular-culture mutant was likely to become an implacable and dangerous enemy. Philip Dick's story "The Golden Man" (1954), representing the Superman as a cunning beast, was, by the author's own admission, inspired by the "buildings marked SHOWERS but which really weren't" (332). But the text that most forcefully interprets the bloodshed of the mid-twentieth century in terms of the confrontation between two kinds of humanity is George Orwell's *1984.* The subject of heated controversy, appropriated (or rather, misappropriated) by opposite political camps, extolled as prophecy and dismissed as crude propaganda, *1984* is a classic dystopia analyzing the nature of utopian subjectivity. The torture scenes in *1984* represent the defeat of the "last man," Winston Smith, by the New Man, O'Brien. The issue that is being settled between Smith and O'Brien is not political compliance but the nature of humanity. For Smith, humanity resides in the body, in its modest pleasures—sex, a comfortable bed, the taste of good coffee—and its painful vulnerabilities. For O'Brien, however, it is precisely Smith's "human, all too human" body that constitutes the locus of his ideological corruption. Stinking, filthy, diseased, the failing body is a self-evident proof of the failure of the mind: "You are rotting away. . . . What are you? A bag of filth. Now turn round and look into this mirror again. Do you see the thing facing you? That is the last man. If you are human, that is humanity" (219).

Winston Smith is the "last man" not because of his political views—those are an implant of the Party, which still needs a fig leaf of ideological deviance to justify its purges. It is his body that rebels, stubbornly refusing to be incorporated into the "national organism." His dissidence is an organic defect. He is persecuted for what he is, not for what he thinks or does. And in the womb of the Ministry of Love he is truly reborn as a subject of ideology. He is not made to adopt a new ideology; he is given a new selfhood. The motto of the utopian transformation of subjectivity is, as O'Brien says, "Thou art" (205). Smith's degradation fills him with profound disgust for his own sick flesh. But his renunciation of his own physicality is not enough: regeneration comes at the moment when he is made to commit—or at least to envision—an act of violence. When he begs for his lover Julia to be subjected to the rat torture instead of him, the betrayal lies not in his inability to resist the torturer but in his ability to identify with him. At least for a moment, he tastes the intoxication of the New Man's power. And this is the moment of transformation: the last man is no more.

The torture scene in *1984* recurs in contemporary investigative dystopias as a submerged site of trauma, revisited and revised over and over again. But in these texts, written after the collapse of the violent utopia, the outcome is different: the defeat of the subject of ideology by the refurbished subject of discipline, of the New Man by the last man.

PRIVATE INVESTIGATION

While the classic utopias and dystopias contain investigative moments, they are submerged in the preoccupations with the politics of the New Man. *1984,* despite its frame-up of Smith, is not really interested in the minutiae of the police work in Oceania. But in contemporary texts dealing with real or imaginary dystopias, the detective aspect is consistently emphasized. Since the end of the Cold War, the police investigation has become a chief modality of dealing with violence in popular culture. As the subject of discipline emerges from the trauma of the detective's protracted confrontation with the subject of ideology, he applies his criminological tools to the defeated and yet still formidable and poorly understood enemy.

Robert Harris's *Fatherland* and *Archangel,* Donald James's *Monstrum,* and Paul Johnston's *Body Politic* are not the only or even the best investigative dystopias written in the last twenty years. However, they are fairly representative, and their joint analysis is facilitated by the fact that they share the same plot structure. The four novels depict the investigation of a series of murders against the background of a dystopian society broadly modeled upon *1984.* The milieu of Johnston's novel is a future Edinburgh turned into an approximation of Plato's *The Republic* by a movement calling itself "the Enlightenment." Inherited from Adorno, the notion that the Enlightenment is to blame for totalitarianism has been simplified here into a vision of the Enlightenment as a dangerously ambitious project of social engineering, culminating in an oppressive and corrupt society. *Monstrum, Archangel,* and *Fatherland* focus on the two twentieth-century "gods that failed": Stalinist Russia and Nazi Germany. *Archangel* takes place in contemporary Russia, occasionally flashbacking into the heyday of Stalinism; *Monstrum* depicts Russia in the near future, devastated by a civil war and poised on the brink of a new round of totalitarian dictatorship; while *Fatherland*—the most famous investigative dystopia of the 1990s—takes place in an alternative history in which the Third Reich has won World War II.

The obvious difference between these novels and *1984* is their choice of targets. Whether Orwell's specific bête noire was Nazism, the Soviet Union, or even postwar England itself, the enemy was immediate and present (even the resurrection of the Third Reich was not beyond imagination in 1948). The situation is radically different today: both Nazism and Communism are dead, while the Enlightenment was never alive in the first place. As opposed to the classic dystopias, which criticized contemporary ideological trends, investigative dystopias are obsessed with the past and with "what might have been" (the last words of *Fatherland*). While incorporating elements of science fiction, they make no serious attempt at extrapolation. Even the ostensible future of *Monstrum* is a thinly disguised allegory of the past, of the turbulent Russia of the 1920s and 1930s. The name of the nascent dictator, Leonid Koba, gives it away. Koba was the Party alias of Stalin.

The analepsis of the detective story uncovers the violent trauma of the past. By transposing dystopia's preoccupation with ideological violence into a detective story format, the investigative dystopia exposes the traumatic foundation of the postmodern self. The downfall of utopia is made to underwrite a resounding triumph of the mythos of liberal democracy. But precisely this need to repeat the story of the New Man's crime and punishment testifies to the anxiety this story still provokes. As Freud points out, repetition is a neurotic symptom of an unhealed trauma, and the trauma of genocide, reawakened by the events in Bosnia and Rwanda, still haunts the resurrected disciplinary subject.

But as we have seen in the last chapter, the narrative strictures of the classic detective story are incapable of fully containing the delirium of ordinary violence. Still less are they capable of taming the sublime violence of ideological slaughter. The failure of the disciplinary plot to come to terms with the subject of ideology leads to some strange twists and deformations in the narrative shape of the investigative dystopia. But it is precisely through these twists and deformations that the true nature of ideological genocide and its perpetrators may be glimpsed. The investigative dystopia is founded on a paradox: it tries apprehending the history of mass murder with the help of patently inadequate narrative tools, whose very inadequacy is a means to grasp the scope and meaning of the atrocity.

The incongruity between the disciplinary narrative model and the history of genocide begins with the figure of the detective. The detective in the investigative dystopia often seems to have wandered into the wrong book. He is a character out of a Raymond Chandler or Dashiell Hammett novel, a Philip Marlowe lost in the belly of the totalitarian Behemoth. Despite their diverse ethnic origins and ideological commitments, Quintilian Dalrymple of *Body Politic,* Constantin Vadim of *Monstrum,* and Fluke Kelso of *Archangel* are uncannily similar, sharing general moodiness, occasional alcoholic haze, and a sort of untidy sexiness. Xavier March of *Fatherland,* despite strong resemblance to his generic brethren, has an additional dimension I will discuss separately. But in all four novels, the detective explicitly flaunts his generic extraterritoriality. In *Body Politic* a friend reproaches Dalrymple with "doing your Philip Marlowe impersonation" (77), and in *Monstrum,* Vadim, on a date with an American woman, chooses a single malt rather than a familiar vodka for a drink because "who ever heard of Humphrey Bogart drinking vodka?" (252).[5]

Philip Marlow and Humphrey Bogart are not quite Sherlock Holmes and Miss Marple. They belong to the hard-boiled thriller and film noir. Raymond Chandler and Dashiell Hammett infuse the detective story formula with the bleak urban atmosphere of America between the two world wars and exaggerate the classic detective's loneliness into existential alienation. Philip Marlowe wanders the dark crime-infested streets of his hometown like a stranger in a strange land. This psychic dislocation allows him, as Fredric Jameson argues in his essay on Raymond Chandler, to fulfill "the demands of the function of knowledge rather than of the lived experience: through him we are able to see, to know, the society as a whole" (128). And it is precisely the function of the detective in dystopia. Since he is up against "society as a whole," through his cynical, disillusioned but still reliable eyes we can see and know the nature of the criminal regime.

Despite his weaknesses, the detective is fundamentally honest. As Geoffrey Hartman puts it, the hard-boiled sleuth is "the heir to a popular American myth—he is the latest of the uncooptable heroes" (in Most 227). But in dystopia this American myth becomes the focus of political dissidence. The clash between honesty and corruption is rewritten as the confrontation between the subject of discipline and the subject of ideology. The moody private eye, smoking, drunk, or in bed with a woman, resists the pull of the sublime body. His shabby corporeality is so patently at odds with the purity of the New Man that his cooperation with the system is simply out of the question. He is a creature of a different species, acting as the locus of the implied reader's relieved identification with a familiar, less-than-perfect subject in the kingdom of murderous supermen. The detective's petty cynicism acts as a counterweight to the sublimity of mass violence. Instead of being disturbing, his alienation becomes comforting, almost cozy.

But the enhanced role of the detective in the investigative dystopia involves a strange reversal of his generic role. In the classic detective story the detective represents order struggling against the chaos of violence and criminality. In the investigative dystopia he is chaos contesting deadly order. In the classic detective story, as Michael Holquist points out, the detective himself is "the essential metaphor for order" (156). But utopia *is* order—the order of perfection opposing the flux and contingency of history. Confronting it, the subject of discipline paradoxically has to defend disorder. Reluctantly and somewhat uneasily, he takes upon himself the unfamiliar role of representing the contingency of history as opposed to the static perfection of utopia. As Morson puts it: "Whereas utopias describe an escape *from* history, these anti-utopias describe an escape, or attempted escape, *to* history, which is to say, to the world of contingency, conflict and uncertainty" (qtd. in Booker 4).

The initial crime in the investigative dystopia appears as an accident or aberration. The state demands that this inexplicable glitch of violence be mopped up as quickly and as discreetly as possible. In *Body Politic* a guardian haughtily comments that Dalrymple's detective skills are unnecessary: "There has been little call for [forensic] expertise recently"(27). The utopian state promises more than just "law and order"; the security it offers is a shield against chance, randomness, and accident.[6] Utopia's claim to eliminate chance involves what might be called "planned contingency." The Third Reich was simultaneously an efficient bureaucratic machine and a mess of conflicting authorities; paradoxically, it united "a chaos, a rule of lawlessness and anarchy" with striving for perfect order (Neumann xii). Similarly, under Stalin, the very same state that protected its citizens from the vicissitudes of market economy also subjected them to random persecution, so that nobody, no matter how ideologically orthodox, could be assured of escaping the Gulag. Since chance cannot be gotten rid of altogether, it has to be incorporated into the system as one of its elements. Utopia, as Wells points out, is to take shape "in a world of uncertain seasons, sudden catastrophes, antagonistic diseases" (1905, 7). It cannot eradicate contingency, but it can make it part of a quasi-divine—because incomprehensible—overall design. As O'Brien explains in *1984,* the state masters nature by insisting that whatever is, must be.

The detective's function is to uncouple chance and necessity. And thus the investigative dystopia's private eye blindly stumbles through improbable coincidences, tangles in the plot's tortuous twists and turns, and reaches his conclusions by pure luck rather than by logic. In *Archangel* the name of the historian turned detective, *Fluke* Kelso, is a giveaway of his role. He is the lucky chance that upsets the deadly order of the once and future totalitarian society he investigates.

However, by taking upon himself the narrative function alien to his generic origin, the detective already registers the uneasy combination of the disciplinary frame with the ideological subject matter. And the strain becomes even more severe as it gradually turns out that the secret he laboriously uncovers is in no need of investigation at all.

THE OPEN SECRET

In all investigative dystopias the initial violence seems to be a private criminal act. *In Body Politic* and *Monstrum* it is a series of atrocious but seemingly motiveless slayings; in *Fatherland* and in *Archangel* it is the murder of an "old fighter." But it quickly becomes clear that what the detective really confronts is the criminal nature of the regime itself. And since he is aware that the state is guilty of mass violence (though he may underestimate its true scope), the detective discovers not only that the perpetrator is known to him but that he himself is an accessory to the crime he investigates.

The circular nature of the investigation that loops upon itself somewhat resembles the structure of *Oedipus Rex,* which has been called "the first detective story" by David Grossvogel. In his book *Mystery and Its Fictions: From Oedipus to Agatha Christie,* Grossvogel suggests that *Oedipus Rex* is different from the standard detective story because it investigates not a shallow secret but a metaphysical mystery: the mystery of Oedipus's own identity, founded on transgressive violence.

But disregarding the obvious difference of artistic merit, the situation of Xavier March in *Fatherland* is not unlike Oedipus's: he too comes to realize—and to admit—his own culpability. By doubling back upon itself, the cognitive dynamics of the detective story is short circuited. Knowledge can no longer neutralize the horror of murder, since all it discloses is the identity of the regulator and the perpetrator.

After a long and laborious investigation, March comes up with the documentary evidence of the extermination of eleven million European Jews (in Harris's alternative history, triumphant Hitler, still alive in 1964, has had sufficient time to carry out his program). But this evidence, for the preservation of which he eventually sacrifices his own life, tells him nothing he has not known before. During his interrogation by a Gestapo officer, who claims, "I did not know any of this!" March says: "Of course you knew! You knew every time someone made a joke about 'going East,' every time you heard a mother tell her children to behave or they'd go up the chimney. We knew when we moved into their houses, when we took over their property, their jobs. We knew but we did not have the facts. . . . Those [the notes] put flesh on the bones. Put bones where there was just clear air" (311).

The shift from "you" to "we" is significant: March, an SS officer, who spent the war in a U-boat, wearing socks made of the hair of death camp inmates, acknowledges his own guilt. The question is why he has participated in, or at least silently condoned, the genocide. And the answer to this question lies in the "we," of which he is a part; in the repression, evasions, and traumas of the utopian body politic, collectively responsible for the crime of the century.

In discussing the "secret" of the Holocaust, historian Walter Laqueur analyzes a peculiar combination of knowledge and denial that structured public discourse—and not only in Germany—during the war. As Himmler famously put it in his Posen speech: "Among ourselves, we can openly talk about it [the extermination], though we will never speak a word of it in public. . . . This is a page of glory in our history that never has been and never will be written" (in Remak 159). The accumulation of oxymorons—talk/silence, page of glory/blank page—outlines the structure of the *open secret:* knowledge that is held in suspension between acceptance and denial, never quite repressed, but never quite integrated into consciousness either. Himmler enjoined absolute secrecy but, as Laqueur points out, "while he was talking the tape recorders were running" (17).

Open secret is a splinter of memory lodged in the collective psyche but so overgrown with the tissue of lies and evasions that it infiltrates the consciousness only as an occasional phantom pain. In *1984,* Orwell's famous description of doublethink—"to know and not to know, to be conscious of complete truthfulness while telling carefully constructed lies" (31)—perfectly captures its irreducible ambiguity. The secret is open because violence has to be simultaneously hidden and displayed. Himmler's speech, with its lingering relish over the growing number of corpses, tacitly assumes that genocide is both ideologically justified and pleasurable, but while the first could be acknowledged, the second could not, if the Nazi New Man was to retain his self-image as a decent human being. And yet without the dreadful aura of large-scale violence, the New Man would be nothing but a decent—that is, feeble and degenerate—human being. Open secret was a way to have one's cake and to eat it, to indulge in ultimate transgression, while clinging to the ordinary mores of middle-class existence.[7]

Both in the Third Reich and Stalinist Soviet Union, the body in pain was simultaneously displayed and denied. Even those who lived in the vicinity of concentration camps and killing grounds could talk about what they saw only through euphemisms, circumlocutions, and indirect hints. The suffering body was forced into the cultural Imaginary, broken into mute and disjointed flashes of vision, retained as a source of sadistic pleasure and occasional nightmare, but denied the voice that could connect it with the values of morality and ethics that the regime still professed.

Daniel Goldhagen in *Hitler's Willing Executioners* claims that the vast majority of the Germans essentially agreed with what was done during the Final Solution and therefore were not overtly perturbed by the information about the death camps. But this is a simplification, for it disregards the numerous witness accounts of the visceral shock pictures and stories of atrocities could induce. Even the executioners themselves were not immune to nervous breakdowns, while the SS tried to prevent dissemination of too graphic descriptions among the general public. SS-Untersturmfuhrer Max Taubner was tried by a disciplinary court in 1943 for taking "shameless and utterly revolting" pictures of massacres and showing them around (qtd. in Klee 199). And yet at the same time such pictures *were* routinely taken and carefully preserved. Much of the iconography of the Holocaust derives from the perpetrators' own documentary evidence. A peculiar double desire seems to be at work here: to hide what is being done under the veneer of stale euphemisms and at the same time to proudly display it in all its gory nakedness.

The issue of the bystanders in Russia is even more controversial, for while the Germans, at least, were assured that they could never be among the victims, the Russians were not. Stalin's Terror was random and contingent, choosing a new group of victims almost every day, fluctuating with the exigencies of internal and external policy, a power struggle within the NKVD (the secret police) or merely the leader's whim. In 1937 nobody in the Soviet Union could feel immune from arrest, torture, deportation, or execution, since anybody could be declared "an enemy of the people" overnight. It seems that such a situation should have provoked a much greater empathy with the victims but, in fact, apart from sporadic acts of human kindness, there was none. Trying to puzzle out the mystery of a people acquiescing in autogenocide, historian Alan Bullock suggests that "a dual consciousness," generated by the "secrecy" of the camps, was partially responsible (503).

This "dual consciousness" is the double structure of the New Man's self. Drunk on the violent sublime, he nevertheless must preserve the rigid structure of his subjectivity through scrupulous adherence to social codes. Wallowing in blood, he must still be "pure"; and the more blood he spills, the more urgent the need for purity becomes. The atrocity may be seen, but it must not be named. The split between sight and story exemplifies the irreducible schizophrenia of the New Man who, in pursuit of sublime unity, becomes like Oedipus a self-deceiver, divided between the deep knowledge of the "terrible secret" and its superficial denial.

In all investigative dystopias the detective's solution of the murders is merely the articulation of the open secret. The detective's culpability as an accomplice is indicated either directly, as in March's musings on his own military past, or symbolically. Quintilian Dalrymple, the detective of *Body Politic,* uncovers the involvement of the utopian state itself in organ trade and sex slavery. The head of the state's council is his own mother. In this quasi-feminist version of *Oedipus,* the hidden sin is not incest but familial complicity in genocide. In *Monstrum* and *Archangel* the detective's guilt is more confused and indirect. Constantin Vadim, the hero of *Monstrum,* is a decent and upright policeman, but he is tainted by his past association with the Soviet system. Fluke Kelso of *Archangel* is a British historian, eventually forced to acknowledge the Western media's involvement in a plot to "resurrect" Stalin.

In the ordinary whodunit the closure is provided by the discovery of the murderer's identity. But in the investigative dystopia the cognitive satisfaction of the whodunit no longer suffices: there is no cognitive satisfaction in having one's prior knowledge confirmed. Instead the genre offers two potential resolutions, both inadequate and each incompatible with the other. In this very confusion is inscribed the unrepresentable historical trauma of genocide.

The first closure is predicated on the liberal value of openness: the belief that silence breeds monsters and that mere airing of secrets, whether personal or collective, will result in therapeutic catharsis. If "glasnost" may be seen as a social equivalent of "talking cure," all investigative dystopias end with the society on the couch. *Body Politic* and *Monstrum* are fairly optimistic that a cure may be effected: Dalrymple actually decides to stay in The Enlightenment's Edinburgh in order to reform the corrupt community in the name of its original dream. But in *Fatherland* and *Archangel* a far darker view predominates: glasnost is seen as part of the problem rather than the solution.

Once March in *Fatherland* discovers the evidence of the Holocaust, his first impulse is to convey it to the West. With the help of Charlie, his American lover, he arranges for the documents to cross the border, risking his own life in the process. Charlie believes that the facts "change everything. Without them you have nothing, a void. But produce facts—provide names, dates, orders, numbers, times, locations, maps, references, schedules, photographs, diagrams, descriptions—and suddenly that void has geometry, is susceptible to measurement, becomes a solid thing" (292). Once people know what has been done in their name, they will rebel and "this society will fall apart" (ibid.). Charlie articulates the view of the classic detective story, the faith in the omnipotence of reason. Like Sherlock Holmes or Augustus Dupin, she believes violence can be adequately dealt with by logic and language. But when she rhetorically asks whether a society can be built on mass graves, March does not answer, perhaps because he knows it can.

The novel is ambiguous not only about the success of March's scheme—we do not know whether Charlie will indeed cross the border—but also about the value of the information itself. After all, the point of an open secret is not that the people do not know the truth, but that they do not want to know it. When March, tortured in the Gestapo, attempts to tell his interrogator—an erstwhile colleague—about his findings, the interrogator says, "I'm not so sure I want to know about it" (314). There is no guarantee that the German people as a whole—or the Americans, with vested interests in détente with the Third Reich—will feel any different.

In *Archangel* the view is even grimmer. Fluke Kelso, an historian following the trail of Stalin's diaries and finding instead the dictator's reincarnation, eventually discovers that the Western media are complicit in the "red-brown" plot to bring about the restoration of Stalinism in Russia.[8] Instead of risking his life to preserve the historical evidence, as March does, Kelso risks his life to destroy it. He attempts—unsuccessfully—to get rid of Stalin's diary, realizing that the disclosure of the dictator's murderous madness will only serve to attract new disciples to his banner.

The classic detective story could pretend that violence held no attraction, that condemnation followed murder as inevitably as day follows night. The genre banked on its readers' solid bourgeois morality with the assurance that was perhaps slightly tinged with anxiety. Still, the disclosure of the murderer's secret identity was deemed sufficient to rectify the evil of the crime. At some point, March attempts to retreat back into the protective rigidity of the parental genre, to be a detective and nothing more than that: "Was history changed so easily? He wondered. Certainly, it was his experience that secrets were an acid—once spilled, they could eat their way through anything: if a marriage, why not a presidency, why not a state? But talk of history—he shook his head at his own reflection—history was beyond him. Investigators turned suspicion into evidence. He had done that" (294).

March tries to pretend that he is dealing with an ordinary crime and ordinary criminals. Scale should make no difference: "if a marriage . . . why not a state?" If one corpse provokes righteous bourgeois indignation, why not millions? But there is a profound difference between ordinary "rational" murder and genocide, and an even greater difference between the disciplinary criminal and the ideological New Man. Identified with the immortal corporeality of the state, the latter cannot be simply hauled off to jail, because jails—and slaughterhouses—are incorporated into his sublime body. To defeat him, to turn intractable history into a comprehensible and disciplined story, private investigation is not enough. And thus *Fatherland* proposes a more radical closure in the detective's self-sacrifice.

The closure of *Oedipus Rex* is not the revelation of the truth but Oedipus's self-blinding. In this terrible gesture of atonement, transgressive violence is turned back onto the perpetrator. And even though Xavier March is hardly the King of Thebes, in *Fatherland* the same logic of atonement dictates a melodramatic ending. In order to divert his pursuers from Charlie, March drives on the autobahn all the way to Poland, to the site of Auschwitz. There is nothing there anymore: the bodies burnt, the buildings blown up, nothing to show that this is the scene of the greatest crime in history. And this is where March takes his last suicidal stand against the pursuing helicopters of the SS.

March's anagnorisis involves the acknowledgement of his own complicity in genocide as a member of the murderous body politic. But by doing so, he decisively removes *Fatherland* from the terrain of the detective story, still inhabited by *Monstrum* and *Archangel*. The failure of discipline in coming to terms with ideological violence is inscribed in the failure of the detective plot. An altogether different narrative modality, that of sacrifice and atonement, concludes the story of a genocidal utopia. Like the ones who walk away from Omelas, March has to repudiate the violent sublime through action rather than ratiocination.

March's complicity is inscribed not through his psychology, which is shallow to the point of nonexistence, but through his corporeality. A war hero with an unblemished war record, March is, above all, a perfect Aryan. The book stresses his racially pure appearance and his snappy black SS uniform. But the giveaway is his unmanly propensity for studying himself in the mirror. This Imaginary self-identification with the regime's corporeal ideal betrays the secret of March's subjectivity: what seems psychic blankness is in fact the utopian purity of the self, cleansed of memory, conscience, and desire.

But all these things surge back, despite Harris's inability to portray as convincingly as Orwell or Zamayatin does, the rebellion of the fallible human body against the inhuman perfection of utopia. March's transformation begins with a vague sense of unease that eventually returns him not so much to true individuality as to the generic mold of the private eye, a hard-boiled knight of justice. The impetus of his Holocaust investigation is the sense of some mystery buried in his own past, "a vague and growing uneasiness that had happened to coincide with his birthday," prompting him "to seek an answer" (33). March's crime scene is memory: he knows how easy it is "to live your life in ignorance of the past, of your world, yourself" (187). Like Oedipus, he digs into the past to find out what he has known all along, the secret of his origin. But if Oedipus discovers the secret in the particular drama of parricide and incest, March's origin lies in the realm of the general. He has no family, almost no human connections of any kind. Stripping away his Philip Marlowe act, one sees a generic "decent" Nazi, with no distinguishing characteristics, one cell in the organic body politic, which is repudiated by this body when it turns unruly. March is not an individual marked by unique fate but a part sharing the fate—and the guilt—of the whole. He is a New Man investigating himself.

In this aporia of subjectivity, the investigative dystopia confronts its own limits. The crime of ideology is supposed to be exposed and punished by the subject of discipline. But in a truly successful ideological state, where would such a subject come from? Winston Smith, the "last man," is fed by memories of his pre-utopian past, but what happens when such memories are gone? Why would a New Man rebel against his own body politic? The generically mixed nature of the investigative dystopia points precisely to its inability to imagine a successful revolt from within utopia's own narrative structure. Xavier March, a savior in the SS uniform, is such a strange and unsatisfactory character precisely because he is a living ideological paradox. Unlike Smith, he successfully withstands torture; his body is as invulnerable to pain as Himmler wanted his paladins to be. But why would such a sublime body—or a sublimely empty mind—experience any empathy with the subhuman victims, sacrificed on the altars of its own divinity? The novel provides no answer because there is none and quickly dispatches March to die a martyr's death before it becomes necessary for him to arrest himself.

THE SALVATION OF HORROR

But, of course, people did rebel, utopias did fall or were never built in the first place, and the self-narrative of the subject of ideology fizzled out in a rush of consumer goods. With the benefit of historical hindsight, we can see that the violent sublime failed to deliver the promised transfiguration of subjectivity. This has led to the resurfacing of a belief in "human nature," so that all too often the liberal subject of discipline appears as the original Man. Despite all the efforts of postmodernist theory, popular culture is serenely confident that capitalist democracy is the rule and everything else—an aberration. However, in delineating the paradox of sublime violence, popular narratives unwittingly betray the shakiness of this assumption. In their generic twists and inconsistencies, postmodern dystopias disclose the origin of the New Man's fall not in the inherent middle-class morality of all human beings but rather in the inevitable and unresolvable clash between the ideological narrative and the experience of violent excess.

Utopian ideologies thrive on violence and yet cannot totally contain it. The irreducible element of horror creeps in, spoiling the brave new subject, rusting his steely purity, undermining the impossible unity of his self. In chapter 1 I discussed the connection between utopia and horror. But this connection, the lure of the violent sublime, is double-edged: while it accounts for the attraction of such ideologies as Nazism, it simultaneously corrodes the rational and scientific underpinnings of these ideologies, preventing them from stabilizing into a self-sustaining body politic. Once released, the sublime cannot be totally controlled by the secret police or reduced to bureaucratic procedures. The excess of horror unleashed by utopia finally destroys it.

Scenes of torture, mutilation, graphic violence are present in most dystopias. In *Monstrum* a new victim of a serial killer is discovered in the middle of Moscow: "I looked back quickly . . . to the concrete block on which the girl was splayed, her bloodied legs wide. It was a statueless plinth. On the side, in bronze letters of running blood I read the name: JOSEPH STALIN" (104).

In this not overly subtle tableau, the mutilated body is displayed as evidence of the regime's criminality. The cut-up corpses in *Body Politic* serve the same function: to demonstrate the hidden violence seething under the surface of a would-be happy society.

But there is a strange displacement in the scene quoted above, since the girl, lying on the plinth of Stalin's memorial, seems to represent not so much the victims of the regime as the missing body of the dictator himself. The same conflation of the victim's and perpetrator's corporeality is evident in *Fatherland,* in the scene of the autopsy of Josef Buhler, one of the architects of the Final Solution, now an overweight and flabby old man, gutted by the medical examiner's knife. And it reaches its peak in *Archangel,* where the body of Stalin becomes the focus of the plot. The novel opens with a description of Stalin's death, in which the omnipotent General Secretary is reduced to a mass of "rotting," smelly, paralyzed flesh (16). The convolutions of the plot eventually lead Kelso to discover, in the frozen wastes of Siberia, Stalin's posthumous son and heir, his father's reincarnation, a savage, stinking, mad killer. Looking at the "careless self-mutilation" with which he hacks off his hair, Kelso realizes he is face to face with "*Homo Sovieticus,* the Soviet Man" (335, 345).

The dynamics of the open secret buries the bodies of the victims under the pall of euphemisms and understatements. But equally central to utopia is the denial of the stubbornly mortal and imperfect bodies of the perpetrators. Le Guin's filthy suffering child represents not just the hidden victims of utopia but also the obverse side of the Omelas citizens' impossible corporeal perfection. Purity is achieved when death, sickness, and suffering of the perpetrators are projected upon the victims and eliminated together with them.

The crime that founds utopia is not just murder but rather the "disappearing" of the body, in the same sense as political dissidents have been "disappeared" in totalitarian and authoritarian regimes. Immured in the foundations of the utopian state, repressed and ritually sacrificed, the individual body of pain guarantees the collective health of the New Man. The investigative dystopia excavates this missing corpus, in all the ugliness of its putrefaction. The bodies of the victim and the perpetrator are fused into one monstrous whole, and this "monstrum" haunts utopia's antiseptic palace, transforming it into the house of horror.

Murder in utopia is the return of the corporeal repressed. The function of the detective is not to identify the perpetrator but to name the crime. In the kingdom of ideological simulacra, he sees the truth of the naked, vulnerable flesh underneath the New Man's utopian clothes. Even nausea becomes a political gesture: March is too squeamish to watch Buhler's autopsy and Vadim flaunts his sensitive stomach like a badge of decency.

It is in relation to the victim's and the perpetrator's bodies that the investigative dystopia becomes an inverted image of the classic detective story. If the latter hides the body under the layers of narrative, the former strips them away. March's investigation begins with the yellowed photograph—of a Jewish family—that he finds in his apartment. The family name is Weiss—"*White. A blank*" (33). The rest of the book is March's attempt to fill in this blank with the bodies of the victims. He has to "put flesh on the bones, put bones where there was just clear air" (317). Odilo Globocnik, one of the perpetrators of the Final Solution, boasts: "There's nothing there anymore, not even a brick" (317).[9] March (who eventually finds some bricks on the site of Auschwitz) is out to disprove him by providing material evidence. He has to show that what lies behind the euphemism of "evacuation to the East" is murder. As long as the terrible sublimity of genocide resides in the ellipsis of the open secret, the "sublime body" of the New Man is invincible. Once shown for what it is, the horror of the slaughter will corrode the utopian body politic. Disgust at the mounds of rotting corpses will overcome ideological indoctrination; the utopian story will be vanquished by terrible spectacle. At least, this is what March—along with Le Guin—hopes for.

If the ordinary detective begins the investigation with the victim's body, March has to end with it. The novel's ending—with March dying on the site of Auschwitz—can be seen as a symbolic self-sacrifice, in which the detective, unable to unearth the obliterated bodies of the victims, offers his own in their stead. But while his gesture is seen as heroic, in Harris's next novel the idea of "substitute" bodies becomes far more ambiguous. In *Archangel,* when Kelso realizes he has been the dupe of a Stalinist conspiracy, he feels completely impotent to prevent the dictator's resurrection. Western logic is irrelevant to Russia, and the revelation of the atrocities is yesterday's news. The only possibility of resolution is offered by the daughter of Stalin's bodyguard, who is about to shoot the dictator's reincarnation in order to revenge her murdered father. His body—and presumably her own, for she is not likely to survive a public assassination—will be a sacrifice preventing the rebirth of the totalitarian monster. But in the light of the fact that Stalin's Terror was unleashed by the public assassination of Kirov, *Archangel* wisely abstains from a happy ending or any ending whatsoever.

If the body of the victim becomes the focus of the repressed horror of the violent sublime, so does the body of the murderer. The merging of the corporeal identities of victim and violator that I noted in horror occurs in dystopia as well, but in a different way. Since both violence and victimization are collective processes, the body of an individual murderer becomes a scaled-down version of the body politic. Its monstrosity represents the monstrosity of a society built on mass graves.

In *Body Politic* the killer is a young female auxiliary who attempts to end the city-state's involvement in sex slavery and organ trade. The detective Dalrymple at the beginning is tempted to interpret her actions as a romantic rebellion: "In the perfect city, the only way to express free will was to commit murder" (332). However, when he finally meets the beautiful and accomplished Amanda, he recognizes her for a New Woman, a member of what he calls "the superior race" that has conquered Edinburgh (341). Amanda sees herself as fulfilling, rather than undermining, the ideology sustaining "the body politic": "I'm a good auxiliary. I wanted to purge the city of the disease that was afflicting it" (327). She is one of the "ten thousand trained killers" who serve the system (60). Her own body is a symbol of the outwardly beautiful but in fact monstrous body politic created by the Enlightenment. She is attractive but freakish, with six fingers and flexible bones.

Unlike *Body Politic,* whose utopia is imaginary, *Monstrum, Fatherland,* and *Archangel* investigate the historical utopian bodies whose monstrosity requires a postmortem rather than remedial surgery. But there is an interesting difference between *Fatherland* and the other two novels, the difference that reflects the disparate attitudes of the West to the Holocaust and the Gulag. *Monstrum* and *Archangel,* dealing with "exotic" Russian history, vacillate between nature and nurture in explaining the utopian monstrosity. Totalitarianism is intermittently perceived as either a Russian national trait or as the result of a common Western tendency, with the decisive slant to the former. This attitude accounts for a peculiarly smug tone, especially evident in *Monstrum,* for the horrors of an alien culture can only imbue one with a pleasant feeling of one's own superiority. *Monstrum* delivers a scathing critique of the Russian failure to develop a democratic society and to come to terms with the crimes of the past. But its historical analysis is intertwined with the clichés of the "darkness in the Russian personality" and "Russian Gothic" (483). Insofar as the totalitarian state is regarded as a specifically Russian perversion, the central image of the book—that of the "Monstrum"—comes to signify a crippled national, rather than social, body. "Monstrum" is the nickname of the serial killer, who cuts out women's uteri. The word itself is linked to the old peasant practice of killing deformed and brain-damaged babies at birth. "In the good old days," says Vadim's informant, "Mother Russia regularly gave birth to a monstrum in every village in the land" (74). The killer, then, is a Russian native son who savagely turns against the Motherland, and as the convoluted plot develops, the Russian state itself—whether Communist or nationalist—becomes a collective Monstrum, a mutated body politic tearing itself apart. If democracy is "founded deep in human nature" (497), then, perhaps, the Russian inability to have a democratic government is related to some natural deficiency.

However, all such speculations about Russia's "special path," all too common in Russia itself, are undermined by the unexpected denouement. The killer, it turns out, is neither Russian nor a son but an American female physician, ostensibly an observer for the UN, actually a dealer in stolen organs and a violent sociopath. As in Johnston's novel, a trade in body parts comes to signify the cannibalistic nature of the body politic, which acquires a spurious corporeality through the violence done to individual bodies. But unlike *Body Politic,* the violence here is due to an outside influence: while Imogen Shepherd is protected by highly placed Russian officials, she herself is not merely a Western import but a Western caricature, an over-the-top femme fatale. If she symbolizes what many Russian nationalists claim is the true cause of Communist violence, the pernicious influence of Western ideas, it is difficult to reconcile her presence with the image of the Russian monstrum. An attempt to please everybody, to intimate that the monstrous body politic of Stalinism is both a Russian mutation and a Western bastard, leads the novel into incoherence.

Archangel, a far more serious and knowledgeable exploration of Stalinism, eventually falls into the same trap of the "mysterious Russian soul." The final explanation of the genocide is, disappointingly, Stalin's madness. His son is a deranged serial killer, trapping and torturing stray tourists for his private satisfaction. But since the son also exemplifies the *Homo sovieticus,* the novel leaves the reader with the obvious conclusion that the USSR was populated exclusively by violent psychopaths and that the "new" Russia, about to welcome another dictator, is no better.

There are, however, no intimations of madness in *Fatherland.* Surprisingly—and this is an issue I will discuss in greater detail in chapter 6—the Holocaust, despite a flood of pieties regarding its ineffable character, is regarded by popular culture as more easily narrativized than the Gulag. There are many reasons for such different attitudes to Nazi and Soviet genocide. But everything else aside, the Holocaust is a better story than the Gulag. Nazi ideology, with its uncompromising racial division of humanity, follows the familiar plot of science fiction and monster movies. Deeply embedded in the bio-ideologies of the nineteenth century, it is "scientific," logical, and self-consistent. Its image of racial utopia resonates with the long Western tradition of the purified and homogeneous body politic. Its New Man is both Nietzschean Übermensch and comic book Superman. Its sublimity is all the more terrifying—and tempting—because it is framed in a compelling plot.

On the contrary, the ideological narrative which governed Stalinist utopia was ad hoc, provisional, incomplete, glued together only by the personality of the Leader. Revised and rewritten many times, the Communist utopia turned into a hybrid body, in which elements of a homegrown national socialism were incongruously coupled with original Marxism. Barely comprehensible even to the Russians themselves, the story of the Gulag cannot be properly told. The sublimity of genocide is lost in a narrative muddle.

This is why popular narratives fare so much better when confronted with "the Enlightenment" or the Third Reich than with the chimera of Stalinism. This is why Hitler and not Stalin becomes the subject of endless novels, films, scholarly treatises, trying to solve the mystery of his "radical evil." In his mammoth book *Explaining Hitler,* Ron Rosenbaum summarizes more than half a century of grappling with the enigma of the man who has come to represent the evil "that places him beyond even the extreme end of the continuum of human nature" (xvi). Hitler is not an ordinary perpetrator of violence but "something else again entirely" (ibid.). This "something else" is the sublime subject of ideology, the purest (perhaps only?) incarnation of the utopian self, entirely constructed by the logic of its own narrative. What makes *Mein Kampf* such a terrible book to read is that there is no sense of humanity, however twisted, beyond the text. What you see is what you get. In the aftermath of the Holocaust, Hitler has become the eidolon of the aborted New Man, while Stalin is perceived as a magnified serial killer, an omnipotent psychopath.

In *Fatherland* Hitler is precisely that "defining absence" that the Holocaust becomes in narratives of history and posthistory. Alive, but unseen, spoken about in whispers, euphemism, circumlocution, the Fuhrer is the black hole whose gravity warps the narrative space. He is as sublime as the ultimate crime he has perpetrated. The final subject of ideology, he has remade himself in the image of the annihilation he has unleashed.

The novel cannot tackle the Fuhrer. The final defeat of the investigative dystopia is that it ultimately backs off from the confrontation with its murderer. All *Fatherland* offers is the unsatisfactory substitute of March himself, a self-contradictory subject, a hero and a criminal, a New Man and a law-abiding citizen, atoning for his own halfheartedness by a bathetic death.

But not all popular narratives are that cowardly. In the next chapter I will look at another New Man who is second in notoriety only to Hitler himself, Dr. Josef Mengele. As we shall see, he has a whole genre to himself. And within its boundaries, he builds his own utopia of torture and mutilation.

5

Doctor Death: From Moreau to Mengele

> *Servatius declared the accused innocent of charges bearing on his responsibility for the "collection of skeletons, sterilizations, killings by gas, and* similar medical matters," *whereupon Judge Halevi interrupted him: "Dr. Servatius, I assume you made a slip of the tongue when you said that killing by gas was a medical matter." To which Servatius replied: "It was indeed a medical matter, since it was prepared by physicians;* it was a matter of killing, and killing, too, is a medical matter."
>
> —*HANNAH ARENDT,* Eichmann in Jerusalem

THE ORIGIN OF THE SUBLIME SPECIES

The last chapter ended with the New Man's demise. I want to start this one with his birth.

The rationale for this inverted order lies in the taxonomy of the violent subject that frames this book. The dystopias I discussed in the last chapter dramatized the clash between the subject of discipline and the subject of ideology. But the subject of ideology, in fact, appeared in them as a defining absence rather than a definitive presence: the melodramatic but improbable O'Brien; the brooding but invisible Fuhrer; the mad but cunningly elusive Stalin Junior. March, a peculiar hybrid between a disciplined detective and a heroic New Man, is interesting only by virtue of the narrative aporia he incarnates. It almost seems that in order to meet the subject of discipline in his pure form we will have to resurrect dead narratives: the *freicorps* writings, as Klaus Theweleit did so brilliantly in *Male Fantasies,* or the Soviet utopias, which are still waiting for their explorer.

However, my focus is genealogical (in the Foucauldian sense, as the history of the present) rather than archeological. The New Man is still present in postmodern culture in two modalities: as an image of the future and a memory of the past. In the following chapter I will discuss the commemoration of the New Man's atrocities. In this chapter I will analyze the way in which the Nazi Übermensch survives through a scientific—and science-fictional—narrative of transcendence that has its roots in nineteenth-century biology. Despite the trauma of World War II, the New Man has been defeated politically, economically, and ideologically but not narratively. I will trace the career of Doctor Death, the New Man as a force of natural selection, from his appearance in a fin de siècle science fiction novel to his present-day persistence as a stubborn ghost of a past menace and a future threat.

The rhetoric of Nazism and its ideological forerunners and fellow travelers are marked by an explicit, sometimes almost obsessive, emphasis on the body. The physical body becomes a target of massive ideological intervention, as a result of which "a new man will once again emerge in Europe, *half from mutation and half from breeding:* the German man," claims writer Gottfried Benn; "the Revolution which is taking place in Europe is total because it is the revolution of the body," says Drieu La Rochelle.[1]

Martin Heidegger provided a respectable philosophical genealogy for the emerging Übermensch in the writings of Nietzsche and indicated his link to modern science and technology. However, the nature of this link has often been interpreted far too broadly, as in the vague discussions of "instrumental rationality." Of course, the genesis, identity, and evolution of the New Man constitute a complex and intricate tangle of political, cultural, and scientific developments. A comprehensive narrative of his origin would have to include the radicalization of political discourse beginning in the 1890s, the shattering impact of World War I on the generation of the trenches, the changing images of gender. But there is one aspect of the New Man's ideologies that, until recently, was ignored altogether and even now is mostly explored by historians of science rather than by cultural scholars.[2] This is the connection between the New Man and the fin de siècle discourses of biology. Political scientists and historians of ideas recognize the importance of the Darwinian revolution in the genesis of fascism and Nazism. Gotz Aly and his collaborators, for example, claim that Nazism as a whole was an attempt to find "a biological solution to a social problem" (Aly 1). Muller-Hill, Lifton, and Lerner chart the social policies based on what Muller-Hill, a practicing biologist himself, called "a murderous science." However, while meticulously documented, their studies often give little attention to the crucial question of how, exactly, the massive shift in the perception of Nature occasioned by Darwin's theory shaped the utopian subjectivity of the New Man. How were this new body, with its impossible perfection, and this new soul, with its dedication to violence, generated by the sober discourse of science?

Literature is wiser than culture studies. Among the more compelling—and persistent—symbols of Nazism today is Doctor Death, a ruthless surgeon, a monster-maker who indiscriminately destroys and creates life. This icon, often related to the real-life Auschwitz physician Josef Mengele, is found in anguished investigations of the Holocaust, such as Rolf Hochhuth's play *The Deputy* (1964); in meditations on the psychology and philosophy of Nazism, such as Jorge Luis Borges's "Deutsches Requiem"; and in thrillers with Nazi "bad guys," such as Ira Levin's *The Boys from Brazil* (1976).

It is through this figure that I want to investigate the evolution of the New Man. This investigation will eventually focus on two key texts: Lucius Shepard's short story "Mengele" (1986) and H. G. Wells's novel *The Island of Dr. Moreau* (1896). The texts are very similar: Shepard's story, in fact, is a condensed rewriting of its famous predecessor. Both describe the arrival of the first-person narrator in an enclave ruled over by a ruthless and enigmatic surgeon who deliberately inflicts terrible pain upon his experimental subjects. The results of his scientific torture are suffering and malformed monsters who worship their creator as God. Moreau is eventually killed, but the Beast-Folk persist in his cult; Mengele is unharmed. The narrators in both texts succumb, with different degrees of conviction, to the philosophy expounded by Doctor Death. But while the historical origins of Shepard's story are sufficiently explained by its title, the prolepsis of Wells's novel is far more puzzling. What is Doctor Death doing in a novel written fifty years before his appearance on the world stage? And in picking Wells's novel as a model for his own parable of Nazism, is Shepard evading the issue or confronting it?

I will argue that the intertextual continuity between Moreau and Mengele, the continuity apparent in almost every fictional text dealing with the butcher surgeon of Auschwitz, indicates more than just postmodern recycling of plots. It outlines the ideological continuity between Nazism and fin de siècle bio-ideologies reflected in Wells's great novel. The transformation of Dr. Moreau into Dr. Mengele parallels the development of the New Man from an aesthetic possibility to a political goal.

The aesthetics of the New Man are predicated on transformation of atrocity into sublime harmony since all the holocausts of totalitarianism "have always been perpetrated in the name of man as harmonious being, of a New Man without antagonistic tension" (Zizek 5). But the specific articulation of this harmony in Nazism is not simply a refurbished version of the Platonic vision of the subject as the microcosm of the ideal body politic that I have outlined in the last chapter. In addition to his remote Platonic descent, the Nazi New Man has a more immediate ancestor: a cluster of fin de siècle discourses of corporeality and subjectivity. This cluster, composed of the bio-ideologies of Social Darwinism and eugenics, generates what I will call "the biological sublime," a particular modality of the violent sublime that combines the ecstasy of murder with the instrumental rationality of science.

At the core of the biological sublime lies the creation of the New Man through imaginary self-identification with Nature's law of pain and suffering. The biological sublime is based on a deliberate manipulation of the experience of the new order of Nature, revealed by Darwinian theory for the ideological purpose of constructing the selfhood of New Man. Darwinism generated an influx of the sublime into culture. This influx had two aspects, corresponding to Kant's distinction between mathematical and dynamic sublime. By opening up the abyss of deep geological time, Darwinism created that vertiginous effect of infinity, which, for Burke, is the "truest test of the sublime" (87). But within these deep vistas of evolution, nature was suddenly perceived as far from serene. Rather, it was seething with pain, "red in tooth and claw," blindly inflicting suffering and death on innumerable living creatures. This infinite abattoir was the sublime of a different order, evoked by "the irresistibility of nature's might [that] makes us, considered as natural beings, recognize our impotence" (Kant 121). But if for Kant the counterbalance to this impotence is to be sought in the mind's inner resources, for the discourse of Social Darwinism and eugenics, the escape from human helplessness and terror lies in identifying with Nature's sublime might. The eugenic New Man seeks "to take over the functions of nature" (Lifton 17).

One of the Nazi goals was to produce what Hitler called "that supreme good: a race created according to the rules of eugenics" (Burrin 26). But despite some sporadic attempts to breed supermen, Nazi science was not up to the actual creation of a new species. Nor was this its real aim. Rather, what was achieved by Nazi biology was an ideological transformation of the existing subject. Its accomplishment was the new sublime body of the elite living in what Lifton calls "the continuous 'high state'" (474), always tottering on the verge of ecstatic self-dissolution and yet mastering this dissolution by an act of will. The experience of the sublime was domesticated for ideological purposes and "transcendence, like everything else, became biologized" (Lifton 475).

The biological sublime is an attempt to harness the sweeping changes inaugurated by evolutionary biology to a particular modality of subjectivity. Thus, it becomes part of what might be called the "politics of humanity," by analogy with the politics of class or gender. Defining humanity in opposition to various other entities—primarily animals on the one hand and machines on the other—has been one of the central concerns of Western culture since antiquity. In the "General Introduction" to the volume *The Boundaries of Humanity,* Morton Sosna points out that there is a long history of "repeated attempts to reduce the human to a single a priori concept, to uncover linkages between moral and natural orders (or disorders), and to create allegories that legitimize a given culture's most cherished beliefs" (3). But Darwinism has thrown a monkey wrench into all such attempts by proving, with a certainty that could be resisted but not seriously contested, that humans *are* animals. It has substituted a narrative of continuity for the allegories of contrast or opposition.

In the wake of the cultural cataclysm that was *The Origin of Species* (1859), the question of the nature of human subjectivity was raised with a new urgency and couched in a new idiom. It is arguable that both Nietzsche and Freud are Darwin's offspring. Without the metaphor of fossils, of the past shaping the present and persisting in the form of enigmatic traces and calcified clues, there would have been no psychoanalysis. Without the new, and often anguished, questioning of Nature there would have been no Übermensch.

The shattering impact of Darwinism is often mistakenly related to the notion of evolution. But, in fact, there was nothing new in this notion. Charles Darwin had been preceded by Erasmus Darwin, Lamarck, Robert Chamber, and many others who had argued for the mutability of the species. Rather it was Darwin's proposed mechanism of evolution, natural selection, that created the foundation for the "transvaluation of values" and eventually, in a paradoxical backlash, gave birth to the New Man.

Instead of the teleological "ladder of progress" leading up to humanity as the pinnacle of the orderly evolutionary process, natural selection projected an open-ended narrative of accident, randomness, and contingency. Darwinian evolution is neither inherently teleological nor progressive, and its main mechanism, natural selection, is cruel and wasteful. There were few nineteenth-century thinkers, excluding Darwin himself and his disciple, T. H. Huxley, who were willing to face squarely the implications of this concept. Neo-Lamarckism, the misnamed Social Darwinism and eventually eugenics, were ways of avoiding the vertigo of the suddenly contingent world. While many biologists attempted to find ways to reintroduce teleology into evolution, philosophers and ideologues sought to conquer Nature by identifying with it.

The New Man incorporates Darwinism's dizzying denial of essential humanness, while at the same time neutralizing its potentially anarchic emphasis on randomness, heterogeneity, and accident. The language of eugenics denies fragmentation, loss, and separation as the necessary foundation of selfhood. This imaginary plenitude, however, is achieved by going back to the bloody Eden of violent, indifferent, amoral Nature. Holding all oppositions in impossible balance, the sublime biological subject transcends the human condition and aligns himself not with the flawed law of the Symbolic but with the ineffable law of Nature: "The sublime is the anti-social condition of all sociality, the infinitely unrepresentable which spurs us on to yet finer representations, the lawless masculine force which violates yet perpetually renews the feminine enclosure of beauty" (Eagleton 54).

The aesthetic paradox is subsumed in the New Man's seamless subjectivity. Produced by disruptive violence, it is nevertheless fully social; transcending representation, it is caught in a web of images and words; aggressively masculine, it "renews" femininity by raping it. And most importantly, while created by scientific manipulation, it assumes the mantle of "naturalness." The eugenic New Man is a technological monster who claims to be a prelapsarian Adam.

In order to understand how Darwinism becomes implicated in this ideological fantasy, we have to uncover the hidden aesthetics of science, the nexus where rational theories tangle with the irrationality of desire and where representations of Nature are infected with the unrepresentability of violence. In the next sections I will show how the sublime biology of the New Man rests on the foundation of the biological sublime.

The Empire of Doctor Death

"National Socialism is nothing but applied biology," said Rudolf Hess, Hitler's deputy.[3] In Robert Jay Lifton's formulation, the Third Reich was a "biocracy" (17). Lifton, Robert Proctor, Richard Lerner, Bruno Muller-Hill, Gotz Aly, and others have dispelled the image of Nazism as mindless, antiscience, and irrational and have shown that the Nazi revolution was based on what the Nazis "considered sound biology and medicine" (Proctor 7).

Nazi biology was not a specifically German phenomenon. Eugenics was a science with international appeal whose influence on the scientific agenda and the social policies in Europe and the United States was enormous in the decades preceding World War II.[4] The father of the New Man is the eugenic perfect Child: "A perfect Child is the symbol of evolution; he represents the highest Nature has produced up to our time—the hope of Man and of God. We must live for him, sacrifice all for him; shape our lives for his benefit; for in this we shall live for the future welfare of mankind—the goal of Evolution" (Armstrong 116).

Thus writes eugenicist Charles Wickstead Armstrong in his book published in England in 1927, while Hitler in *Mein Kampf,* a couple of years earlier, exhorts his countrymen to sacrifice everything in order to "safeguard the existence and reproduction of our race and our people, the sustenance of our children and the purity of our blood" (214). It is not likely that either of these authors was aware of the existence of the other. But in analyzing ideologies, parallels are more important than straightforward appropriations. Martin Pernick points out that the parallels between eugenicist discourses outside Germany and Nazism "do not depend for their significance on . . . direct links of intellectual ancestry. Rather, the similarities are important because they illuminate how Nazism built upon internationally shared eugenic concepts and images" (167).

Nor would it be possible to draw a clear line between science and pseudoscience in unraveling the spider web of deadly rhetoric that almost strangled Europe. Mario Biagioli argues that the horrors of Nazi concentration camp experiments were "a form of science rather than its aberration" (186). Historically contingent, the boundaries of science are shifting and uncertain: racial hygiene blurs into eugenics that blurs into the legitimate study of heredity; the torture chamber may double as a laboratory; Doctor Death may anxiously work on his postdoctoral project (as Mengele, in fact, did during his service in Auschwitz). It is tempting for contemporary biology to treat Nazism as a tragic accident, an inexplicable swerve from the normal, perfunctorily regretted and easily forgotten. Such a gesture ostensibly preserves the purity of scientific endeavor from the contamination of politics. But history is not a disease that can be warded off by intellectual quarantine. And the history of Nazi ideology amply demonstrates the link between evolutionary science and genocide.

Eugenics, the science of human breeding, had two aspects, positive and negative , the first attempting to increase what it saw as the genetically superior part of the population, the second to eliminate the "unfit." The latter included both social rejects and inferior races: in accordance with its profoundly deterministic, hereditary view of human nature, eugenics regarded any kind of social deviance (including simple poverty) as a biological flaw. In official proclamations of eugenicists, positive eugenics was seen as paramount, while negative eugenics, whether in the shape of sterilization or extermination (which was being advocated as early as 1900), was often apologetically shrugged off as a regrettable necessity.[5] However, in the actual policy of Nazi Germany the goals were reversed: while there were some halfhearted attempts to increase fertility and stimulate the reproduction of "true Aryans," all of the state's power became invested in the projects of negative eugenics, first as the euthanasia program and then as *die Endlösung*.

The death camp and the medical experiments performed there constitute one of the most horrifying chapters in what Steven Bruhm calls "the history of pain." As I have argued above, pain, whether experienced or witnessed, "materializes" the body. Narrativized, pain becomes a "culturally mediated experience through which authors and characters come to 'know,' in some sense, their own bodies" (Bruhm xx). But the medical torture practiced by the Nazi physicians went beyond the knowledge of the body; it became a ritualized praxis of self-transformation.

There is something so chilling in the mere catalogue of the senseless but meticulously documented surgeries, mutilations, and baroque executions performed in Mengele's laboratory that one can understand Rolf Hochhuth's image of him as "His Satanic Majesty." In his play *The Deputy,* the evil of Nazism is represented by the sinister Doctor, explicitly modeled upon Mengele. In his notes to the play, Hochhuth seriously claims for the Doctor a superhuman, demonic status: Mengele has "the stature of Absolute Evil, far more unequivocally . . . than Hitler" (31–32). Hochhuth is taken to task by various critics for regarding a murderer as a supernatural force of evil. However, are the alternative labels "gangster" or "thug" any more illuminating?[6] Despite Bertold Brecht's attempt to cut the Nazi Übermenschen down to size by treating them as criminals, it seems impossible to relate to "the Angel of Death from Auschwitz" as if he were mere flesh and blood. Robert Lifton attempts to juxtapose the "real" Mengele—son, husband, and father, a good-looking scion of a Bavarian family that made their money by producing agricultural tools—with the Doctor Death of the legend. But he has to admit that many Auschwitz inmates who knew the real man all too well also perceived him as "a nonhuman evil force" (345). In order to account for his aura, Lifton suggests that Mengele was an incarnation of the ideology that built Auschwitz; that his harmony with this factory of pain "rendered him unique into himself, *sui generis*" and at the same time representative of Nazism as such (346). There is, in other words, no hidden human truth to be discovered by dissociating Dr. Josef Mengele from Doctor Death: the two are the same.

The source of Mengele's fascination is the combination of limitless cruelty and scientific rationality. As opposed to the serial killers I discussed in chapter 2, his selfhood was not ruined by the raw impact of the violent sublime. Mengele never suffered as much as a nervous breakdown; for thirty years after the war he remained steadfast in his convictions. Ted Bundy, stammering through broken self-explanations, is a monster. Mengele, clean-shaven and industrious, cheerfully filling cardboard boxes with human eyes to be sent to his scientific patron in Berlin, is a dark angel, if not a dark God. In the words of a prison doctor who knew him well, Mengele indeed "wanted to be a God—to create a new race" (qtd. in Lifton 359).

This self-divinity is sought not simply in the brute power of knife and fist. This is a disciplined, productive transcendence—"to create a new race." But even Mengele himself should have realized that his "experiments," such as injecting brown eyes with a blue dye to create a more "Aryan" appearance, were worthless.[7] The science of the death camp is simultaneously more disciplined than ordinary scientific research—Mengele's inmate assistants were executed for a single mistake in copying anthropometric data and epistemologically futile. It is not a question of morality, such as is ordinarily asked in the discussions of the "limits of science," but of simple utility. Stem cell research might appear morally problematic to some, but there is no question that it works. There was not a single significant discovery coming from

Auschwitz and even the raw data that were collected could have easily been obtained without torture. It seems that Hochhuth is right when he insists that suffering is not a by-product of the Doctor's research but its goal, as his character gleefully proclaims:

> I'm already doing enough
> to perpetuate racially pure humanity.
> I cremate life,
> I create life—
> and always I create suffering. (237)

Pain, not knowledge, was being sought in endlessly repeated and endlessly elaborated rituals of scientific murder. Representations of Mengele emphasize this "sadistic" aspect of Doctor Death: in Shepard's "Mengele," for example, the narrator says: "I had not understood what scientific purpose could have been served by this sort of mutilation" (278). The same production of pain is the dominant feature of Wells's Dr. Moreau. Moreau, ostensibly aiming at the creation of supermen, ends up producing pitiful monsters whose only function is to suffer. It is not a "mistake," as with Frankenstein, who does not realize what an ugly and unfit creature he has made until it is too late. Both Moreau and Mengele *want* to create pain through unnecessary and mutilating surgery.

It is easy to imagine Doctor Death as a B-grade movie's "mad scientist": disheveled hair, jury-rigged electric installations, eyes glazed with lust for power. This image is a great relief. Priest Riccardo in *The Deputy* hopefully asks the Doctor: "Are you only a lunatic?" (247), and Rosalynn Haynes assimilates all murderers with a Ph.D. into the stereotype of the "mad, bad scientist." However, Hochhuth's Doctor does not even deign to answer the priest, while Moreau brushes off the imputations of both madness and evil, eventually managing to convince the novel's narrator that his project is both rational and right. And if we understand the nature of this project, we might be tempted—hopefully, not for long—to assent. For Doctor Death is indeed logical, consistent, and very far from either the confusion of madness or the vaguely sexual pleasures of sadism. He does want to create a "new race," though not with the inadequate tools of test tubes and genetic charts. Technology is limited; but Doctor Death harnesses the power of science as ideology. The sublime subject, the New Man that he wants to create, is himself.

In attempting to come to terms with Mengele's astounding cruelty, Lifton emphasizes the role of ideological investment in the formation of the self: "none of Mengele's behaviours—least of all his capacity to inflict pain and feel nothing for victims—can be understood separately from his involvement in ideology" (377). This is the ideology that utilizes the violent sublime in order to produce a new subject. The anthropological transformation that Nazi "biocracy" strove to achieve was not so much physiological or genetic as psychological. Science, especially the science of biology, was the blueprint for a new psyche rather than for a new body. Whatever wondrous results eugenicists—and not only in Germany—promised in the future of scientifically regulated breeding, underlying their texts is the utopian urgency of becoming Nature's highest form themselves, here and now.

Eugenics can be seen as a Foucauldian "technology of the self" rather than a technology of reproduction. The Nazi failed "revolution of the body" was a pretext for a revolution of the soul, which used atrocity for purposes of self-transformation according to Nature's plan. The actual breeding of the blond blue-eyed superman was a chimera, but a species of the New Man did come into being in concentration camps:

> believing Nazis saw themselves as "children of the gods," empowered to destroy and kill on behalf of their higher calling, as men who claimed "spurious attributes of divinity." All Nazis staked some claim to this transcendent state, but doctors could buttress their omnipotence with those bizarre and compelling claims made in the name of biology, evolution, and healing. The Auschwitz self could feel itself to be tapping the power source of nature itself in becoming the engine of the Nazi movement, or nature's engine. (Lifton 449)

This "Auschwitz self" includes but transcends what Klaus Theweleit calls the "corporeal ego" of the fascist male: the image of the "man of steel," locked in his invulnerable, rigid, insensitive body armor, "a man with machinelike periphery, whose interior has lost its meaning," a man anesthetized to pain and desire (2, 162). As we shall see, immunity to pain is indeed an important prerequisite of Doctor Death. But it has to be supplemented with an ability to inflict pain on others: not just in the orgasmic violence of the battlefield but channeled into an elaborate, measured, highly structured activity, which builds up the violator's divinity in the exact proportion to the abjection of his victims. Torture becomes both science and art. Foucault's discussion of "*scientia sexualis,*" the transformation of sexuality into a field of knowledge, provides a model for the development of the science of violence, or rather of science *as* violence.

It is important to stress that genocide did have practical goals outside the self-deification of the killers. The ideological complex of "biology, evolution, and healing" involved the physical transformation of the body politic by cleansing it from the Jewish "pestilence" and encouraging the propagation of the biologically superior Aryans. But equally, and inseparably from this physical task, it involved the psychical transformation of the elite into eidolons of divinity. By identifying with Nature, "a doctor playing God" becomes "the embodiment of a larger spiritual principle, the incarnation of a sacred Nazi deity" (Lifton 379). This deity is Nature. Nazism's ideal subjects "owe their higher existence . . . to the knowledge and ruthless application of Nature's stern and rigid laws," says *Mein Kampf* (288).

There is still some unease experienced by many people when they try to reconcile the scientific ideology of Nazism with its delirium of violence. Mindless storm troopers, brutish brownshirts, sadomasochists in black uniforms—all those fit very well with the idea of the Third Reich as a barbarian horde. After the Eichmann trial, however, this was counterbalanced by the image of a vast bureaucratic machine presided over by little paper pushers, some of them in academic gowns. On the one hand, "one could argue that a corrupt and inherently distorted science lent Nazism a specifically 'academic' and 'scientific' character" (Burleigh and Whippermann 56). On the other hand, counters Dominick LaCapra, we should "at least entertain the possibility of a Nazi sublime that, in a fascination for radical transgression, complicated the desire for a 'beautiful' and rational totality that would exclude Jews" (1994, 95). It is precisely because "radical transgression" is seen in inherent opposition to the academic and the scientific that Doctor Death becomes such an enigmatic character. The solution to the enigma lies in the realization that the two are interconnected.

When radical transgression is repressed, the Holocaust perpetrators become dehumanized, depersonalized robots, bureaucrats of genocide, so blinded by "obedience to orders" that they saw no difference between corpses and office circulars. An unfortunate consequence of Hanna Arendt's *Eichmann in Jerusalem,* with its catchphrase "the banality of evil," this view has only recently been challenged by new historical studies. Even Tzvetan Todorov in his recent book *Facing the Extreme,* which attempts to present a more morally nuanced view of the universe of camps, still talks of the perpetrators in terms of "fragmentation" and "instrumental thinking" (177), as if they were somnambulists of murder, killing in a fit of absentmindedness. Obviously, this is the image of themselves the surviving perpetrators are eager to present, since it absolves them of responsibility. But what Todorov reads as the flat effect of psychic fragmentation in Rudolf Hoess's autobiography can also be read as the ecstatic intrusion of the sublime, which cannot be voiced, just as the ecstasy of a mystic cannot be voiced. The mystic appeals to his God to grant him the tongue of fire that can speak the ineffable. At the time Hoess is writing, his god is dead.

It is not as bureaucrats but as "children of the gods" that the Nazi elite saw themselves. Doctor Death is "a god or, at least, a demigod" because "he is master over flesh and spirit, life and death" (Amery 35–36). And this mastery comes not because the torturer cannot empathize with the pain of the tortured but precisely because he can. The victim, recovering from all but unbearable pain, but still alive, can say to himself: "I have experienced the ineffable" (Amery 38). The torturer can say: "I have made another person experience the ineffable on my behalf, I have the power to send a messenger over the border into the kingdom of death and to bring him back, and all with no harm done to myself." The torturer becomes a vampire of transcendence.

Daniel Goldhagen's *Hitler's Willing Executioners* (1997), despite the criticism many historians leveled at it, had the advantage of emphasizing the agency of the perpetrators and arguing that they were not obedient automatons but willing and often eager torturers and murderers. However, Goldhagen's explanation of this eagerness in terms of a specifically "virulent" character of German anti-Semitism suffers from an obvious flaw, which was not pointed out in the heated debates over the book. These debates centered on what was erroneously perceived as Goldhagen's blanket accusation of the German nation as a "mad" people, a nation of serial killers and lust murderers. He replied he was talking about a special character of German culture and not about some immutable biological trait in German blood. But, in fact, the very terms of the debate, ideology or blood lust, nurture or nature, were inadequate to the issue at hand. Even assuming all the Holocaust perpetrators were passionate believers in Nazi ideology, this still does not address the phenomenological quandary of how a sane man could look at a child and see "vermin," a "parasite," shape-shifting alien, or whatever else the Jews were supposed to be. Goldhagen's book fails in penetrating this transition from the "cognitive models" of an ideology to the actual carrying-out of atrocity. He explains how the moral and social prohibitions of murder were undermined by an ideology that offered a new "cognitive scheme." But what about the instinctive reluctance to kill, especially to kill an unarmed defenseless creature at close quarters? That this reluctance existed in full force is testified by the fact that gassing was first tried because shooting took too heavy a psychological toll on the perpetrators.

Ideology was necessary as a narrative model that framed the perpetrators' subjectivity in a socially acceptable way. But at the core of this self-narrative of the decent *Volkish* comrade lay the dark core of the violent sublime. The cognitive frame of scientific racism was the stepping-stone toward the plunge into the ineffableness of mass killing. Nazi science denied the humanity of the victim and yet covertly acknowledged it in its own incredible brutality.

If the torturer did not identify with the corporeality of his victim, there would be no "divinity" in transcending his own weakness. A member of SD Einzatzkommando, Felix Landau, describes in his diary his reactions to shooting naked women and children. He is surprised at his own fortitude; he claims to be "completely unmoved"; he is congratulating himself on his "toughening" into a perfect Party comrade. And yet at the same time his heart "beats faster" when he recalls having been in a similar situation to that of his victims: as a participant in the failed Austrian coup in 1934, he had to face "the machine-gun barrels" of the police. Now he can taste the sweetness of his own survival by vicariously experiencing the fear of his victims: "And here I am today, a survivor, standing in front of others in order to shoot them" (in Klee 96–97).

To sustain this murderous balancing act of identification and disavowal, the violator must perceive himself as justified and supported by a higher power. The heady experience of violence, in which his old self is battered and dissolved, is seen as communion with this power, as emergence into a higher state of being. Ideology supplies the perpetrator with a social narrative that allows him to integrate the high state of murderous exaltation with everyday functioning. The sublimity of violence eats through the old narratives of identity built on ethics and discipline. But at the same time, by "spurring on" the production of new modalities of representation, violence encourages new forms of selfhood that strive for murderous transcendence. Entering the social space, the pain of the victim gives birth to the sublime self of the murderer.

But this is not the inarticulate, socially mute self of the serial killer, whose sublimity is indistinguishable from unintelligibility. Because it is held together by the "skin" of a shared ideological narrative, the sublime self of the subject of ideology ultimately expands to identify with that very symbolic authority that underwrites its violence, be it God, history, or nature. And the more clear, logical, and incontrovertible this narrative appears, the greater its success in engendering such sublime subjects who combine dedication to slaughter with keen social skills.

The bio-ideology of Nazism is far more efficacious in incorporating the violent sublime than the comparatively utopian ideology of Stalinism. The two regimes shared the salient features of the ideal subject I outlined in the last chapter—identification with the body politic, self-worship, and disgust with democracy. However, they differed in the nature of the ultimate symbolic authority that underwrote their violent excesses. Consistent and scientific, Nazi racism could represent the victim as literally, not metaphorically, nonhuman. The Jews were aliens, not enemies, of the people. By reshaping the concept of Nature, Nazism could imbue its adherents with the belief that their violence was part of the natural pattern of existence, while empathy was degenerative and sick. Stalinism, which adulterated the initial Marxism with whatever additions took the leader's fancy at any given moment, could never be as efficient in producing New Men as its rival. Precisely because Stalinism was a piecemeal, "weak" ideological construct, it never reached the heights of

Nazi baroque cruelty, even though it managed, in its own fitful way, to kill off more people. Moreover, the neo-Lamarckian emphasis on "nurture" was deeply ingrained in its master narrative, causing the notorious ban on genetics. Since the dividing line between the victim and the deified murderer could never be drawn with a biological precision, Stalinism did not have its equivalent of Doctor Death.

The Nazi collaboration between ideological rationality and the intoxication of the sublime is perfectly expressed in the infamous slogan at the entrance to Auschwitz, *Arbeit Macht Frei,* "Work makes you free." Often seen as pure cynicism, it was apparently meant by its inventor, Rudolf Hoess, "not as a mockery . . . [or] a false promise that those who worked to exhaustion would eventually be released, but rather as a kind of mystical declaration that self-sacrifice in the form of endless labor does in itself bring a kind of spiritual freedom" (Friedrich 2–3). Hoess was a workaholic himself, and in the mystical identification with his victims, he promised them that their sacrifice would set him free. But this identification has to be constantly checked by the construction and reconstruction of difference, or the murderer will drown in the sublime, emerging from his baptism of blood as a monster rather than the Angel of Death. The mingled horror and intoxication of killing could get out of hand as attested by several documented cases of psychotic breakdowns among members of the *Einzatzgruppen.* So the perpetrators of genocide had to be reassured that their sublime bodies were different from the abject corporeality of the victims. Shaved, tattooed, starved, beaten, dressed in ridiculous uniforms, the victims were made to look as unlike their torturers as possible. Their abjection acted as a foil to the New Man's "impermeable body" (Bruhm 25). Such a body was constructed through the immediate aesthetic contrast with the bleeding, messy, opened-up corporeality of his victims. This contrast was institutionalized in concentration camps. Looking scarcely human, the prisoners set off the neatly uniformed bodies of their masters that seemed to transcend physical wear and tear.

By identifying with the Law of Nature rather than with the merely human law of the Symbolic, Doctor Death positions himself beyond the judgment of words. However—and this is where the irony of Doctor Death's cultural genealogy lies—his vision of Nature as a sublimely cruel force is founded on a culturally specific evolutionary narrative, which, moreover, is open to a very different interpretation from those imposed upon it by the "men of steel."

THE NATURAL HISTORY OF PAIN

Nazi science is not a Nazi invention. There is nothing original or even specifically "German" about Mengele's worldview. What distinguishes him from his British, American, and French colleagues is the single-mindedness with which he and the racist state that he represented transformed the platitudes of eugenics and the utopian mood of the radical intelligentsia into a social fact. Nazi "sacred science" (Lifton 472) originates in what George Bernard Shaw calls "the religion of evolution," the fin de siècle blending of biology and mysticism that took all of Europe by storm (1903, 151). Pernick cogently describes the process whereby "the scientific method [was viewed] as the foundation of a new objectively true religion, in which the laws of nature were truly morally binding 'laws'; not neutral facts but ethical imperatives" (Pernick 98). And like any other religion, this new scientific dispensation had a mystical side, appealing to the desire for transcendence.

In this section we step back from Auschwitz and the historical Mengele to look at their ideological roots. The mold of subjectivity that Mengele filled with such chilling precision had been created long before he drew his first breath, and it persists, now indelibly stamped with his name, after his anonymous death by drowning. In order to understand how the "sacred science" of eugenics produced Doctor Death, we have to understand the two features that distinguished it from ordinary experimental pursuit of knowledge. First, it was indeed based on worship of Nature; second, this was a new post–Darwinian Nature, filled with pain and violence.

The collaboration between science and pursuit of transcendence is described by the famous British biologist J. B. S. Haldane in his 1924 essay "Daedulus" as the "substitution of the doctor for the priest," whereby the "biological invention then tends to begin as a perversion and end as a ritual supported by unquestioned beliefs and prejudices" (49–54). Haldane might have had in mind the views of Ernst Haeckel (1834–1919), Germany's most important Darwinist and the founder of the Monist League, whose ideology "combined an almost mystical, religious belief in the forces of nature (i.e., natural selection as the fundamental law of life) with a literal, if not analogical, transfer of the laws of biology to the social and political arena" (Lerner 24). And just a short time before Haldane's essay, biologist Albert E. Wiggam published in America a best-selling volume, *The New Decalogue of Science,* which disseminated "the biological Golden Rule" and enlisted Jesus on the side of eugenics. Wiggam's rhetoric, while extreme, is by no means atypical:

> Yet the new dispensation is just as divine, as sacred, as inspired as the old. It is filled with warnings of wrath, both present and to come, for the biological ungodly, as well as with alluring promises for them who do His scientific will. These warnings should first make you tremble; they should, secondly, make you pray; they should, thirdly, fill you with the militant faith of a new evangel. (22)

Nature as revealed by science becomes a new gospel, a guide to both private and public conduct. This is the bedrock of eugenics, which propagated its prescriptions for the biological regeneration of humanity with the fervor of prophecy rather than with the calmness of expert opinion, yet at the same time enlisted the authority of knowledge to shield itself from ethical criticism: "The revelation to which I refer . . . is Nature . . . wherever our ethical notions come into conflict with natural law it is our ethics that need correction, not natural law . . ." (Armstrong 99).

Nazism faithfully reproduced this duality of eugenics in its everyday ideological discourse. Martin Bormann, for example, in his secret instructions to the party's district leaders, deflected Christian attacks on Nazi policies by blasting religious superstition and proudly claiming that "National Socialism . . . rests on a scientific foundation." Yet, as he went on to explain, the natural law incarnated in the Third Reich was also invested with sacredness, precluding any blasphemous attempt to try it with the acid of "corrosive" Jewish reasoning: "The power of nature's law . . . is what we call the omnipotent force, or God" (in Remak 103).

By the 1940s, this is a cliché. Already in 1872, Walter Bagehot formulated what later became the main doctrine of Social Darwinism and eugenics: the methods of Nature should be emulated in human society, "what was put forward for mere animal history may, with a change of form but an identical essence, be applied to human history" (43–44). And later on, with the traditional power structures in disarray, the fin de siècle fastens upon the "normative idea of Nature—Nature as a model of human existence" (Stern 48). However, this is Nature that has undergone profound transvaluation as a result of Darwinism.

In 1860 Darwin wrote to Asa Gray:

> I own that I cannot see as plainly as others do, and as I should wish to do, evidence of design and beneficence on all sides of us. There seems to me too much misery in the world. I cannot persuade myself that a beneficent and omnipotent God would have designedly created the Ichneumonidae with the express intention of their feeding within the living bodies of Caterpillars, or that a cat should play with mice. (1993, 124)

The shocking (even to himself) impact of Darwin's words can only be appreciated against the background of natural theology—a trend in early nineteenth-century natural history that attempted to read God's design in the data of science. William Paley's celebrated book *Natural Theology* (1803) summarized its goal: to muster sufficient examples of beneficial adaptation in the natural world to prove, in the words of the later *Bridgewater Treatises,* the

"Power, Wisdom and Goodness of God in the Works of Creation" (qtd. in Bowler 85).

After *The Origin of Species* power and wisdom of sorts are still evidenced by the world, but goodness is in very short supply. Charles Darwin, a reluctant revolutionary, was influenced by natural theology in his youth. He still attempted to interpret the book of nature in terms of purpose and design. But the inescapable conclusion of his own theory seems to be that the only purpose that stands out clearly from the confused scribbling of evolution is infliction of pain. Natural selection works by discarding millions of lives in order to achieve even a minor adaptation, and this winnowing out of the unfit is accompanied by relentless suffering. Paley's famous metaphor for the beautifully designed, harmonious natural order was a watch. In the post–Darwinian world, a rack appears to be a better symbol. Darwin writes in 1856 to Joseph Hooker: "What a book a devil's chaplain might write on the clumsy, wasteful, blundering, low, and horribly cruel works of nature!" (1990, 178). This devil's book, a radical revision of *Natural Theology,* is jointly written by scientists, writers, and ideologues in the second half of the nineteenth century.

In 1888, T. H. Huxley, Wells's teacher at the Normal School of Science, assesses natural theology's "evidences of benevolence" and ironically asks: "But if so, why is it not equally proper to say of the equally numerous arrangements, the no less necessary result of which is the production of pain, that they are evidences of malevolence?" (196). Many fin de siècle intellectuals, especially biologists well versed in the vulnerabilities of the flesh, were inclined to agree. George Romanes, another famous scientist and man of letters, turns the findings of evolutionary theory into an indictment against the creator of nature.

> For in the human mind the sense of right and wrong—with all its accompanying and constituting emotions of love, sympathy, justice, etc—is so important a factor, that however greatly we may imagine the intellectual side of the human mind to be extended, we can scarcely imagine that the moral side could ever become so apparently eclipsed as to end in the authorship of such a world as we find in terrestrial nature. Most of the instances of special design which are relied upon by the natural theologian to prove the intelligent nature of the First Cause, have as their end or object *the infliction of painful death* or the escape from remorseless enemies; and in so far as the argument in favour of the intelligent nature of the First Cause is an argument against its morality . . . it does appear that the scheme [of nature], if it is a scheme, is the product of a Mind which differs from the more highly evolved type of human mind in that it is immensely more intellectual without being nearly so moral. (76–79)

However, the very magnitude of suffering that evolutionary theory uncovers in Nature precludes mere condemnation. Pain on such a scale becomes dazzling, breathtaking, as sublime as the starry sky. Nature, as it emerges from Romanes's writings, may still be "horribly cruel," but it is no longer "clumsy and low."

In this covert admiration for the sheer scale of Nature's brutality lie the seeds of "sacred science." One possible philosophical attitude to Nature that followed from Darwinism was radical dissociation between the natural world and human civilization. This attitude, brilliantly expounded in T. H. Huxley's seminal essay "Evolution and Ethics" (1894), claimed that the greatness of civilization lies in its being unnatural. Evolution cannot provide a guide to social conduct. We prove our humanity by challenging Nature with such artificial inventions as justice, mercy, and compassion. Huxley presciently saw where eugenics was heading and warned in no uncertain terms against the consequences of any human body investing itself with the "natural" authority to winnow out "the unfit." H. G. Wells, Huxley's student, was profoundly influenced by his teacher's views, and this influence is clear in both *The Time Machine* (1895) and *The Island of Dr. Moreau* (1896). But Wells, as his subsequent utopian leanings clearly demonstrate, could not face being suspended in the void of human freedom, with no "symbolic authority" to guide us in the building of a better world. His very long career could be mapped out in terms of the conflict between his Huxleyan pessimism and his own attempts to reconstruct a meaningful nexus between Nature and history that eventually brought him into some unsavory political company. This ambivalence is already felt in *The Island of Dr. Moreau,* as we shall see. However, Wells, a biologist by training, remained constrained by the clear message of Darwinism that evolution is nonteleological. But in order to articulate his own version of "the religion of evolution," George Bernard Shaw had to ditch Darwinism altogether. His long Introduction to *Back to Methuselah* is an astounding argument in favor of neo-Lamarckism on political grounds. If natural selection cannot underwrite utopia, natural selection has to go.

However, most post–Darwinian biologists chose a less radical path of trying to reconcile natural selection with some version of teleology. The scientific details of these fascinating developments, such as theories of orthogenesis, and various combinations of natural selection and some form of in-built evolutionary progressionism (or emphasis on mutations), are beside the point now. What science tried to do was to make Nature, as brutal and uncaring as it is, into a guide for human progress. And science's ideological spin-offs, Social Darwinism and eugenics, magnified this trend by ascribing to Nature's cruelty a positive moral value.

If evolution is seen as teleological and progressive, pain and suffering become ennobled by being tools of evolutionary transcendence. An early example of this attitude, which constitutes the emotional bedrock of Social Darwinism, is Winwood Reade's *The Martyrdom of Man* (1872). The book is a sweeping survey of cosmic and human history as a ceaseless striving for progress governed by "a law which in itself is murderous and cruel" (406):

> But it is when we open the Book of Nature, that book inscribed in blood and tears; it is when we study the laws regulating life, the laws productive of development—that we plainly see how illusive is this theory that God is Love. In all things there is cruel, profligate, and abandoned waste. Of all the animals that are born only a few can survive; and it is owing to this law that development takes place. The law of murder is the law of growth. Life is one long tragedy; creation is one great crime. (519)

Instead of indignation, however, this grim picture of a universal abattoir evokes admiration. Evolution, after all, is one inexorable rise to divinity. From the amoeba to the ape to the "savage" to the European, mankind "is becoming more and more noble, more and more divine, slowly rising towards perfection" (522). The way to see Nature's cruelty as sublime is to shift the focus from the individual body writhing in agony to the collective body of humanity which, by virtue of its sheer enormity, overwhelms the senses and drowns sympathy and pity in the calm contemplation of evolution's irresistible power.

Thus the sublime body of eugenics is born—the body of the collective that subsumes and cancels out the pain of individual members, the body of the race, the "national organism," that needs to be cured and purified—even, and in particular, at the price of its components' suffering. The impervious, immortal body that the New Man wishes to don is constructed through the phantasmagoric self-identification with the "human whole," which, of course, excludes those "cells" deemed cancerous, inferior, diseased.

The post–Darwinian inversion of benevolent natural theology into a gospel of cruelty paves the way for the sacred science of massacre. The chosen few may escape Darwin's universal hecatomb by identifying both with the goal and with the methods of evolution. The sublime of violence is available to any murderer but only as a shattering and mute experience of limits. Incorporated into a political ideology and propped up by the authority of science, however, it becomes a tool of individual and collective transcendence, a dissecting knife wielded with a sense of righteousness by the priest of a new biology-based religion, "conscious of his ghastly mission, and proud of it" (Haldane 93).

THE TWO SURGEONS

In Lucius Shepard's short story "Mengele," the first-person narrator named Phelan crashes his plane in the Amazonian rainforest where he is saved by a scientist who brings him to the enclave populated by misshapen humanoid creatures, the product of the scientist's experiments. Phelan has a long confrontation with the scientist in the course of which the latter explains his motivations. Phelan attempts to kill the Doctor, fails, and ultimately succumbs to his grim philosophy. The scientist is Dr. Josef Mengele.

The plot of the story is identical to the plot of *The Island of Dr. Moreau.* This similarity is not accidental. Striking parallels between Dr. Moreau's vivisection and Nazi concentration camp science have been noted by writers and critics alike. Frank McConnell, for example, sees in Moreau's "chaste sadism . . . the origins of a peculiarly modern institution. The concentration camp is becoming possible" (92).

For McConnell, however, parallels between Moreau's island and Auschwitz are only vaguely conceptualized in terms of "sadism." My emphasis, on the contrary, is on the ideological continuity that accounts for their similarity. Dr. Moreau is one of the first portrayals of the New Man of eugenics who later evolves into the New Man of fascism. Both the island and the camp are factories of pain, manufacturing the sublime body, and neither can be understood outside the ideological rationale for its existence. The cruelty of Moreau and Mengele is not the cause but the effect of their involvement with "a peculiarly modern institution" of ideologically motivated torture.

H. G. Wells's novel is remarkably prescient in its analysis of the interaction between ideology and cruelty. Prendick, the first-person narrator, arrives on Moreau's private island after the shipwreck that has exposed the raw violence people are capable of in extreme situations. What he sees on the island first seems to him to be a continuation of his nightmare of primitive brutality: the misshapen and suffering Beast-Folk and the charnel house of Moreau's laboratory. His response is abhorrence and fear. The pain he witnesses causes him an almost physical distress but at the same time evokes an emotional empathy with the victims of Moreau's vivisection.

But after he meets Moreau and the latter has a chance to expound his philosophy, Prendick undergoes a complete about-face. He is enthralled, confused, and ultimately convinced. Their conversation centers precisely on the issue of pain, Prendick having just witnessed the ghastly spectacle of a cut-up bleeding body stretched on a rack. When Prendick indignantly asks Moreau: "Where is your justification for inflicting all this pain?" the latter gives a double answer, by turns disparaging pain and glorifying it, shifting from sober physiological evaluation to sadomasochistic ecstasy: On the one hand: "Oh,! but it [pain] is such a little thing. A mind truly opened to what science has to teach must see that it is a little thing. . . . Why, even on this earth, even among living things, what pain is there?" (106). On the other hand: "Each time I dip a living creature into the bath of burning pain, I say, This time I will burn out all the animal, this time I will make a rational creature of my own" (112).

Pain is both a "little thing," accidental to the issue at hand, which is the transformation of animals into human beings, and at the same time, the mystical baptismal font, which is to effect this transformation. This is the double-speak of the scientific ideologue combining the striving for rationality with radical transgression. But what is even more unsettling is the effect this has on Prendick. Once the immediate danger to himself is over, he drifts around, passively soaking up Moreau's philosophy. When he was personally threatened, his reaction was defiance, but the more secure he feels, the more he falls under Moreau's spell.

When Prendick looks at Moreau at the close of their conversation, he sees not the madman or the criminal he expected to find but an iconic figure of wisdom, "a white-faced, white-haired man, with calm eyes. Save for his serenity, the touch almost of beauty that resulted from his set tranquility and from his magnificent build, he might have passed muster among a hundred other comfortable old gentlemen" (114). What is striking is the abstractness of this description, as if Prendick saw an ideal incarnated rather than the body of an individual. Similarly, Phelan in Shepard's "Mengele" views Mengele as an embodiment of a general "Mengele principle." And even the historical Mengele was enveloped in the mystique of generality, deliberately cultivating an image of himself as an "abstraction" rather than an individual human being (Lifton 380, quoting testimony of a survivor). In the eyes of those who come under his spell, Doctor Death is seen not as the perishable, irrevocably individual flesh but as the sublime body.

Wells's great novel demonstrates exactly where the divinity of the torturer comes from. Power, even absolute power, is not enough: the sadistic camp guards evoked fear and revulsion but nothing like the equivocal admiration surrounding Doctor Death. What is necessary in order to produce a sublime body is a particular ideological interpretation of the power of violence.

Simply to torture, maim, and murder is only the beginning; one needs a symbolic authority that integrates violence into a comprehensive worldview. One needs a cause. For Moreau, as for all the subsequent New Men, the cause is the renaturalization of society. When Prendick asks Moreau "Why?" the latter replies: "The study of Nature makes a man at last as remorseless as Nature" (106–108). Moreau's project, as he sees it, is based not on Faustian hubris but on obedience to natural law. Later Moreau offers a classic formulation of the precepts of "sacred science": "Then I am a religious man, Prendick, as every sane man must be. It may be, I fancy, I have seen more of the ways of the world's Maker than you—for I have sought His laws, in *my* way, all my life, while you, I understand, have been collecting butterflies . . ." (106).

One of the contemporary reviews of the book saw the author's object as "parody[ing] the work of the Creator of the human race" (in Parrinder 56). McConnell also reads the novel in theological terms, with Moreau being "a post–Darwinian Christ" (97). And this is indeed how Moreau sees himself, regarding his butchery as *imitatio dei.* Not only is vivisection a path to the divine but it is the only true path. Pain is the gospel of "the world's Maker," while innocuous butterflies are just a gaudy screen, a diversion hiding God's stern visage. Similarly, Shepard's Mengele explains his activities in terms of a higher principle, except that in the post–Auschwitz world even he cannot call this principle anything other than evil: "Evil was not—as it had been depicted for centuries—the tool of chaos. Creation was the chaotic force . . . [Evil] was simplicity, it was system, it was the severing stroke of a knife. And most of all, it was inevitable. The entropic resolution of good, the utter simplification of the creative. Hitler had always known it, and National Socialism had always embodied it" (281).

By identifying with "the world's Maker," the New Man becomes divine. Moreau is worshipped by his creatures whose litany of praise for their torturer is one of the most wrenching scenes in the book:

> *His* is the House of Pain.
> *His* is the Hand that makes.
> *His* is the Hand that wounds.
> *His* is the Hand that heals. (85)

There are echoes of Shakespeare's *The Tempest* in Wells's depiction of the island ruled over by a near omnipotent magician-cum-scientist. But it is *The Tempest* for the age of ideology, in which the Calibans praise their Prospero rather than curse him. And yet the Beast-Folk ultimately rebel, goaded on by their unbearable suffering. They are, as Moreau never ceases to point out, not human enough, mere animal meat for the scientific Superman to practice his craft on. They are enslaved, not converted. Moreau's true disciple is neither the brutish Speaker of the Law, whom his creator despises with the same frigid cruelty with which he despises all of his subjects, nor the drunken dissolute Montgomery, his human assistant, who feels furtive pity for the tortured animals. Moreau's apostle is the intellectual Prendick, who at the beginning felt immeasurably superior to the bloody filth of the island: a gentleman in the colonial Heart of Darkness.

In the scene of reading Moreau's Law, Prendick, an outsider, joins in the chorus of the Beast-Folk. Having witnessed terrible violence, he is shocked and traumatized, and belief in Moreau's divinity offers the only possibility of reconstituting his shattered self. To cope with the violent sublime, he identifies with the sublime object of power rather than with its abject victims. His own liberal values exploded by what he witnesses on the island, Prendick eagerly grasps at Moreau's sacred science as the alternative system that can make sense of the dreadful senselessness of the Beast-Folk's suffering. Moreau's "divinity," first seen as an absurd imposture, soon becomes for him an article of faith. After the Doctor's death, he reimposes it upon the Beast-Folk. He claims this to be a matter of self-preservation, but it is not difficult to see in his contempt for Moreau's victims an acceptance of the vivisectionist's values. His only regret is that he is, after all, too weak to emulate Moreau's self-transcendence: "Had I kept my courage up to the level of the dawn, had I not allowed it to ebb away in solitary thought, I might have grasped the vacant spectre of Moreau, and ruled over the Beast People. As it was, I lost the opportunity, and sank to the position of a mere leader among my fellows" (170).

After his escape from the island, he transmutes the brutal shock of his experience into an epiphany, which allows him to view Moreau's House of Pain as part of the eternal order of Nature: "There it must be, I think, in the vast and eternal laws of matter, and not in daily cares and sins and troubles of men, that whatever is more than animal within us must find its solace and its hope" (192).

However, his lofty identification with the "vast and eternal laws of matter" is merely a rephrasing of Moreau's creed. Prendick strives to translate the sublime experience of the island into the language of concepts, and the result is his intellectual enslavement to Moreau. The despised Beast-Folk retain more independence, for they eventually kill their creator. If the House of Pain is meant to teach obedience, the only one to learn the lesson is Prendick whose body escapes Moreau's knife. The victims rebel; the witness becomes a collaborator.

An even starker description of the same process is given in Shepard's "Mengele." Phelan decides to kill Mengele but runs away when he finds out that Mengele has "transformed himself into a monster" (285), leaving his face old but rejuvenating his body. The horror of bodily mutilation first shocks him into surrender—"the sight of that shrunken face perched atop a youthful body was enough to shred the last of my rationality" (285)—and then opens him up to the acknowledgement of the inevitability of "Mengele's principle" (289). In his moment of epiphany, traumatized by the sight of yet another monstrous cripple, he realizes Mengele represents the supreme order of Nature and his cruelty is merely a limited contribution to the inexorable cosmic process: "I doubted his efforts were essential to that gray principle underlying the factory air, the principle he worshipped, whose high priest he was. He had been right. Good *was* eroding into evil, bright into dark, abundance into uniformity" (288).

For both Phelan and Prendick the power of Doctor Death becomes as irresistible, as self-evident, and finally as amoral as the power of Nature and just as little to be resented or rebelled against. Prendick moves from the sublime of power and pain to the calm, disinterested, elevating sublime of vastness and infinity. He now contemplates Moreau's charnel house as if it were a distant star. He accepts Moreau's "tranquility" at face value, as the serene indifference of Nature. In doing so, he, as much as Phelan who gives up his search for Mengele, becomes an accomplice to atrocity.

Prendick's narrative itself can be seen as an attempt to overcome the trauma of the sublime experience, to translate it into language, to say the unsayable. But what he ends up saying has been determined by Moreau. The whole aimless project of vivisection becomes a sort of macabre teaching device. The glimpse of a wounded creature "bound painfully upon a framework, scarred, red, and bandaged" (73), initially served as a visual shock to shatter the defenses of the symbolic order. By the end of Prendick's education in the pain of the Other, a new symbolic order has been erected on the ruins of the old one and the tortured body has become its transcendental signifier.

Moreau's subjectivity has been shaped by the new Law, which bestows upon him the sublime immunity from pain and pleasure: "Pain! Pain and pleasure—they are for us only as long as we wriggle in the dust . . ." (107). And to prove to Prendick that he has indeed reached the evolutionary stage of the "man of steel," Moreau unflinchingly sticks a penknife into his own thigh. This masochistic gesture draws attention to his own corporeality and at the same time disavows it. He is body, true, but a body invulnerable to pain, impervious to agony, perfect and immortal, the body of the "One Man," the future goal of evolution: "Then with men, the more intelligent they become the more intelligently they will see after their own welfare, and the less they will need the goad [of pain] to keep them out of danger" (106–7).

What drives Moreau's quest for the sublime body is the fear and revulsion toward the real flesh polluted by what he calls "the mark of the beast." He is an ascetic of sadomasochism whose only pleasure, he claims, is "the strange colourless delight of . . . intellectual desires" (107). He seeks numbness by making the Beast-Folk writhe in torment; transcends the body by violating it; and purifies himself by exposing the unsightly mess of blood and viscera in his victims. Moreau's ideal is the body without sensation and without interiority, the steely carapace, which later becomes forged into the armor of the soldier male.

It has been argued that Moreau is a new Frankenstein, and his insensitivity is the result of blind pursuit of knowledge.[8] But, in fact, Moreau is uninterested in knowledge or rather, like Mengele, he uses procedures of scientific inquiry as an alibi for his own self-fashioning. On his deathbed, Frankenstein talks with enthusiasm about the possible application of science, but when Prendick asks Moreau what possible practical results he could hope to achieve, since "The only thing that could excuse vivisection to me would be some application . . . ," Moreau dismisses him with a contemptuous "You are a materialist" (105). Unlike other famous vivisectionists, such as Claude Bernard, Moreau has no practical goal in sight.[9] Instead, he pursues the intangible "something" which seems to be forever eluding his grasp: "something in everything I do that defeats me, makes me dissatisfied, challenges me to further efforts" (112). Thus, his surgery becomes autotelic, pain for pain's sake. His aimless creation of "thing[s] of pain and fear" (108) is caught in a circular logic: Moreau's cruelty is justified by the cruelty of Nature, which is demonstrated by the cruelty of Moreau.

It is precisely in their ritual character that Moreau's experiments differ from Frankenstein's. Frankenstein belongs to a different ideological configuration altogether, and any attempt to construct a unified genealogy of the "mad scientist" overlooks a sharp break brought about by Darwinism and the emergence of bio-ideologies. Frankenstein is a solitary Romantic hero, who becomes obsessed with his creation; their relationship is essentially psychological, a trope for the split psyche, the divided soul. Moreau, churning out monsters on an almost industrial basis, is brutally indifferent to the Beast-Folk, enslaving them with a kind of absentminded efficiency that eerily prefigures Mengele's "detached, haughty air" and "his frigid cruelty" (Lifton 345, quoting testimony of a survivor). It is their bodies that interest him, not their souls, which he dismisses as the primitive "souls of beasts" (113). He needs the anonymous suffering flesh in order to recreate himself in the image of cruel and sublime Nature. The Beast-Folk are simply reservoirs of pain which Moreau uses to elevate himself from the plane of the merely individual to the cosmic level of "One Man." The new self he fashions for himself is the very antithesis of Frankenstein's split psyche: it is unified, impermeable, supreme.

However, Wells's and Mary Shelley's novels do share one significant feature: both are records of failure. Even though Moreau leaves behind an ambivalent disciple in Prendick, his own project collapses. The Beast-Folk ultimately revolt, kill their deified torturer, and then revert to animality. Moreau himself foresees the "return of the beast": "And they revert. As soon as my hand is taken from them the beast begins to creep back, begins to assert itself again . . ." (113).

The resistance of the Beast-Folk is unconscious, almost like the physiological process of healing, the stubborn flesh broken and rearranged by Moreau's scalpel growing back into its former shape. Frankenstein's monster rebels, goaded by injustice; the Beast-Folk are unaware of such abstract concepts. Their revolt is the revolt of the body.

And yet it is precisely the corporeality of their resistance that offers the only bulwark against the rapacity of the biological sublime. As Prendick's and Phelan's surrenders demonstrate, moral ideals are too fragile to withstand the onslaught of "sacred science." But since his search for the sublime body is inescapably tied to the real flesh, Moreau's project refuses to dissolve in the rarefied reaches of the mathematical sublime. The sublime body is haunted by the sentient body, the body of pleasure and pain. For Moreau such corporeality is bestial, for only the steely armor of the New Man deserves the name of humanity: "As long as visible or audible pain turns you sick, as long as your own pains drive you, so long as pain underlies your propositions about sin, so long, I tell you, you are an animal, thinking a little less obscurely what an animal feels" (105).

The novel, however, compellingly shows that no humanity is possible without the "mark of the beast." The Beast-Folk's transformations, from animality to humanity and back again, graphically demonstrate the unbroken continuity between the human and animal estates. It is the very animality of the Beast-Folk that makes them human: "seeing the creature there in a perfectly animal attitude, with the light gleaming in his eyes, and its imperfectly human face distorted with terror, I realized again the fact of its humanity" (136).

In two parallel chapters entitled "The Crying of the Puma" and "The Crying of the Man," Prendick hears the sounds of pain which he first takes for animal ululation and then for the articulate sobbing of a human being. But it is the same pain and the same voice. This continuity of anguish undermines Moreau's dream of escaping the beastly flesh.

Pain expresses the kinship of all living things that Moreau attempts to transcend by inflicting pain. Such a paradox is negotiable only by a strict separation between the ordinary bodies of man-animals that feel pain and the sublime body of the "One Man" that does not. In Moreau's project, the pain of the victims is read as proof of their inhumanity, while the superior humanity of the surgeon-priest rests on his exemption from suffering. Pain becomes a just punishment for the ability to feel pain. Similarly, the scars and mutilations of the vivisection function as an after-the-fact legitimization for inflicting them, for nobody so ugly could possibly deserve any better. Moreau's surgery is meant not to reconfigure his victims into a human shape but to disfigure them, creating the grotesque hybrids of the Ape Man, the Dog Man, the Hairy Gray Thing whose ugliness appalls Prendick. It is clear that the "plasticity" of living forms, Moreau's ostensible subject, does not require the imposition of human likeness onto such unsuitable subjects as sheep, pumas, and llamas. Prendick calls his choice of the human form "a strange wickedness" (105), but there is nothing strange about it in terms of Moreau's ideological needs. The Beast-Men are made to look deformed, so their humanity will be seen as tainted, while Moreau's superiority is established by his "touch of beauty." This is the aesthetics of the concentration camp in which the dehumanization of prisoners served to support the original biodiscourse "which made it possible to exclude a group of people from within the borders of the human race" (Biagioli 201).

But such exclusion is sustainable only until the New Man's sublime body is revealed as the ideological phantom it is by the irrefutable fact of mortality. Moreau's exalted corpus turns into ordinary carrion, just as bloody and disgusting as the bodies of vivisected animals, its head "battered in by the fetters of the puma" (151). Pain creates the fiction of power but it can also dispel it by acting as "the sign of a radically new and wholly secular truth: the truth of the material body" (David Morris 233). This "secular truth" belies the sacred science of pain and the fantasies of evolutionary transcendence predicated on the repression of the New Man's own corporeality. The torturer must keep himself pure from imputations of being like the tortured; otherwise, pain spreads across the sterile edge of the scalpel and corrodes power rather than creates it. Moreau's own body becomes both the incarnation of the biological sublime and the arena of its defeat.

Moreau wages a losing battle against the stubborn physicality of the body, the persistence of pleasure and pain that drags his creatures down the evolutionary gradient, back into the morass of beasthood: "First one animal trait, than another, creeps to the surface and stares out at me . . ." (112). While the Beast-Folk's minds are molded by Moreau's religion, their bodies unconsciously resist his Law. Individual bodies, with their own irreducible dynamics of pain and pleasure, reject their allotted role as empty vehicles for fantasies of the biological sublime. Insofar as such fantasies always require the body, they are always defeated by their own dependence on it.

DEAD RINGERS

In Ira Levin's *The Boys from Brazil* (1976), Mengele (who was, in fact, still alive when the book was published) puts his twins experiments in Auschwitz to good use. Twenty years before Dolly, the cloned sheep, he produces ninety-four cloned Hitlers. The action of the novel, a taut and well-plotted thriller, centers on his plan to kill the adoptive fathers of the boys when they reach fourteen, so as to create the right psychological conditions for the maturation of the Fuhrer, whose tyrannical father died when young Adolf was that age. Mengele is eventually foiled by Yakov Liebermann, a Nazi hunter, but the boys remain at large.

Identical twins are natural clones and Mengele's well-documented obsession with them, which led him to "collect" twins from the incoming transports, might have been based on some project to increase Aryan fertility. But twins are also monsters in the purely biological, nonjudgmental sense. In human beings twin births are, by definition, rare and abnormal—monstrous. In her Introduction to a book about twins, Penelope Farmer, a twin herself, writes: "my researches as well as my experience have led me to think more and more that we twins really are in some respects wholly peculiar, other, beasts" (7). Levin's Mengele, thus, is both the would-be father of a new world, the hopeful demiurge of the once and future Reich, and the creator of monsters.

In Levin's book, one of the first contributions to the present upsurge in Nazi pop-mythology, the historical relationship between Hitler and Mengele is inverted to produce a new archetype. The Angel of Death was, after all, just one of the many physicians in Auschwitz, not a member of the Nazi political elite, and hardly somebody to be on intimate terms with the Fuhrer. But the dross of history is discarded in favor of the tinsel of legend. Mengele, his dreadful aura maintained in the collective imagination by the stories of his atrocities, eclipses the Goerings and the Speers as Hitler's second-in-line, his chosen henchman, his most loyal servant. But even this is not enough and Mengele—many years younger than the historical Hitler—becomes the Fuhrer's father and creator. This is why Levin's character constantly stresses that he has personally delivered the boys from Brazil. In the timelessness of the cultural unconscious, Moreau and Mengele coalesce into one sinister figure, Doctor Death, who gives birth to the monstrous kingdom of pain. While the real Mengele is a forgotten exile in South America, Levin's Mengele has an army of assassins at his beck and call. One of them is perturbed by his strange assignment but quickly gives in—the doctor knows best:

> Farnbach shrugged and looked at his sheet again.
>
> "You're . . . the doctor", he said.
>
> "So I am," the man in white said, still smiling as he turned to his briefcase. (25)

Not just a doctor, but *the* doctor, the "man in white," Mengele with his clones is the most potent image of the deadly New Man, doubly threatening because he seems to link the archaic mystique of the Third Reich with the futuristic dangers of biotechnology. The demonic energies of Hitler can only be released through his monstrous midwifery.

But Levin's book ends on a paradoxical note. Mengele is killed not by his nemesis, the camp survivor Liebermann, but by one of the cloned Adolfs who sets his Dobermans upon the doctor after having been told of his own genesis. Is this a sign of the radical innocence of postmodernity born in the bloody travails of World War II, or of its radical entanglement with the New Man's historical crimes?

Twin research is central to the scientific adjudication of the rival claims of heredity and environment.[10] The old conundrum of nature versus nurture is now revived by the stunning successes of the human genome project. Data on identical twins are used to buttress claims about the hereditability of various psychological and physical traits (and the same data, suitably reinterpreted, are cited in support of the environmental argument). *The Boys from Brazil* is positioned in the focus of this debate, yet manages to evade taking a definite position. Levin seems to want to have his cake and eat it too. A Hitler child dispatches Mengele, thus proclaiming his independence from the dark genome of history. But the very cold-bloodedness with which he murders his creator has something chilling in it, a premonition of future atrocities. And even more ominously, the novel ends with another clone imagining himself as a crowd-commanding demagogue.

Liebermann destroys the list of Hitler clones to prevent a radical Jewish organization from killing them. His decision is moral since they are, after all, only children. He believes in the primacy of the environment: growing up in a better milieu, these children will overcome Mengele's heritage. But the novel itself seems to be skeptical about his optimism, and in the twenty-five years since its publication, the hereditarian view of human nature has grown much stronger.[11] Hitler reborn becomes a figure for the rebirth of the bio-ideologies that inspired the Nazi genocide. If Mengele is just a deluded lunatic, he is frightening but also pathetic: an obsessive snubbed by his former comrades, as he appears in some scenes in Levin's novel. But if he is right, if even one of the boys becomes a simulacrum of the Fuhrer, Nazi eugenics is vindicated, and Mengele is a prophet, the omnipotent "doctor," presiding at the birth of the Übermensch.

Created and recreated by Mengele, Hitler becomes both the ultimate New Man and the ultimate monster. The Immaculate Conception of cloning cleanses him from the last taint of corporeal vulnerability. When the Hitler child asks Mengele who his parents were, the latter triumphantly replies: "You have none!" (243). Mengele longs to be "blessed" by this budding Antichrist, whose future Aryan empire he describes in the language of the Apocalypse. But at the same time, like Moreau's Beast-Folk, the cloned

Hitlers are Mengele's creatures, called into being without consideration for their own needs and desires. And like Moreau, Levin's Mengele is torn apart when his creatures rebel.

Looking at his mangled corpse, the white of bone, the red of blood, Liebermann feels profound satisfaction that the Angel of Death has been reduced to carrion. So far, at least, the lessons of history have been efficacious: the glamour of Doctor Death is not what it used to be. However, Mengele's children are alive and well. One of them is drawing a spellbound crowd and the TV cameras focus on the face of the speaker, "someone fantastic, a *really good person* that they loved and respected" (268), someone who could change people's lives, inspire them, reshape them in his own image, a real New Man.

6

The Singularity of History

The present narrator has three kinds of data: first, what he saw himself; secondly, the accounts of other eyewitnesses (thanks to the part he played, he was enabled to learn their personal impressions from all those figuring in this chronicle); and lastly, documents that subsequently came into his hands. He proposes to draw on these records whenever this seems desirable, and to employ them as he thinks best. He also proposes.

—*ALBERT CAMUS*, The Plague

FRAGMENTS OF GENOCIDE

This chapter is inspired by the Wilkomirski affair: the publication of Binjamin Wilkomirski's *Fragments: Memories of a Wartime Childhood* which purports to inscribe the author's childhood memories of survival during the Holocaust and which is now believed to be a confabulation. This chapter is not about the Wilkomirski affair. Rather, it is about the notion of memory fragments itself and about the force that is responsible for memory's collapse. The reason why Wilkomirski's book, despite its many inconsistencies with the historical record, was afforded an enthusiastic reception was, precisely, its broken, ruptured discourse, its absence of any adult viewpoint to integrate what the author calls "shards of memory with hard knife-sharp edges," its seemingly immediate inscription of the unimaginable trauma of a child's suffering, which artlessly gives up "on the ordering logic of grown-up" to cry out its pain (4). These are the new criteria of authenticity, which have supplanted the outdated notions of accuracy and objectivity. And as if to underline the break between the new discourse of memory (traumatic memory) and the old discourse of history, it turns out that for shards of memory to draw blood they need not have been shattered by any real event.

The *New York Times Book Review* called *Fragments* "a struggle for memory," and indeed, both its writing and reception reflect the struggle for memory in postmodern culture. Emancipated from the confinement of "master narratives," the memory fragment becomes the cornerstone for a new historiography of trauma. Released from the truth, memory seeks authentication in the intensities of individual pain. But it does not thereby escape the entanglement with politics. The jubilation of Holocaust deniers over the Wilkomirski affair is enough to prove that traumatic memory is as much a subject of ideological cooptation as narrative history. My exploration of the problematic of traumatic memory follows the metaphor of memory collapse. Starting with mere cracks in the edifice of the coherent past, it culminates in what modern physics sees as the ultimate fragmentation of both space and time: the black hole. The black hole has become the master trope at the intersection of history, memory, and trauma. But in adopting the physical concept that describes the destruction of the very fabric of space–time, the discourse of trauma unwittingly reveals its own dangers. The vortex of the violent sublime lying at the heart of the uncritical celebration of traumatic memory threatens to consume history.

PHYSICS OF MEMORY COLLAPSE

A time traveler disappears in Auschwitz. Her colleague comments: "That place is the black hole of history, man. No such thing as getting out" (Dunn 309).

A woman approaches a therapist, perturbed by the memory of a long-ago summer when something terrible happened in her extended family. She says: "I've been thinking about my golden, golden childhood and a black hole in the middle of it" (French 69).

A scientist explores the virtual simulation of her comatose sister's blasted psyche and encounters a mysterious vortex of nothingness: "Beyond the flame is blackness. Not the gallery wall, not an opening to the outside memoryscape. Simply an opening. A void. A black hole" (Wilson and Costello 146).

Psychoanalyst Dori Laub, who coauthored with Shoshana Felman a book on testimony in literature and history, describes the black hole as the locus of memory and forgetting, "both the gaping hole of genocide and the gaping hole of silence" (Felman and Laub 65). The black hole is the ever open wound of traumatic memory that cannot be articulated within the structure of rational discourse. Such memory demands transformation into testimony that, paradoxically, becomes testimony to its own impossibility: "As a relation to events, testimony seems to be composed of bits and pieces of a memory that has been overwhelmed by occurrences that have not settled into understanding or remembrance, acts that cannot be constructed as knowledge nor assimilated into full cognition, events in excess of our frames of reference" (5).

Traumatic memory is the nemesis of narration. If it is articulated at all, it is only through a discourse of rupture and fragmentation that mutely gestures at what cannot be encompassed by the discredited structures of causality, continuity, and closure. The postmodern burial of history, announced so often nobody shows up for the wake anymore, has left individual memory in sole possession of the past. And this memory, traumatized by the battering of the Real, speaks in the glossolalia of pain. Trauma has become the template of our relationship to history.

> I would propose that it is here, in the equally widespread and bewildering encounter with trauma—both in its occurrence and in the attempt to understand it—that we can begin to recognize the possibility of a history that is no longer straightforwardly referential (that is, no longer based on simple models of experience and reference). Through the notion of trauma, I will argue, we can understand that a rethinking of reference is aimed not at eliminating history but at a resituating of it in our understanding, that is, at precisely permitting *history* to arise where *immediate understanding* may not. (Caruth 1996, 11)

The writing of "traumatized history" produces a discourse that undercuts its own tendency to generate meaning. The refusal of referentiality becomes not merely a regrettable necessity but a moral imperative in the face of the historical disasters of the twentieth century. Felman inveigles against any "totalized, settled, understood, and closed account" which falsifies the raw experience of horror (158).

But what is history without understanding, referentiality, continuity, history based on the ecstasy of memory dissolution and the intensity of individual suffering? Is this history, in fact, ethical, as Felman and Laub claim, because it gives voice to the victims' pain, or is it immoral because it denies them the consolation of meaning and justice? How can the discourse of trauma cope with an individual memory in which the issue of accuracy is at stake and how can it underwrite a collective commemoration of an historical catastrophe? In his even-handed appraisal of the issues of memory and narrativity, Michael Roth points out that trauma both precludes forgetting and stalls any kind of cognitive response to the past: "the traumatic event draws one to it even as it demands acknowledgement that one can never comprehend what happened at that time in that place" (107). Thus, trauma is a modality of "piety" in relation to such momentous historical catastrophes as the Holocaust. Narrativity, however, erases the very past it strives to recapture: "Historical representation is taken as a sign of forgetting" (108). And yet, paradoxically, that very forgetting is inseparable from freedom. While trauma locks one in the timelessness of the "past present," narrativity situates the past within the temporal chain leading to the future and thus simultaneously erases and preserves it: "Narrative memory . . . *transforms* the past as a condition of retaining it" (Roth 111).

Should we choose piety or freedom, obsessive reliving of the incomprehensible past or its falsification through the discredited master-narratives? I suggest that the very terms of this apparently insoluble dilemma should be reformulated. Trauma does not grant a direct access to the raw reality of pain and suffering at the core of history, piercing the dead accretions of just-so stories. Instead, it generates a discourse of the sublime that is just as vulnerable to political manipulation as any totalizing narrative of history, if not more so. The past only exists as traces scribbled across the field of the present, and whether we employ memory or history in deciphering them, we are engaged in a hermeneutic endeavor. In choosing between trauma and narrativity, we choose not between the persistence of the past and its erasure, but rather between two modalities of the existence of the past in the cultural present. And by elevating memory over history, trauma over narrative, silence over words, we participate in a dangerous war on temporality whose first casualty may be the ethical discriminations of violence. The metaphor of the black hole embodies the ruination of temporality implicit in the discourse of trauma. Stephen Hawking in *The Brief History of Time* describes the black hole as "a region of space–time, from which it is not possible to escape to reach a distant observer. This region is what we now call a black hole. Its boundary is called the event horizon and it coincides with the paths of light rays that just fail to escape from the black hole" (90). A black hole is created by a collapsing star whose mass, squeezed into smaller and smaller volume, punctures the fabric of space–time, producing a singularity in which physical laws break down. The singularity "wraps" gravity around itself, allowing neither light nor matter to escape. Later in the book Hawking employs a telling metaphor to describe the heart of a black hole: "One could well say of the event horizon what the poet Dante said of the entrance to Hell: 'All hope abandon ye who enter here.' Anything or anyone who falls through the event horizon will soon reach the region of infinite density and the end of time" (94).

In the language of mathematics, singularities are no more intrinsically hopeless than any other natural phenomenon. But inserted into common discourse, the black hole amasses a satellite ring of metaphors. Prominent among them are images of hell, careening away from their religious orbit and seeking a new cultural primary. The black hole becomes the ultimate prison, brimming over with contained pain but allowing no escape, in which time is reduced to an endless "now."[1] Thus, it designates a traumatic memory, which can be neither integrated into a narrative nor abandoned altogether. Lawrence Langer describes the difference between what he calls "chronological" and "durational" time in Holocaust survivors' testimony: "the chronological current, which flows until we channel it between the permanent banks of historical narrative, and durational persistence, which cannot overflow the blocked reservoir of its own moment and hence never enters what we call the stream of time" (16).

Kali Tal suggests that trauma "is enacted in a liminal state, outside of the bound of 'normal' human experience" (15). Traumatic memory, like a black hole, is both "a special set of events" and "a region of space–time" in which the past is imprisoned in all its horrible vividness. A physical black hole is invisible; its presence is betrayed by gravitational anomalies. Similarly, a traumatic memory manifests itself in psychic disturbances, while remaining "repressed" or "unrecovered." As Cathy Caruth suggests, "trauma seems to be much more than a pathology, or the simple illness of a wounded psyche: it is always the story of a wound that cries out, that addresses us in the attempt to tell us of a reality or truth that is not otherwise available" (4).

It is precisely the exceptionally painful nature of traumatic memory that serves as guarantee of its authenticity. While narratives of "chronological time" are greeted with postmodern distrust, the stasis of "durational time" is sacred. The Real can only be glimpsed in the blinding ecstasy of trauma. To reach the truth one has to perform the impossible feat of plunging into the black hole and coming out on the other side as "survivor," so that grasping history is tantamount to the harrowing of hell. This hell of history is created by violence. Memory shapes itself into a simulacrum of the violated body that challenges the consoling fictions of meaning, progress, or manifest destiny. Mutilated, fragmented, scattered, repressed memory bears witness to the Real of violation.

But by representing memory as an analogue of the body in pain, we are already engaged in the metaphorical erasure of the "incontestable reality" of physical suffering. Every representation of violence in language, including the language of the victim himself, is necessarily a falsification of the experience itself. Every memory, no matter how traumatic, is filtered through discourse. The sight of the body in pain may constitute the rupture in the Symbolic through which the Real is momentarily glimpsed. But the relation of remembered pain to the body is much more problematic. This is indicated by what might be called the dissemination of trauma.

In describing her pedagogical experience of teaching a literary course on trauma and testimony, Felman reaches an astounding conclusion: rather than learning about witnessing, her students become witnesses themselves.

Confronted with videotaped testimonies of Holocaust survivors, the students, understandably enough, undergo an emotional upheaval, which Felman uses to admonish them to bear "testimony" to their own experience. They do so by turning in a paper, which is "an amazingly articulate, reflective and profound statement of the trauma they have gone through and of the significance of their assuming the position of the witness" (52). But witness to what? Their own discomfort at hearing other people's stories of genocide? If anybody can be a witness, testimony becomes a species of role-playing game or group therapy. The separation of memory from the discourse of historical truth, contrary to its professed intentions, devalues trauma and cheapens suffering, leading to what Kali Tal calls "the appropriation of survivor experience" (59). But though Tal is highly critical of Felman, her own conceptualization of trauma also rests on the "intensity" of individual pain which is not to be profaned by any tests of accuracy or historical content, thus paradoxically resulting in the very process of "depoliticizing the survivor and then medicalizing her condition" which she deplores (Tal 59). While to be a survivor of a genuine disaster implies a certain kind of chosenness (even bad luck can be seen as elitist), intensities of transference and imaginary identification are available to all. Trauma ushers in a new democracy in which the pursuit of psychic pain makes all world kin. By discounting the nature of the trauma and divorcing its subjective perception from its objective parameters, "trauma studies" undermine their own foundations. If, to take Felman's examples, the testimonies of Dostoevskii, who faced the firing squad; of Paul Celan, who faced the Holocaust; of Mallarmé, who faced neither; and of Felman's students, who faced their teacher, are equally evidence of "a radical human condition of exposure and vulnerability" (5), who can escape bearing witness? If "human vulnerability" is enough to inflict a trauma, everybody is traumatized, and the discourse of wounded memory becomes simply a tedious tautology. The black hole seems to be an inadequate metaphor, for only a star of particular mass and density can produce a singularity, while trauma is accessible to all.

But the laws of cultural space are different from the laws of physics. The insistence of "trauma studies" on the ubiquity of trauma may be justified, after all, if the inassimilable kernel at the core of memory's black hole turns out to be produced not by memory but by desire. An imaginary mass would fail to dent the fabric of space–time, but an imaginary trauma may indeed tear apart the psychic fabric of the subject. Michael Roth insists that the choice between memory and narrativity hinges on the exploration of "the awkward and painful question of what desires (and interests) are served by the need to return repeatedly to the origins of pain" (108). In the following sections I want to investigate the nature of the collective, and therefore political, desire that manufactures black holes of memory.

THE GRAVITY OF THE SUBLIME

Here are two stories that demonstrate attractions and perils of remembrance. The first one is Jorge Luis Borges's "Funes the Memorious." The eponymous character is a young man who, after a trauma (he falls off a horse and becomes paralyzed), suddenly acquires eidetic memory. His recollections are as sharp and vivid as actual sensations: "Each visual image was linked to muscular sensations, thermal sensations, etc" (64). He relives every moment of his uneventful life, while gradually wasting away on the cot in his shabby room.

Some hail Funes as "a precursor of supermen" (59), but the narrator of the tale considers him hardly human. For him, Funes's memory has taken away his capacity for analytical thought, making him "almost incapable of ideas of a general, Platonic sort." Instead of giving him insight into his own condition, memory impoverishes Funes because "to think is to forget differences, generalize, make abstractions" (66).

The second story is Dan Simmons's science fiction novella "Flashback." Its premise is the creation of a drug that allows everybody to become like Funes, to "flash back" to the most pleasant, potent, or significant memories of one's life. As a result, America becomes a ghost land of memory junkies, incapable of any significant effort in the present because of the always beckoning escape into the vividness of the past. If Funes is physically paralyzed, the characters of "Flashback" are psychologically incapacitated by the addiction to memory.

Memory is additionally compromised in Simmons by violence and falsification. While Funes simply looks for refuge from the bleakness of the present, Simmons's characters search for more substantial thrills. The heroine's fifteen-year-old son, together with his buddies, commits a senseless murder for the sole purpose of reliving it during flashbacks. Her father, on the other hand, obsessively flashes back to the murder of President Kennedy and his own failed attempt to prevent it. The trouble is, he had never been there. The memory, as vivid, detailed, and compelling as any other, is totally false.

Simmons's story, published in 1993, is obviously a topical response to what has been called "the memory wars" of the early 1990s. The real-life equivalent of "flashback" is the recovered memory movement, with its claim to uncover through therapy horrific memories of incest, satanic abuse, or alien abductions, which, its critics contend, are false. The central premise of the movement is precisely that "the memory can be recovered *intact*—filled not only with all the visual and sensory detail of the original event but with all the emotional and cognitive material as well" (Ofshe 43). This recovery, moreover, is considered therapeutic; Simmons mocks this claim through the character who wants to flash back his entire life in order to "reintegrate" it, an undertaking that will be completed by the time he is senile. But the similarity between Simmons's satire and Borges's much earlier fable indicates that both sides in the "memory wars" draw upon well-established precedents in the conceptualization of memory and its relation to history. While the defenders of recovered memory appeal to the Romantic notion that recollection of the past constitutes the only solid basis of subjectivity, its opponents see memory as both seductive and dangerous. "To think is to forget" and to be forever locked in the memory of a trauma is to lose the capacity to judge its meaning. And yet both Funes and Simmons's junkies prefer the delirium of false memory to the humdrum and uncertain reality of the present, even though what awaits them in the past is the trauma of violence endured or inflicted.

The heated debate about the veracity of recovered memories has long ago crossed the boundaries of a scientific controversy and has become a political playing field where the opposing sides clash over the central issue of history and posthistory: the relation between individual memory and historical truth. It is precisely the urgency of this issue that animates the debate. Insofar as it might be seen as a displacement of the general problematic of the truth of history in the age of simulacra, what is central to it is the attempt to ground individual history in the intensity of pain rather than in the "objectivity" of truth. For the defenders of recovered memory the imperative to believe the survivor overrides any other consideration. And what makes the survivor's speech so inherently believable, what invests it with unimpeachable authority, is, paradoxically, the underlying layer of silence, the voiceless cry of a trauma.

While not claiming that all recovered memories are false, one cannot escape the accumulated evidence that, as the psychologist Michael Nash suggests, "we . . . cannot tell the difference between believed-in fantasy about the past and viable memory of the past. Indeed there may be no structural difference between the two" (quoted in Loftus 166). But whether fantasy or genuine recollection, the most prominent thing about recovered memories is their catastrophic character. In bringing to light visions of incest, satanic abuse, alien abductions, they seem to reshape the landscape of individual lives in the image of the wasteland of twentieth-century history. And yet this wasteland becomes invested with the urgency of desire, as "believed-in fantasies" follow the lead of collective traumas.

The connection between memory and desire forms the crucial nexus of the "memory wars," with one side trying to uncouple the two and the other insisting that they are essentially identical. This nexus is articulated through the divergent metaphors that are used to conceptualize memory. The defenders of the authenticity of recovered memories liken memory to an automatic recording system such as videotape: "Our favorite and most familiar metaphors emphasize the accuracy and efficiency of memory. Memories, we imagine, are . . . recorded on blank videocassettes, properly labeled and filed away for future use" (Loftus 73).

Elizabeth Loftus, a memory researcher, however, insists that memory is more like the Internet, in which the circulation of information is governed by its sensation value rather than its veridicality. Memory is a self-contained virtual world, always vulnerable to false information, slippage, mistakes, or viral infestations: "Nets get tangled, knots develop, frays and holes begin to rip apart the intricately knotted fabric" (Loftus 75).

The automatism implicit in the "videotape" image contrasts sharply with the agency posited as responsible for the selection and processing of information in the memory net. Thus, the memory war is ultimately a war over the status of the subject versus history. Psychoanalyst Jeffrey Prager, for example, criticizes the passivity of the subject assumed by recovered memory and trauma specialists: "Those with MPD [multiple personality disorder] or PTSD [posttraumatic stress disorder] are ever victims of their memories, haunted by the past. And the past is not of their own making: they are, if you will, victims of history" (130).

Whether history is seen as a vague, all-encompassing menace to "human vulnerability" or a localized and specific act of violence, the "victim of history" is bound to replay its effects like a looped recording. Those, however, who insist on the primacy of unconscious confabulation in the process of remembering, prefer to speak of victims of memory. Memory does not passively register a trauma but actively manufactures it, with or without external stimuli. Both psychoanalysts and neurophysiologists marshal convincing proof of memory's creative power, and both insist that a simplistic one-way connection between trauma and external events denigrates the autonomous subjectivity of the victim. If we are seen as passive "recordings" of history, we become not so much witnesses as evidence.

But why would anybody crave the subduing of subjectivity? Why do victims of memory seek out the black hole of the past, risking the coherence of one's psyche in the crushing gravity of its embrace? In her book *Hystories* Elaine Showalter relates the epidemic of recovered memories to "the hidden fantasies, myths, and anxieties that make up the current hysterical crucible" (207). But what is the fantasy behind the willing abdication of one's subjectivity to the external and incomprehensible forces of history?

A number of psychologists have argued that recovered memories serve the function of constructing a self-narrative for the victim and thus giving shape and meaning to the victim's life. However, from the many case studies quoted by Loftus, Ofshe, Prager, and others, it is clear that recovered memories are just as likely to blow the victim's life to pieces. At best, radical memories of violence can create a parallel life narrative, which refuses to square with the victim's previous self-representation. At worst, memory can become the fragment-strewn field of trauma. Neither Borges's Funes nor Simmons's characters are engaged in streamlining their biographies; on the contrary, their obsessive flashing back of unrelated episodes ruptures the narrative coherence of their lives beyond repair. Narrative implies the chronological time of past, present, and future, moving toward a closure. The traumatized memory lives in the perpetual "now" of durational time, in the eternal return of nightmare: "Trauma survivors live not with memories of the past, but with an event that could not and did not proceed through to its completion, has no ending, attained no closure, and therefore, as far as its survivors are concerned, continues into the present and is current in every respect" (Felman and Laub 69).

The only appropriate aesthetic modality for such a state is the sublime. In surrendering to the sublime, the subject is rewarded by the ecstasy of dissolution that we have seen in horror's monsters. But another, more mundane, reward is the renunciation of responsibility. Recasting himself as a victim of history involves a certain kind of absolution from the ethical problematic of choice. Falling into the black hole may be seen as preferable to the futility of trying to close it. And as opposed to the heady pleasures of monsterhood, the paralysis of memory is also safe. The advantage of reliving over living is that the former is risk-free, for the very fact of remembering means that the subject has survived the trauma. When the access to the sublime is sought in traumatic memory, the subject both abdicates responsibility for the past and avoids the risks of acting in the present. The sublime filtered through rituals of nostalgia becomes almost cozy. But this renunciation of temporality and narrativity has a strange effect on self-representation. If the self cannot be apprehended through time, it becomes frozen in space. Memory becomes not a temporal chain of events, but a space of trauma. The focus on the external and uncontrollable trauma, Prager argues, leads to "an assault on subjectivity" in which the "interpretative . . . self" is overrun by the traumatizing environment. Contemporary traumatic psychology is "driven exclusively by the external" (132–33). Divorced from the imagination, memory becomes sinister and alienated, a terra incognita surrounding the black hole of the violent sublime. The self-as-story turns into the self-as-setting.

MEMORYSCAPE

This drive for the externalization of memory finds its expression in the image of "memoryscape," the mysterious landscape of the past in which the present self wanders like a fantasy hero armed with some dubious psychoanalytical spells and a phallic-symbol sword, out to slay the monster of a remembered or misremembered trauma. In this section I want to explore the implications of this spatialization of memory and the relation of memoryscape to the black hole of the sublime, primarily through reference to two detective novels, Nicci French's *The Memory Game* (1998) and Wilson and Costello's *Mirage* (1996). Both deal with the subject of false memory and both employ the metaphor of memoryscape.

In *The Memory Game,* which is highly critical of recovered memory therapy, the spatialization of memory is conveyed through a consistent parallel between the literal and the psychic landscape. The novel begins with the heroine, Jane, a professional architect, accidentally digging out the skeleton of her childhood friend Natalie who disappeared twenty-two years ago. Jane, who grew up with Natalie's extended family and married her brother, eventually goes into therapy and, under the hypnotic prompting of her therapist, "uncovers" a false memory of witnessing her friend's murder by her father. The therapist's main tool is the suggestion that Jane should put herself "back into the landscape from where Natalie disappeared" (184) and explore this dark land.

Mirage is a science fiction whodunit, in which the memoryscape becomes real. Julie, the heroine of this novel, is a neurophysiologist whose erratic twin sister, Samantha, lapses into a mysterious coma, apparently linked to the death of the girls' parents in a fire during their childhood. Julie creates a virtual reality simulation of her sister's memory and explores this dangerous, devastated terrain in search of the buried secret of their joint past. Both novels rest on the trope of subjectivity-as-space, which goes back to Freud's representation of the psyche.

In *Civilization and Its Discontents* Freud tropes the psyche as the "the eternal city" of Rome:

> There is certainly not a little that is ancient still buried in the soil of the city or beneath its modern buildings. This is the manner in which the past is preserved in historical sites like Rome.
>
> Now let us, by a flight of imagination, suppose that Rome is not a human habitation but a psychical entity with a similarly long and copious past—an entity, that is to say, in which nothing that has once come into existence will have passed away and all the earlier phases of development continue to exist alongside the latest one (17).

But no sooner does Freud erect his architectural trope that he demolishes it with a devastating critique: memoryscape cannot be an accurate representation of the psyche because for the past and present to be equally vivid in the psychic space we must assume that two objects can occupy the same space: "If we want to represent historical sequence in spatial terms we can only do it by juxtaposition in space: the same space cannot have two different contents" (17–18). Thus, either the concept of memory survival or its representation through architecture is wrong. Surprisingly, Freud does not opt for the obvious solution of searching for a better metaphor but qualifies the concept itself: "Perhaps we are going too far with this. Perhaps we ought to content ourselves with asserting that what is past in mental life *may* be preserved and is not *necessarily* destroyed" (18). It seems that the architectural metaphor is more important than the notion of the preservation of memory itself. Why? Perhaps because its retention allows Freud to introduce the image of memory ruins and to figure himself as an archeologist of the psyche. Obviously, the only way in which several buildings can occupy the same space is in the form of an archeological dig: layers upon layers of collapsed and ruined structures, with the oldest, most primal ones buried deeply under assorted rubble, necessitating a prolonged and careful work of excavation and reconstruction. If memory were indeed a sort of hologram, instantly accessible to the subject, the work of the psychoanalyst would be menial at best: a tour guide among the splendidly preserved edifices of the psyche. But Freud and his followers, even those abjuring the orthodoxy of psychoanalysis, would rather see themselves as intrepid explorers, hawk-eyed treasure hunters or, best of all, keen detectives piecing together scattered clues.

In *Mirage* Samantha's ruined memoryscape is literally in ruins. It is a bleak, scorched terrain dotted with the rubble of "memory nodes," "the land of the dead" (69). But it also, as Julie soon finds out, a multilayered country, with progressively deeper strata holding more and more devastating secrets. As she journeys down the circles of the memory hell, she approaches the ultimate secret, the deepest-buried memory, the undead past.

The metaphor of "digging for the past" is so widespread as to become virtually nonmetaphoric. As Loftus points out, the very word "repression" nowadays "whispers of dark secrets and buried treasures" (48). The therapist in *Memory Game* suggests Jane's decision to enter therapy is tantamount to the determination to "dig up your own past, to disinter your own secret" (88). Moreover, he equates this "digging" with the physical act of the disinterment of Natalie's body from its hiding place in the family garden.

Both the grave and the body are drained of their physical reality, transferred into the memoryscape. The therapist explains: "Some of us may have bodies in our minds, hidden, waiting to be discovered" (71). The conflation between the physical terrain and the terrain of the mind ensures that the therapist's work is the discovery of the truth, that his "follow[ing] the clues" of Jane's supposedly repressed memory will end up producing tangible results in the real world, and that by filling up the "strange dark holes" in Jane's memory, the yawning hole of the victim's burial place will also be filled (154).

In *Mirage* Julie's quest through the subterranean world of her sister's memory, which starts as a therapeutic intervention, ends up as a full-fledged criminal investigation. The therapist metamorphoses into an archeologist-cum-detective whose unearthing of ruins, fossils and shards of memory is simultaneously a modality of healing and a search for the truth. By pursuing oblique leads and pasting together seemingly unrelated memory fragments, the therapist relies on what Carlo Ginzburg calls "the evidential paradigm," the conviction that "infinitesimal traces permit the comprehension of a deeper, otherwise inaccessible reality" (101). To emphasize how central the idea of the "clue" is to psychoanalysis, Ginzburg quotes Freud's essay "The Moses of Michelangelo" with its famous line about psychoanalytical method being "accustomed to divine secret and concealed things from unconsidered or unnoticed details, from the rubbish heap, as it were, of our observations" (Ginzburg 99).

This "rubbish heap" is precisely the rubble of memory Julie is sorting through in search of the solution to the crime that devastated her childhood. But "rubbish" has a double meaning; it is simultaneously a remnant of something and a health hazard. And "the evidential paradigm" combines the two. The truth shall make you healthy. When Jane undergoes a crisis after "recovering" her memory of the murder, Alex reassures her: "Think of it as your body trying to expel a quarter of a century of poisons and impurities that have been trapped inside you" (French 256).

The rubble of memory is a toxic dump, and the therapist is an archeologist, gravedigger, and sanitation worker rolled into one. A triple metaphorical structure is born, whereby memory becomes first a space and then a thing: "why do we expose ourselves to the risks of digging up the buried material? Because the shards and fragments of the past will continue to penetrate our present-day lives, causing piercing pain and grief. Not until we unearth the memory, file down its jagged edges, and carefully slide the smoothed-out pieces into our expanded sense of the self will we experience relief and release from the past" (Loftus 145). If the psyche is a city, therapy is urban restoration.

However, in the end both *The Memory Game* and *Mirage* deliver an unexpected blow to the very metaphor that underpins their plots. Sensitive to the memory wars, both texts side with the widespread skepticism about the validity of recovered memories and both retreat from their initial valorization of trauma. In *Mirage* the unearthing of the secret memory does indeed bring "release from the past" and the restoration of selfhood. The hidden pathogenic memory turns out to be of a crime committed by Julie and Samantha's father, and at some point Julie becomes convinced the crime is something as "mundane and tawdry" as sexual abuse. Though most "so-called repressed memories are fiction," she is "dealing with the real thing this time" (271–72).

However, the notion of recovered memory is broached only to be rejected. The father is a monster, to be sure, but of a sci-fi kind: not a pedophile but a mad scientist who conducts neurochemical experiments on his daughters. The Gothic architecture of the twins' memoryscapes turns out to be the result of his deliberate intervention and not a spontaneous product of repression. Memory is fragile, malleable, subject to chemical falsification, and the memoryscape is revealed not as the "eternal city" but as a disposable backdrop in a virtual reality game.

The Memory Game is even blunter in attacking the identification between memory and history. Jane's well-explored memoryscape is an imaginative construct, the land beyond the looking glass (she remembers everything as a mirror image, making her recollection of the murder a physical impossibility). In order to find out the truth, she has to get out of her head and start digging in the real ground. In an ironic twist on the metaphor of "digging up the past," she has to excavate the hole where Natalie's body is found in order to discover material clues to the unexpected identity of the killer. Memory is useless for the solution of the crime whose perpetrator, Natalie's brother and Jane's former husband, relied on old-fashioned misdirection rather than repression to avoid being caught. The supposed trauma, the hidden collapsed star at the core of the black hole of Jane's memory, turns out to be nonexistent.

Once memory is seen as unreliable, memoryscape mutates into dreamscape. When Jane wakes up to the impossibility of her recollection of the murder, she goes to another psychiatrist who explains to her that memories are not like solid ruins. Rather, they are like "a sandcastle on a beach"—capable of being washed away by tides of forgetting and reconstructed in new forms by the hands of the imagination (362). Samantha's memoryscape in *Mirage* becomes increasingly surreal, filled with vivid hallucinatory images: living pictures, a lion on fire, a boy biting into a severed hand. Eventually Julie realizes that everything she sees is subjective, and what she really explores is her sister's unconscious fantasy (83).

The trauma at the heart of memory's black hole becomes the wound of the imagination. Both the longing for, and the fear of, the violent sublime collide in that "toxic spot" which Julie sees as a poisoned circle on the grounds of her own memoryscape. It is no longer the burial place of memory's rotting body but the hatchery of the imagination's murderous fantasies. This is the spot in which the correspondence between imagination and truth, memory and history, breaks down and where the memoryscape, predicated on such a correspondence, begins to unravel. The space–time singularity cancels the physical laws that enable its existence; the singularity of trauma explodes the memoryscape constructed to enable its exploration. But this is where the limits of the metaphor become glaringly obvious, for as opposed to a physical black hole the black hole of memory may have wrapped itself around total emptiness. As Julie suggests: "It could be there's no single incident that sent [Samantha] into her own black hole" (268). The most traumatic revelation is that there has been no trauma at all.

WITNESS FOR THE ABSOLUTION

The cultural imagery of trauma feeds upon the vocabulary of the sublime in crediting the "survivorship" of violence with special powers whose essence is incommunicable to the nontraumatized. "Trauma is a transformative experience," says Kali Tal (119). Those who have not experienced the purifying touch of the sublime are barred from criticizing or doubting survivors' narratives: "We must carefully distinguish between texts written by the survivors of a particular trauma, and texts by writers who describe or detail traumatic situations they have not experienced" (132). The insight granted by trauma is the result of the "shattering" of "personal and national myths" (ibid.). The wound of the Symbolic speaks with the voice of the Real. Survivors are not witnesses to the specific crime of their victimization but prophets, testifying to the ineffable—and thus universal—truth: "What happens when a traumatic event forces someone to 're-cognize' a disturbing reality? There is a transformation, a change in the terms of representation—even a revision of what constitutes an 'event,' both in perception and in storytelling" (134).

The three groups Tal discusses are the Holocaust survivors, Vietnam veterans, and victims of sexual abuse. Such a choice disregards not only the specific historical situation of each group but even the content of the trauma itself. It is only the fragmentation of memory and the transformation of perception that they are supposed to have in common. But even assuming that all three groups equally suffer from PTSD, the exclusive focus on the psychological aftermath of trauma overlooks the specific way in which the subject makes sense of its pain. The politics of the Holocaust, the soldier's moral dilemmas, the structure of family power, all are sacrificed to the epiphany of the unrepresentable. With the historical circumstances of the trauma edited out, what is left is the sense of rupture, discontinuity, of entering "the catastrophic environment of trauma through the 'membrane' that separates sense from nonsense" (Tal 15). The trauma memory is hypostatized purely as the experience of narrative and symbolic lapse, as a psychic singularity.

It is clear from Tal's own account, however, that many survivors are not happy with the role of a mute testimonial to the unrepresentable. Rather, they actively attempt to represent their experience, to bear witness not to the universality of trauma but to the particularity of a crime or injustice. The aesthetics of the sublime seems to hold a greater attraction for the scholars of victimization than for the victims themselves. Paradoxically, Tal, while insisting on the privileged status of traumaspeak, faults those survivors who speak too much, such as those Vietnam veterans who "have rejected, repressed, and revised most of their war experiences until the parts that they can recall seem to be consonant with the greater body of national myth" (130). But a trauma, obviously, does not guarantee enlightened politics. The trench generation of World War I, traumatized beyond imagination, was instrumental in the rise of fascism, and Hitler himself, having suffered from hysterical blindness after a gas attack, could be classified as a trauma survivor. Thus, Tal's objections seem to be not so much to a particular narrative of a traumatic memory but to narrativity itself: those survivors are "inauthentic" who, not satisfied with fragments, incoherence, the ruins of the sublime, attempt to "revise" their experience and to tell a story.

But the need to tell a story, to reintroduce causality into a world voided of meaning by a catastrophe, to tame the sublime, is precisely the need that sustained the survivors of camps, massacres, and genocide. Primo Levi's famous dream in *Survival in Auschwitz* shows how people caught in the muteness of the black hole hunger for speech. In the dream he is back home with his family and attempts to tell the story of the camp, only to realize to his horror that people are not listening. The dream is repetitive and insistent, "the pain of every day translated so constantly into our dreams, in the ever-repeated scene of the unlistened-to story" (54). Cold, starvation, backbreaking work, dirt, disease, selections for the gas chambers, all these constitute the duration of Levi's ordeal which is cut off from the chronological time of ordinary human existence: "For us, history has stopped" (107). Without history, without reason or explanation, without shared language to describe what he is going through, Levi's only hope is to rejoin humanity through the bridge of storytelling. The dream is not—as some have seen it—an emblem of the incommunicability of trauma, a call for reverend silence, and uncritical attention to the testimony of pain. What Levi craves is not sympathy but understanding; what sustains him is not silence but words. At one point he recites *The Divine Comedy* to a fellow inmate, quickly, before both of them are killed, for it "is vitally necessary and urgent that he listen, that he understand" (104).

In commenting on this scene Tzvetan Todorov emphasizes the moral value of shared beauty amid the ugliness of the camp, but perhaps just as important is the intelligibility of Dante's hell as opposed to the senseless hell of Auschwitz. Levi's own book, written in tight, controlled, crystal-clear prose, is another guide to the Inferno, and like Dante, he searches for answers. Perhaps there are no answers; perhaps, like fellow Auschwitz prisoner Jean Amery, Levi ultimately comes to the conclusion that in the death camps the mind smashes against its limits. But both continued to write, after all; both clung to language, if only to struggle with its impotence, and to the intellect, if only to decry its bankruptcy.

A number of ordinary prisoners, both of Auschwitz and the Soviet Gulag, fought to pass their stories on, writing diaries, hiding manuscripts, helping one person to escape, so he will reveal the truth about the death of a multitude. What they hoped to preserve was not only memory but meaning, "a possibility for narrative" (Todorov 97). At some point Levi discusses the question whether Auschwitz would be better forgotten altogether and decides against it: not out of regard for the victims' suffering but for the sake of the abstract truth. With stunning detachment, he writes: "To this question [whether the memory of the Holocaust should be preserved] we have to reply in the affirmative. We are in fact convinced that no human experience is without meaning or unworthy of analysis, and that fundamental values, even if they are not positive, can be deduced from this particular world which we are describing. We would also like to consider that the Lager was preeminently a gigantic biological and social experiment" (79).

But precisely this detachment points to the black core of incommunicable suffering that smolders under the polished surface of his prose. It is possible to argue that, despite its cohesion, the writing of Levi and other survivors is the discourse of trauma, after all, that *Survival in Auschwitz* represents that very moment of deceptive stability before the final memory collapse. George Klein, a scientist and Holocaust survivor, describes the dilemma of the "traveler returning from hell" in one of his essays, structured around his meeting with Rudolf Vrba, the man who escaped from Auschwitz to alert the indifferent world. Klein is in awe of Vrba, the "authentic hero," the man who dedicated his life to bearing witness, writing books, testifying at trials of Nazis, appearing in Lanzmann's *Shoah.* The hero's only fear, according to Klein, is that he would not be believed, that his stories of hell would fall on deaf ears. But Klein is also aware that Vrba "knows" something, which cannot be put into any human language: "Only the dead could have more to tell" (128). Speaking for the dead is incomprehensible to the living. Vrba himself says later: "No one who has not experienced it can understand. None of the many books ever written about it, not even my book, could convey the sense of what it was really like" (in Klein 133).

Perhaps it is in this lapse of meaning, in the acknowledgement of the impossibility of speech, in submission to the trauma, that Levi's, Klein's, and Vrba's own stories achieve their power of testimonial. Perhaps Levi's faith in reason is misplaced and we should see through it to the internal fragmentation of his narrative; perhaps indeed, as Langer insists, the only legacy of the Holocaust "when truly faced" is "an internal disordering" of "images from the past" (40). However, the problem is that precisely the same dialectic of detachment and hurt, of causality and disorder, of the need for speech and the curse of silence can be found in stories written not by victims but by perpetrators. Murderers can also "bear witness" to a trauma. Rudolf Hoess, the commandant of Auschwitz, also considered the Lager "a gigantic biological and social experiment." His narrative is also marked by a flat affect, vacillating between objectivity and horror, smooth narrative flow and the stuttering of the incommunicable. What he calls "the story of my innermost being . . . reconstruct[ed] from memory" becomes a story of memory destroyed, shattered to pieces by the unbearable weight of violence (1).

Narratives of perpetrators, as both Todorov and Gilbert, the Nuremberg psychologist, point out are marked by psychological fragmentation. Members of *Einsatzgruppen,* engaged in hands-on killing of Jews, often suffered from PTSD, as Himmler acknowledged in several speeches and memoranda. If the content of the trauma is of no particular importance in determining the fragmentation of memory and if, as Cathy Caruth writes in the Introduction to the anthology *Trauma, "the* pathology [lies] solely *in the structure of its experience* or reception" (4), then there is no way to discriminate among morally opposite varieties of traumatic discourse. Both Hoess's and Levi's narratives struggle to encompass the black hole of the unspeakable and both fail in similar ways. The absolute and irreducible difference between them is that one is a murderer and the other is an innocent victim. But this is the difference, which the experiential framework of trauma can neither encompass nor express.

In discussing the "crisis of truth" brought about by the mutual imbrication of trauma and history, Felman dismisses the juridical model of such a crisis being resolved by a verdict as "contained" and "institutionalized," incapable of encompassing "a horror . . . whose effects explode any capacity for explanation or rationalization" (4–6). But here, it seems, an epistemological problematic is substituted for a moral and political one. Perhaps nobody can truly bear witness to the event of the Holocaust, but the crime of the Holocaust is a different matter.

In a remarkable exchange with the members of the Western New England Institute for Psychoanalysis in 1990, Claude Lanzmann excoriated what he called "the obscenity of the very project of understanding" (in Caruth 1996, 205). Commenting on a Dutch film about the chief medical officer of Auschwitz, Eduard Wirths, Lanzmann vehemently rejected all such projects to "understand" the Nazi soul as somehow implying forgiveness of the Nazi crimes. Any attempt to understand the Holocaust is a sacrilege; the only way to honor the victims is by acknowledging the unbridgeable gap, "an abyss," between intelligibility and massacre. It is not difficult to see why cheap absolutions of Nazi criminals, along the lines of "but he was a good family man," would provoke revulsion. But is it true that to understand is to forgive? The opposite case might just as easily be made: that by refusing understanding, we grant unwarranted absolution to the murderers. Shadowed by their alien motives, they become demons and evil demigods, far above the paltry reach of human justice. Nazi ideology, too, turns into a mystique, preserving and even increasing its dangerous allure. But as Todorov puts it, "the crimes are inhuman but the criminals are not" (138). To think otherwise is to accept the self-deification of the "master race."

One such would-be Superman, an Auschwitz guard described by Primo Levi, has become an unexpected cultural hero of trauma studies, endlessly quoted by scholars and writers. "*Warum?*" asks Levi and the guard replies, "*Hier ist kein warum*" (there is no why here). What is generally omitted is the pettily sadistic context of this pearl of Lager wisdom: the guard brutally snatches away the icicle with which Levi tried to slake his thirst, hardly an incomprehensible act for anybody familiar with schoolyard bullying. That the prisoners' experience in the camps soon accelerates beyond any measure of ordinary cruelty does not mean that the perpetrators' reasons are beyond understanding. Levi's guard is lying, or rather, speaking only half of the truth. "Whys" are quite real in Auschwitz, but they are reserved for members of the master race; it is part of the Jews' exclusion from the commonality of the human species that they are denied the epistemological privilege of meaning. The SS-man knows very well why Jews have to die; he has scientists to explain to him that their killing is of no more moral consequence than the extermination of lice. The death of meaning in the camps is the obverse side of the insane hypertrophy of meaning in Nazi ideology, which managed to obviate the basic instinct of human solidarity. By glorifying the black hole of nonsignification, we tacitly condone the crime of its making.

As junkies of the sublime, the concentration camp killers willingly plunged into the black hole of violence, craving the ecstatic dissolution of the self. But in the cold aftermath of defeat, intoxication became trauma. Suffering from the hangover of "radical transgression," the perpetrators may seek refuge in the silence of the unspeakable. What they achieve, if such a refuge is granted, is parity with the victims. Walter Benjamin's angel of history, seeing the past as "one single catastrophe which keeps piling wreckage upon wreckage and hurls it in front of his feet" (1969, 257), is an angel of trauma. One can easily imagine its wings trembling over the head of Rudolf Hoess as he contemplates the scorched earth of his memoryscape where millions are buried. The task of the historian, however, is not to submit to the angel of history but to wrestle with it: "Only that historian will have the gift of fanning the spark of hope in the past who is firmly convinced that *even the dead* will not be safe from the enemy if he wins. And this enemy has not ceased to be victorious" (Benjamin 1969, 255).[2]

THE CHILDREN'S CRUSADE

In a court of law the verdict is rendered through a competition of the stories offered by the defense and prosecution to account for the facts of the case. The relation of these stories to the truth has been a concern of legal studies, with many critics pointing out that judicial storytelling is subject to the laws of genre. It seems that the best chance of winning the case belongs to a strong narrative that follows an instantly recognizable structural paradigm. But, of course, this does not mean that such a narrative will be any closer to what actually happened than a weak, fragmented, contingent tale of accidents.

There is a traditional comparison between history and jurisprudence: the historian must act as judge, belatedly rendering justice to the victims of historical crimes. Edith Wyschogrod, however, criticizes the model of narrative discrimination underlying both historiography and jurisprudence: "It may be concluded that depriving historical groups of speech is a juridical wrong but that it lies beyond the strategies of rectification within most Western juridical systems" (22). Narrative, both historical and juridical, cannot recognize the irreducible singularity of genocide: "If the cataclysm is beyond magnitude, events are singular. How are we to imagine the cataclysm as 'expressing' a singularity. . . . The other's death is by virtue of the other's alterity always already more than what can be given in my representation, more than what my imagination could present" (46).

Narrative can bear witness to the black hole of "the cataclysm" only by being wormholed with ellipsis. But such a narrative has, by definition, given up on the very possibility of competing in a court of law. It has conceded its incapacity to rectify the victims' wrong even before the trial has begun. While clinging to "the truth of the other's alterity," it has virtuously abjured the instrumental truth of political efficacy. What about the opposite: the narrative that flaunts its own falsity yet claims to represent the victims' rights?

In Begnini's film *Life Is Beautiful,* the father in the death camp hides the horror of reality from his small son by telling him fairy tales. The boy does not see the selections, the crematoria, the brutality of the guards but only the enchanting world of games, competitions, and small miracles his father spins out for him. The film has been severely criticized for falsifying the experience of the Holocaust, but this falsification is precisely its theme. The camp shown in *Life Is Beautiful* is just as much a fairy tale as the stories told to the boy. The documented reality—even leaving aside the issue of "representability"—was a thousand times worse. But showing it "as it really was" would, of course, make it impossible for the film to be what it is: an exceedingly popular combination of comedy and the fairy tale. There are films and books trying to depict the atrocity in all its horror, but none of them achieved even a fraction of the popularity of *Life Is Beautiful. Schindler's List,* another Holocaust blockbuster, goes a little further in the direction of historical accuracy, but obviously owes its popularity not to the harrowing scenes of the mass execution in the ghetto, but to Schindler's melodramatic heroism. The film's black-and-white color scheme corresponds to its black-and-white morality, which is the uncompromising—and as many would argue, simplistic—morality of the fairy tale: there are heroes and villains, with little in between.

The fairy tale is one of the oldest—and strongest— narrative genres. So rigid is its narrative scheme that it was the favorite target of formalist and structuralist criticism, from Propp on. So clear-cut is its moral scheme that it was the genre of choice for stern Victorian preachers, such as George MacDonald. Imposing this genre on the Holocaust seems like the ultimate betrayal of the cataclysm's "singularity." But this is the narrative that stands the best chance of winning in a court of law or in the court of public opinion. The viewers of *Life Is Beautiful* and *Schindler's List* have no difficulty in identifying the good and the bad, the victims and the perpetrators. In terms of historical justice—not to mention the dangers of neo-Nazism—this is a clear gain. But this gain is bought at the price of the inevitable falsification of the horror of genocide.

The increasing popularity of Holocaust fairy tales testifies to the cultural need for judgment. As opposed to horror, such texts do not flaunt the violent sublime through disturbances and rifts in the narrative fabric. On the contrary, they use a rigid narrative formula to combat the disintegrating pull of the cataclysm. The black hole is covered up by the black-and-white moral scheme. No therapy to the survivors here; instead, the court is in session, dispensing punishment in the never-never land of historical justice. And yet, most such texts are aware—though to different degrees—of their own inevitable failure to convey the truth of what happened. Some of these Holocaust *Märchen,* such as Jane Yolen's *The Devil's Arithmetic,* are meant for children. Most are not. But as in *Life Is Beautiful,* the child is often the central figure: a personification of tough and stubborn innocence, untainted by the prevarication of the corrupt adult world. While the discourse of trauma and recovered memory views the child's psyche as fragile, easily splintered by adult violence, these fairy tales revert to the older, almost Dickensian, notion of the child as the angel of judgment. She stands outside the adult world, pitilessly exposing its sins of omission and commission. Instead of being a victim of history, the child becomes its judge.

Cherry Wilder's "The House on Cemetery Street" (1988) is a gruesome

Christmas carol, in which the children of a famous German writer, who spent the years of World War II in "inner emigration," discover the bodies of three Jewish babies immured in the attic of their family home. The children, Lucy and Jo, stayed in the United States during the war and so come back to Germany "cleansed" of their Aryan taint, a couple of all-American teenagers who are forced to confront the lies, evasions, and complicity of their elders. Their final verdict is that the family house "is no better than one of those concentration camps" (26), even though their father and aunt killed the children not out of active malice but out of cowardice, literally "forgetting" about their existence because it was convenient to do so. Here traumatic forgetting is seen as an act of ultimate betrayal, while the recovery of memory is an act of justice.

Taking place on Christmas Eve, the story equates the babies' corpses with the corpus Christi. But there is no redemption. Innocence and forgiveness are as soiled as his childhood toys Jo recovers from the noisome hole where the babies died. Unlike Tiny Tim or other Victorian Christ-children, dispensing goodwill under the Christmas tree, Jo acts as both prosecutor and judge in forcing his family to confront their crime.

"The House on Cemetery Street" judges the traumas of the perpetrators. Lisa Goldstein's "Breadcrumbs and Stones" (1993) does the same to the traumas of survivors. The story uses the "Hansel and Gretel" plot to pit a survivor's daughter against her mother. Here the trauma itself is the crime, for what is being condemned is the inability of the survivor to tell the right story. In hiding the horror of her past and her unwilling complicity in her brother's death, the mother has abandoned her daughter in the dark forest of history, with only the perishable breadcrumbs of fantasy to mark the way instead of the durable stones of the truth. The mother's rich repertoire of fairy tales excluded the one tale she had to tell, the tale of the brother and sister brought to the place of the ovens. In not telling it, she is guilty of a failure of courage. Even more cruelly, the story suggests that the same failure contributed to her brother's arrest by the Gestapo. The story goes very far in the direction of blaming the victim: the opposite syndrome to the exculpation of the perpetrator, implicit in the pieties of silence. Which one is better?

In Jane Yolen's short novel *Briar Rose* (1992), the answer is clear: salvation lies in storytelling, and the only way out of the black hole of genocide is through finding the right tale and clinging steadfastly to it. The heroine's grandmother, the only woman survivor of the extermination camp of Chelmno, has her memory wiped clean by the horror of her experience. The only thing she remembers—and ceaselessly tells her granddaughters—is the story of the Sleeping Beauty or the Briar Rose, the romantic tale of a pretty girl woken from deathlike sleep by a prince's kiss. Investigating her grandmother's past, the youngest granddaughter discovers that the tale is true in every particular but also horribly, grotesquely false. The fairy-tale castle is the processing center of extermination (there was really a castle on the grounds of this Nazi slaughterhouse); the spell of sleeping is the exhaust pumped into the sealed vans; the blush on the faces of the sleepers is caused by carbon monoxide; and the prince who saves the Sleeping Beauty is a minor Polish aristocrat, a persecuted homosexual who becomes a Righteous Gentile by default.

The romance of the most nauseatingly saccharine of all Disney-marketed fairy tales mocks itself, juxtaposed with the reality of Chelmno. And yet it is precisely in this constantly emphasized disparity between the unrepresentability of horror and the representational strategies of the fairy tale, worn smooth by centuries of repetition, that the novel seeks a means to convey the Holocaust. Even though we can never tell what it was "really like," we have to try. The process of storytelling itself, regardless of the truth of each particular story, constitutes a defense against the black hole of violence. The Prince of *Briar Rose* tells the granddaughter how, during the war, people "had cared more about making a powerful story than about life itself" (182). Perhaps in extremis it is better to be a fairy-tale hero, no matter how inauthentic, than a traumatized victim, no matter how genuine.

In all three texts moral judgment is linked to narrativity. Those who tell the right stories are acquitted; those who keep silent are condemned. Whether perpetrators or victims, those who use trauma to run away from historical responsibility are guilty; those who hold fast to their tales are heroes. However, the relation between this tale and the truth of what happened is equivocal at best; the Prince in *Briar Rose* raises the possibility that his tale might be an elaborate mystification. And in any case, as the author's note prefacing the novel flatly states, the truth of the matter is that no woman ever escaped from Chelmno alive. And yet, while acknowledging the inability of stories to contain history, Holocaust fairy tales insist that history can only be apprehended through story.

This apprehension is not only—or even primarily—intellectual but moral. We need the black-and-white morality of the fairy tale, with shining heroes and darkest villains, to bring justice into the realm of genocide. *Schindler's List,* with its unabashed melodrama, follows the moral scheme and partially even the narrative structure of the fairy tale to create the most successful Holocaust narrative of the last decade. And this is precisely why in the eyes of so many critics all these texts, from *Briar Rose* to Spielberg's film, are inauthentic, exploitative, insulting. It is not only that the plots offered are time worn and unseemly, but a stronger argument is often made that any plot for the Holocaust is a blasphemy. Rejection of narrativity goes hand in hand with the rejection of formal justice. Failure of storytelling automatically implies failure of judgment based on competing stories. This, according to Langer, is precisely the "lesson" of the Holocaust: those who are "offended" by the numerous miscarriages of justice in the Nuremberg trials should finally accept that "the logic of law can never make sense of the illogic of extermination" (171). This is because words and stories and verdicts are helpless before the violated body: "What system of justice can render homage to the mounds of corpses being shoved into a mass grave by a giant British bulldozer?" (172).

The question, however, is whether silence can render homage to these corpses any better than words. If stories are rejected as a means of taming the black hole, will pious quietude resurrect the bodies that have been swallowed by it? Or will it just bury them all the more securely?

THE SHROUD OF SILENCE

The memory of violence is always linked to the body. As the therapist in *The Memory Game* says, there are "buried bodies" in the black hole of trauma. Words, by necessity, obscure the reality of the body mangled by violence. But what is the relationship of the body and silence?

In her defense of the silence of traumatic memory—more particularly, of the silence of Paul Man regarding his collaborationist past—Shoshana Felman sets up the crucial distinction between the speaking narrative of history and the muted testimony of trauma. This distinction, which is central to the discourse of the Holocaust, hinges on the relation to the body. For Felman, the narrative of history is inauthentic: it is "a totalized, settled, understood, and closed account" which, in attempting to provide "a semblance of the historical reading of the Holocaust," turns into "a speech act of disposing of the scandal of the bodies" (158). Silence, though, such as that of Man, is a true testimony that "invokes the Holocaust as the very figure of silence, of a historical forgetting, which our very efforts at remembering—through the unwitting use of ready-made cultural discourses—only reenact and keep repeating" (164). It is through silence that the martyred bodies can be made present, while speech—any speech—simply reenacts their extermination. But examination of the figure of silent memory in Felman and other critics suggests precisely the opposite: traumatic silence reinscribes the action of the violent sublime, which denies the independent existence and the ethical stature of the Other. Narrative history, however, by opening itself to revision, correction, rewriting, and the test of veridicality, enters the dialogical realm of ethics in which the corporeality of the victim may be acknowledged, though never manifested. Adorno's famous statement about the impossibility of poetry *after* Auschwitz has been interpreted to mean the impossibility of poetry (or any kind of descriptive language) *about* Auschwitz.

In *Probing the Limits of Representation,* a volume edited by Saul Friedlander, a number of literary critics, historians, and philosophers claim that any kind of representation cheapens the Holocaust. Dominick LaCapra, for example, suggests that "[Auschwitz] may reduce one to silence. Silence that is not a sign of utter defeat, however, is itself a potentially ritual attitude; but in this sense it is a *silence survenu* intricately bound up with certain uses of language" (126). If for LaCapra "certain uses of language," framing the silence, give to it its validity as a sign of mourning, for Eric Santner, another contributor to the same volume, it is silence that validates the language in which it is embedded. Santner argues that "Nazism and the 'Final Solution' need to be theorized under the sign of massive trauma, meaning that these events must be confronted and analyzed in their capacity to endanger and overwhelm the composition of individual and collective identities that enter into their deadly field of force" (151). The implicit metaphor of the black hole is unmistakable here. Any narrative that resists the fragmenting pull of the sublime in an attempt to retain its coherence is therefore suspect. Santner warns against what he calls "narrative fetishism": "By narrative fetishism I mean the construction and deployment of a narrative consciously or unconsciously designed to expunge the traces of the trauma or loss that called that narrative into being in the first place" (144).

Even though Santner actually criticizes only certain kinds of narratives, his attack on "narrative fetishism" makes it possible to view any kind of Holocaust speech as illegitimate. The victims cannot speak because they have been struck dumb by the horror; the bystanders should not speak because their speech is unsanctified by the searing touch of the sublime. Any kind of narrative knowledge becomes the accomplice of the perpetrators' supposed "instrumental rationality." As Maurice Blanchot puts it in *The Writings of the Disaster:* "But the danger (here) of words in their theoretical insignificance is perhaps that they claim to evoke the annihilation where all sinks always, without hearing 'to be silent' addressed to those who have known only partially, or from a distance, the interruption of history" (84).

Knowledge of horror becomes, for Blanchot, the horror of knowledge, the collaboration of voice with violence, which can only be dispelled by silence. "Knowledge which goes so far as to accept horror in order to know it, reveals the horror of knowledge, its squalor, the discrete complicity which maintains it in a relation with the most insupportable aspects of power" (82).

This scathing denunciation of storytelling, however, is illustrated by a story. The story is of a young Auschwitz prisoner who was asked how he could bear having been forced to hold the victims' heads during SS executions. He is supposed to have replied that he "observed the comportment of men before death." Blanchot's response is the flat "I will not believe it" (82).

The prisoner's tale seems to him far too rational, his refuge in detachment of knowledge somehow false, perhaps even unworthy of the sublimity of his experience which can—must?—be honored only by the delirium and dissociation of PTSD. Trauma here functions as an ideological touchstone used to invalidate the response of a bona fide survivor. Instead of muting all speech, the discourse of trauma becomes a measuring rod, wielded to distinguish between "authentic" (fragmented or delirious) and "inauthentic" (rational and coherent) narratives.

In *Facing the Extreme* Tzvetan Todorov also has a story to tell. The story is about Maurice Blanchot. Todorov rebukes the intellectual he once admired for not having ever acknowledged in print his own involvement in the anti-Semitic *Action française* in the late 1930s. Later, after an ideological change of heart, Blanchot excoriates others, such as Valéry and Heidegger, for their complicity with anti-Semitism and fascism. But for Todorov, Blanchot's speech is morally invalidated by that single instance of silence.

In Shoshana Felman's essay on Paul Man, on the contrary, silence becomes the only proper response to the trauma of history. But paradoxically, in taking the discourse of silence to the extreme, she deconstructs it, to reveal at its core not merely abdication of responsibility, but denial of history itself as the realm of difference and subjectivity. Reverend silence becomes a mirror of the empty voracity of the violent sublime that grinds individual bodies and minds into the uniformity of the unrepresentable. As opposed to Todorov who, in the similar case of Blanchot, sees the silence as far graver than the original offense, for Felman it is paradoxically what redeems Man and even makes him into an exemplary and tragic figure. In attempting to judge Man in the reductive terms of good and evil, we deny our personal stake in his dilemma: "[The judgment] thus fails to grasp what is essentially at stake: how Man articulates *our silence*; how today we are all implicated in Man's ordeal and his incapacity to tell us more about it; how, having faced what he faced, Man chose an inevitable syntax and an inevitable understated (silent) language" (124).

But why should "we" (whoever we are) find ourselves implicated in Man's suppression of his unsightly personal past of writing for a collaborationist newspaper in Nazi-occupied Belgium? Because his "ordeal," according to Felman, is not a particular action but the trauma of history itself which is equally shared among all. The choice of words in describing Man's past is revealing: "ordeal," "having faced what he faced," "radical loss—or death—of self" (135). Blown to such cosmic proportions, the initial trauma requires an equally cosmic response, and so Man's silence, "our" silence, becomes not avoidance or escape but a heroic gesture of resistance directed at the ultimate enemy: truth, meaning knowledge.

> In the testimony of a work that performs actively an exercise of silence not as simple silence but as the absolute refusal of any trivializing or legitimizing discourse (of apology, of narrative, or of psychologizing explanation of recent history), Man articulates . . . the incapacity of apologetic discourse to account for history as Holocaust, the ethical impossibility of *a confession that, historically and philosophically, cannot take place.* (152)

A cynic might say that such a philosophy is custom-made for tax evaders. But more is at stake in Felman's argument than Man's personal morality. Under the blanket of silence, subjective differences are suffocated; political distinctions eroded; and history, rather than being saved from "abstractions," is swallowed up by the empty signifier of "trauma." The black hole finally devours the very substance of memory, leaving nothing behind but the verbal wreckage of the sublime. Felman's discourse of trauma, instead of articulating our responsibility for history in terms of specific subject positions, denies that such positions even exist. Felman's repudiation of "judgment" (123) is more than a refusal to consider legalities—irrelevant in any case, since Man was exonerated by a Belgian court. Rather, it is the denial of the ethics and epistemology of historically specific difference.

The generalized "trauma" of history makes it possible to equate Man's wartime collaboration with the survival in Auschwitz. Man's silent "testimony" of his own "catastrophic experience" is glossed by Primo Levi's words, which Man could "borrow," about the suspect nature of memory (140). Quite apart from the moral repulsiveness of such equivalence, Levi's statement is taken from a body of works which, stubbornly and against the perceived impossibility of telling "how it really was," attempt to bear witness. The core of silence in Levi's work is encased in words, which create a fragile but necessary defense against the rapacity of the Holocaust's annihilation of meaning. Levi's acknowledgment that memory is unreliable leads him to conclude that it has to be shored up by what he calls "considerations" which, for Felman, would be precisely those "trivializing or legitimizing discourses" that Man abhors. Levi is a traveler returning from hell, whose speech is a testimony to the unspeakable; Man's silence hides the fact that he, at best, averted his eyes from the hell-in-making, at worst, contributed his spark to its fires. To suggest that the two are the same is to sacrifice the very possibility of meaningful action on the altar of bloated and unspecified "trauma." Not only is the dynamics of "traumatization" opposed to the discourse of objective truth, as in the recovered memory movement, but the rememberer is conveniently absolved even from demonstrating his or her suffering. Felman infers the existence of Man's trauma from the special "quality" of his silence, but if words are ambiguous, their absence is no less so. Who is to say that Man regarded his past as painful rather than, say, merely embarrassing?

The discourse of trauma becomes abhorrent when it conflates Man's experience with that of the survivors; it becomes ridiculous when it aligns him with the worst of the perpetrators. Felman's apology might be read as an indictment. With its inflated rhetoric of the "apocalypse," it emphasizes Man's supposed "realization that there can be no way back from what has happened, no possible recuperation" (135). This is the realization more appropriate for a Mengele or a Rudolf Hoess, one would think. Writing an anti-Semitic article is hardly the same as throwing children into flames. But it is precisely the connection between trauma and the discourse of the sublime that invests an ordinary moral failure with the grandeur of radical evil, while at the same time denying the ethical dimension of their suffering to the survivors.

The black hole of silence accomplishes what Felman accuses historical narratives of doing: it erases the body. It is most glaringly obvious in Felman's comparison between Man and Walter Benjamin, whose lives, she admits, seem total opposites: "Man collaborates while Benjamin is persecuted as a Jew" (157). Nevertheless, there is a profound similarity, for both "experience the events of the Second World War essentially as a mistake, as a historical misreading that leads both men to a misguided action" (ibid.). The "misguided action" is Man's collaboration and Benjamin's suicide.

What falls through the cracks of this comparison is precisely what Felman calls "the scandal of the bodies" (158). Benjamin's Jewish body is marked for death, while Man's is exempt from destruction. Of course, Nazi racial theory is a "mistake" to the extent to which a Jew's body is not intrinsically different from anybody else's. But once inscribed with the sign of ideological alienation, this body, in its irreducible suffering, becomes testimony to "the material . . . way in which linguistic utterances have real effects (make history), without any relation to their meaning, their intention, or their content" (Felman 148). Insofar as Man's anti-Semitic article participates in Nazi "linguistic utterances," its effect is to produce a radical difference between the two men, which is manifested in the wartime fate of their bodies, one dead and one living.

The erasure of all moral, political, and ideological distinctions in the discourse of trauma leads to a vitiation of subjectivity. The closer one approaches the black hole of the sublime, the more is one's unique subject position distorted by its all-consuming pull. Hayden White criticizes the notion of the objective historical truth, external to the narrative emplotment of history writing. He suggests that the appropriate modality of Holocaust narration is what he calls, following Barthes, the "middle-voice" of literary modernism or a "distance-denying discourse," which subverts the realistic conventions of referentiality by collapsing the distinction between the writing subject and the object of narration (48).

Like Felman's vicarious "witnessing," the distance-denying discourse is available to everybody, regardless of the historical, cultural, and ideological positioning of the subject. It projects a kind of free floating, sovereign subjectivity that, cut loose from history, can pick and choose its own modality of trauma. Both the glorification of silence and the pseudotherapeutic flood of "trauma talk" are underwritten by the refusal of "Why," the renunciation of the intellect. But this renunciation does not lead to the confrontation with the naked pain of the suffering body. Instead it produces the hypertrophy of the psychological, which erases what Scarry calls the "incontestable reality" of a specific, concrete human body in pain. The mass-accessible ecstasy of trauma becomes a way to avoid coming to terms with the history of atrocity.

In the course of his conversation with Rudolf Vrba, who escaped from Auschwitz, George Klein, also a Holocaust survivor, asks him whether his Canadian colleagues—for Vrba is a professor of neuropharmacology in Vancouver—know what he has gone through. Vrba tells him a story: having seen Lanzmann's *Shoah,* one of his colleagues got very upset and asked Vrba, who appeared in the film, whether the "horrible things" he said are really true. "I don't know," replied Vrba. "I was only an actor reciting the lines." "How strange," said the colleague. "I did not know you were an actor. Why did they say the film was made without any actors?" (Klein 133).

What is the point of this story? For Klein it is that the "children of paradise" cannot understand the "children of hell." Insofar as "understand" means "share the experience of," he is undoubtedly correct. But if "understanding" also means, as the dictionary has it, "perceive the significance or explanation or cause of," then Vrba's devastating irony is directed not at the colleague's inevitable failure of empathy but at his refusal of knowledge. It is more comforting to think *Shoah* is a fictional film. For the thrill of a vicarious trauma, it is, perhaps, of no significance whether Vrba mouths a script or not. The "middle-voice" of fake personal involvement is unaffected by the subject's real position in relation to the events described. But it is clear that for Vrba's colleague the question "Was it real?" is a defense against the devastating implications of the fact that it did happen. The Holocaust deniers are unwilling witnesses to the profound moral significance of facts, for they understand very well that the power of the "horrible things" to affect us hinges on their being true. As Terence Des Pres puts it:

> For the victims of the Holocaust I cannot speak. Their agony, which to this day is visible in the millions of scratches made by fingernails on the ceilings of the gas chambers, is theirs with a finality none of the living could know. But

> for us who dwell in its aftermath, the most awful thing about the Holocaust is simply that it happened. It entered the world not of fantasy or science fiction, but of fact, of history, the world that is real and present and ours. (54)

TRAVELER IN HELL

How can a narrative, especially a self-declared fantastic narrative, recover the bodies buried in the black hole of the violent sublime? J. R. Dunn's *Days of Cain* (1998) takes place precisely in the "world of fantasy or science fiction" Des Pres singles out as the opposite of history. And yet, while hardly an artistic masterpiece, *Days of Cain* is interesting precisely in the way in which it utilizes the generic tools of science fiction to come to terms with the violent physicality of twentieth-century history.

Literature of the fantastic in general, and science fiction in particular, literalizes the master tropes of the collective imagination. In *Mirage* the memoryscape is a physical terrain. In *Days of Cain* the black hole of atrocity becomes an actual place to visit, to explore, and to redeem. Or rather, to attempt to do so, for the redemption fails, defeated by the scale of the genocide. By taking to the extreme the trope of the black hole, *Days of Cain* serves as a compendium of paradoxes that the Holocaust has bred in postmodern culture. The plot of the novel follows the convention established by Isaac Asimov's *End of Eternity:* a vast intertemporal organization called the Extension, with operatives recruited from different historical eras, is charged with preventing deviations of history from its appointed course. It is done in the name of the "Moiety," which is "the ultimate union of consciousness in the late epochs of the universe"(Dunn 12). The Moiety is literally the "master narrative," the self-aware pattern of development that polices history to ensure its own emergence.

A number of operatives, led by a woman named Alma Lewin, have gone renegade, attempting to change the pattern by preventing the Holocaust from happening, first by assassinating Hitler and then by sabotaging Auschwitz, where Lewin voluntarily goes as an inmate. The plot follows the intervention of the protagonist, Gaspar James, who manages to foil the renegades' plans and to preserve the integrity of history by allowing the Holocaust to take place. The "continuum" in which the Extension's operators work is the collective memoryscape. It is the totality of the past, bounded by its determinate beginning and ending. The relation between the agents of the Extension, who freely roam across space–time, and ordinary human beings, frozen within particular temporal "cells," is the relation of people to their memories. Like images of the past, ordinary humans are unknowingly bound to reenact the script of that which has already happened: "the primary metaphysical quality of the Extension was that it effectively deprived all entities within the continuum of free will. Space–time had been transformed into a deterministic system, the only intelligences possessing agency those of the Extension itself" (314). Yet what grants them agency is precisely the existence of the history script, which is to culminate in the unimaginable but surely benevolent entity of the universal intelligence. However, this narrative is undermined by the unstoppable tide of violence. Shocked by the immensity of suffering, the novel's characters come to realize that history is simply a charnel roll call, an "eternal string of deaths, one after another. That's what history is" (202).

Gaspar's metaphor for this infinite slaughter is the Great Wheel, mindlessly rolling across millennia, "a vast wheel churning out death and horror and blood" (217). The teleological, linear narrative of history is bent into a circle, in which even the Moiety that is supposed to redeem all the suffering is reimagined as simply "the casing of the Wheel, its last inert outer layer" (202). And the axle of the Wheel is a black hole. The Channel that the Extension uses to travel across time is "itself a singularity—the source singularity, the cradle of everything—created at the moment of primal inflation, a flaw in superspace similar to the cosmic walls and strings of normal space, but along a temporal rather than spatial axis" (67). Time is pierced by a black hole, the emptiness at the core of history. This literal black hole which appears first as a doorway of darkness, observed by young Hitler on the battlefield of World War I, gradually becomes conflated with the figurative black hole of "the original sin of history," the Holocaust.

Against the background of cosmic millennia, the characters of the novel debate essentially the same question as the German historians of the local "historians' debate": whether, to use LaCapra's formulation, the Holocaust is "unique," or "comparable" to other events of the same nature (1992, 111). Rather unexpectedly, the Extension's consensus is that it is unique. One of the monitors explains: "The Holocaust differs from other historical events, both in degree and in nature" (33). Gaspar meets a creature from an epoch so far ahead in time that it no longer looks even remotely human. And yet this is an advanced "upliner" of "the sin of Auschwitz" (73).[3] It is as if the traumatic memory of the Holocaust grew, rather than diminished, with time, devouring more and more of Western culture's collective memoryscape. Whether this will be true for the future eons is debatable, but it is certainly true for the last twenty years, which is all the eternity a popular novel can envisage.

But in positing the historical uniqueness of the Holocaust, the novel undermines its own premise of the consistent, intelligible, and total narrative of history. Gaspar originally views the Holocaust as just another event, which is to be processed in accordance with his primary commitment to the "continuum." The novel charts the breakdown of his professional detachment until he ends up as a self-exiled "ghost," voluntarily resigned from the Extension. Shaken by his tour of Auschwitz in the guise of an SS officer, horrified by the "ungodly hole the Germans have created," by "the foulness, the viciousness, the *pointlessness* of it . . . " (243), Gaspar rejects his more "advanced" superior's explanation that the Holocaust is, in fact, a historically beneficent phenomenon because it created "a benchmark of human behavior, an abyss that must not be approached" (254) and thus prevented humanity's suicide. And when at the end Gaspar, shattered by Alma's death in the oven, and by his own success in preserving the existence of Auschwitz, is approached by "the author of Moiety," the godlike universal intelligence, and offered what amounts to a technological version of the Judgment Day, he reacts with revulsion and violence. He will not accept a consolation of meaning, because any such consolation is a betrayal of Alma's ashes. "He'd cling to his own damnation. At least it was his" (314).

The consistency of master-narrative is rejected in favor of the fragmentation of grieving. As the master-plot disintegrates, the black hole comes to the fore as the only appropriate figure for the Holocaust. Alma's metaphor, irreducible to any general scheme of reasonableness, is the one that remains: "She saw it as a great shadow, falling across history from its point of origin, distorting everything it touched. . . . The shadow grows as time passes, tainting and debasing all it contacts, even the Moiety itself" (32).

And later Alma, already a prisoner in the camp, explains it to an uncomprehending Jewish girl: "That's what history is, you know—a vast wheel churning out death and horror and blood. . . . The way it was, is, will be. Right until the final state. . . . Oh yes: this is the center. Right here. This camp. It does not get worse than here, ever. This is the end point, the final exit, the axle of the Wheel" (217–18).

At this point the novel, which strives to reconcile the piety of silence and the judgment of storytelling, lapses into incoherence. Falling back on the irreducible paradox of the physical black hole, it seems to be content to display its own narrative mutilation as the unavoidable badge of violence.

However, as a popular fiction, the novel still has one option left. Its characters, living in a fictional world where trauma and memory become physical objects, can act upon them with a physical force. And act they do. If neither words nor silence can cope with trauma, perhaps actions can. The time travel solidifies history into the "continuum," but at the same time opens it up to revision. This paradox is incarnated in the convention of the time loop or chronoclasm: actions in the past may affect the present and thus cancel themselves out.[4] Like memory, the past in time-travel science fiction is simultaneously solid, inescapable, immutable, and pliant, vulnerable, open to revision. Alma sets out to rewrite the narrative of history by closing the black hole of genocide: "They'll track us, sure enough. Run us down eventually. But they'll have to take us upline then. . . . To the final state? The real power? What a scary thought that is. But at least then I'll find out what they're actually up to. What it all means, what they aren't telling us (218).

Her actions are on an epic scale, the undertaking of a hero who is trying to force the hand of God. She is perceived as a larger-than-life figure, able to inspire a dedicated band of followers to accompany her in her harrowing of hell. She is a saint, says another monitor, "a saint without a Deity, without a church," responsible only to the prompting of her own conscience (31). It almost looks, in fact, as if she is about to manufacture her own brand of the sublime, to oppose transcendent atrocity with transcendent self-sacrifice.

However, once in Auschwitz, Alma becomes merely another prisoner, an ordinary human being whose strength is broken by the machinery of death. All her superior powers are useless against the Lager. Ironically, her most potent weapon is not some supergadget but mundane greenbacks with which she manages to bribe wardresses and minor officials, thus participating in the sordid economy of the camp, which Primo Levi calls "the complex network of thefts and counter-thefts" (77). But the money soon runs out, and Alma, the product of an unimaginably advanced civilization, is subjected to the routine process of abuse and dehumanization. She is beaten, starved, and finally burnt—like everybody else.

Before her death, however, Alma's goals have shifted. She still dreams of the grand melodrama of the camp liberation, fire from the sky falling upon the murderers, the prisoners led to freedom through the benevolent black hole of a temporal portal which will cancel out the black hole of death. But what she actually does, in the weeks before her murder, is to take care of the inmates of her block. Against all rational considerations, and jeopardizing her own master plan, she decides to preserve one girl's pregnancy and allow a healthy baby to be born in the camp. The baby is born and thrown into the oven, while the mother is killed with a phenol injection.

In his book on the morality in the concentration camp universe, Todorov wrestles with the dilemma of whether what he calls the heroic virtues of hopeless rebellion and self-sacrifice, or the ordinary virtues of individual caring and preservation of dignity, are of more value in counteracting atrocity. He comes to the conclusion that caring for an individual human being is morally superior to a sacrifice in the name of an abstract cause. Alma's story seems to confirm this conclusion. But it also starkly outlines the limits of ordinary virtues, the same limits that are pointed out by Primo Levi and Jean Amery. Alma does not succeed in saving anybody, including herself; even Rebeka, her protégé, survives only because of a spontaneous and unexpected act of kindness on the part of the SS man Reber. Neither the heroic rebellion against the master narrative of history nor the microethics of caring and compassion are of much use when facing Auschwitz. Even the third venue of resistance, justice, while seemingly endorsed by Reber's death vision of the "Moiety of the righteous," is undercut, as Gaspar contemptuously slams the phone on the Universe's would-be supreme Judge.

Days of Cain transposes into narrative aporia the postmodern paradoxes of the violent sublime, successively undermining all possible epistemological, discursive, and moral frameworks for dealing with genocide. But it does tell a story. Moreover, within the text itself, storytelling is presented as the only activity that resists the destructive pull of the black hole. Before the final abdication, Gaspar writes a tale for his granddaughter. It is about the Great Wheel of cruelty and violence:

> rolling across history through all the periods and epochs, never seen or described, known only by the desolation it left behind. Only two could stand against it: the saint and the monitor, a young woman and a man of first age, bound by oath never to rest until the Wheel was broken at last. They possessed powers, these two; they moved behind the curtains of space and time, always a step ahead of the Wheel, always turning it aside, leading the victims from Judaea, and the steppes, and Ireland, and the camps, to the one safe place, the sanctuary guarded by their friends the flickering clouds. And though the battle was never finished and victory far away, they were very happy. . . . (313)

Novels, films, comic strips, fairy tales are the "event horizon" of the black hole of genocide. They cannot close it, but they can mark its boundaries and act as beacons of warning: here be monsters. By disregarding their warning and plunging straight into the voracious maw of the violent sublime, traumatic memory courts the infinity of second-hand suffering. Perhaps it risks an even worse fate: the infinity of boredom.

Conclusion: Peacescripts?

RUNNING WILD

In J. G. Ballard's novella *Running Wild* (1988), a group of children brutally massacre their parents. The children, the progeny of highly paid, caring, and conscientious professionals, are brought up with kindness and consideration and given all the right toys to play with and all the right activities to pursue. They experience the perfect balance of parental supervision and respect for their autonomy. Their parents not only lavish expensive gifts on them but, fortified with the latest in psychological research, set out to provide their kids with a conflict-free, nurturing environment. No dark secrets in Pangbourne Village, no hidden child abuse, no kiddie porn, no trauma festering under the surface of loving family life. Nevertheless, the children of paradise are a group of ruthless killers, psychotic in their detachment from human reality, exterminating their parents without a flicker of horror or remorse and embarking on a crusade of accelerating violence.

The explanation, according to the narrator of this postmodern morality play, is that without tragedy or fear in their lives, the children grow up severely handicapped. Deprived of the knowledge of pain and mortality, they crave violence as the reprieve from the intolerable blandness of their existence. But even parricide fails to provide the stimulus they need: lacking the story of Oedipus—or any tragic story, for that matter—they cannot situate their actions in a meaningful context. Their parents' benevolent tolerance and boundless understanding turned out to be worse than excessive strictness. They did not warp their children's emergent selves; they just did not provide them with any. Incapable of feeling and unburdened by conscience, the children are hooked on violence in the vain hope of experiencing the guilt that might fill the aching void inside. But instead, murder and terror only serve to empty out their already shriveled psyches, producing glassy-eyed assassins.

Ballard's strange and disturbing tale goes against the grain of the contemporary wisdom that locates the source of violence in childhood abuse and trauma. It suggests that people kill because they want to kill, because killing offers an experience so potent that it is worth the risk of the reciprocal violence of the law. This experience is seen as an escape from the meaningless routine of suburban existence. But the escape is deceptive; running wild, the murderer only outruns his or her humanity.

RUNNING SCARED

Desire, as Lacan perceptively noted, is like a railway track stretching toward the unreachable horizon. But the murderer's desire is looped into a circle, speeding away from the victim's corpse, only to end up at another crime scene.

The narratives of violence we have encountered range far and wide: from Dostoevskii to dystopia, from Dickens to Clive Barker, from graphic horror to fairy tale. Its subjects are as motley a crew as the reader is likely to encounter anywhere. And yet Frankenstein's monster, Professor Moriarty, and Dr. Mengele do have one thing in common: the murderer's desire. Whether expressed in all its naked rapacity, as the serial killer's body count, or disguised as the search for profit or purity, this desire propels all the narratives I have discussed in this book. And the proof that it is the same desire, despite its chameleonic transformations, lies in the one structural feature all bloodscripts share. This feature is the lacuna, the ellipsis, the stumble, and the incoherence that figure and disfigure the story of a murderer. Like the scar of a freshly dug grave, this lacuna betrays the presence of a hidden body. But adorned with a tombstone, a grave becomes a holy place. The pit of violence is at the same time a site of transcendence, of spiritual self-aggrandizement—the site of the sublime.

Biologists, psychologists, and criminologists argue about the origins of the desire to kill; but while different, many of their models acknowledge the irreducible ambiguity built into human violence. In Robert O'Connell's discussion of the origin of war, for example, he recognizes the existence of "a strong and innate human inhibition against killing members of our own species" and suggests that various forms of "cultural mediation" were developed in the Neolithic age to disarm this inhibition by convincing the aggressor that "the victim was not actually human and was, therefore, subject to predation." This mediation is so powerful that it "is capable of overwhelming . . . the reporting of our senses as to the true nature of the victims" (110–11). Goldhagen's "ordinary Germans" did, perhaps, see aliens in place of women and children. But such self-delusion cannot be seamless and complete without escalating into psychosis. And so the perpetrator of violence is locked in a peculiar double state of knowing and not knowing, accepting the victim's humanity and denying it. This vacillation, this inevitable splitting of the perpetrator's selfhood in the act of violence, is what accounts for the shattering impact of killing on the coherence of the self. But precisely because the self exists only in, and through, discourse, this shattering is mistaken for the liberation from the "prison-house of language." Violence appears as communion with the Real, beyond the shifting illusions of the Symbolic. But in fact this communion is the greatest illusion of all.

Like any sociobiological speculation, this one is a just-so story of origin. But whatever the ultimate source of what I called the "violent sublime," it exists. It sends raw recruits into fits of weeping after their first combat, but it also transforms Vietnam veterans into adrenaline junkies. It inspires Ted Bundy–like nonentities to taste the divine in rape and torture, and it seduces would-be scientists into identifying with Nature red in tooth and claw. It makes the concentration camp builders shed tears when confronted with the spectacle of their handiwork, but it also makes them build the camps in the first place. Killing somebody, even if it happens only once, even if it is unintentional or justified, in self-defense or in defense of others, marks the killer forever. It is as irrevocable as the loss of virginity: "the act of killing changes the person who has performed it, from then on he is a different person living in a different world" (Kott 72). Having killed, an ordinary subject becomes a subject of violence.

But subjectivity is not located only in a subject's individual body; it is created in, and through, discourse. No society is free of violence, but no violence is free of society either. The self-narratives of violent subjects unfold within the generic matrix of socially circulating stories, and it is this matrix that the book analyzes.

Hunger for the violent sublime is expressed differently in each category of murderers that I discussed. Frankenstein's creature, Dracula, the Invisible Man, and Barker's Cabal are embodiments of this hunger at its most extreme, emptying those it possesses of all semblance of humanity. Horror's creatures are cautionary metaphors of what I called the subject of torture, the speechless monster from beyond the social pale. Their serial killer counterparts retain the human form that the generic conventions of horror allow the monster to discard. But like fictional monsters, serial killers lose the coherence, the social intelligibility that defines a human subject. The story of a monster automatically situates the perpetrator in opposition to society, as the deviant, the outcast, the Other. No matter how deeply the subject of torture plunges into the ecstasy of violence, he will eventually float up as social carrion. Even in Foucault's premodern spectacle of the scaffold, the executioner was an untouchable. Power needed him, used him, and threw him away. Stripped of its narrative husks, presented as a gory spectacle, the act of violence mangles the body of the victim and the story of the perpetrator.

Precisely because of this radical disenfranchisement, the subject of torture is sometimes regarded with certain awe and even admiration. Film audiences cheer for Freddie Krueger, and the intellectuals absolve serial killers of responsibility with Auden's worn-out line about those to whom evil has been done. Surely, a person who pays such a horrifying price for murder must somehow be compelled to commit it! And the same logic is applied to murderous martyrs and suicide terrorists.

What I tried to emphasize in the first and second chapters is the free desire that impels the subject of torture to engage in rape, mutilation, and horrifying slaughter. Fictions of horror reveal this desire: would Mr. Hyde roam the dark streets of London if Dr. Jekyll did not labor to bring him forth, or would Basil Hallward be dead if Dorian Gray's longing to be a painted thing were less overwhelming? Criminological treatises and true-crime books, however, often persist in denying it. Supposedly "emptied" of their subjectivity by the onslaught of the media or traumatized beyond repair by humdrum childhoods, serial killers are presented as impotent slaves of social and psychological scripts not of their choosing because it is simply too unsettling to view them as actively and knowingly writing their own scripts in the blood of their victims. But the very same texts inadvertently reveal the serial killers' agency through the blatant inadequacy of all explanations. A recent book on the career of Dr. Harold Shipman, perhaps the most prolific serial killer in British history, is a perfect example of the aporia of determinism, for try as they might, the authors can find absolutely nothing in Shipman's average childhood, sexuality, or lifestyle that would account for the staggering trail of dead bodies he left in the wake of his house calls. Eventually, they resort to a standard horror's ploy by labeling him "unremittingly evil" (Whittle and Ritchie 362)—in other words, a monster. But this ploy may be more illuminating than all the experts' opinions they quote, for it indicates that Shipman freely chose a self-narrative which cast him in the role of an evil alien. This is a position of power, which Shipman undoubtedly cherished; but perhaps more importantly, it is a position of transcendence. Shipman, like any other serial killer, has escaped social and cultural determinations into the wordless realm of the sublime, where the narrative definitions that shackle each of us to a chain of identities fall apart. He is a man, a husband, and a father, a doctor, but more than that, something unspeakable, unimaginable, a thing, a creature, an angel, inhabiting a world of the Real. A killer with no qualities, he epitomizes all motiveless murderers' transformation into ciphers. Unintelligible to others, he is equally unintelligible to himself; and in this self-unreadability lies the murderer's nemesis. The drill of the superego is more easily disregarded than Freud imagined. But even if some people may do without conscience, dispensing with consciousness is a different matter. If the script of the self is obliterated by random and uncontrolled bloodshed, the self will eventually vanish.

Instead of plunging headlong into the wound that violence opens in language, other killers try to suture it. Discipline and ideology promise sublimity and coherence, transcendence and intelligibility, transgression and the Law. They promise it in different ways, however. Discipline aligns with the existing Law by allotting to the subject of violence a place in the rational, orderly, and comprehensible universe of discourse; a bad place, to be sure, a jail, but a jail of one's own. Ideology has grander goals: the jail will be transformed into paradise, and rather than inhabiting the necessary but uncomfortable margins of society, the killer will be enthroned at its center.

Discipline requires physical violence as its opposite, the dark double of the rational world of calculable risks and affordable rewards. But in its omnivorous desire to reach everywhere, discipline turns every citizen into a potential murderer. Rather than being concentrated in the emblematic figure of the monster, ritually displayed and sacrificially expelled, violence becomes an invisible poison seeping into reason and contaminating it from within. Instead of a pariah, the violent subject of discipline becomes Everyman.

C. Auguste Dupin, Sherlock Holmes, Hercule Poirot, Father Brown offer a safe route into the kingdom of bloodscripts: enjoy murder and call it fine art; touch the sublime and pretend you are only solving a puzzle. But they, and their adversaries, so often indistinguishable from the detectives themselves, bear witness to the irrepressibility of the violent sublime by the very labor expended in building defenses against it. The perfect form of the classic detective story is a temple of reason raised over the sewer of horror.

In the wake of Foucault, discipline has gotten a bad name. But the confrontation between the classic detective story and the dystopia reveals that the rational murderer is not the worst thing to bump into in the dark alleys of history. Beyond the subject of discipline looms the shadow of the subject of ideology who has already turned twentieth-century textbooks into bloodscripts and has plans for the new century as well. And the confrontation between the two restores an ethical scale to the problematic of violence, which tends to be blurred by understandable indignation at any act of murder. But if all murderers are evil, some are more evil than others. When the aging Hercule Poirot battles idealistic killers; when the private eye stumbles into a state-sponsored torture chamber; when Xavier March treats the Holocaust as a crime to be investigated and penalized, we are reminded that jail is preferable to genocide.

What is a private transcendence for the subject of torture becomes a collective transformation for the subject of ideology. The violent sublime will be unleashed, turning ordinary, limited and mortal human beings into New Men. Any ideology that promises the millenarian metamorphosis of the self-divided human consciousness into what Zizek calls "the sublime subject" requires violence. Regardless of its overt political platform, regardless of the historical conditions, regardless of the ostensible goals and the real or imaginary grievances, the search for a radical millennium generates radical tribulations. And just as the millennium in the Book of Revelation is continuously postponed, while the count of the tribulations mounts, the sublime subject never quite emerges from the womb of history, which meanwhile continues to bleed. The Holocaust, the Gulag, the genocide in Cambodia, Rwanda, and elsewhere are all necessary outcomes of their respective ideologies to forge a new, racial, social, or ethnic sublime subject.

That the scale of such ideological violence exceeds anything achieved either by freelance criminals or by the disciplinary state is due to ideology's management of the violent sublime, far more efficient than either release or repression. In an ideological state, such as Nazi Germany, the "cultural mediation" of violence becomes so powerful that it blinds the perpetrators to the bloody spectacle of the body in pain and thus allows this spectacle to be repeated endlessly, hidden away from the ordinary citizens in some *anus mundi,* and yet titillating those same citizens with its half-acknowledged presence.[1] The familiar argument that the visibility of violence in the media provokes more violence avoids the historical experience of genocidal regimes, where the invisibility of violence acted as a spur to its escalation. There was no pornography of violence—or any other pornography—in the kingdoms of the New Men, the Third Reich or Stalin's Russia. Their censorship acted with admirable efficiency against any kind of decadent entertainment, such as horror movies. The use of SS paraphernalia in sadomasochism is a triumph of the imagination over history, for hardly anything could be more puritanical than this organization, in which marriage and eugenically perfect children were a prerequisite for membership. But precisely because the narrative universe of the Nazi killers presented them with the utopia of happiness and health, their exultation at having the power to kill, maim, and torture was unchecked by the shuddering recoil that destroys the subject of torture. A serial killer eventually gets out of control, descending into what in the jargon of profiling is called "the disorganized stage," sometimes actually begging to be caught. A disciplined assassin will either be caught or retire, perhaps occasionally bothered by a nightmare or two. But a junkie of the sublime will need more and more of his drug. He will only stop if his society as a whole shifts into a different narrative modality, returning to discipline and repressing the age of ideology. And then the ruins of the utopia will crawl with hitherto unknown serial killers, such as the notorious post–Soviet mass murderer Chikatilo, who perhaps long for the time when violence was not a forbidden pleasure but a social duty. Empires come and go, but the impulse to write a utopian narrative in blood remains an integral part of Western—and nowadays global—culture, with the new breed of terrorists proving that a state apparatus is not a prerequisite for mass violence but an ideology is.

It is here that the lessons of the bloodscripts that I have investigated diverge sharply from much of postmodern theory. From Adorno on, the mainstream of theory has blamed the Enlightenment and its product, the bureaucratic nation-state, for the Holocaust and all the other mass killings of the last century. "Instrumental rationality" is widely held to foster violence; in Copjec's summary, Enlightenment concepts are "responsible for bringing about the very disasters they pretend to ward off" (ix). This would be true if the Holocaust were perpetrated by conscientious bureaucrats or if, indeed, the Twin Towers were brought down by a committee. I have argued above against Arendt's concept of the "banality of evil" as being in any way adequate for representing the Nazi subject. From Hoess's autobiography to *Mein Kampf,* from Borges's Linde to the Hitler clones, from Moreau to Mengele, representations and self-representations of the subject of ideology insist on his full awareness that murder, torture, extermination are not banal but sublime. And Moreau and Mengele's misuse of science demonstrates that for Nazism rationality and discipline become means rather than ends, reason enslaved to power the machinery of murderous ecstasy.

Such popular fictions are more radical than Habermas's philosophical defense of the Enlightenment, for they do not claim that reason is innocent but only that it is necessary. He argues that the Enlightenment has been perverted to serve the ends of violence; they show that a kind of violence is indeed inseparable from reason, but that there are worse kinds. Discipline breeds its own killers; bureaucratic democracies wage wars and execute criminals. But utopian and apocalyptic ideologies generate mass-scale violence not as a by-product of their functioning but as their raison d'être. To refuse to discriminate between the two, to condemn, for example, both sides in the Second World War because both committed war crimes (which is perfectly true) is to abandon ethics altogether. Moral absolutism may in practice be more dangerous than nihilism. Philip Gourevitch, in his book on the genocide in Rwanda, shows how Western refusal to make a moral distinction between ideological slaughter and partisan war led to complicity with the perpetrators of genocide. Such complicity, or course, was supported by cynical geopolitical interests, but without a tendency in the media to airbrush the genocide into a "tribal war," it would not have worked.

The glorification of trauma, the subject of my last chapter, reveals the serious political danger of treating violence as absolute, divorced from its historical, cultural, and ultimately narrative setting. If violence is everything and everywhere, it is also nothing and nowhere. Acknowledging, along with Kant, the universal human potential for radical evil is not the same thing as claiming the universality of guilt, for the latter ends, as with Shoshana Felman's defense of Paul de Man, in blanket absolution for everybody. If the bloodscripts, with their finely tuned generic distinctions, teach us anything, it is the necessity of discrimination, which is also the necessity of judgment.

RUNNING FOR COVER

"Must we burn Sade?" famously asked Simone de Beauvoir. Must we burn the bloodscripts? In the world beset by war, terror, crime, genocide, ethnic cleansing, the morality of a project such as mine is inevitably open to question. It is bad enough that people read such books; should we afford them the dignity of a scholarly investigation as well? Investigation, not castigation, for the latter is regularly found in both the academic and the general discourse on representation of violence. The most powerful component of this discourse, reiterated with various degrees of moral fervor and intellectual sophistication, is the call to ban all bloodscripts, or at least as many of them as happen to fall within the author's purview. In particular, this call is heard when the focus is, as it is in this book, on the genres of violence. Hardly anybody would demand censoring *Oliver Twist* (if for no other reason than because it is old and remote enough to have acquired the status of a "classic"), but the horror movie industry is a different matter. And even if horror becomes the subject of scholarly analysis, it is with an eye to its "subversive" potential. Violence is only acceptable if read as rebellion and preferably within the safe confines of a movie theater. But when a real-life serial killer sets out to imitate Barker's monsters, cultural scholars join the politicians in blaming pictures and books for disseminating the taste for murder. With certain apocalyptic smugness, recalling Dickens's "it was the best of all times, it was the worst of all times," theoreticians of postmodernity claim the scope and nature of violence today exceeds anything known to Rome, the Golden Horde, or the crusaders, and point the finger at the proliferation of bloodscripts, aided and abetted by the electronic media. In such a climate, my book is bound to provoke dissent, not just because of its subject matter, but because the generic approach I espouse seemingly makes ethical discrimination among narratives of violence impossible. By placing Dickens and Barker or Wells and *Mein Kampf* in the same generic categories, I extend the aesthetic protection of the former to the latter. And indeed, if "protection" means refusal of censorship, I do.

Regardless of the complex theoretical framework erected around the critical defense of "silence" that I critiqued in the last chapter, there is a simple human impulse behind it. If we do not talk about horror, it will disappear. If we do not see it, it will go away. If we do not show it, our children will grow up innocent and peaceful. "Aggression is contagious," says Rosalind Miles, "watching it, taking part in it, reading about it, and expressing it will never reduce it" (298). Violence is a disease that we catch through the eyes mesmerized by the high-tech spectacle of extermination; through the ears that listen to the staged moans of the victim; and most of all, through the mind that is so perversely seduced by stories of murder and mayhem. The still ongoing feminist debate about pornography centers on the contagion of violence against women that hard-core pornography supposedly disseminates by its very existence, by the simple fact of its availability, even though its actual consumers may be a tiny minority. All the sophisticated feminist arguments that have been rallied against this contention and the legal actions it inspired founder on the rock of common sense. Men who see violence done or read about it will become violent themselves. Isn't it self-evident?

It is self-evident that we should beware of self-evident truths. It was common sense, bolstered by the unquestionable authority of science, that made Mengele believe that the Jews were a dangerously defective, nonhuman race. It is common sense that prompts criminologists to search for a hidden deviation in ordinary men who commit unspeakable atrocities. It is common sense that tells us that if people are fed, they will not go to war.

We are still caught in the double myth of the Garden of Eden and the Fall of Man. If children are corrupted by horror comics and violent television shows, does it mean that left to their own devices, they will grow up nurturing and cooperative? This Rousseau-like view, popular in the 1960s and 1970s, is increasingly giving way to the sociobiological argument that aggression is inherent in the human genetic make-up. But those are two sides of the same coin. In both cases violence is seen as a single definable entity, either a germ that infects primal innocence or a hereditary disease that civilization can cure. In both cases, representation of violence serves as a vector of transmission, either dropping the venom of corruption into the pristine mind or awakening the dormant pathogen. Just ratchet up the movie rating system, ban violent pornography, tone down literary mayhem, and society will be cured.

Metaphors are dangerous tools of thought. As we have seen above, radical attempts to cure the body politic of violence led to bloodshed, and the search for absolute health ended in the sickness of persecution and genocide. Violence is not a "contagion." It is neither a disease of language nor the genetic inheritance of our beastly ancestors. It is a human possibility, a form of behavior that humans can engage in, just as they can engage in love, politics, art, stamp collecting, or transcendental meditation. It exists not because we are burdened with animal instincts but because we are not. Humans are "flawed," incomplete animals, making up with extraordinary learning capacity for the weak or absent biological programming. There are presumably some forms of behavior that are outside the realm of human nature, but we will never know what they are, because anything somebody can imagine, somebody else will do.

Civilization, as T. H. Huxley so presciently recognized while all around him scientists, writers, and intellectuals hurried to prop up their pet utopias with the symbolic authority of Nature, is profoundly unnatural. Freedom of choice sounds somewhat old-fashioned, squeezed between the post–Foucaldian primacy of discourse and the post–Human Genome Project primacy of the hard-wired brain, but it is nevertheless indispensable if we are ever to understand violence. Serial killers kill because they want to kill, says John Douglas, with some chagrin at being unable to discover any deeper secret after a lifetime of profiling violent criminals. And bookstores do a brisk trade in Douglas's titillating autopsies of the victims' bodies and the killers' minds, because people want to read them.

The desire for violence is part of human freedom and thus it can never be eliminated, only confronted. Reading Kant through Lacan, Joan Copjec claims: "Human freedom makes radical evil a structural inescapability" (xxvi). And if violence is embedded in the structure of the subject, it is equally embedded in the structure of the narrative through which the subject constructs himself. Whatever form the bloodscripts take, they are present in any conceivable cultural configuration in which human beings apprehend the fact that they are capable of making other human beings bleed. To ban narratives of violence, we would have to ban narrative altogether.

In *Demonic Males* Richard Wrangham and Dale Peterson, drawing on the evidence of our genetic closeness to the chimpanzees, suggest the explanation for human violence is the "coalitionary bonds among males" (167). Predation is widespread in the animal world but intraspecies violence as a choice is rare. Male chimps, however, formed into party gangs, kill other chimps for no obvious reason (incidentally, female chimps can be violent too, engaging in infanticide and mutual fighting). Is this the biological bedrock of aggression? But one might just as well claim that the behavior of street gangs in the Bronx explains the killings among rival chimp bands. In other words, genetic closeness cuts both ways: we cannot deny freedom of choice or even glimmerings of self-consciousness to our nearest simian relatives. Perhaps what set us on the road to freedom is precisely the weakening of the inhibition against killing members of one's own species, along with the loosening of the other inherent regulators of behavior. Perhaps the chimps are following in our footsteps rather than our helplessly repeating the simian patterns of the evolutionary past.

But to the best of our knowledge, chimps do not tell each other stories, and thus animal violence cannot become embedded in a cultural matrix. We live in, and through, language, whether it is conceived as a prison house or as an infinite playground. Once violence becomes a possibility of action, it also becomes a possibility of language, and therefore, of narrative. A loop is formed, in which a subject's choice of violence is reinforced by the violent narratives of his culture, while these narratives are fed by such choices. It seems seductively simple, then, to end a journey through bloodscripts with a pious hope that somewhere in the brighter future this loop will be cut, ushering in the millennium of peace. And if I refuse to do so, it is not only because I believe this hope is unrealistic—all hopes are—but because I think it is dangerous.

Setting the elimination of all violence as its goal, society might encourage the apocalyptic quest for purity that would end up washing away the stain of human imperfection with blood. For the seduction of the sublime subject is precisely this: the end to inner division, ambiguity, contingency, to the makeshift nature of the human self, provisionally constructed in language and narrative. And it is seduction all the more powerful since it is never—nor can it be ever—consummated.

The source of the violent sublime is the human body, vulnerable, aching, and mortal. To inflict agony and death on another human being produces in the perpetrator a sense of transcendence, which is also the sense of escape from the limitations of his own embodied self. But this escape is temporary; eventually, the murderer has to return from the realm of the sublime into the realm of language. Nobody is born a killer (though in some cultures every male is predestined to become one). But having once experienced the loss of self in violence, a killer has to fit it into a self-narrative, to rewrite his life-story. Culture offers him a number of templates: a tough guy, a smooth operator, a soldier of the Motherland, a holy warrior, a New Man. But no story can quite soak up the sight of the torn and bleeding flesh, the impact of the body, once as alive as the body of the killer and now as irrevocably dead as his body will one day be. We are all brothers and sisters under the skin. And the killer himself lives with the knowledge of narrative's duplicity, both accepting his new identity and often proud of it and yet at the same time recognizing its deception. The only way to escape this aporia is to plunge, over and over again, into the wordless ecstasy of violence, in which momentarily all ambiguities of language are obliterated.

Educators might hope to teach children the danger of addiction to the violent sublime; feminists might fight the fictions of masculinity that equate courage with mindless aggression; dreamers might imagine a world in which economic spurs to violence are minimized. But any attempt to provide a final solution to the problem of violence will bring about the usual catastrophic results of a final solution because it will attempt to do the impossible: to eliminate free choice from human behavior and free play of meaning from human language.

RUNNING FREE

And yet the ethically minded would rebel at the thought that there is nothing to be done and that violence, like the poor, will always be with us. If not elimination, what about resistance? On what ground can the resistance to violence fight its battle? Censorship breeds underground pornography, education—guns in the classroom, and persuasion—ridicule. It almost seems preferable to declare, with a fashionable kind of apocalyptic gloom, that all discourse is violent by definition and that there is no difference between violent speech and violent action. This position, however, is vulnerable to the same kind of refutation as the one employed by Dr. Johnson against Bishop Berkeley: namely, a kick.

When Foucault in his last works gropes toward defining a position of resistance to power and knowledge, he attempts to situate it in the human body itself. The body's vulnerability is the source of the violent sublime and yet, paradoxically, it might also offer the last-ditch defense against its seduction. Adorno in *Negative Dialectics* sets the materiality of the body against what he sees as the murderously "metaphysical" nature of the Holocaust by claiming that "the course of history forces materialism upon metaphysics" (365). Andrew Hewitt, in his discussion of Adorno, points out that it is not only the body's mortality but also its capacity for pleasure, the "flows and functions" of its survival, that constitute a bulwark against ideology (77). But both attend to the body of the victim; I would shift the focus to the body of the perpetrator. Whatever pain or pleasure the victim experiences in his body, it is incommunicable and thus cannot offer resistance to the murderous power. It is only when the perpetrator's and the bystander's bodies thrill or cringe in empathic identification that corporeality enters the social circulation of meaning and becomes capable of infecting and weakening the metaphysical edifice of ideology. This identification, as I have argued, creates desire for violence in the first place, for without it, there would be no sublime subjects. If violence were *only* instrumental, Auschwitz would not have been built. But it is also a site—perhaps *the* site—of resistance, for through the shiver, the recoil, the nausea, the perpetrator recognizes his own "functions and flows" in the terminal convulsions of the victim.

And insofar as the bystander, the witness, the reader of the bloodscripts, shares in the perpetrator's pleasure, he also shares in his abasement. This abasement, conveyed through the convulsion of narrative, concedes the ultimate victory of the body. Glimpsed through "those ejaculations of language that no terror could eradicate" (101), the shared corporeality of the victim, the perpetrator, and the bystander offers not a hope of totally eradicating violence—such a hope can only lead to more terror—but a limit to its power.

In Ballard's fable that I discussed at the beginning of this chapter, the children of utopia kill because they have never learnt to recognize their own mortality in the mortality of others through the medium of bloodscripts. They have not shared in the bloody exploits of It or the Wolfman, only to recoil from the monster at the end. They have not followed Sherlock Holmes on the trail of Victorian evildoers, only to recognize that while the murderer is neutralized, murder is not. They have never seen Nazi demigods, strutting around in their Star War uniforms, only to watch their downfall into abjection. Violence for them becomes both meaningless and inescapable. Running away from the antiseptic narrative of happily-ever-after forced upon them by their parents, the childern kill and kill again, futilely trying to find themselves in a story of their own.

The bloodscripts, whether high art or pop culture, provide a frame to express, define, and delimit violence. Consciously or not, they reveal the truth underlying the false promise of omnipotence inherent in the act of murder. This truth is the dead body itself, immune to the regulating power of discourse, taunting the killer with its unsubdued materiality. In discussing the writings of Sade, de Beauvoir rhetorically asks: "But what would the tyrant do with this *inert object,* a corpse?" (31). The answer is nothing except recognize his own potential inertness in this chunk of the flesh, and this is the recognition no tyrant is willing to face. Promising manhood to the impotent, strength to the weak, divinity to the downtrodden, violence delivers nothing but what is available to every human being anyway: mortality.

Notes

Notes to Introduction

1. I use "subject" and "subjectivity" to designate the culturally and socially endorsed image of the self. In other words, a subject is a way in which a person is perceived by others and by themselves within a specific social configuration.

2. By narrative representation I mean simply storytelling in the broadest sense of the word. Narrative, as it is widely accepted today, constitutes one of the main ways in which human beings apprehend themselves and their world. We make sense of our experience by telling stories; in other words, by constructing narratives according to the generic rules of our culture.

3. Except for special cases, I use the third-person masculine pronoun in referring to violent subjects. This reflects the simple fact that most violent subjects analyzed in this book are men. However, this does not mean I endorse the often-voiced claim that violence is somehow endemic to male sexuality. Later in the book I argue against this contention, as articulated by Rosalind Miles, Maria Tatar, Cameron and Frazer, and Robin Morgan in *The Demon Lover*. Violence is a human activity that may be freely chosen by both male and female subjects. Women, despite social and physical limitations, have participated in wars, executions, and genocide. Even with regard to the most extreme and sexualized forms of violence, there have been several widely publicized cases, such as the Moor murders of Brady and Hindley and the activities of Fred and Rose West in which a male and a female murderer worked in tandem, with the female partner being every bit as sadistic as the male. But the social construction of gender makes it very difficult for women to find an appropriate script for their violent behavior. Most cultures, including Western culture, have circumscribed female physical violence by an array of taboos. The indisputable fact that a majority of violent offenders are men testifies to the cultural gendering of self-transcendence as masculine rather than to any innate proclivity of women to pacifism. Aggression, short of actual murder, is written into the narratives of masculine sexual identity in a way that makes it much easier for a male to slide into extreme violence, often directed against women. However, precisely because this intersection between violence and male sexuality has been so insistently portrayed and so extensively analyzed, I want to displace it by looking at the dynamics of violence that both underlies and subverts gender.

4. The distinction between narrative and historical truth is made by Donald Spence with regard to the stories told by patients in therapy: the narrative truth is a psychologically satisfactory script that emerges in the process of therapy, while the historical truth is the actual facts of the patient's life.

5. The American psychologist at Nuremberg G. H. Gilbert described him as "a man who is intellectually normal but with the schizoid apathy, insensitivity and lack of empathy that could hardly be more extreme in a frank psychotic" (Gilbert 239).

6. Again, we might be skeptical about such claims. But in the case of the Holocaust perpetrators, recent historical studies have conclusively shown that the worst mass killers in modern history were, as in the titles of the books by Daniel Goldhagen and Christopher Browning, "ordinary" Germans or "ordinary" men, depending whether the emphasis is on the historical specificity of the Holocaust or on the general human vulnerability to evil. It must be stressed, however, that such "ordinariness" does not equal Hanna Arendt's "banality of evil," which, as I will argue in chapter 5, completely distorts the ideal subjectivity the Nazi killers strove to possess. They did not see themselves as bureaucrats of extermination. They were "ordinary" only in the sense of not suffering from any mental disorder.

7. *Lingua Tertii Imperii: The Language of the Third Reich,* is a book written by Victor Klemperer, a Jewish scholar who survived in Nazi Germany by going underground. The book, published in 1949, describes the Nazi misuse of language.

8. Derrida, *Of Grammatology.*

9. See Rhodes on the concept of "violent meaning" as the way in which the perpetrator explains his act to himself.

10. The existence of such inherent mechanisms limiting aggression in both animals and humans has been recognized by biologists, anthropologists, and historians. See, for example, O'Connell's *Ride of the Second Horseman*.

11. Probably unwittingly, the veteran repeats the words of the terrorist Chen in Malraux's *La Condition Humaine*: "A man who has never killed is a virgin" (qtd. in Kott 72).

12. I will occasionally use the Lacanian terminology of the Symbolic, the Imaginary, and the Real but only as useful metaphors for the different phenomenological or cultural registers, or both, that I will discuss. For Lacan's own definition of these registers, see his *Écrits*. Fredric Jameson gives what, in my opinion, is the most lucid exposition of the Lacanian "three orders" in his essay "Imaginary and Symbolic in Lacan." According to Jameson, the Imaginary is a "configuration of space . . . which swarms with bodies and forms . . . whose fundamental property is . . . to be visible . . . to be, as it were, already-seen, to carry their specularity upon themselves like a color they wear or the texture of their surface" (1977, 355). The Imaginary is an archaic region of fluid and unformed subjectivity, of perpetual exchange of places, but also of "struggle, violence, and antagonism" (ibid. 356). The Symbolic is the discursive register, in which a stable and law-abiding self is formed. The Real, the most enigmatic term, is the "remainder" outside language, "that which resists symbolization." Jameson identifies the Real as "History itself" (ibid. 384). "History itself" is not necessarily a more illuminating term than "the Real," but Jameson's analysis makes it clear that the Lacanian terminology is a convenient shorthand that may be used for approaches remote from psychoanalysis, as is the case with Jameson's own neo-Marxism. My own approach is neither psychoanalytical nor Marxist, but I follow Jameson in making use of the Lacanian terms for my own purposes when it seems appropriate to do so.

13. Dickens knew the power of this scene and always included it in the public readings he gave during the last years of his life, invariably causing some members of the audience to faint.

14. See Friedrich Nietzsche, *Human, All Too Human.*

15. See *Eichmann in Jerusalem,* by Hannah Arendt, and *Radical Evil,* edited by Joan Copjec.

16. By narrative dynamics I mean the unfolding of a narrative of the self in time.
17. See Jameson's *The Political Unconscious.*

Notes to Chapter 1

1. I am going to use the neutral pronoun for the monster, just as horror texts often do. Below, I will consider in greater detail the monster's subversion of gender identity.

2. The recent film *The Hollow Man* reduces Wells's complex exploration of violence and nonconformity to a run-of-the-mill warning against the dangers of science. However, the focus on the body's interiority and the connection between visibility and pain are preserved in the film's few good scenes, which use contemporary special effects techniques to stage Dr. Sebastian Caine's transformations.

3. The precursor of horror fiction is the Gothic novel of the late-eighteenth century (whose popularity was greatest in the period from the 1780s to the 1820s). Born with the publication of Hugh Walpole's *The Castle of Otranto* (1780) and developed by such writers as Ann Radcliffe, "Monk" Lewis, Charles Maturin, and others, the Gothic novel revolutionized literature by introducing hitherto prohibited themes—supernatural, violence, incest—and employing a variety of startlingly innovative techniques, including multiple and unreliable point of view, embedded narratives, and play with fiction/nonfiction divide. The overall aesthetics of the Gothic novel were influenced by the contemporary discourse of the sublime, resulting in an attempt to find a fictional equivalent to the theories of Longinus and Burke. Contemporary horror has inherited many Gothic narrative techniques and so have "higher" literary genres. But the horror as we know it today originates in the fin de siècle, its generic parameters defined by Robert Louis Stevenson's *The Strange Story of Dr. Jekyll and Mr Hyde* (1886), H. G. Wells's *The Invisible Man* (1896), Bram Stoker's *Dracula* (1896), and many others, including novels and short stories of Arthur Machen, M. R. James, and later William Hope Hodgson and Algernon Blackwood.

4. Following Freud's own lead in his analysis of E. T. A. Hoffmann's horror tale "The Sandman" in *The Uncanny,* theories of horror have strip-mined the genre for illustrations of psychoanalytic concepts, dutifully matching its conventions with repressed infantile desires, Oedipal traumas, and toilet-training scars.

5. Like all vampires, Carmilla does not age. She is actually Laura's distant ancestor. But what is even more significant, Laura remembers Carmilla's face watching over her cradle in her early childhood. Mothering becomes a prelude to murder.

6. See, for example, Philip Martin's "The Vampire in the Looking-Glass."

7. The current fashion of seeing serial killers as victims of childhood abuse (which I will discuss in detail in the next chapter) is a peculiar application of this narrative trope of horror to the enigma of the real-life violent psyche.

8. Benjamin, trying to escape the Nazi persecution of the Jews, killed himself in 1940.

9. In this novel the progeny of Dracula have taken over the Communist bureaucracy of Causescu's Romania. Dracula, appalled by the large-scale excesses of this institutional monstrosity, eventually engineers a coup. In staging this confrontation between an old-fashioned individual monster and a monstrous body politic, Simmons is keenly aware both of the generic tradition of "classic" horror and of its subterranean connection to utopian ideologies. See Dan Simmons's *Children of the Night.*

Notes to Chapter 2

1. With regard to serial killers, even more so than with regard to ordinary murderers, the

issue of gender seems to be inevitable. Many (though not all) serial murders contain an explicitly sexual element in the rape or sexual torture of the victim. Most (though not all) serial killers are male. Popular culture underscores the sexual character of serial murder, as in the baroque near-pornography of *Kiss the Girls.* However, I would be extremely wary of drawing the seemingly obvious conclusion that there is a direct causal link between male sexuality and serial murder, as does Morgan in *The Demon Lover.* Cameron and Frazer's more nuanced suggestion that serial killers pursue a special kind of transcendence, which Western culture designates as masculine, seems to me much closer to the mark. Though they do not define it as such, this "transcendence" in many ways parallels my concept of the violent sublime. It seems that in the self-scripts of serial killers violence not so much develops out of, as replaces, sexuality, so that initially gay perpetrators, such as Jeffrey Dahmer, choose male victims.

2. Many serial murderers enter into a quasi-symbiotic relationship with the media, becoming enamored of their own notoriety. Moreover, even before being caught, they sometimes attempt to manipulate their own media image, either by writing letters to the police, as did the original Jack the Ripper, or committing more murders, as Ted Bundy claimed to have done. After being captured they often willingly cooperate with psychologists or journalists. Bundy's communication skills were noted by the media and his biographers alike whom he seemed to enjoy manipulating. Nilsen's cooperation with his biographer, on the other hand, suggested an attempt to understand his own behavior. In any case, both of them had no difficulty in speaking the language of their society.

3. Moreover, they are also story characters. Douglas sees himself and his colleagues as direct descendants of the nineteenth-century Great Detectives, stating that "our [criminal profilers'] antecedents actually do go back to crime fiction more than crime fact" and devoting a considerable amount of space to a knowledgeable discussion of Poe, Wilkie Collins, and Arthur Conan Doyle (1996, 32–33).

4. Polygenesis was the belief that different human races had independent evolutionary origins in the transition from hominids to humans and thus were, in effect, different species.

5. In the recent film *Red Dragon,* Dollarhyde's physical monstrosity is minimized (just a harelip), and he is saddled instead with a slew of traumas, outlandish delusions, and plain meanness, making him into yet another patchwork and incoherent self.

6. This is the Lecter of *Silence of the Lambs.* The Lecter of the recent *Hannibal* is quite a different matter. He is furnished with a life story, so muddled and improbable as to make sense only in terms of pop-mythology. In these terms, Lecter, a victim of Nazism (!), is firmly assimilated to the victimization paradigm and made to battle a monster so grotesque that we are supposed to see him as a sort of dark Christ, smiting violence with violence. Instead, however, he becomes ridiculous, his affair with Clarice Starling descending into bathos, and the cannibalistic Eucharist he shares with her is more likely to upset the reader's stomach than to provide any metaphysical insights. Apart from the failure of the author's imagination, there is a structural reason for the failure of *Hanniba*l the novel and the subsequent film. The attraction of the original Lecter lies precisely in his challenge to narrativity. Any narrative sequel, in trying to "develop" the character, is bound to destroy him.

7. Unlike the unflappable Lecter, Brady became seriously disturbed during his incarceration.

Notes to Chapter 3

1. The ears belong to the spinster's youngest sister, Mrs. Browner, and her lover, both murdered by her husband. The husband blames the middle sister, who was in love with him,

for leading his wife astray and mails her the gruesome package, which by mistake arrives at the eldest sister's, the only one not involved with the tragedy.

2. Chesterton's religious worldview resonates with the theology and worldview of St. Thomas Aquinas. This Scholasticism (based ultimately on Aristotle) saw the universe and belief itself as "reasonable." Every aspect of this theological system revolves around Ratio. "Supernaturalism" flies in the face of this faith: first, because access to the Divine is through Christ and the Church; second, because the chaos of the supernatural could be led by the Evil One. There are, of course, profound mysteries which humans cannot really fathom: the Incarnation, the Eucharist, the Resurrection. But there are attempts to make them "reasonable": it was said, for example, that in Transubstantiation, the form remains the same but the substance is the Body of Christ. Thus, Father Brown becomes a kind of teleological detective, discovering the pattern and meaning that was there all the time (I am grateful to Dr. Stephen A. Weninger for this information and insight).

3. See Stephen Jay Gould, *Ontogeny and Phylogeny,* for a detailed exposition of this concept and its history.

4. Of course, toward the end of his career, Poirot should have been more than 120 years old. Reflecting the longevity of his creator, his unchanging age (for he is equally described as "elderly" in the 1920s and the 1970s) adds to his ghostly aura.

5. Giles Deleuze, a French philosopher, described what he called "a body without organs," an imaginary corporeality of pleasure, in his book *Anti-Oedipus,* co-authored with Felix Guattari.

6. See Kelves and Proctor on eugenics and Nazi medicine. Also see chapter 5.

Notes to Chapter 4

1. In a 1992 article, Krishan Kumar takes issue with this point of view. He denies that "the fate of utopia is tied to particular social philosophies and social practices" (1993, 71). However, later he somewhat contradictorily argues that modern—that is, nineteenth- and twentieth-century—utopia, is a product of a specific ideology, namely socialism. National Socialism is not mentioned immediately, but ultimately Kumar concedes that "fascism is a utopia; so too is Communism in its Soviet form" (65). The question of the violence of these two regimes and its link to the utopian ideologies is raised implicitly but never explicitly addressed. See also Moylan's discussion of the "critical utopia."

2. See Griffin 202–203. Griffin's reader on fascism emphasizes the creation of the New Man as one of the primary goals of fascism in all its varieties. Insofar as fascism (including National Socialism) was utopian and not simply repressive, its endlessly reiterated goal was the birth of the new subject of history which Otto Strasser, one of the *volkish* ideologues, calls "the new type of human being" (qtd. in Griffin 115).

3. On the place of women and femininity in Nazism see Claudia Koonz's *Mothers in the Fatherland.* This volume argues that while the social politics of Nazism were uniformly reactionary, the symbolic role of femininity in Nazi discourse was very important, split between the covert disgust I describe in this section and the eugenicist glorification of motherhood, not that different from Shaw's. On the development of the argument about the politics of metaphor, see my "Hard and Wet," 199–223.

4. This is probably the single most unjustified political accusation ever hurled at Stalin, who was at this point on the brink of seizing complete control of the party and eradicating whatever "democratic taint" was still left.

5. His date, of course, turns out to be the criminal. Vadim's very name is a mark of his foreignness to his textual universe. Vadim is a first name that cannot be a family name in

Russian. It is, however, evocative of the French actor Roger Vadim, who was very popular in the Soviet Union, thus indicating the character's adopted "Frenchness," reinforced by his occasional musings on existentialist philosophy.

6. E. M. Cioran writes in *History and Utopia:* "In a perfect city, all conflict would cease; human wills would be throttled, mollified, or rendered miraculously convergent; there would reign only unity, without the ingredient of chance or contradiction" (87).

7. The survival of these mores in the Third Reich, alongside the regime's utopian attempts to restructure family life and to separate children from parents, is well known. The same dynamics obtained in the Soviet Union under Stalin. The last years of his power were marked by a resurgence of almost-Victorian attitudes, with separate schooling for boys and girls, emphasis on the sacredness of the family, and so on.

8. The "red-brown" is the popular name for the common front of Communists and Neo-Nazis in Russia.

9. Globocnik, Buhler, and several other characters in *Fatherland* are historical figures who died or were executed after the war. Their presence in the fantastic world of the text, like the mythologizing of Josef Mengele I will discuss in the next chapter, testifies to the centrality of the Third Reich and the murderous utopia it represented in the collective imagination rather than merely collective memory.

Notes to Chapter 5

1. Gottfried Benn's quote is from *Der neue Staat und die Intellektuellen* ("The New State and the Intellectuals"), published by Deutsche Verlags-Anstalt in 1933. Pierre Drieu La Rochelle's essay "Renaissance de l'homme européen" is part of *Notes pour comprendre le siècle*. The last two texts are excerpted in Roger Griffin's *Fascism*, 136 and 203 respectively.

2. I refer here to numerous studies of eugenics and its aftermath. See Kelves, Proctor, and Pernick.

3. Hess made this statement at a mass meeting in 1934. See Lifton 31.

4. On the role and scope of eugenics outside Germany, see Daniel Kelves's *In The Name of Eugenics.* Proctor, Burleigh, and Whippermann discuss the amalgamation of eugenics and Nazi racial science, while Pernick discusses some of the implications of the similarities between respectable "mainline" eugenics in the English-speaking world and Nazism.

5. W. Duncan McKim, in his eugenicist treatise published in 1900, advocated "a gentle and painless death" by carbonic gas for an amazing variety of deviant types, including tramps and housebreakers.

6. See the essays in *The Deputy Reader,* Schmidt and Schmidt, eds., that accurately reflect the contemporary debate over Hochhuth's representation of the Doctor.

7. Lifton and Proctor both consider the validity of the scientific work done in death camps, and both come to the conclusion that, at best, it was puerile, at worst, fake. Mengele's research on twins was indeed a continuation of an important trend in eugenics and human genetics, but he did not achieve anything that could not have been achieved with more or less orthodox methods. On the nature of his experiments, see his surviving subjects' testimonies in Lucette Matalon and Sheila Dekel's *Children of the Flames.*

8. See, for example, Haynes and McConnell, both deriving the figure of Moreau from Frankenstein, even though McConnell is more aware of the contemporary relevance of Wells's "mad scientist."

9. In the debate over vivisection, physiologists' general argument was pragmatic: infliction of pain on animals might be regrettable, but it was necessary to alleviate human suffering and to obtain knowledge. Claude Bernard's *Experimental Medicine* promoted this approach.

10. Twin research was central to racial hygiene and anthropology in the Third Reich. Eugen Fischer, a prominent Nazi eugenicist, called twin studies "*the* single most important research tool in the field of racial hygiene," while Otmar von Verschuer, Mengele's scientific patron to whom the latter submitted all "research material" from Auschwitz, claimed it was "the sovereign method for genetic research in humans." All multiple births in the Reich were registered expressly "to isolate the effects of nature and nurture in the formation of the human racial constitution" (Proctor 42–43).

11. Despite the unquestionable primacy of social constructionism in the humanities, the trend in biology, psychiatry, psychology, and even anthropology is the opposite, strengthened by the stunning developments in human genetics. To take an example almost at random, the *Herald Tribune* of October 4, 2001 published a small news item announcing the discovery of a gene, FOXP2, that is linked to language development. The item nonchalantly announces that the discovery raises hopes "that the genetic revolution is closer to identifying roots of conscious thought and, perhaps, refining what it means to be human" ("Gene Tied to Language is Found," 4). Although, of course, no such identification is possible on the strength of a single gene, the humanities would do well to pay attention to such developments and expose them as a continuation of the long and unsavory history of bio-ideologies. However, is there a point to building an elaborate edifice of theory on the foundations of de Saussure and Freud, if both language and the structure of the mind are shown to be genetically determined to a much greater extent than was previously believed?

Notes to Chapter 6

1. The recent film *Event Horizon* literalized the metaphor of the black hole as hell, with results remarkable for both spectacular special effects and plot incoherence.

2. The scandalous response of the West to the genocide in Rwanda was marked precisely by the unwillingness to study its historical and ideological roots and thus to see it for what it was: not a "tribal war" but a political mass murder. As a result, humanitarian help was offered not to the victims but to the perpetrators, when the latter fled the country and became refugees. Impressed by the killers' trauma of uprooting and homelessness, humanitarian agencies refused to judge their past deeds and thus became accomplices in one of the twentieth century's worst ideological slaughters, on a par with the Holocaust and the autogenocide of Cambodia. See Gourevitch's *We Wish to Inform You That Tomorrow We Will Be Killed with Our Families . . . Stories From Rwanda.* and Keane's *Season of Blood: A Rwandan Journey*.

3. An "upliner" in the novel is a person from the protagonist's future.

4. The chronoclasm is also known as "the grandfather's paradox" because of the following illustration: one can travel into the past and kill one's grandfather, thus preventing oneself from being born, which in turn would make it impossible to kill one's grandfather.

Note to Conclusion

1. "Anus mundi," "the anus of the world," is the way Auschwitz is described in Lifton's book, based on his interviews with survivors.

Works Cited

Adorno, Theodor. *Negative Dialectics.* Translated by E. B. Ashton. New York: Continuum, 1987.

Alford, C. Fred. *What Evil Means to Us.* Ithaca, NY: Cornell University Press, 1997.

Aly, Gotz, Peter Chroust, and Christopher Pross. *Cleansing the Fatherland: Nazi Medicine and Racial Hygiene.* Translated by Belinda Cooper. Baltimore: Johns Hopkins University Press, 1994.

Amery, Jean. *At the Mind's Limits: Contemplations by a Survivor on Auschwitz and Its Realities.* Translated by Sidney Rosenfeld and Stella P. Rosenfeld. Bloomington: Indiana University Press, 1980.

Arendt, Hannah. *Eichmann in Jerusalem: A Report on the Banality of Evil.* New York: The Viking Press, 1963.

———. *On Violence.* New York: Harcourt, Brace and World, 1970.

Aristotle's Poetics. Translated by Leon Goldman. Englewood Cliffs, NJ: Prentice-Hall, 1968.

Armstrong, Charles Wickstead. *The Survival of the Unfittest.* London: The C. W. Daniel Company, 1927.

Armstrong, Nancy, and Leonard Tennenhouse, eds. *The Violence of Representation: Literature and the History of Violence.* London: Routledge, 1989.

Ashfield, Andrew and Peter de Bolla, eds. *The Sublime: A Reader in British Eighteenth-Century Aesthetic Theory.* Cambridge: Harvard University Press, 1996.

Ashheim, Steven E. *The Nietzschean Legacy in Germany 1800–1900.* Berkeley: University of California Press, 1992.

Auden, W. H. "The Guilty Vicarage." In W. H. Auden, *The Dyer's Hand and Other Essays.* London: Faber and Faber, 1963.

Babener, Liahna Klenman. "The Shadow's Shadow: The Motif of the Double in Edgar Allan Poe's 'The Purloined Letter.'" *Mystery and Detection Annual* 1 (1972).

Bagehot, Walter. *Physics and Politics: Or Thoughts on the Application of the Principles of 'Natural Selection' and 'Inheritance' to Political Society.* London: Henry and King Co., 1872.

Baldick, Chris. *In Frankenstein's Shadow: Myth, Monstrosity, and Nineteenth-Century Writing.* Oxford: Clarendon Press, 1990.

Ballard, J. G. (1988). *Running Wild.* London: Flamingo Books, 1997.

Bann, Stephen and Krishan Kumar, eds. *Utopia and the Millennium.* London: Reaktion Books, 1993.

Barker, Clive (1984). *Books of Blood: Volume One.* New York: Berkley Books, 1986a.

———. (1984). *Books of Blood: Volume Two.* New York: Berkley Books, 1986b.

———. (1984). *Books of Blood: Volume Three.* London: Sphere Books.

———. (1984). *The Inhuman Condition* (first published as *Books of Blood: Volume Four*). New York: Pocket Books, 1987.

———. (1984). *In The Flesh* (first published as *Books of Blood: Volume Five*). New York: Pocket Books, 1988.

———. (1984). *Books of Blood: Volume Six.* London: Sphere Books, 1985.

———. "The Hellbound Heart." In *Night Visions: The Hellbound Heart.* Edited by George R. R. Martin. New York: Berkley Books, 1988a.

———. *Cabal: The Nightbreed.* London: Fontana/Collins Books, 1988b.

———. *Imajica.* London: Fontana Books, 1992.

Barker, Clive, Murray Close, and Stephen Jones. *Clive Barker's The Nightbreed Chronicles.* London: Titan Books, 1990.

Barker, Francis. *The Culture of Violence: Essays on Tragedy and History.* Chicago: University of Chicago Press, 1993.

Barthes, Roland. *Image, Music, Text.* Translated by Stephen Heath. New York: Hill and Wang, 1977.

Bataille, Georges. *Essential Writings.* Edited and translated by Michael Richardson. London: SAGE Publications, 1998.

Baudrillard, Jean. "The Ecstasy of Communication." In *The Post-Modern Reader.* Edited by Charles Jencks. London: Academy Editions, 1992.

Benjamin, Walter (1921). "Critique of Violence." In *Walter Benjamin, Selected Writings, Volume 1 (1913–1926).* Edited by Marcus Bullock and Michael W. Jennings. Cambridge: Belknap Press of Harvard University, 1996, 236–53.

———. *Illuminations: Essays and Reflections.* Translated by Harry Zohn. New York: Schocken Books, 1969.

Berger, James. *After the End: Representations of Post-Apocalypse.* Minneapolis: University of Minnesota Press, 1999.

Bernard, Claude (1865). *An Introduction to the Study of Experimental Medicine.* Translated by Henry Copley Greene. New York: Dover Publications, 1957.

Bersani, Leo. "Is the Rectum a Grave?" In *AIDS: Cultural Analysis, Cultural Activism.* Edited by Douglas Crimp. Cambridge: MIT Press, 1988, 197–223.

Biagioli, Mario. "Science, Modernity, and the 'Final Solution.'" In Friedlander 1992, 185–206.

Bjerre, Andreas. *The Psychology of Murder: A Study in Criminal Psychology.* London: Longman, Green and Co, 1927.

Black, Joel. *The Aesthetics of Murder: A Study of Romantic Literature and Contemporary Culture.* Baltimore: Johns Hopkins University Press, 1991.

Blanchot, Maurice. *The Writings of the Disaster.* Translated by Ann Smock. Lincoln: University of Nebraska Press, 1995.

Booker, Keith M. *The Dystopian Impulse in Modern Literature.* Westport, CT: Greenwood Press, 1994.

Borges, Jorge Luis. *Labyrinths: Selected Stories and Other Writings.* Edited by Donald A. Yates and James E. Irby. New York: New Directions Books, 1964.

Boscaglia, Maurizia. *The Eye on the Flesh: Fashions of Masculinity in the Early Twentieth Century.* Boulder, CO: Westview Press, 1996.

Bowler, Peter J. *Evolution: The History of an Idea.* Berkeley: University of California Press, 1986.

Bradbury, Ray. "Skeleton." In *The Vintage Bradbury.* New York: Vintage Books, 1965, 179–97.

Brooks, Peter. "Godlike Science/Unhallowed Arts: Language, Nature, and Monstrosity." In *The Endurance of Frankenstein: Essays on Mary Shelley's Novel.* Edited by George Levine and U. C. Knoepfmacher. Berkeley: University of California Press, 1979, 200–14.

Browning, Christopher R. *Ordinary Men: Reserve Police Battalion 101 and the Final Solution.* New York: HarperCollins, 1992.

Bruhm, Steven. *Gothic Bodies: The Politics of Pain in Romantic Fiction.* Philadelphia: University of Pennsylvania Press, 1994.

Bullock, Alan. *Hitler and Stalin: Parallel Lives.* New York: Vintage Books, 1993.

Burke, Edmund (1757). *A Philosophical Enquiry into the Origins of Our Ideas of the Sublime and the Beautiful.* Edited by Adam Phillips. Oxford: Oxford University Press, 1990.

Burleigh, Michael, *Ethics and Extermination: Reflections on Nazi Genocide.* Cambridge: Cambridge University Press, 1997.

Burleigh, Michael, and Wolfgang Whippermann. *The Racial State: Germany 1939–1945.* Cambridge: Cambridge University Press, 1991.

Burrin, Philippe. *Hitler and the Jews: The Genesis of the Holocaust.* London: Edward Arnold, 1994.

Burroughs, Catherine B., Jeffrey David Ehrenreich, and Carlo Ginzburg. *Clues, Myths, and the Historical Method.* Translated by John and Anne C. Tedeschi. Baltimore: Johns Hopkins University Press, 1989.

Burroughs, Catherine B., and Jeffrey David Ehrenreich, eds. *Reading the Social Body.* Iowa City: University of Iowa Press, 1993.

Butler, Judith. *Gender Trouble: Feminism and the Subversion of Identity.* London: Routledge, 1990.

———. *Bodies that Matter: On the Discursive Limits of 'Sex.'* London: Routledge, 1993.

Cameron, Deborah, and Elizabeth Frazer. *The Lust to Kill.* London: Polity Press, 1987.

Canter, David. *Criminal Shadows: Inside the Mind of the Serial Killer.* London: HarperCollins, 1994.

Carr, Caleb. *The Alienist.* New York: Bantam Books, 1994.

Carroll, Noel. *The Philosophy of Horror, or Paradoxes of the Heart.* New York: Routledge, 1990.

Caruth, Cathy, ed. *Trauma: Explorations in Memory.* Baltimore: The Johns Hopkins University Press, 1995.

Caruth, Cathy. *Unclaimed Experience: Trauma, Narrative, and History.* Baltimore: Johns Hopkins University Press, 1996.

Cawelti, John G. "Canonization, Modern Literature, and the Detective Story." In Delamater and Prigozy, eds., *Theory and Practice of Classic Detective Fiction,* 5–17.

Cheney, Margaret. *Why—The Serial Killer in America.* Saratoga, NY: E Publishers, 1992.

Chesterton, G. K. *The Complete Father Brown.* London: Penguin Books, 1986.

Christie, Agatha (1926). *The Murder of Roger Ackroyd.* London: Fontana/Collins, 1974.

———. (1931). *Peril at End House.* London: Fontana Books, 1971.

———. (1936). *Cards on the Table.* London: Pan Books, 1972.

———. (1937). "Dead Man's Mirror." In *Murder in the Mews.* London: Fontana Books, 1971, 100–68.

———. (1938). *A Holiday for Murder* (originally published as *Murder for Christmas*). New York: Bantam Books, 1973.

———. (1939). *Ten Little Indians.* New York: Pocket Books, 1967.

———. (1940). *One, Two, Buckle My Shoe.* London: Fontana Books, 1972.

———. (1942). *The Body in the Library.* London: Fontana Books, 1973.

———. (1956). *Dead Man's Folly.* Fontana/Collins, 1978.

———. (1961). *The Pale Horse.* London: Fontana/Collins, 1973.

———. (1969). *Hallowe'en Party*. London: Fontana/Collins, 1969.

———. *Curtain: Poirot's Last Case*. London: Fontana Books, 1975.

Cioran, E. M. *History and Utopia,* London: Quartet Books, 1987.

Connor, Steve, ed. *Charles Dickens*. New York: Longman, 1996.

Conrad, Joseph. *Heart of Darkness*. Edited and introduction by Paul O'Prey. London: Penguin Books, 1985.

Copjec, Joan, ed. *Radical Evil*. London: Verso, 1996.

Cornwell, Patricia. *Post-mortem*. New York: Avon Books, 1990.

———. *From Potter's Field*. London: Warner Books, 1996.

Crawford, Marion E. (1911). *For the Blood Is the Life and Other Stories*. Clarkston, GA: White Wolf Publishing, 1996.

Crispin, Edmund, ed. *Best Detective Stories*. London: Faber and Faber, 1959.

Crowe, Catherine (1848). *The Night-Side of Nature*. London: The Aquarian Press, 1986.

Currie, Mark. *Postmodern Narrative Theory*. London: Macmillan Press, 1998.

Darwin, Charles. *The Correspondence of Charles Darwin. Vol. 6, 1856–1857*. Cambridge University Press, 1990.

———. *The Correspondence of Charles Darwin. Vol. 8, 1860*. Cambridge: Cambridge University Press, 1993.

De Beauvoir, Simone. *The Marquis de Sade*. London: New English Library, 1972.

Delamater, Jerome H., and Ruth Prigozy, eds. *Theory and Practice of Classic Detective Fiction*. Westport, CT: Greenwood Press, 1997.

De Quincy, Thomas. *On Murder Considered As One of the Fine Arts and On War. Two Essays*. London: Doopler Press, 1980.

De Quiros, C. Bernardo. *Modern Theories of Criminality*. Translated by Alfonso de Salvio. Boston: Little, Brown and Company, 1911.

Derrida, Jacques. *Of Grammatology*. Translated by Gayatri Spivak. Baltimore: Johns Hopkins University Press, 1976.

Des Pres, Terence. *Writing into the World*. New York: Viking Press, 1991.

De Vries, Hent, and Samuel Weber, eds. *Violence, Identity, and Self-Determination*. Stanford: Stanford University Press, 1997.

Dick, Philip K. "The Golden Man." In *The Golden Man*. London: Methuen, 1981, 35–54..

Dickens, Charles (1837). *Oliver Twist*. London: Penguin Books, 1980.

———. (1843). *Martin Chuzzlewit*. London: Oxford University Press, 1951.

———. (1859). *A Tale of Two Cities*. Edited by George Woodcock. London: Penguin Books, 1988.

———. (1864). *Our Mutual Friend*. London: Penguin Books, 1986.

Docherty, Thomas. *Alterities: Criticism, History, Representation*. Oxford: Clarendon Press, 1996.

Dostoevskii, Fyodor Mikhailovitch (1866). *Prestuplenie i nakazanie* [Crime and Punishment]. Moscow: Belarus, 1969.

Douglas, John and Mark Olshaker. *Mindhunter: Inside the FBI Elite Serial Crime Unit*. London: Mandarin, 1996.

———. *Journey into Darkness*. New York: Pocket Star Books, 1997.

Doyle, Arthur Conan. *Sherlock Holmes: The Complete Facsimile Edition*. Hertfordshire: Wordsworth Editions, 1997.

Dreyfus, Hubert L., and Paul Rabinow. *Michel Foucault: Beyond Structuralism and Hermeneutics*. Chicago: University of Chicago Press, 1982.

Drieu La Rochelle, Pierre. "Renaissance de l'homme européen." In *Notes pour comprendre le siècle*. Paris: Gallimard, 1941.

Dunn, J. R. *Days of Cain.* London: Hodder and Stoughton, 1998.

Eagleton, Terry. *The Ideology of the Aesthetic.* Oxford: Basil Blackwell, 1990.

Eco, Umberto, and Thomas A. Sebeok, eds. *The Sign of Three: Dupin, Holmes, Peirce.* Bloomington: Indiana University Press, 1983.

Farmer, Penelope. *Two or the Book of Twins and Doubles: An Autobiographical Anthology.* London: Virago, 1996.

Felman, Shoshana, and Dori Laub, M.D. *Testimony: Crises of Witnessing in Literature, Psychoanalysis, and History.* New York: Routledge, 1992.

Ferri, Enrico. *Criminal Sociology.* New York: D. Appleton and Company, 1900.

Foucault, Michel (1961). *Madness and Civilization: A History of Insanity in the Age of Reason.* New York: Vintage, 1973.

———. (1963). *The Birth of the Clinic: An Archeology of Medical Perception.* London: Routledge, 1989.

———. (1966). *The Order of Things: An Archaeology of the Human Sciences.* London: Tavistock Publications, 1970.

———. (1975). *Discipline and Punish: The Birth of the Prison.* Translated by Alan Sheridan. London: Penguin Books, 1987.

Fox, James Alan, and Jack Levin. *Overkill: Mass Murder and Serial Killing Exposed.* New York: Plenum Press, 1994.

Frank, Gerold. *The Boston Strangler.* London: Pan Books, 1967.

Fraser, John. *Violence in the Arts.* Cambridge: Cambridge University Press, 1974.

French, Nicci. *The Memory Game.* London: Penguin Books, 1998.

Freud, Sigmund. "Medusa's Head" (1922 [1940]). In *The Standard Edition of the Complete Psychological Works of Sigmund Freud.* Vol. 18. Edited by James Strachey. London: The Hogarth Press and the Institute of Psychoanalysis, 1962, 273–74.

———. *Civilization and Its Discontents.* Translated by James Strachey. New York: W. W. Norton and Co., 1961.

Friedlander, Saul. *Reflections on Nazism: An Essay on Kitsch and Death.* Translated by Thomas Weyr. New York: Avon Books, 1986.

Friedlander, Saul, ed. *Probing the Limits of Representation: Nazism and the 'Final Solution'.* Cambridge: Harvard University Press, 1992.

Friedrich, Otto. *The Kingdom of Auschwitz* (1994). London: Penguin Books, 1996.

Genette, Gerard. *Narrative Discourse.* Translated by Jane E. Lewin; foreword by Jonathan Culler. Oxford: B. Blackwell, 1980.

Giannangelo, Stephen J. *The Psychopathology of Serial Murder: A Theory of Violence.* Westport, CT: Praeger, 1996.

Gilbert, Elliot L., ed. *The World of Mystery Fiction.* Bowling Green, OH: Bowling Green State University Popular Press, 1983.

Gilbert, G. M. (1947). *Nuremberg Diary.* New York: Signet Books, 1961.

Gilman, Sander. "'Who Kills Whores?' 'I Do,' Says Jack: Race, Gender, and Body in Victorian London." In Burroughs et al., eds. *Clues, Myths, and the Historical Method,* <p nos?>

Goebbels, Joseph (1925). *Michael: A Novel.* Translated by Joachim Neugroschel. New York: Amok Press, 1987.

Goldhagen, Daniel Jonah. *Hitler's Willing Executioners: Ordinary Germans and The Holocaust.* New York: Vintage Books, 1996.

Goldstein, Lisa. "Breadcrumbs and Stones." In *Snow White, Blood Red.* Edited by Ellen Datlow and Terri Windling. New York: Avon Books, 1993.

Gomel, Elana. "Hard and Wet: Luce Irigaray and the Fascist Body." In *Textual Practice* 12, no. 2 (1998): 199–223.

Gould, Stephen Jay. *Ontogeny and Phylogeny.* Cambridge: Belknap Press of Harvard University, 1977.

———. *Wonderful Life: The Burgess Shale and the Nature of History.* London: Penguin Books, 1989.

———. "Literary Bias on the Slippery Slope." In *Bully for Brontosaurus: Further Reflections in Natural History.* London: Books, 1991.

Gourevitch, Philip. *We Wish to Inform You That Tomorrow We Will Be Killed with Our Families . . . Stories From Rwanda.* New York: Picador, 1998.

Griffin, Roger, ed. *Fascism.* Oxford: Oxford University Press, 1995.

Grixti, Joseph. *Terrors of Uncertainty: The Cultural Contexts of Horror Fiction.* London: Routledge, 1989.

Grossman, Dave. *On Killing: The Psychological Cost of Learning to Kill in War and Society.* Boston: Little, Brown and Company, 1995.

Grossvogel, David J. *Mystery and Its Fictions: From Oedipus to Agatha Christie.* Baltimore: Johns Hopkins University Press, 1979.

Grunberger, Richard. *A Social History of the Third Reich.* London: Penguin Books, 1983.

Halberstam, Judith. *Skin Shows: Gothic Horror and the Technology of Monsters.* Durham, NC: Duke University Press, 1995.

Haldane, J. B. S. *Daedalus or Science and the Future.* New York: E. P. Dutton and Co., 1924.

Harris, Robert. *Fatherland.* New York: Random House, 1992.

———. *Archangel.* London: Arrow Books, 1999.

Harris, Thomas (1989). *The Silence of the Lambs.* London: Mandarin, 1991.

———. *Red Dragon.* New York: Dell Books, 1981.

Hawking, Stephen. *A Brief History of Time: From the Big Bang to Black Holes.* New York: Bantam Books, 1988.

Haynes, Rosalynn D. *From Faust to Strangelove: Representations of the Scientist in Western Literature.* Baltimore: Johns Hopkins University Press, 1994.

Heidegger, Martin (1961). *Nietzsche.* San Francisco: Harper and Row, 1984.

Heller, Terry. *The Delights of Terror: An Aesthetics of the Tale of Terror.* Urbana: University of Illinois Press, 1987.

Helman, Cecil. *The Body of Frankenstein's Monster: Essays in Myth and Medicine.* New York: W. W. Norton Company, 1992.

Hewitt, Andrew. "The Bad Seed: 'Auschwitz' and the Physiology of Evil." In Copjec, ed., *Radical Evil,* 74–105.

Hitler, Adolf (1925). *Mein Kampf.* Translated by Ralf Manheim. Boston: The Houghton Mifflin Company, 1972.

Hochhuth, Rolf. *The Deputy.* Translated by Richard and Clara Winston. New York: Grove Press, 1964.

Hoess, Rudolf (1951). *Commandant of Auschwitz: The Autobiography of Rudolf Hoess.* Introduction by Lord Russell of Liverpool, C.B.E., M.C. Translated by Constantine FitzGibbon. New York: Popular Library, 1959.

Holder, R. W. *A Dictionary of Euphemisms.* Oxford: Oxford University Press, 1995.

Holquist, Michael. "Whodunit and Other Questions: Metaphysical Detective Stories in Postwar Fiction." In Most and Stowe, 149–75.

Huet, Marie-Helene. *Monstrous Imagination.* Cambridge: Harvard University Press, 1993.

Huhn, Peter. "The Politics of Secrecy and Publicity: The Function of Hidden Stories in Some Recent British Mystery Fiction." In Delamater and Prigozy, 39–51.

Huxley, Thomas Henry. *Evolution and Ethics and Other Essays.* London: Macmillan, 1894.

Ignatieff, Michael. *The Warrior's Honor: Ethnic War and the Modern Conscience.* London: Vintage, 1999.

Jackson, Rosemary. *Fantasy: The Literature of Subversion.* London: Methuen, 1981.

James, Donald. *Monstrum.* London: Arrow Books, 1998.

James, M. R. *The Ghost Stories of M. R. James.* London: Edward Arnold, 1983.

Jameson, Fredric. "Imaginary and Symbolic in Lacan: Marxism, Psychoanalytic Criticism, and the Problem of the Subject." In *Literature and Psychoanalysis. The Question of Reading: Otherwise.* Edited by Shoshana Felman. Baltimore: Johns Hopkins University Press, 1977, 338–96.

———. *The Political Unconscious: Narrative as a Socially Symbolic Act.* Ithaca, NY: Cornell University Press, 1981.

———. "Progress Versus Utopia; or, Can We Imagine the Future?" *Science-Fiction Studies* 9 (1982): 147–59.

———. "On Raymond Chandler." In Most and Stowe, 122–49.

Johnston, Paul. *Body Politic.* London: New English Library, 1998.

Kafka, Franz. "In the Penal Colony." In *Black Water: The Book of Fantastic Literature.* Edited by Alberto Manguel. New York: Clarkson N. Potter Inc., 1983.

Kant, Immanuel (1790). *Critique of Judgement.* Translated by Werner S. Pluhar. Indianapolis: Hackett Publishing Company, 1987.

Keane, Fergal. *Season of Blood: A Rwandan Journey.* London: Penguin Books, 1995.

Kelves, Daniel J. *In the Name of Eugenics: Genetics and the Uses of Human Heredity.* London: Penguin Books, 1985.

King, Stephen. *Danse Macabre.* New York: Berkley Books, 1981.

Klee, Ernst, Willi Dressen, and Volker Riess, eds. (1988). *"The Good Old Days": The Holocaust As Seen by Its Perpetrators and Bystanders.* Translated by Deborah Burnstone, foreword by Hugh Trevor-Roper. New York: Konecky and Konecky, 1991.

Klein, George. *Pieta.* Translated by Theodore and Ingrid Friedmann. Cambridge, MA: MIT Press, 1992.

Koonz, Claudia. *Mothers in the Fatherland: Women, the Family and Nazi Politics.* New York: St. Martin's Press, 1987.

Kott, Jan. *Shakespeare, Our Contemporary.* Translated by Boleslaw Taborski, preface by Peter Brook. London: Methuen, 1967.

Kristeva, Julia. *Powers of Horror: An Essay on Abjection.* Translated by Leon S. Roudiez. New York: Columbia University Press, 1980.

Kucich, John. "Repression and Representation: Dickens' General Economy." In Connor, ed., *Charles Dickens,* 197–211.

Kumar, Krishan. *Utopia and Anti-Utopia in Modern Times.* Oxford: Basil Blackwell, 1987.

———. "The End of Socialism? The End of Utopia? The End of History?" In *Utopia and the Millennium.* Edited by Krishan Kumar and Stephen Bann. London: Reaktion Books, 1993, 63–78.

Lacan, Jacques. *Ecrits.* Paris: Seuil, 1966.

LaCapra, Dominick. "Representing the Holocaust: Reflections on the Historians' Debate." In Friedlander, ed., *Proving the Limits of Representation*, 108–28.

———. *Representing the Holocaust: History, Theory, Trauma.* Ithaca, NY: Cornell University Press, 1994.

Landau, Misia. *Narratives of Human Evolution.* New Haven: Yale University Press, 1991.

Langer, Lawrence L. *Admitting the Holocaust.* New York: Oxford University Press, 1995.

Laqueur, Walter. *The Terrible Secret: Suppression of the Truth about Hitler's 'Final Solution.'* London: Penguin Books, 1980.

Lawrence, D. H. *Apocalypse* (1931). Introduction by Richard Aldington. London: Penguin Books, 1974.

Le Fanu, Joseph Sheridan. *Best Ghost Stories of J. S. Le Fanu.* Edited and introduction by E. F. Bleiler. New York: Dover Publications, 1964.

LeGuin, Ursula K. *The Wind's Twelve Quarters.* Toronto: Bantam Books, 1976.

Lem, Stanislaw. *His Master's Voice.* Translated by Michael Kandel. San Diego: Harcourt Brace Jovanovich, 1983.

———. *The Star Diaries.* Translated by Michael Kandel. New York: Avon Books, 1977.

Lerner, Richard M. *Final Solutions: Biology, Prejudice, and Genocide.* State College: Pennsylvania State University Press, 1992.

Lesser, Wendy. *Pictures at the Execution.* Cambridge: Harvard University Press, 1993.

Levi, Primo (1958). *Survival in Auschwitz.* Translated by Stuart Woolf. New York: Collier Books, 1961.

Levin, Ira. *The Boys from Brazil.* New York: Dell Publishing, 1976.

Lifton, Robert Jay. *Nazi Doctors: Medical Killing and the Psychology of Genocide.* New York: Basic Books, 1986.

Ligotti, Thomas. *The Nightmare Factory.* New York: Carroll and Graf Publishers, Inc., 1996.

Loftus, Elizabeth, and Katherine Ketcham. *The Myth of Repressed Memory.* New York: St. Martin's Griffin, 1994.

Lombroso, Cesare. *Criminal Man According to the Classification of Cesare Lombroso.* Summarized by Gina Lombroso Ferrero, introduction by Cesare Lombroso. New York: G. P. Putnam's Sons, 1911.

Lyotard, Jean-François. *The Inhuman.* Translated by Geoffrey Bennington and Rachel Bowlby. Stanford: Stanford University Press, 1991.

———. *The Postmodern Condition: Report on Knowledge.* Translated by Geoff Bennington and Brian Massumi. Minneapolis: University of Minnesota Press, 1984.

———. (1988). *Heidegger and 'The Jews'.* Translated by Andreas Michel and Mark Roberts, introduction by David Carroll. Minneapolis: University of Minnesota Press, 1990.

Machen, Arthur. *Tales of Horror and the Supernatural.* London: The Richards Press, 1949.

Maples, William R., and Michael Browning. *Dead Men Do Tell Tales: The Strange and Fascinating Cases of a Forensic Anthropologist.* London: Mandarin Paperbacks, 1994.

Markman, Ronald, and Dominick Bosco. *Alone with The Devil: Famous Cases of a Courtroom Psychiatrist.* New York: Bantam Books, 1989.

Martin, Philip. "The Vampire in the Looking-Glass: Reflection and Projection in Bram Stoker's *Dracula.*" In *Nineteenth-Century Suspense.* Edited by Clive Bloom et al. London: Macmillan Press, 1988.

Matalon, Lucette L., and Sheila C. Dekel. *Children of the Flames: Dr. Josef Mengele and the Untold Story of the Twins of Auschwitz.* New York: Morrow, 1991.

Matsuda, Matt K. *The Memory of the Modern.* New York: Oxford University Press, 1996.

McConnell, Frank. *The Science Fiction of H. G. Wells.* Oxford: Oxford University Press, 1981.

McDermid, Val. *The Mermaids Singing.* London: HarperCollins Publishers, 1999.

McGowen, Randall. "Punishing Violence, Sentencing Crime." In Armstrong and Tennenhouse, eds., *The Violence of Representation,* 140–57.

McKim, W. Duncan. *Heredity and Human Progress.* New York: Knickerbrocker, 1900.

Miles, Rosalind. *The Rites of Man: Love, Sex and Death in the Making of the Male.* London: Paladin, 1992.

Miller, D. A. *The Novel and the Police.* Berkeley: University of California Press, 1988.

Mishra, Vijay. *The Gothic Sublime.* Albany: State University of New York Press, 1994.
Moretti, Franco. *Signs Taken for Wonders: Essays in the Sociology of Literary Forms.* Translated by Susan Fischer, David Forgacs, and David Miller. London: Verso, 1983.
Morgan, Robin. *The Demon Lover: On the Sexuality of Terrorism.* New York: Norton, 1990.
Morris, David B. *The Culture of Pain.* Berkeley: University of California Press, 1991.
Morris, Mark. *The Secret of Anatomy.* London: HarperCollins Publishers, 1995.
Morris, William (1890). *News From Nowhere.* London: Routledge and Kegan Paul, 1976.
Most, Glenn W., and William W. Stowe, eds. *The Poetics of Murder: Detective Fiction and Literary Theory.* San Diego: Harcourt Brace Jovanovich, 1983.
Moylan, Tom. *Demand the Impossible: Science Fiction and the Utopian Imagination.* New York: Methuen, 1986.
Muller-Hill, Bruno. *Murderous Science: Elimination by Scientific Selection of Jews, Gypsies and Others, Germany 1933–1945.* Translated by G. R. Fraser. Oxford: Oxford University Press, 1988.
Neumann, Franz (1944). *Behemoth: The Structure and Practice of National Socialism, 1933–1944.* New York: Harper Torchbooks, 1966.
Nietzsche, Friedrich. *The Philosophy of Nietzsche.* Translated by Thomas Common. New York: Random House, 1927.
———. *Human, All Too Human: A Book for Free Spirits.* Translated by R. J. Hollingdale. Oxford: Oxford University Press, 1986.
Norris, Joel. *Serial Killers: The Growing Menace.* London: Senate, 1997.
O'Connell, Robert L. *Ride of the Second Horseman: The Birth and Death of War.* Oxford: Oxford University Press, 1995.
Ofshe, Richard, and Ethan Watters. *Making Monsters: False Memories and Sexual Hysteria.* London: Andre Deutsch Limited, 1995.
Onions, Oliver (1911). "The Beckoning Fair One." In *The Pocket Book of Best Ghost Stories.* Edited by Philip Van Doren Stern. New York: Pocket Books, 1956, 23–106.
Orwell, George (1949). *1984.* London: Penguin Books, 1969.
———. *A Collection of Essays.* San Diego: Harcourt Brace Jovanovich, 1953.
Paley, William (1803). *Natural Theology; or Evidences of the Existence and Attributes of the Deity Collected from the Appearances of Nature.* 5th ed. London: Faulder, n.d.
Parker, Tony. *The Violence of Our Lives: Interviews with American Murderers.* New York: Henry Holt and Company, 1995.
Parrinder, Patrick, ed. *H. G. Wells: The Critical Heritage.* Boston: Routledge and Kegan Paul, 1972.
Patterson, James. *Kiss the Girls.* New York: Warner Books, 1997.
Pernick, Martin S. *The Black Stork: Eugenics and the Death of 'Defective' Babies in American Medicine and Motion Pictures Since 1915.* New York: Oxford University Press, 1996.
Pick, Daniel. *Faces of Degeneration: A European Disorder, c.1848–c.1918.* Cambridge: Cambridge University Press, 1989.
Plato. *The Republic.* Translated by Benjamin Jowett. Cleveland: The World Publishing Company, 1946.
Poe, Edgar Allan. *The Complete Tales and Poems of Edgar Allan Poe.* New York: Vintage Books, 1975.
Pollack, Rachel. "Angel Baby." In *Future on Fire.* Edited by Orson Scott Card. New York: Tom Doherty Associates, Inc, 1991, 136–59.
Prager, Jeffrey. *Presenting the Past: Psychoanalysis and the Sociology of Misremembering.* Cambridge: Harvard University Press, 1998.
Priest, Christopher. *The Extremes.* New York: St. Martin's Press, 1998.

Proctor, Robert N. *Racial Hygiene: Medicine under the Nazis.* Cambridge: Harvard University Press, 1988.

Reade, Winwood. *The Martyrdom of Man.* New York: The Truth Seeker Company, 1872.

Remak, Joachim, ed. *The Nazi Years: A Documentary History.* New York: Simon and Schuster, 1964.

Rendell, Ruth (writing as Barbara Vine). *A Fatal Inversion.* London: Penguin Books, 1987.

———. (1991). *Kissing the Gunner's Daughter.* London: Arrow Books, 1993.

Rhodes, Richard. *Why They Kill: The Discoveries of a Maverick Criminologist.* New York: Vintage Books, 2000.

Romanes, George John. *Thoughts on Religion.* Edited by Charles Gore, M.A. London: Longmans, Green and Co., 1895.

Rosenbaum, Ron. *Explaining Hitler: The Search for the Origins of His Evil.* New York: Random House, 1998.

Rosenfeld, Alvin H. *A Double Dying: Reflections on Holocaust Literature.* Bloomington: Indiana University Press, 1980.

Roth, Michael S. "Trauma, Representation, and Historical Consciousness." *Common Knowledge* 7, no. 2 (fall 1998): 99–111.

Routley, Erik. *The Puritan Pleasures of the Detective Story.* London: Victor Gollancz Ltd., 1972.

Russo, Mary. *The Female Grotesque: Risk, Excess, and Modernity.* New York: Routledge, 1994.

Santner, Eric L. "History beyond the Pleasure Principle: Some Thoughts on the Representation of Trauma." In Friedlander, ed., *Probing the Limits of Representation,* 143–55.

Sartre, Jean-Paul. *Anti-Semite and Jew.* Translated by George J. Becker. New York: Schocken Books, 1948.

Scarry, Elaine. *The Body in Pain: The Making and Unmaking of the World.* Oxford: Oxford University Press, 1985.

Schmidt, Dolores Barracano, and Earl Robert Schmidt, eds. *The Deputy Reader: Studies in Moral Responsibility.* Chicago: Scott, Foresman, 1965.

Sebeok, Thomas A., and Jean Umiker-Sebeok. "'You Know My Method': A Juxtaposition of Charles S. Peirce and Sherlock Holmes." In Eco and Sebeok, eds., *The Sign of Three,* 11–55.

Sedgwick, Eve Kosofsky. *Epistemology of the Closet.* Berkeley: University of California Press, 1990.

Seltzer, Mark. *Serial Killers: Death and Life in America's Wound Culture.* New York: Routledge, 1998.

———. "Serial Killers (1)." *Differences: A Journal of Feminist Cultural Studies* 5, no. 1 (1993): 93–127.

Serial Killers. By the Editors of Time-Life Books. Time-Life Books, 1992.

Shaw, George Bernard (1903). *Man and Superman.* New York: Dodd, Mead, 1930.

———. *Back to Methuselah: A Metabiological Pentateuch.* Leipzig: B. Tauchnitz, 1922.

Shaw, George Bernard, et al. (1889). *Fabian Essays.* London: George Allen and Unwin Ltd., 1962.

Shay, Jonathan. *Achilles in Vietnam: Combat Trauma and the Undoing of Character.* New York: Atheneum, 1994.

Sheleff, Leon Shaskolsky. *Ultimate Penalties: Capital Punishment, Life Imprisonment, Physical Torture.* Columbus: The Ohio State University Press, 1987.

Shepard, Lucius. "Mengele." In *The Jaguar Hunter.* New York: Bantam Books, 1987.

Shiner, Lewis. "Love in Vain." In *Jack the Ripper.* Edited by Susan Casper and Gardner Dozois. London: Futura, 1988, 363–84.

Showalter, Elaine. *Hystories: Hysterical Epidemics and Modern Media.* New York: Columbia University Press, 1997.

Simmons, Dan. "Flashback." In *Lovedeath.* London: Headline Books, 1993.

Simmons, Dan. *Children of the Night.* New York: Warner Books, 1993.

Sosna, Morton. "General Introduction." In *The Boundaries of Humanity: Humans, Animals, Machines.* Edited by James J. Sheehan and Morton Sosna. Berkeley: University of California Press, 1991.

Spence, Donald P. *Narrative Truth and Historical Truth: Meaning and Interpretation in Psychoanalysis.* New York: W. W. Norton, 1982.

Stallybrass, Peter, and Allon White. *The Politics and Poetics of Transgression.* London: Methuen, 1986.

Stapledon, Olaf (1936). *Odd John.* New York: Berkeley Publishing Corporation, 1965.

Staub, Ervin. *The Roots of Evil: The Origins of Genocide and Other Group Violence.* Cambridge: Cambridge University Press, 1989.

Stern J. P. *Hitler: The Fuhrer and the People.* London: Fontana Books, 1975.

Stoker, Bram (1896). *The Annotated Dracula.* Introduction by Leonard Wolfe. New York: Ballantine Books, 1973.

Storr, Anthony. *Human Destructiveness.* New York: Grove Weidenfeld, 1991.

Sturgeon, Theodore. *More Than Human* (1953). New York: Vintage Books, 1999.

Symons, Julian. *Bloody Murder. From the Detective Story to the Crime Novel: A History.* London: Penguin Books, 1974.

Tal, Kali. *Worlds of Hurt: Reading the Literatures of Trauma.* Cambridge: Cambridge University Press, 1996.

Tani, Stefano. *The Doomed Detective: The Contribution of the Detective Novel to Postmodern American and Italian Fiction.* Carbondale: Southern Illinois University Press, 1984.

Tatar, Maria. *Lustmord: Sexual Murder in Weimar Germany.* Princeton: Princeton University Press, 1995.

Theweleit, Klaus. *Male Fantasies: Volume I.* Translated by Steven Conway. Minneapolis: University of Minnesota Press, 1987.

———. *Male Fantasies: Volume II.* Translated by Chris Turner and Erica Carter. Cambridge, MA: Polity Press, 1989.

Todorov, Tzvetan. *Facing the Extreme: Moral Life in the Concentration Camps.* Translated by Arthur Denner and Abigail Pollak. New York: Henry Holt and Company, 1996.

Walker, Robert W. *Darkest Instinct.* New York: Jove Books, 1996.

Watson, Colin (1971). *Snobbery with Violence: English Crime Stories and Their Audience.* London: Methuen, 1987.

Wells, H. G. (1896). *The Island of Dr. Moreau.* London: Penguin Books, 1961.

———. (1905). *A Modern Utopia.* Lincoln: University of Nebraska Press, 1967.

———. (1927). *Democracy Under Revision.* London: L. and V. Woolf at the Hogarth Press, 1927.

———. (1932). *The Shape of Things to Come.* London: Corgi Books, 1967.

———. *The Scientific Romances of H. G. Wells.* London: Victor Gollancz, 1933. (Includes *The Invisible Man, The Time Machine,* and *The War of the Worlds.)*

White, Hayden. "Historical Emplotment and the Problem of Truth." In Friedlander, ed. *Probing the Limits of Representation*, 37–53.

Whittle, Brian, and Jean Ritchie. *Prescription for Murder: The True Story of Dr. Harold Shipman, the Biggest Serial Killer of Modern Times.* London: Warner Books, 2001.

Wiggam, Albert Edward. *The New Decalogue of Science.* Indianapolis: The Bobbs-Merrill Company, 1922.

Wilde, Oscar. *The Complete Works of Oscar Wilde*. London: Hamlyn, 1983.

Wilder, Cherry. "The House on Cemetery Street." In *Best New Horror*. Edited by Stephen Jones and Ramsey Campbell. London: Robinson Publishing, 1990.

Wilkomirski, Binjamin. *Fragments: Memories of a Wartime Childhood*. Translated by Carol Brown Janeway. New York: Schocken Books, 1996.

Williams, Linda. *Hard Core: Power, Pleasure, and the "Frenzy of the Visible."* Berkeley: University of California Press, 1989.

Wilson, Colin, and Donald Seaman. *The Serial Killers: A Study in the Psychology of Violence*. London: Virgin Publishing Ltd, 1996.

Wilson, F. Paul, and Matthew Costello. *Mirage*. New York: Warner Books, 1996.

Wrangham, Richard, and Dale Peterson. *Demonic Males: Apes and the Origins of Human Violence*. Boston: Houghton Mifflin Company, 1996.

Wyschogrod, Edith. *An Ethics of Remembrance: History, Heterology, and the Nameless Others*. Chicago: University of Chicago Press, 1998.

Yolen, Jane. *Briar Rose*. New York: Tor Books, 1992.

Zizek, Slavoj. *The Sublime Object of Ideology*. London: Verso, 1995.

Index

The Theory and Interpretation of Narrative Series

James Phelan and Peter J. Rabinowitz, Editors

Because the series editors believe that the most significant work in narrative studies today contributes both to our knowledge of specific narratives and to our understanding of narrative in general, studies in the series typically offer interpretations of individual narratives and address significant theoretical issues underlying those interpretations. The series does not privilege any one critical perspective but is open to work from any strong theoretical position.

Misreading Jane Eyre: A Postformalist Paradigm
Jerome Beaty

Invisible Author: Last Essays
Christine Brooke-Rose

Narratologies: New Perspectives on Narrative Analysis
Edited by David Herman

Telling Tales: Gender and Narrative Form in Victorian Literature and Culture
Elizabeth Langland

Matters of Fact: Reading Nonfiction over the Edge
Daniel W. Lehman

Breaking the Frame: Metalepsis and the Construction of the Subject
Debra N. Malina

Framing Anna Karenina: Tolstoy, the Woman Question, and the Victorian Novel
Amy Mandelker

Surprised by Shame: Dostoevsky's Liars and Narrative Exposure
Deborah A. Martinsen

Politics, Persuasion, and Pragmatism: A Rhetoric of Feminist Utopian Fiction
Ellen Peel

Narrative as Rhetoric: Technique, Audiences, Ethics, Ideology
James Phelan

Understanding Narrative
Edited by James Phelan and Peter J. Rabinowitz

Before Reading: Narrative Conventions and the Politics of Interpretation
Peter J. Rabinowitz

Narrative Dynamics: Essays on Time, Plot, Closure, and Frames
Edited by Brian E. Richardson

The Progress of Romance: Literary Historiography and the Gothic Novel
David H. Richter

A Glance beyond Doubt: Narration, Representation, Subjectivity
Shlomith Rimmon-Kenan

Psychological Politics of the American Dream: The Commodification of Subjectivity in Twentieth-Century American Literature
Lois Tyson

Ordinary Pleasures: Couples, Conversation, and Comedy
Kay Young